HOLLY'S HEART
Collection Three

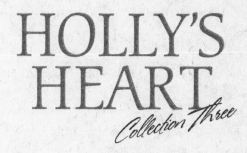

BEVERLY LEWIS

HOLLY'S HEART
Collection Three

BETHANYHOUSE
Minneapolis, Minnesota

© 2003, 2008 by Beverly M. Lewis

Published by Bethany House Publishers
11400 Hampshire Avenue South
Bloomington, Minnesota 55438
www.bethanyhouse.com

Bethany House Publishers is a division of
Baker Publishing Group, Grand Rapids, Michigan.

Printed in the United States of America

Updated and revised for 2008 edition.

Previously published in four separate volumes:
   Freshman Frenzy © 2003, 2008 Beverly Lewis
   Mystery Letters © 2003, 2008 Beverly Lewis
   Eight Is Enough © 2003, 2008 Beverly Lewis
   It's a Girl Thing © 2003, 2008 Beverly Lewis

ISBN 978-0-7642-0460-9

Library of Congress Cataloging-in-Publication Data is available for this title.

Photographer: Mike Habermann Photography, Inc.
Cover design by Eric Walljasper

About the Author

BEVERLY LEWIS, born in the heart of Pennsylvania Dutch country, fondly recalls her growing-up years. A keen interest in her mother's Plain family heritage has inspired Beverly to set many of her popular stories in Amish country, beginning with her inaugural novel, *The Shunning*.

A former schoolteacher and accomplished pianist, Beverly has written over eighty books for adults and children. Five of her blockbuster novels have received the Gold Book Award for sales over 500,000 copies, and *The Brethren* won a 2007 Christy Award.

Beverly and her husband, David, make their home in Colorado, where they enjoy hiking, biking, reading, writing, making music, and spending time with their three grandchildren.

Books by Beverly Lewis

GIRLS ONLY (GO!)*
Youth Fiction

Girls Only! Volume One
Girls Only! Volume Two

SUMMERHILL SECRETS†
Youth Fiction

SummerHill Secrets Volume One
SummerHill Secrets Volume Two

HOLLY'S HEART
Youth Fiction

Holly's Heart Collection One†
Holly's Heart Collection Two†
*Holly's Heart Collection Three**

www.BeverlyLewis.com

*4 books in each volume   †5 books in each volume

HOLLY'S
HEART

For my cool niece
Amy Birch.

And . . .
for a very special fan
in Roseville, Minnesota—
Beth Alexander.

Chapter 1

My freshman year was doomed, thanks to the Dressel Hills, Colorado, school board.

"How can they do this?" I wailed, watching Mom prepare a casserole for supper.

"Well, try looking on the bright side." She offered a comforting smile. "You get to go to high school a whole year early."

"That's exactly the problem!" I argued.

She continued. "And don't forget, now you can see your tenth-grade friends every day."

That's cool, I thought. Friends like Danny Myers . . . and Stan Patterson, my brousin—cousin-turned-stepbrother.

I could almost see it now, Stan sneering down his sophomore nose at me. Probably all year long, too! I couldn't wait *not* to go.

Of course, my twin girl friends, Paula and Kayla Miller, would be there. An encouraging thought. But in spite of the togetherness aspect, it didn't change the fact that I was being cheated out of my last, fabulous year of junior high. Top of the heap was an honor. Something to look forward to. Something to remember . . . forever.

Lofty freshmen had always ruled the corridors of Dressel Hills Junior High. Paula and Kayla were constantly talking about how cool it was last year. Now, just when it was my turn to be in the highest class on campus, I was being shoved out—off to high school, returning to the bottom of the barrel.

I stared at Mom's creamy chicken-and-rice casserole.

It smelled perfectly delicious, even with the broccoli bits not-so-subtly mixed in. But my appetite had vanished. How could the voting public possibly think this was a good move? So what if the junior high was too crowded? I mean, come on—it was a rip-off for us freshmen. Didn't we deserve our rightful privilege?

I must've sighed or something. Anyway, Mom glanced at me. "You're taking this too hard, Holly-Heart."

"I don't know how else to take it, Mom! I just can't deal with it. It's just so . . . so . . ."

The sparkle faded from her cheerful eyes. "What?"

"It's so unfair!" I blurted.

"Life's not always fair. You and I both know that." She turned around to set the oven timer.

I shrugged and headed upstairs to my room. Mom was too glib. Sure, she'd been through her teen years and lived to tell about it—eons ago. How could she possibly remember how it felt to be my age?

I hurried upstairs to my desk. I owed someone a letter. A very special someone—sixteen-year-old Sean Hamilton. The boy I'd met last Christmas while visiting my dad in California. Sean was the sweetest guy I'd ever met. Best of all, he was a Christian.

I'd surprised myself and faithfully answered each of his letters since returning home five weeks ago. In fact, my correspondence with Sean was very interesting. His letters were friendly, and he was open about his life goals and other things.

I reached for a box of pastel pink stationery and picked up my pen.

Thursday, August 29
(Four days of freedom before school starts!)
Dear Sean,

Hey. How's everything out there? Did you get your car fixed? If not, are you still jogging to your summer job at the radio station?

I guess there's not really much to write about. I mean, there is—it's just that I'm not sure if you'd be that interested. Okay, I can hear you saying, "Go ahead and tell me."

Well, to begin with, the schools here are overcrowded, and sixth graders are being moved up to the junior high, now the middle school. That pushes the freshmen like me up to high school. And, you guessed it, I'll have to deal with initiation and stuff. Worse than that, I'm going to miss being top dog in junior high. Being on the low end of the totem pole doesn't sound like much fun. But, oh well, I guess I'll survive. I have no choice, right?

School starts next Tuesday.

I was wondering, did you have to go through high-school initiation as a freshman? If you did, what kinds of things did they do to you? I'm dying to know, so I can prepare myself. Ha!

Actually, it's not very funny. When I think about it, sometimes I feel like crying. That might sound dumb to you, but it's true.

Anyway, life stinks here.

Hope your school year's better than mine!

> *Your friend,*
> *Holly*

I reread the letter and decided it sounded almost too personal, especially the crying part. I thought about rewriting the whole thing. Then I got the idea to dig out Sean's letters to see how he'd expressed some of his concerns about life.

After looking through them, I decided to let my words stand as written and sealed the envelope. Personal or not, Sean would be reading it in about three days. Mom hadn't understood my feelings about school. I hoped Sean Hamilton would.

Chapter 2

After supper I walked to the mailbox to mail my letter. Since it was still light out—and I wanted to avoid another conversation at home—I continued walking down the brick sidewalk.

The sky was full of small, shredded clouds floating across deep-blue space. Summer was winding down in more ways than one. Everywhere I looked, families on Downhill Court— my street—were outdoors grilling hamburgers. The final relaxed moments of summer would soon dissolve into a hectic hustle of kids bustling back to school.

Three blocks down, I came to Aspen Street—the only stretch of road leading into and out of town. Compared to the bumper-to-bumper traffic during ski season, the street seemed lonely now.

A musty, nostalgic feeling swept the air—a hint of fall, I guess—accompanied by an unexpected breeze. I shivered a bit. The minute the sun set in Dressel Hills, things began to cool off. Even in late August.

Colorado mountain towns are like that. After all, we aren't far from the continental divide. Top of the world.

Just not top of the heap.

I sighed, thinking about my old junior high. And the lost ninth-grade, top-dog status. Gone forever! The more I thought about it, the more frustrating it seemed.

Then, just as I was about to explode, I noticed my best friend, Andrea Martinez, coming out of the doughnut shop. She wore her church camp T-shirt and faded blue jean shorts. Her hair framed her face in dark curls. "Hey, Andie!" I called.

"Hey!" She waved back.

I had to know what she thought about the school mess. "Heard the latest?"

"Unfortunately." She wrinkled up her nose. "What's going to happen to us lowly freshmen?"

"That's what I'm worried about." I began to tell her how I'd flung my concerns on my mom.

Andie nodded. "My mom thinks it's too soon—moving us to high school a year early. She wishes I could stay in junior high another year. But then, she's a helicopter mom—you know, always hovering."

Andie's mother was more than overly protective. She was an outright worrywart.

"What they should do is give us freshmen our own wing of the school or something. Then we'd have something to claim and rule."

"Yeah," I agreed, "but who's going to suggest something like that?"

Andie fluffed her curly locks. "I will."

"Excuse me?"

"You're looking at the president-to-be of the Dressel Hills High freshman class!"

"Don't you wish." I studied her, waiting for the usual hilarious outburst. But she was confident, smiling. "When did you decide this?"

"Oh, a bunch of us were talking at the Soda Straw a little while ago."

"Today?" A strange, left-out feeling poked at me.

"Uh-huh." She glanced at me. I could tell by the recognition in her eyes she'd caught on. She knew how lousy I was feeling. Growing up as someone's best friend tends to give instant insight to the other person's feelings. "Aw, c'mon, it's not like we planned a meeting or anything," she said, obviously trying to back away from the subject. "It just happened."

"So . . . who all was there?"

"Just people."

"Right." Now her private little planning party had been reduced to "people." I stared at her bag of doughnuts. "What's going on?"

"Honestly, nothing. Paula and Kayla Miller were there having sundaes with Billy Hill and Danny Myers. All of us were kicking around some ideas."

I was all ears. "And?"

"Someone said I ought to run for freshman class president . . . that I'd make a good one. You know, a strong Christian voice in the school and on the student council." She grinned.

I agreed on *one* thing: Andie had a strong voice.

She continued. "Then Jared Wilkins and Amy-Liz Thompson showed up. When they heard what we were discussing, Jared came up with the idea that a bunch of us from church ought to think about running for student offices—we could evangelize the school."

I nodded, listening to her explain, although somewhat distracted. Jared and Amy-Liz—together?

Andie kept talking, but I tuned her out. It was easy to see she was off on one of her fantasy tangents. No way could she get voted in. Shoot, I hated to think this about my best friend, but there were lots of other, more popular, kids who stood a way better chance.

"Earth to Holly?"

I snapped out of it. "Huh?"

"Well, what do you think?"

I was still half dazed. "About what?"

"Will you be my campaign manager?"

Andie was serious about this running for president thing. I could see it in her eyes. "Uh . . . well, I guess I could. But, hey, wait a minute—how do you know *I* don't want to run?" I faked a good laugh. "I just might, you know."

"Oh, Holly," she groaned. "Give me a chance—just this once?"

I waited for her to stop whining. "Look, you don't have to worry. I'm going to be too busy adjusting to high school. You know how I am about my grades," I assured her.

"Yeah, you actually study!" she snickered.

"Just give me a year to settle in," I said. "Then watch out!"

Andie's eyes danced. "So you promise not to run?"

I nodded. "I really couldn't care less about all this. If you want to run, I'll manage your campaign."

She grabbed my arm and squeezed. "Oh, thank you! You won't be sorry, I promise!"

"What a relief," I teased, pulling the doughnut bag out of her hand. She chased me all the way to Downhill Court. We stopped running and started giggling in front of my next-door neighbor's house.

Mrs. Hibbard was entertaining her sewing-circle friends on the front porch. "Hello, girls," the elderly woman called to us.

Andie and I waved politely. "How are you doing, Mrs. Hibbard?" I replied.

"Oh, not too bad," she answered. "Won't you girls come join us for pie?" The thoughtful woman stood up and leaned on the porch banister. "Holly?" she called again without waiting for my reply.

I wanted to say no, but out of respect—and it was obvious she wanted us to come—we climbed the steps leading to her porch. "Hello," Andie and I greeted all her lady friends.

"Now, you just have a seat, girlies," Mrs. Hibbard said, hobbling off to get some pie. Soon she was back with an enormous piece of apple pie a la mode for both of us. "Here we are."

"Thank you," I said, conscious of five wrinkly faces staring at us. How long had it been since these senior citizens laid eyes on teen girls? Decades? Maybe longer? It sure felt that way, having five sets of eyes bore into me and my every move.

I slid my fork into the pie and tasted the fabulous dessert. "Mmm! Delicious," I said as they observed.

"Would you care for some tea?" one of them asked, leaning forward.

"No, thank you." I glanced over at Mrs. Hibbard and noticed that her eyes were transfixed on my hair. Reaching up, I felt the top of my head. Nothing unusual.

Mrs. Hibbard kept staring. "Your hair is so long and pretty, Holly," she said. "I remember seeing you as a wee girl, your hair flying free in the wind or gathered into a ponytail. Just the way you have it now."

Hearing her mention my childhood and associating it with my long hair made me feel uneasy. Here I was, on the verge of high school, wearing my hair the same old way. Maybe it was time for a change.

"Well, I've thought about doing something different with it. But the urge to change it comes and goes." I almost told her about going with my stepmom to an exclusive beauty salon in Beverly Hills while I visited in California last month. Saundra had nearly convinced me to have a spiral-wrap perm. She thought the crisp, vertical waves would look good in long, thick hair like mine. Daddy said so, too. But at the last minute I'd chickened out.

Mrs. Hibbard frowned a bit. "Don't you like your hair, Holly?"

"Oh, it's okay, I guess. I'm a little bored with it."

One of the other ladies chimed in. "I used to wear my hair

down to my waist, too. But it got to be so heavy . . . bothered my neck."

"Well," I said, "I haven't had that problem. Not yet, anyway."

By now Andie was grinning like a Cheshire cat. For years she'd tried to get me to whack off my waist-length locks.

Mrs. Hibbard spoke up. "Well, my goodness, why would you want to cut your hair?"

I hadn't said anything about cutting it. Thoughtfully, I balanced my fork on my plate. "I'm not thinking of getting it cut—just permed."

"Oh, some curls," one of them said, flopping her hand forward in midair. "Well, why didn't you say so?"

I took another bite of pie.

Soon all of them were twittering about the pros and cons of perming. That's when Mrs. Hibbard offered to perm my hair for me. "I do my sister's hair all the time," she boasted. "There's nothing to it, really."

Gulp! The innocent look on her face frightened me. How could I get out of this gracefully?

I looked at Andie for moral support, but she was laughing so hard she nearly choked on her pie!

FRESHMAN FRENZY

Chapter 3

Without the slightest help from Andie, I salvaged Mrs. Hibbard's dignity and said thanks but no thanks to her offer to perm my hair.

"Close call," I said as Andie and I hurried across the lawn to my house.

"No kidding." She eyed me. "Don't tell me. This hair thing, it's about high school, right?"

Andie was like that—thought she knew what I was thinking before I ever said it. "Well, maybe," I said. "But it *is* time for a new look."

"So, what're you going to *do* for your new do?"

I giggled. "Ever hear of a spiral wrap?"

"Oh no! Not that!" She clutched her throat.

"Come on, Andie—it'll be fine, you'll see."

"Your hair's way too long for that," she insisted. "It'll fry!"

The thought of that wiped me out. Who'd want to go to high school looking like a surge of electricity had hit? "Are you sure?" I asked.

"C'mon, Holly. Perms can do damage."

"What about conditioners and moisturizers—stuff like that?"

No way was I ready to dismiss this perm business simply because of Andie's scare tactics.

"Fine," she huffed. "Go ahead; be a frizzy freshman. Just don't say I didn't warn you."

"Whatever," I muttered.

When Andie left I called to make an appointment with my mom's hairdresser. Unfortunately she was booked solid all day. Tomorrow too. I was stuck. What could I do?

"I might be able to squeeze you in on Monday," the hairdresser said.

"You're working on Labor Day?" I asked.

The woman chuckled. "It's Labor Day. Somebody has to work."

So I agreed to have my hair done on Monday, one day before the first day of school. I must've been crazy to chance it like this. Andie's words rang in my ears. And I worried. *What if my hair does frizz?*

♥ ♥ ♥

I sat in the swivel salon chair, gazing at the plain, wide mirror in front of me. Family snapshots were scattered around the edges. Strange as it seemed, not one of the people in those pictures had a single curl!

I reached for my purse and found my brush. Last chance to whisk it through my hair with long, sweeping strokes. The silky feel, the length . . . it was all I'd ever known. Was I doing the right thing?

When my shampoo was finished, I spoke up. "My hair's never been permed before," I said. "In fact, except for the times you've trimmed it, it's never been cut."

The chubby woman smiled reassuringly. "Are you having second thoughts, hon?"

"Uh . . . sorta."

"Well, I could shorten the time for the perming solution."
She rolled up her sleeves.

"Will that help?" I asked, feeling more and more unsure of
myself.

"You seem worried."

I told her what Andie had said, and she promised to keep
a close eye on things. Carefully, she sectioned off my hair and
began to wrap the ends of my hair around each curler. It took
over an hour to roll all my hair—one skinny strand at a time.

While I waited for the solution to do its thing, I read my
new Marty Leigh mystery. I kept glancing up from my book,
wondering what time it was. Listening for the timer . . . looking
for Mom's spunky hairdresser.

I guess when you worry, you set yourself up for the very
thing you fear to happen. Anyway, my hair frizzed up big time,
exactly the way Andie said it would!

The hairdresser tried to smooth things over. "Don't worry,
your hair will tame down, Holly. If it's like most newly permed
hair, it should be quite manageable in about a week . . . with
these." And nonchalantly, she dumped a handful of conditioner
samples into my purse.

A week?

She acted as though there was absolutely nothing wrong with
that amount of time. I started to say I wanted my money back . . .
no, what I really wanted was my old, straight hair back. But she
was too busy greeting her next customer to notice my panic.

Frustrated, I paid and left. The instant I arrived home, I called
Andie. "You have to come over!"

"Why? What's wrong?"

"Just hurry," I pleaded, filling her in on the horrid details.

She came over. Faster than ever before. With her makeup
bag and scissors in tow.

When she started pulling the scissors out and snipping the
air around my hair, I backed away. "Wait!"

"A little trim should help things." She seemed to be dying for the opportunity to whack away.

I peered into my dresser mirror. My hair had turned wild, all right.

Carrie, my flesh-and-blood sister, almost ten, poked her nose into my room. Stephanie, age eight, my youngest cousin-turned-stepsister, was right behind her. "Hey, who fried your hair?" Stephie asked.

Carrie and Stephie stood there, staring at me, their eyes growing wider with each second. "Eewie, reminds me of some wild animal!" Carrie shouted.

I reached out to grab her, but Uncle Jack, my stepdad, appeared in the hallway. (He wasn't a blood relative. The uncle part came from the fact that he'd been married to my dad's sister before she died.)

Carrie yelled, "Don't touch me!"

I slammed the door. Muffled, anxious tones floated through the cracks, but I held my breath, hoping nobody would investigate. No one did.

Turning around, I pleaded with Andie for moral support.

"You've got to do something before tomorrow," she advised. "And fast." She'd situated herself on my window seat, stroking Goofey, my old tabby cat.

"So . . ." I began. "Besides cutting it all off, what do you suggest?"

"A light trim will do." Andie got up and pranced over to where I stood fussing with my mane. She held up her scissors. "Show me how much to trim."

I frowned and held my fingers about an inch apart. "This much?"

Andie shook her head. "Nope, that won't even cut it."

We both burst into giggles. Mostly nervous ones.

"Honest—I didn't mean to make a pun." She waved the scissors at me.

I pulled a piece of hair forward, let it brush against my face, then let it fall. The texture was unbelievably coarse. Even with the sample moisturizers from the beauty salon, I couldn't imagine ever getting my hair back to its normal, healthy sheen. "It's perfectly hopeless," I whispered.

"Not if we get the dead, dry ends off."

I sighed. "How many inches?"

She fooled with the back of my hair. After a few seconds she said, "At least six."

"Six inches?" I whirled around. "No way!"

"Don't freak," Andie said. "Now turn around, and I'll tap on your back where your hair would come."

I could feel her hand bumping my spine below my shoulder blades. "I don't know," I muttered. "Feels awfully short."

She picked up a strand of hair and held it high. "Look at this mess. Cutting it is the only possible remedy. And it's not the end of the world," she reminded me. "Hair always grows back."

She had a point. Only I didn't want to think about waiting for my hair to grow. "Cut no more than three inches," I commanded, watching nervously as she wielded her scissors.

Without another word, Andie began to snip away.

Chapter 4

"So . . . what do you think?" Andie asked when she was finished.

I reached for a hand mirror and turned around, checking the back of my hair. "It's still too bushy."

"But you have to admit, it's better."

I combed through. "It's uneven, though—look!"

She inspected it. "You're right. Here, hold still, I'll straighten things out."

I was nervous. In fact, I shook with fright. Maybe having Andie cut my hair wasn't such a good idea. Maybe I should call a halt to things right now. Have it cut professionally . . .

"Uh, wait, Andie," I ventured.

She stopped cutting and looked at me in the mirror. "Why, what's wrong?"

"I don't think you should cut off any more," I said.

"Do you really think I'm going to let my campaign manager run around looking like Einstein?" she said, laughing it off. "You've got to look cool if you're going to help me solicit votes."

"Right." I'd almost forgotten about managing her campaign.

It seemed so trivial at the moment. "Look, maybe it would be better to have someone professional even it up."

"It'll be okay," she insisted. "I'll be careful not to cut off too much. I promise." I held my breath again, cringing with the sound of each snip of the scissors.

At last she was finished. A wave of relief rushed over me as she placed the scissors on the dresser.

"Now it's lots better," she said with delight.

I looked in the hand mirror, inspecting the trim job. My heart sank as I stared in horror. My hair, my beautiful hair, looked like a brier thicket. And the length? It came to about mid-back. My greatest fear had come true!

♥ ♥ ♥

In order to nurse my wounds, I asked Mom if I could eat supper in my room. No sense exposing myself to snide remarks from my brousins. Stan, nearly sixteen, Phil, just turned eleven, and Mark, age nine, were sure to find my frizzle-frazzle hair a target for jokes.

"Aw, honey, just pull it back in a braid or something," Mom suggested.

"And what do I do with the rest of it?" I said, referring to the puffiness on top of my head. "It's like a bush!"

Mom tried to be helpful. "I'll run to the store after supper. Maybe I can find a hair reconstructor . . . something to treat the problem."

I sighed. Now my own mother was calling my hair a problem! "But is it okay if I eat in my room?" I pleaded.

She set the salad bowl down, her eyes squinting. Uh-oh, she was upset. "You should know better than to ask that, Holly-Heart. We're one big, happy family around here."

Happy for her, maybe. She hadn't been the brunt of constant teasing. And pranks. From the minute my uncle Jack married Mom last Thanksgiving, my cousins—his four kids—had seized every opportunity to make my life miserable. Starting with little miss snoopy Stephie and my diary. And Mark and Phil were constantly trying to get out of kitchen duty, not to mention hiding the TV remote so they could concentrate on their nonstop computer games. Last, but not least, was sneery Stan, who at his age should've known better than to humiliate me at every turn.

This was happy?

"Oh, Mom," I groaned. "Please let me?"

But she pointed to the dining room. "You heard me. Supper's on the table."

I ran upstairs to tie my hair back, steeling myself against insults sure to come.

And come they did. Beginning with the way Phil prayed over the food. "Dear Lord, bless this food to make us healthy and strong. And while you're at it, could you bless something else, too?" He paused dramatically. I could feel it coming . . . right down to my fried follicles!

Phil, of course, did not disappoint me. He barreled right on through. "Please, dear Lord, do something quick to help Holly's, uh . . . hair."

"Mom!" I blurted.

"Philip Patterson!" my stepdad said.

The prayer was over; that fact was obvious. Uncle Jack reprimanded Phil sternly, even made him apologize to me. Still, I resented being present at the table with everyone staring—or trying not to stare.

After supper, Mom was kind enough to let me off the hook for kitchen cleanup. I snickered when she chose Phil to take my place scraping dishes. Justice!

I reached for an extra sugar cookie and headed for my room, even though I longed to sit out on the front-porch swing. But it wasn't worth the risk. You never knew who might stroll by on an evening like this.

Back in front of my dresser mirror, I gawked at my mop. I

couldn't remember spending this much time in front of a mirror . . . not ever.

I reached back and took out my hair band, then started brushing. Would the natural oils in my scalp kick in after a hundred strokes? Two hundred?

I brushed vigorously, then stopped to check. No oil, no nothing. After three hundred brush strokes and a very sore arm, I knew this frantic approach wasn't doing the trick. In fact, the brushing made my hair stick out even worse.

Then I remembered the sample conditioner packets and found my purse. "These better work," I mumbled to myself.

My image was on the line. Tomorrow was my first day as a high-school freshman.

With faint hope, I trudged to the bathroom.

Chapter 5

Tuesday, September 3—2:00 A.M.: Here I am, sitting on my window seat in the middle of the night, waiting for the tenth dose of moisturizer to actually work on my hair. It's so quiet in the house, and it's strange being the only one awake. Shoot, I have to be up and ready for school in five hours. What a nightmare!

Andie, Paula, and Kayla will probably be wide awake and alert tomorrow, looking perfectly stunning in their new school clothes, having spent just a few minutes on their hair. . . .

I'm reading the back of the sample packet, and it honestly guarantees that rich botanical reconstructive ingredients will repair hair to its smoothest, shiniest, and most manageable state of health.

Yeah, well, I can only hope.

I'm going to leave this smelly goop on for another five minutes, and if it doesn't work, I'm shaving my head!

I can see it now—Andie freaking out. "How could you DO such a stupid thing?" she'll say.

"But . . . isn't slick bald in?" I'll answer, acting naïve, which I sort of am anyway.

Her eyes will do their roller-coaster number. "You can't be serious, Holly." She'll probably avoid me for the rest of the year. (And all I wanted to do was get a HEAD start!)

Enough—my humor is sick and so is my hair. It's time to go back to the bathroom and rinse this stuff out. I can't wait to see if this is the end of the fuzz. Here's hoping!

Chapter 6

Mrs. Hibbard was outside sweeping her front walk when I passed her house the next morning. "Holly, your hair looks lovely," she called. "You must've gotten a good perm."

"Thank you," I replied, ignoring her comment about the perm being good. A power-perm oozing with oomph, able to leap long follicles, was a better way to describe it!

But, miraculously, my hair had turned out semi-okay. Thanks to a night spent applying a zillion moisture treatments. This morning I'd used Mom's hot styling brush. My hair was still a little too fluffy, but the shine and flexibility had returned. I was a walking, breathing hair reconstructor ad.

Mrs. Hibbard hadn't said anything about the bags under my eyes, but I knew they were obvious. What a way to start my freshman year. I'd grabbed two cans of caffeine-packed pop on my way out the door and stashed them in my schoolbag. The caffeine would keep me going at least till lunch.

As I boarded the bus, I searched for Andie, Paula, and Kayla. Mostly older kids—upperclassmen—sat in the back of the bus. I found a seat close to the front, wondering if my friends had gotten a ride to school.

Stan had.

Somehow, my stepbrother had talked Mom into letting him catch a ride with an older friend for the first day of school. But had he included me? Guess that's what happens when tenth graders get pushed up to the second rung of the high-school ladder. One rung higher made a big difference—in attitude.

What if . . .

I daydreamed about how things might've been. This moment, I might be riding off to my last, fabulous year of junior high. Top of the totem pole. Right where Andie and all the rest of us cool freshmen belonged.

The bus came to a stop across from Dressel Hills High School. As I waited to get off, I noticed the Miller twins standing on the school steps with Danny, Billy, and Andie.

Andie spotted me as I came off the bus. "Holly!" she called, and I ran across the street to meet her. "Wow, your hair looks great!"

"What you really mean is it looks poofy."

"C'mon, Holly, it's not that bad."

"Thanks," I said, "but you won't believe what I went through to get it semi-manageable."

She cocked her head and studied me. "You look wiped out, girl."

"You'd be tired, too, with just five hours of Zs."

Andie grinned. "You're here; that's all that matters."

I sighed, glancing at the twins heading up the school steps. "Getting stuck riding alone on the bus the first day of school when your best friend is—"

"Don't give me grief over that," Andie interrupted. "It wasn't my idea."

I felt foolish for saying anything. "Just forget it," I muttered. And we turned toward the steps of the enormous old high school. I, for one, was definitely not looking forward to this day.

Once inside, we headed for our lockers, assigned during

recent registration. Andie's was close to Paula and Kayla Miller's—a random assignment from the school office. The threesome chattered about the day and their schedules while Danny and Billy hovered nearby. My locker was practically a mile away, down the hall. I trudged off by myself, feeling lonely. And puffy haired.

A pit stop in the bathroom confirmed my worries. My hair was not only puffy, it had started to frizz up—and out! Now that it was shorter, there wasn't enough length to weigh it down.

I decided to brush it out and pull it back against my head in a tight, single braid. Running the hot water, I held my brush under the faucet. Frantically, I plastered my hair against my temples, as wet and straight as possible.

Perfect. Now if I could just do this after every class. Sure, it was a hassle, but it beat looking like something out of a circus freak show.

♥ ♥ ♥

Homeroom, Room 202, with Mr. Irving seemed strange. A male homeroom teacher? It just didn't fit. Not for me, anyway. Oh, there'd been male teachers in junior high—Mr. Ross, the infamous science teacher with only one necktie, and the adorable student teacher last spring, Mr. Barnett. But homeroom? Never!

Maybe that's why things were so unsettling. But maybe it was something else. Andie was down the hall in Room 210—Miss Shaw's homeroom. My best friend and I had never been separated in school like this.

I took a deep breath, trying to push out negative thoughts. Once seated, I got my backpack situated and located a pen and my three-ring binder just as Jared and Amy-Liz entered the classroom holding hands. The sight of them together struck me hard. I mean, ever since I'd first met Jared in November of seventh grade, he'd flirted with me. Even long after we'd decided to be just friends, he never seemed willing to let me go. Until now . . .

Jared and Amy-Liz sat across from each other, and I saw that he had eyes for only her now. Cute, with naturally wavy, blond hair, my petite friend also had a high, clear soprano voice, not to mention a sparkling personality.

The thought of my first crush interested in someone else made me feel even worse. I guess when it came right down to understanding why I felt this way, I was basically in the dark. But I knew one thing so far: Life as a freshman stunk!

"Good morning," Mr. Irving said. "I have a number of things to pass out to you today. Please bear with me as I do the required paper pushing."

Bear with me? Paper pushing? Where'd they find this guy? But the more I studied him, the more I realized he reminded me of someone's uncle. He was almost parental, I guess you could say.

There were zillions of things to be announced, and my attention wandered a bit while Mr. Irving listed various deadlines, mostly for the return of the papers he'd just distributed. But something about him—maybe his ongoing humorous remarks—reminded me of Uncle Jack.

My ears perked up when he mentioned the election of freshman officers for student council. Jared and Amy-Liz seemed to pay attention for the first time, too.

"One week from now—and you'll be hearing more about this," Mr. Irving explained, "we'll be running student council election-campaigns for this year's freshman class."

Jared raised his hand. "Can anyone run?"

"Absolutely," Mr. Irving said. "America is still a free country." Laughter splashed through the classroom.

I glanced at Jared, who was whispering something to Amy-Liz. Was he going to run? And if so, would Amy-Liz handle his campaign?

I'd already promised to help Andie and had assured her I wouldn't run. Maybe I should've thought it through. Maybe it wasn't too late to change my mind and run against Andie and Jared. And beat them both!

♥ ♥ ♥

I was feeling totally stressed out by lunchtime. On top of everything—bad hair day included—I had landed tons of homework. High-school teachers sure knew how to pile it on. They weren't easing us lowly freshmen into high-school life very gradually.

My hair newly wet down and rebraided, I settled in at a table in the cafeteria. I'd saved three places, hoping Andie, Paula, and Kayla might show up and share the woes of their first morning back at school.

Suddenly I noticed a pixie-haired girl standing motionless in the doorway of the cafeteria. Her eyes were a blank stare. A beautiful dog—a golden retriever—stood at her side.

I watched as the dog deftly guided her through the maze of tables and students to the teacher-monitor. Observing the girl, I felt ashamed. My feelings of contempt for these halls of higher learning and the cruel way life had seemingly treated me—forcing me out of my cozy junior-high nest, not to mention the over-perming of my hair—well, all that seemed unimportant as I watched the blind student.

I began to eat my lunch, contemplating life without the fabulous sense of sight—thinking how it would be having to depend on another person or a guide dog for my mobility. Whew! The thought of such a thing made the imposed move to high school seem trivial. Ditto for hair problems.

Chapter 7

Curious about the blind girl, I started to get up to go introduce myself. That's when Andie and Paula showed up.

"Hey, Holly," they said together, each of them pulling out a chair across the table from me.

Andie seemed a bit startled when she looked at me. "What happened to your hair?" she asked. "It looked really good this morning."

"It started frizzing out, so I decided this was the best I could do."

"Oh, but it's very stylish," Paula offered.

"Wish I had some hair product to weigh it down." Quickly, I told Paula the perm story, playing it down in light of the blind girl who sat a few tables away.

"Thank goodness for modern hair repair," Andie said, laughing. "Holly was up all night applying moisturizers."

There was a glint of recognition in Paula's eyes. "I've certainly had my share of such discouraging things."

I smiled at her comment. Paula and her twin, Kayla, had a very unique way of expressing themselves.

Suddenly I noticed there were no lunch trays or brown bags for either of them. "Not eating lunch today?"

They glanced at each other, smiling. "Oh, we just had burgers with some guys," Andie said.

"What guys?" I looked around.

Andie explained. "Actually, it wasn't just guys. Amy-Liz and Kayla were along, too."

"Oh yes, it was really very surprising how it all came about," Paula spoke up.

"How *what* came about?" I asked.

Paula continued. "A group of us got charged up about student council elections—"

"In two weeks," Andie interrupted.

"Yes," Paula said, "and we decided to have sort of a prayer conference about it. So all of us zipped over to the Soda Straw, you know, and prayed about how we could influence our school for God."

"Over burgers?" I asked.

Andie's dark eyes twinkled. She stopped for a moment and spoke to Paula, but I couldn't hear what she was saying because I was chewing potato chips.

Paula burst out an explanation. "Since we couldn't have group prayer on school grounds, we took our meeting to a public eating place."

"Who's we?" I asked, wondering why I'd been excluded.

"Jared, Amy-Liz, Kayla, and us . . . you know, the kids most interested in running for student council," Paula said.

"Oh." I'd told Andie a few days ago I wasn't interested. Not this year—too much homework. And I had to keep up my grades. Obviously she thought I didn't care about any aspect of it.

"So," Andie piped up, "we decided that as many Christians should run as possible. What do you think, Holly?"

I nodded, feeling completely left out at this point. "Well, I think it's a great idea. Hey, why don't we turn the elections into a crusade?" My words gave me away. I sounded way too sarcastic.

"Holly? What's wrong?" Paula asked.

I shrugged. "High school's just a little overwhelming, I guess. Haven't *you* gotten tons of homework already today?"

Paula shook her head. "It may seem rather unfair, but being a sophomore helps. Honestly, I can't say that I've experienced the same sort of homework load that I hear most ninth graders talking about."

"Don't call us ninth graders," Andie retorted. "We're freshmen."

Paula smiled, and when her lips parted, I noticed her perfectly straight, white teeth. I don't know why I always noticed that part of Paula and her twin, but somehow their pearly whites always got my attention.

"Did you and Kayla wear braces when you were younger?" I asked.

"We never wore them," Paula cooed.

"Let's face it," Andie said. "They have teeth to die for. And poor me—I just found out I have to get braces. Can you believe it? At my age? I've got to wear them for nearly *three years*—ugh!"

I laughed. "Well, your smile should be beautiful in time for senior year."

She sighed. "At least I'll have *one* year of high school without braces."

"Well," Paula said, glancing at her watch, "I have a class now. See you two later."

"Bye." I expected Andie to stay a few minutes and chat, but to my surprise, she followed Paula right out of the cafeteria with only a fleeting wave back to me.

I finished off my Jell-O salad and cookie, wondering how things between Andie and me could've gone from a super-tight friendship . . . to this. What had happened?

On my way to the kitchen to return my tray and dump my

trash, I noticed the blind girl again. She was sitting at a table with several other kids. Not one of them was talking to her. I wanted to go over and start a conversation, but I bumped into Billy Hill near the kitchen.

"I'm thinking of running for class treasurer." He rubbed his hands together. "You know how money and I mix."

"When did you decide this?"

"Today at the Soda Straw." He shifted his weight from one foot to the other, like he was too shy to continue.

"Billy, what is it?"

"Well, I heard you were helping Andie with her campaign and stuff, but I thought I'd ask." Billy's tall, muscular frame hovered over me, his blond bangs flopping across his forehead.

"Ask what?"

"For some expert advice about slogans. Paula says you're good at making up things like that."

Paula said that? I was shocked.

"I'll see what I can do," I said.

"Thanks," he called as I hurried off.

My next class was French, but I wanted to make a quick trip to the girls' rest room. I could feel my hair drying out.

Searching for my schedule, I discovered that Room 202—my homeroom—was the location for French I. And Mr. Irving was the teacher.

♥ ♥ ♥

In the space of two minutes, I learned the correct way to pronounce *oui, n'est-ce pas, mademoiselle,* and *au revoir.* By the end of the hour I was asking questions in French, like, What time is it? What is your name? How are you? and Do you speak French?—with the right amount of throaty sound to my *R*s. It was more fun than I ever dreamed. In fact, there was only one problem with my first encounter with French: Andie hadn't shared it with me.

Weeks ago we'd had a major discussion about foreign languages. Andie had tried to convince me that she shouldn't take French since she was fluent in Spanish. "Why bother?" she'd said.

"If you want to go to college and study music," I argued, "you need four years of instruction in some language."

"Then it should be German—the language of the great composers," she'd decided. But when it came time to register, she had ignored the language classes.

The truth was, at least the way I saw it, Andie hadn't really decided to take the college prep track. For as long as I could remember, Andie had talked of getting married and being a mother someday. That was her number-one goal in life. That and teaching a few piano students.

Andie's goal was perfect for her. Sometimes hearing her talk about raising a large family and cooking great Mexican meals for them made me wonder if I was doing the right thing by reaching for a career in freelance writing. Andie's uncomplicated, cozy future-to-be appealed to me. *Some* days.

💙 💙 💙

After school, Andie, Paula, and Kayla stopped at my locker. "We need to start planning my campaign," Andie said. "You know, get a jump on things."

"Okay, so plan," I answered, laughing.

Andie grinned. "You've always been more popular than me, Holly. But I have every confidence that your fab-u-lous handling of my election campaign is going to make me president of the freshman class."

Kayla interrupted us, reaching over to touch my hair. "This is definitely permed," she said.

"No kidding," Andie said, launching off on her explanation of how I'd spent all night taming it.

"Oh dear." Kayla put her hand over her heart. "You must be fairly exhausted."

Andie stepped closer. "Are you tired, Holly-Heart?" she asked, using the nickname my mother gave me long ago.

"Well—" I yawned—"I guess I'm too tired to plan strategy for your election campaign tonight, if that's what you mean."

"It can wait." Andie shifted her books.

I closed my locker door. "Tomorrow?"

"Sure," Andie said rather grudgingly. And the threesome headed up the hall to their lockers.

Paula and Kayla started chattering about making banners and signs as they walked away. I tried not to let it bother me. But that was supposed to be the campaign manager's job. *My* job.

Chapter 8

Thursday after school Andie and I met at her house to make banners and, in general, plan her campaign. "I think we need lots more help," she said. "Don't you?"

I agreed. "I can round up plenty of kids." I glanced around at the kitchen table. "But what about supplies? I don't think there's enough poster board here to make—"

"Can't we get started with what we do have?" she interrupted.

I shrugged. Something was obviously bugging her. "Sure, whatever."

We made large, vertical posters and wide, horizontal pennants that tapered to a point. Some with sayings she'd thought up, others with more humorous slogans from my zany brain. One was *Vote for Andie, She'll Come in Handy*.

"That's too weird, Holly," she said. "Besides, you're showing off. This isn't a creative-writing class, you know."

I shook my head. The girl was behaving like a spoiled brat. Refusing to fight, I bit my tongue. "Have it your way," I replied and reached for the glue.

And that's precisely how things were between us for the

whole first hour. A negative and not-so-subtle undercurrent was evident.

After five posters were completed, we tried to discuss her campaign speech. Andie had made up her mind about that, too. "You're going to write it," she insisted.

"But it's your speech."

"You're the writer," she whined.

Now I was really upset. "Look, Andie, can't you do something to solicit votes? After all, it was *your* idea to run for office."

Andie gave a disgusted grunt. "Fine, don't help me. I'll get Paula to write my speech."

"Hey, that'll work . . . if you want to sound like something out of *Jane Eyre*," I spouted. "Go ahead."

"What?" Amazingly, she didn't get it, so I pointed out the way the Miller twins talked.

"Yeah, I see what you mean," she agreed, twirling a dark curl. "Won't you please, please write my speech?"

Andie was desperate. So I budged—an inch. "Okay, I'll edit it," I said. "But I won't write it."

She grinned, obviously pleased. However, her change in attitude didn't last long. Paula and Kayla Miller showed up a few minutes later and, honestly, Andie began to side with them. On everything.

I was furious. For one thing, she liked their suggestions better than mine. For another thing, I felt a cliquish thing going on between them—creating a swell in the current. The undertow was growing to tidal-wave proportions—and I was getting sucked out to sea.

♥ ♥ ♥

To make matters worse for Andie, on Friday the very cool Jeff Kinney tossed his hat into the race. Posters kept showing up everywhere—*Don't Be a Ninny, Vote for Jeff Kinney.*

On top of that, Jeff was making campaign promises. Big ones.

Stuff like a pizza bash at his election party. And free pop every Friday for the whole year!

Such a smooth talker. Jeff had it all over Andie in that department. Not that Andie wasn't articulate, but Jeff had a real way with words—something akin to a used-car salesman.

I wondered how Andie could compete. Of course, I knew the answer. There was no way.

Funny thing. People kept coming up to me, saying I should run. "Why don't you?" Jared asked without flirting—probably because my hair looked so pathetic.

When I explained my reasons—the homework, especially algebra, and the grade thing—he seemed to understand. Sort of. Then, right as he was about to leave, he said something obnoxious. "That's you under all that . . . uh, fuzz, isn't it, Holly?"

"Get lost," I muttered.

"C'mon, I was only joking."

"Yeah, right," I blubbered. "Go joke with Amy-Liz." And I turned on my heel.

♥ ♥ ♥

Later that afternoon, Marcia Greene, one of the student editors for the high-school paper, *The Summit,* told me she was glad I wasn't running for student council. "Because," she said, "you're a good writer, and I'm going to need lots of freshman-related articles this semester. Maybe some teacher profiles, too."

As an eighth grader I'd played journalist and loved it. Even interviewed a handsome student teacher once . . .

That seemed like decades ago. But writing for a high-school paper? Now, that would be really fabulous. If only I could get my mind off Andie and the weird way she and the Miller twins were acting.

I was beginning to think that the close friendship Andie, Paula, and I had experienced during the past few months was only a dream. And it hurt.

Chapter 9

I loved Saturdays.

These days, Mom usually let us sleep in. Things had been much different before Mom married Uncle Jack, though. Carrie and I would get up and clean our rooms, help with other chores, then go with Mom to get groceries in the afternoon.

Now on Saturdays we still cleaned our rooms but only after a hearty family brunch and kitchen cleanup. And that was the extent of the chores. The rest of the day we were free to hang out, talk on the phone, go to the mall . . . do whatever.

Mom no longer worked at the law firm as a paralegal—Uncle Jack supported us now. Mom loved being a full-time wife and mother. Often, she made trips to the grocery store three or four times a week, since cooking for eight took three times the food. But Saturday was never a grocery day anymore. And all the other chores got divvied up among six kids, to be done during the week. So things zipped along quite smoothly at 207 Downhill Court.

Weekends were an event at the Meredith-Patterson household. Try getting six kids and two adults to agree on an activity or a game. *Any* activity or game. Getting all of us to show up for brunch at the same time was a miracle.

Fortunately, Stephie, Mark, Phil, and Stan had always been close cousins to Carrie and me. Even though they'd lived with their parents in Pennsylvania before Aunt Marla died—and we were out here in Colorado—we had always loved getting together during summer and at Christmas. Every year.

The hardest part about having four cousins turn into stepsiblings was the way it increased the decibel level in the house. Frequently on Saturdays I'd awaken to Carrie and Stephie giggling loudly in their room down the hall. Or to Stephie's MP3 player going full blast—the reason why I was awake this very minute!

Besides that, my brain hurt as I thought about Andie. Her stubbornness was getting out of hand. Rolling over, I grabbed the blanket and pressed it over my ear. Stephie's silly music kept going. I tried to block out the sound and resume my sleepy state by thinking of pastures of wild flowers, lovely mountain streams—anything to relax. No use. Stephie's tune went straight to my brain.

Frustrated, I leaped out of bed and made a mad dash to the bedroom down the hall. "Okay, you two," I said, leaning against the door, "cut the noise."

I pushed the door open, but the room was empty. I hurried to the bookshelf near Stephie's bed and turned off the obnoxious song.

Silence.

Perfect. I sat down on Carrie's unmade bed, wishing it were this easy to stop the noise in my head about Andie. She'd become so demanding, only wanted things her way.

My ideas weren't good enough anymore. So . . . basically, I didn't care. Paula could run the show for her. Or Kayla. Or even Amy-Liz. Except Amy-Liz was campaigning for Jared, of course. He was running for vice president. Couldn't quite figure that out, because Jared would easily win over Andie. He was far more popular. And when it came to student council, popularity got the votes.

As for Andie, she didn't stand a chance. Not against Jeff Kinney.

Suddenly Carrie screamed. "Mommy! Holly's in our room."

"Yeah," Stephie hollered. "Make her get out. It's supposed to be private."

I leaped off Carrie's bed and hurried out of the room.

The little twerps followed me down the hall and into my bedroom before I could close the door.

Carrie put her hands on her hips and glared at me. She was a mini-image of me. Except now her hair was the longest in the house. "Okay, confess—what were you doing?"

Stephie frowned, her chestnut hair brushing against her cheek. "Were you snooping?"

I sat on my four-poster bed and smiled. "Look, girls, it's as simple as this. I was daydreaming."

Stephie's freckles twitched. "You mean you weren't trying to find our top secret—"

"Shh!" Carrie blurted.

Stephie looked worried. "What? I didn't spoil anything, did I?"

"Just be quiet," Carrie commanded.

Stephie nodded. "On my princess honor," she said, raising her right hand.

"Don't say that!" Carrie howled, grabbing Stephie by the arm and pulling her out of my room.

I grinned, peeking down the hall. Before I closed my door I heard Carrie reprimand Stephie further. Only now in a whisper. "You don't want anyone to know about our secret pact, do you?"

Settling down on my cozy window seat, I thought about Carrie's words and smiled.

It hadn't been so long ago that Andie and I had our own secret pact. A pact of friendship called the Loyalty Papers.

Funny, as you get older, those kinds of things—although heartfelt at the time—become virtually unnecessary. But in a childish sort of way, I was glad I'd saved our old pact. It was special beyond words. At least, that's how I'd always viewed it.

I went to look for the box of childhood treasures stowed under my bed. Sure enough, the Loyalty Papers were tucked away for posterity, and I pulled them out for a comforting escape into the past.

Andie? She'd been a true-blue best friend for the most part up until around seventh grade. That's when I'd freaked out and torn up our Loyalty Papers. But, angry as I was, the bond of friendship had shone through in the end. Thank goodness there had been a copy of the pact hidden under my mattress.

These days, Loyalty Papers were no longer in effect. We'd grown past our need for strict rules for conducting a perfect best friendship. Way past. Maybe so far past that a glimpse into the carefree days of our childhood—together—might help things between us.

I ran downstairs to the kitchen, grabbed the portable phone, and called Andie.

She answered on the first ring. "Hello?"

"Hey," I said. "I was just thinking."

"Yeah?"

"You remember those Loyalty Papers we wrote in third grade?"

She gasped. "Holly! You have to be reverting."

"I'm what?"

"You know, you're going backward," she said. "Is it the high-school thing? The trauma of being pushed out of junior high?"

"The what?"

She tried to explain. "Sometimes people revert to a safer,

more secure moment in their past to . . . uh, buffer their present situation. Is that it, Holly? Think about it, please?"

"Look, all I wanted to do was have you come over sometime today, just for old times' sake."

She exhaled into the phone. "I'm so busy. In case you forgot, I'm running for the highest office of the Dressel Hills freshman class."

"Oh." She knocked the wind out of me.

Neither of us spoke for a moment. Then she said, "Are you coming to *my* house? Paula and Kayla are here helping with more posters and stuff."

"Why should I? You're not interested in my suggestions anyhow."

The silence made my heart pound. I wanted her to coax me, to plead with me to come.

"Fine. Have it your way," Andie said finally and hung up.

Devastation set in, but it was my own fault. The Miller twins and Andie were having a party-down weekend. Without me.

Chapter 10

After brunch the mail came, and with it, snail mail from Sean. I ran to my room and opened the envelope.

Dear Holly,

> *Thanks for your letter. It's always great to hear from you.*
>
> *I'm going to be honest with you. I don't think you have anything to worry about as far as high school is concerned. Maybe by now you've found that to be true.*
>
> *Looking back on my freshman year, I remember feeling twinges of anticipation and worry. Mostly about the grading scale, I think. A score of 94 was a B+—that took some getting used to. What's the grading scale there?*
>
> *About initiation, I suppose the worst thing that could happen is you forget next year what it was like being a freshman and dish out some of the same stuff yourself.*
>
> *But I have faith in you, Holly. You have a good heart. And always will.*

I stopped reading and remembered the craziness I'd initiated during summer youth camp. Wow, I wondered what Sean would think of that.

Turning the page of his letter, I read on.

*Just be on the alert to what might (or could) happen. I'll bet
your friend Andie will help watch out for pranks, too. How's
she doing, by the way?*

I stopped reading again and thought about my trip to see
Daddy in California this past summer. Andie and I had gone
there together. What a crazy time that was, too, but we'd learned
some important things about life . . . and about avoiding little
white lies, no matter what.

Sean would be surprised to know that Andie was running
for class president. The fact still surprised me. I turned back to
Sean's letter.

*Let me know how your first week of high school goes. What's
your favorite class so far? Do you have any interesting teachers this year?*

*My calculus teacher is having chemotherapy. He's really
a terrific guy. We've had a couple private talks about the Lord
after school. Unfortunately, Mr. Fremont has cancer. His hair
is starting to come out, and several students have decided to
shave their heads. What do you think? Should I shave mine?
Tell me the truth, okay?*

I really miss you, Holly. Please write back soon.

Yours, Sean

I refolded the letter and carefully slipped it back inside the
envelope. What a great guy! Too bad Sean didn't live in Dressel
Hills or at least somewhere in Colorado. Somewhere closer.

I glanced fondly at the cream-colored envelope and his handwriting. Clean, strong strokes and easy to read, unlike some
guys' I knew.

Dear Sean, I thought. *He wants me to decide if he should shave his head.* A thoughtful gesture, a noble plan. And not a bad idea, especially since I wouldn't have to witness it. A cop-out, though. What if I did have to see it every day? Would that make a difference?

This talk of head shaving made me think about my own kinky mess. Would my hair grow back curly or straight if I shaved it off? A frightening thought—a bald girl. Yikes!

Quickly, I got up and looked in the dresser mirror. My hair looked worse than ever—sticking out everywhere—even with a couple of days' worth of scalp oil. Usually I washed my hair every other day. It wasn't as oily as some girls' hair. Amy-Liz for one. She had to wash her hair every time she turned around. If I had to wash mine every day, with hair as thick as this, I'd spend half my life drying it.

With that thought, I grabbed my robe and headed for the shower. If I washed my mop several times today, maybe the shampoo would weaken the perm. It was worth a try!

♥ ♥ ♥

Later that afternoon Andie called. "Can I come over?"

"Sure," I told her, even though I was still peeved at her. The girl sounded frantic.

I waited out on the front porch, letting the air dry my damp hair. The sky was scattered with high, feathery clouds that Daddy had always said were for the angels. Featherbeds. I smiled, glad that Daddy was a Christian now. And to think that Sean's older brother had been partly responsible. Prayer really does change things . . . people, too.

Finally Andie arrived. I watched her get off the city bus and run across the street. I stood up and went to meet her. "What's wrong?" I asked.

"Everything. Jeff Kinney's making all those promises, you know." She marched up on the porch and sat down on the swing. "I heard his dad's a soda dealer; they'll stock the pop machines, no problem." Her words spilled out. "Oh, Holly, it's hopeless. There's no way I can compete!"

"So what's wrong with good, solid representation? You know, listening to students' pet peeves? You could make a complaint box and promise to read every letter. Then do whatever it takes to change things . . . solve the problems."

"That's hokey." Andie stopped the swing and stared at me. "You sound like I'm a Miss Fix-It. I'm not running a Dr. Laura show here, for your information."

I nodded. "But there's nothing wrong with offering—and promising—to do your best to represent the wishes of the freshman class."

She shrugged, then pushed her toe against the porch floor. "It's just that I can't compete with a rich kid. Jeff's got the kind of backing I could only dream of."

"I know," I said softly. "It doesn't seem fair."

She talked about how rotten it was for Jeff Kinney to run his campaign like that. Bribery. And not knowing what else to say, I agreed.

We sat in silence for a few minutes. Then I said, "Why do you think Jared's not running against you?"

"I don't know. Guess he's trying to be nice—for a change. He's running for vice president, and so far no one's competing against him. And did you hear? Amy-Liz is running for secretary."

"Really?" This was news.

"Yep, she wants to make sure she sticks close to Jared. Personally, I think they make a good couple."

Better than you and Jared, she was probably thinking.

"Well, I hope he's treating her better than he treated me. It gets old knowing your guy friend's flirting with every girl in the school."

Andie faced me. "That's the amazing thing, you know. Jared's actually quit flirting. It's like some miracle."

I laughed. "I wouldn't go that far, but he does seem more

mature. But then, I thought that about him last year. Maybe we should wait and see if the newness wears off."

"Speaking of new, how's Sean Hamilton?" She studied me with her dark, inquisitive eyes.

"I got another letter today," I said. "He's answered all my letters so far—email messages, too. And he asked about you."

Her face broke into a wide grin. "He did?"

"Uh-huh. Hold on. I'll read it to you." I hurried inside.

When I came back, Stan was sitting on the front-porch step. He'd brought out some soda for Andie and was guzzling a can of his own. But he wasn't making eye contact with her, so I knew he was being a jerk.

I folded the letter from Sean and stuffed it inside my jeans. Andie patted the spot beside her on the swing, and a few minutes later Stan left.

"What's with him?" I asked.

"Try madly in love." She laughed. "With himself."

I snickered. Andie's comment was a fitting diagnosis of Stan's problem. When I was sure he was gone, I pulled the letter out of my pocket and began reading.

At the end of the letter, when I read that Sean missed me, Andie carried on. "Aw, how sweet," she said. "It must feel really great having a guy who cares enough to write you letters like that."

I held the letter against my heart. "Sean's the best."

She was grinning. "So when will you see him next?"

"Wish I knew. But for now, since I'm too young to date, this might be the best thing. A long-distance friendship."

"C'mon, you can read between the lines, Holly. This guy likes you—really likes you!"

"Well, who said anything's wrong with starting out as good friends? I think I prefer it to the mushy stuff."

For a moment Andie didn't respond; then she looked at me

sadly. "I guess I thought Stan and I had a chance for a solid friendship like that."

"Maybe you will someday," I offered. "But you two went separate ways, right?"

She nodded. "And honestly, things feel good this way—boyfriendless."

"Having a guy in our lives—especially at our age—is over-rated. Besides, two weeks from now you could be freshman class president and too busy." I meant it to cheer her up.

"If I could just think of something to promise—a really great campaign pledge. Maybe then I'd have a fighting chance." She leaned back in the swing and stared at the sky.

With all my heart, I wished I could give her that. A fighting chance. My childhood best friend deserved it.

I couldn't help but grin as we sat there. It felt like old times between us as the afternoon sun shone down on Dressel Hills.

I was getting caught up in the feeling of having her back—that Andie and I hadn't lost anything, not really—when the most amazing idea hit me. The perfect campaign promise for Andie's speech.

"I've got it!" I jumped out of the porch swing. "I guarantee this'll get you elected."

Andie couldn't sit still. "What?" She got up and started dancing around the porch with me before I could even speak the words.

Chapter 11

When Andie calmed down I told her my plan. "Here's what you have to promise the freshman class," I said.

"Out with it," she hollered.

"You have to promise to do away with initiation this year. You know, get us freshmen off the hook."

Her eyes grew wide. "That's incredible! But how do I pull it off? I mean, won't I have to talk to a bunch of seniors about this? Especially the most popular ones?"

"Probably. They're the ones who set up the pranks and stuff that goes on," I said. "Then it filters down through the juniors and sophomores . . . like that."

She twirled around in the middle of my porch. "This is so cool. You're a genius."

"Thank you, thank you." I bowed repeatedly, hamming it up.

Suddenly Andie scooted up onto the porch railing, balancing herself there. "There's only one problem. How will I do it? How can I possibly bribe the seniors?"

"Somehow you have to get them to waive initiation this year," I replied. "It's not fair in the first place because we're supposed to be in junior high. You could start out by reminding them of that."

Andie's eyes dropped. "I just don't know how we could talk them out of it. Maybe it isn't such a good idea, after all."

"We could suggest that they initiate the sophomores—they'd be getting it now if we hadn't been moved up," I said, thinking of Stan.

"Hey, you're right. Maybe I'll talk to Marcia Greene. Doesn't she have a brother who's a senior?"

"What about Shauna and Joy?" I said. "Don't they have older sisters—seniors, too?"

"And there's a bunch of seniors in the church youth group"—Andie was getting excited again—"maybe they'd help us."

We dashed inside for some ice cream. Time for celebration.

Mom was sorting through the kitchen pantry when we slid up to the barstools. She turned and smiled. "You two certainly look happy."

Andie and I grinned at each other. "I think we've stumbled onto something to help get Andie elected," I said.

Mom simply had to hear what we were up to. "Sounds like a big undertaking to me," she said after we filled her in. "I'd hate to be the one to approach those haughty seniors at Dressel Hills High. Especially that Zye Greene."

"Zye?" Andie and I said in unison. "You mean Marcia Greene's brother?"

Mom nodded, her eyes squinting a little. "Zye Greene the second. He pretty much runs the show over there."

I wasn't sure how Mom knew so much. "How do you know this guy . . . Zye?"

Andie burst into laughter.

Mom chuckled a little. "Well, Zye Sr. is a highly respected member of the Dressel Hills school board. In fact, he's the one who got the ball rolling for the ninth graders to move up to high school."

"Freshmen," Andie and I said together.

"Yes, you are definitely freshmen," Mom acknowledged. "It's just a little difficult for a mother to adjust to these sophisticated labels." She went back to organizing the pantry.

"Wow." I headed for the freezer. "What do you think? Could we get Marcia's brother to help us call off initiation?"

"We'll give it our best shot." Andie reached for the phone book.

"Who're you going to call?" I asked, dishing up some strawberry ice cream for two.

"Zye, the guy—our main man."

"Good thinking."

Andie scooped up a spoonful of ice cream while she looked in the phone book under the *G*s. "There aren't any Zye Greenes listed," she said, looking up.

"The number might be unlisted," Mom explained. "Maybe you should talk to Marcia on Monday."

"Aw, Mom!" I wailed. "We have to get things rolling now, or we'll never get Andie's campaign speech ready."

Andie was smiling like a chimp, showing all her teeth. "Hey, this is good news, Holly-Heart. You're worried about my speech. Does this mean you'll help me write it after all?"

"I'm speechless, er . . . you know." Oops, wrong choice of words.

Andie stared at me. "C'mon, Holly, I need you. Please?" Our eyes met. And all at once we were very close. Like little kids. I felt that I had a best friend forever. Andie needed my writing to make her speech fly. And I was the writer, like she said.

"Okay, Andie, you win," I said at last. "I'll write your speech."

"Yes!" She raised her hands high over her head.

I grabbed a tablet off the desk in the corner of the kitchen. "Now all I need is a sharpened pencil."

Andie hopped off the stool and found a pencil in a can on the desk. "This is so cool," she announced, hugging me.

Not for one second did I wish I were running against her. Not anymore. I actually wanted to do this—write my best friend's speech, be Andie's campaign manager. With all my heart I wanted to.

Nothing else mattered.

Chapter 12

Monday morning. Bad news.

Andie stopped at my locker first thing. She looked depressed. "We've got a problem," she said. "I talked to Zye Greene this morning. Man, what a jerk. How can his sister be so sweet? Anyway, this guy . . . he's got a major case of senioritis."

I groaned.

Andie continued. "He made it *so* obvious that he did not want some puny peon freshman asking him dumb questions. Zye said no senior alive—at least not in Dressel Hills—would agree to dump initiation. In fact, he let me in on a little secret."

I closed my locker door. "What's that?"

"He said this year's initiation was going to be tougher than ever." Andie's eyes bugged out. "Because, as he put it, 'freshmen have never darkened the doors of this high school.' Are we in for it or what?"

I didn't know what to say. It looked like my plan had fallen flat. And to make things worse, I'd spent most of the weekend writing Andie's speech, focusing on the promise of no initiation. "So . . . now what do we do?"

Paula and Kayla were headed our way. "Have you discussed

this with anyone else?" I asked Andie, nodding in the twins' direction.

"Being sophomores, Paula and Kayla loved your idea," Andie said. "They think none of us—not even tenth-grade students—should get initiated this year. It's degrading to the human spirit."

Sounded like something the Miller girls would say.

"Well, they'd be going through it if we weren't here," I whispered.

"It's either us or them," Andie said, meaning our sophomore friends.

Now the Miller twins were standing on either side of us. "Good morning," Paula said, sporting a new pair of jeans and a pink shirt. Kayla had opted for a slim-fitting outfit in more neutral colors.

"Hey," I said.

Andie smiled. "We've run into a slight snag."

The twins leaned in for the details, and while Andie explained things, I pushed my baseball cap down hard on my head. Wearing a hat worked quite well these days; it smashed down the kinks in my hair.

Kayla must have noticed. "How goes the war?" she asked, eyeing my head.

I ignored the lame comment.

Paula, however, was a bit more sympathetic. "The tomboy look is very in, you know."

"Perfect," I cooed back.

But Andie had the jitters. She wanted to discuss our next move, so I paved the way for her to talk. "What about the seniors at our church . . . remember? Shouldn't we talk to them about initiation?"

"Haven't decided yet," Andie said. "Maybe if enough of us got together it would help. How many churchgoing freshmen do we know in this school, anyway?"

We listed the Christian kids from our church—Jared, Amy-Liz, Billy, Shauna, Joy, Andie, and me. Seven of us.

"Well, that's a good start," Andie said. "But we have to get going on this, because tomorrow's our class meeting."

"You're right," Kayla said, blinking her made-up eyes. "I've been hearing that Jeff Kinney's making some pretty impressive promises."

"Yeah, we heard," I said glumly.

"So what'll we do?" Andie asked.

"Let's try and have lunch with some seniors today," I suggested. "You know, just casually—get to know them."

"Cool," Andie said.

"We'll help spread the word," Paula said.

Spreading the word would be a relatively easy chore since the high school was reflective of our ski village. Small. There were only about three hundred students total—counting freshmen.

The bell rang. Andie, Paula, and Kayla sped off to their individual homerooms. I hurried to Room 202, hoping my newly attained bond with Andie would not dissolve in a brush with senioritis.

In homeroom I sat through announcements. My ears perked up when Mr. Irving began talking about freshman initiation. He called it Freshman Frenzy.

I groaned.

"Several students have already been caught—upperclassmen, of course—for stealing clothes during PE." He smiled with kind, sympathetic eyes. "I thought it was wise to warn all of you—not to alarm anyone. Just be on the lookout."

I raised my hand. "What sort of initiation stunts should we watch for?"

He held his finger near his mouth. "Every year there are cases of books missing, kids being locked inside lockers, salt replaced for sugar in the cafeteria—things like that. Last year, however, someone nearly drowned when a dunking stunt got out of hand.

We certainly don't want any of our freshmen to feel endangered."
He paused, looking more serious now. "However, this sort of
thing is usually done by mid-September, so be especially on the
lookout during the next two weeks."

Once announcements were over, I was torn between answering Sean's letter and rewriting Andie's campaign speech. I sighed
and stared out the window, feeling concern for Andie. The odds
were stacked against her. I couldn't imagine any senior jumping
on board with our idea. Shoot, if I were a senior, would I let
initiation slip through my fingers?

It was impossible to jump ahead three years into the future
and know for sure what I'd be thinking. Three years from now . . .
let's see. I'd be starting my senior year, still getting top grades,
hopefully, and being a person who would be willing to listen
to a lowly freshman. And Sean? Would he still be in my life—
writing great letters, maybe arranging to fly out and ski some
weekends?

"Holly Meredith." Mr. Irving was calling my name.

I jerked to attention. "Uh . . . yes?"

"The principal would like to see you." He came down the
row to my desk. "You're not in trouble," he assured me.

I knew that. People know when they're in trouble. I hoped
no one was sick at home or anything. Quickly, I grabbed my
backpack.

The office was not as crowded as I expected. Instead, it was
populated by two secretaries and a couple of kids waiting to
see the counselor.

I was talking to one of the secretaries when Mr. Crane came
out of his private office. "You must be Holly Meredith." He
extended his hand.

"Yes . . . hello." I shook his hand, feeling a little strange
about this formality.

He led me into his office and pulled out a chair. I sat down,
wondering what this was all about. Mr. Crane, my new principal,

sat behind his wide desk. Then he leaned forward and folded his hands. "One of our student editors, Marcia Greene, has been telling me about you and your terrific writing," he began. "And it occurred to me that perhaps you'd be interested in befriend-ing another writer—a new student. We've taken her under our collective wing, so to speak, mainly because she happens to be handicapped . . . blind."

I couldn't get a handle on any of this. Why was he talking to me?

Finally he made himself clear. "Marcia thinks you are a good choice for a part-time student aide for Tina Frazer."

I listened intently.

"Tina has a high academic rating and is being mainstreamed into regular classes as a four-week experiment. Are you interested in an assigned friendship?" He chuckled somewhat nervously.

A high academic rating . . . an assigned friendship. The whole thing sounded too impersonal. I remembered the pixie-haired girl I'd seen in the cafeteria. She'd seemed lonely; no one had talked to her that first day. "Does Tina know about the experi-ment?" I asked.

"As a matter of fact, she volunteered for it."

Now I was more interested, knowing that she wasn't an unknowing guinea pig. "Did she attend the School for the Deaf and the Blind?" I asked.

"She's always been one of their top students," he explained. "But the school is becoming overcrowded as more handicapped students move here from Denver. Parents are concerned about big-city crime; they want to live in a quieter, less hectic place."

Dressel Hills was the ticket—an ideal place for families. I could see why parents would choose to live here.

I was definitely interested in volunteering to be Tina's aide, but I wondered how tending to a blind student's needs would fit into my campaign plans with Andie.

Mr. Crane sensed my hesitation. "Think about it for a couple of days. In the meantime, Marcia will be assisting Tina."

I wondered why Marcia couldn't continue; then I remembered. She had more responsibility than ever, being on the student staff of the school paper.

I thanked the principal for thinking of me and headed back down the hall. That's when I spotted Tina Frazer and her wonderful dog. The two of them were waiting outside the nurse's office. Alone. Marcia Greene was nowhere in sight.

Not wanting to startle the girl, I scuffed my shoes across the floor as I approached her. "You're Tina, aren't you?"

She smiled. "That's right."

"My name is Holly Meredith. I'm glad to meet you."

Tina held out her hand and I shook it. "Thanks, it's nice to talk with someone who's not afraid to strike up a conversation."

I gazed at her beautiful guide dog. "What a gorgeous dog you have."

She nodded. "Everyone thinks so. Her name is Taffy and she adores people."

"I can see that." Then I realized what I'd said—about seeing—and instantly felt stupid.

The nurse opened the door and Tina turned to me. "I hope I'll see you again, Holly."

"Same here," I said, trying to deal with her usage of "see."

My walk back to homeroom was more leisurely than my wild pace had been minutes before—prior to meeting Tina. What a delightful person. I couldn't get over how outgoing she was. I guess I'd mistakenly pegged blind people as being shy and withdrawn. But Tina was very friendly. And that guide dog of hers—Taffy—what an amazing animal.

By the time I set foot in Mr. Irving's homeroom, I'd almost forgotten the problems Andie faced with her election campaign. Almost, but not entirely.

Lunch hour held the key.

Chapter 13

The weather had turned warm by noon. As warm as any Indian summer I'd experienced this close to the Rocky Mountains. I suggested to Andie that we have our meeting with the seniors outside, but she had other ideas.

"We need to meet them on their own turf," she insisted.

"Are you sure?" I pleaded. "It feels like summer again."

"Relax, Holly. Let's do it my way for a change." There was an icy edge to her words.

Jared and Amy-Liz showed up. Together, naturally. But it was still weird adjusting to them as a couple.

Billy, Shauna, and Joy came into the cafeteria a few seconds later. Paula and Kayla seemed to want to hang around and be involved, too. Even though they had nothing at stake in this, Andie decided they should stay. "For moral support," she said. That was the first blow to my ego, and I should've seen what was coming.

Andie worked her charm with two senior boys from our church. They didn't care either way about curbing initiation. They just seemed jazzed to be seniors. Who wouldn't?

After they left, Andie and the rest of us headed across the

cafeteria—to the back, where the windows offered a panoramic view. Zye Greene and a whole group of seniors sat waiting, most of them drinking soda from cans. Guess it wasn't cool for seniors to eat lunch—at least not in the presence of freshmen. Anyway, the upbeat aspect of things quickly dissolved.

Zye sat there like King Tut. His lips curled into a disdainful sneer. "Look . . . uh, Andrea, is it?"

Andie's face reddened but not from embarrassment. She was mad. "C'mon, you know who I am."

Hang in there, Andie, I thought.

Zye leaned back in his chair and cracked his knuckles. "I think I'm beginning to see who you are." His fingers drummed the table impatiently.

Andie stood firm. "As you know, we were supposed to be in junior high this year." She glanced at all of us. "So if you really want to be cool about things, you'd realize that fairness is in order here. And you seniors are the ones to get the ball rolling."

Wow, was she bold!

I thought by the way Zye was unbuttoning his top shirt button that maybe he was getting hot under the collar. Andie, after all, was coming across like a pro.

"Fairness has never been a consideration in the past." Zye stood up. He reminded me of an Elvis impersonator with his black pants and boots and that leather bomber jacket.

"So are you saying there's no room to negotiate?" I heard Andie say.

"You're hearing it right, girl." Zye cracked his knuckles again.

"Well, that's really a shame," Andie said. "I can see we're not dealing with typical seniors here—seniors with *class.*"

I thought she was pushing it and tugged on the back of her shirt. "Forget it," I whispered.

Another guy stood up. "Hey, you've got a lot of gall, talking that way. Don'tcha have no respect?"

Zye clicked his fingers and the other kid sat down. "This conversation's done. We're outta here," he said.

Good riddance, I thought. Not only was the guy an arrogant jerk, his friend needed grammar lessons.

"We tried," Andie said when it was over. And there we sat, a bunch of whipped freshmen, too baffled to move. Zye and his entourage had exited loudly to the sitting area outside.

I stared out the huge cafeteria window at the students outside. Some of the senior girls were sunning themselves on the flagstone walkway. Others stood around talking and laughing with guys.

Zye sauntered around while sharing his soda with a blond cheerleader. Then I noticed a familiar figure approach him. Medium height, mousy brown hair . . .

I studied him. Then I called to Andie. "Hey, look who's hanging out with Zye." I pulled her over to the window.

"You're kidding," she whispered. "I thought Ryan Davis was history."

Ryan was either a junior or a senior; I didn't know which. I hadn't seen him around school until now. He had that know-it-all upperclassman attitude and a letter jacket that smacked of machismo.

I'd first met Ryan last summer when Stan brought him home for supper after a swim meet at the Y. Now, however, it looked as though Ryan was linked up with Zye. "And I thought that opposites attract!" I said a bit too loudly.

Paula and Kayla came rushing over. "What's going on?" Paula asked as the twins peered at the gruesome twosome.

Kayla clutched her throat. "Oh, say it isn't so."

"I knew that Zye fellow reminded me of someone," Paula interjected.

"Right," I agreed, hoping the thing between Zye and the freshman delegation had nothing to do with the color of Andie's skin. Ryan had slung some disgusting racial slurs at Andie last summer.

"This is *so* sick," Andie said, staring at Ryan.

"Don't let it freak you out—about Ryan, I mean. We both know what he's about."

"He's prejudiced," she persisted.

I wanted to change the subject, to get Andie's mind off what had happened between her and Ryan last summer. "Look, I'm proud of you." I touched her shoulder. "You handled things really well just now."

"Thanks," she said, sounding discouraged.

"You did your best and that's what counts," Paula said, trying to cheer her up.

♥ ♥ ♥

After school, Billy Hill stopped by my locker. "Did you think up any clever sayings for my campaign?"

"Yep." I pulled out my notebook. "Here you go. Billy Hill's No Hillbilly—Vote for a CLASS Act—Class Treasurer."

He grinned. "That's cool. Thanks, Holly."

"Any time." I closed my locker.

"Man, we need some decent leadership around here," he said. "After the way those seniors acted today at lunch . . ."

"I know what you mean."

"So . . ." He seemed hesitant. "I thought maybe you could write up something about me in *The Summit*. You know, just a blip on an unknown freshman running for office."

"I'd love to, Billy. It's just that I'm not officially on the paper staff yet." I didn't want to tell him about Marcia's comments about having me write an occasional piece for the paper. Mainly because I was still wondering how complicated it would be to juggle everything. Grades came first.

Billy shrugged his shoulders. "Oh well, I thought it wouldn't hurt to ask." He turned to leave.

"Billy!" I grabbed his arm. "Don't get the wrong idea. I'll gladly campaign for you. Hey, we want to see how many Christian kids we can get into office, right?"

"Thanks." He smiled broadly. "That'll be cool."

"Want me to nominate you tomorrow?" I asked as he waited for me to get my books.

"Actually, Paula already offered. Thanks anyway."

"Okay."

"Maybe you should be the one to nominate *Andie,* since she's your best friend," he suggested just as Paula came walking over.

"Oh, I'm planning to," I said, all smiles.

Paula shook her head. "Too late. It's already set."

"What is?" I asked.

"Amy-Liz is nominating Andie at your class meeting tomorrow," she said rather haughtily.

I frowned. "But she's running for secretary, right?"

Paula nodded confidently, like she was aware of other privileged information.

"I don't get it." I tried to suppress the hurt.

"Well, I'm sure you understand the saying 'one good turn deserves another'?"

I hadn't the faintest clue what she was getting at. "What's that got to do with this?"

"Plenty. Andie's nominating Amy-Liz." And with that, she and Billy left to catch the bus.

I stood there, gasping. Why did it seem that every time I turned my back, Andie had conducted some private meeting? Without me.

Chapter 14

Monday, September 9
Dear Sean,

I got your letter two days ago. It was interesting, espe-cially the part about your wanting me to decide about your hair! Please feel free to do absolutely anything you want to. I'm thinking of doing something different with my newly permed hair, too. Something to get rid of all these curls!

How's your calculus teacher, Mr. Fremont? I'm sorry to hear about his cancer. Does he have much pain? I always worry when I hear that someone has cancer. Dad's sister died from it two years ago this coming February. My favorite aunt was too young to die—around my mom's age. Anyway, I'll be praying for your teacher.

So much has happened since I wrote you last. Remember all those initiation questions I had? Well, this year it's come down from the top (seniors, of course!) that there's going to be fierce initiation. But, lowly freshmen that we are, we've decided that the sophomores are the ones who really deserve it.

I went on to explain how the sophomores of Dressel Hills High had experienced last year what we were missing now—top of the heap. So in our minds, that meant we shouldn't be punished twice. It made perfect sense!

> *About the grading scale here, we have the same as you do. I*
> *can't get used to a 94% being a high B—it's six points away*
> *from 100, for pete's sake!*
>   *Andie's running for president of the freshman class. She*
> *wants me to write her campaign speech, and I promised I*
> *would, but now . . .*

I read the last two sentences and decided not to tell Sean about Andie's and my differences. I used white correction fluid to cover my words and rewrote the last sentence.

> *She's turning into a regular social bug. It was unbelievable*
> *how she handled herself today at lunch with some of the*
> *world's worst egomaniacs ever! Stay tuned . . .*
>   *I met an interesting girl today. Her name is Tina Frazer,*
> *blind from birth. She's here for an experiment—mainstream-*
> *ing a handicapped student—and I personally hope it's going*
> *to be successful.*
>   *Well, I have lots of homework tonight, so I'd better end*
> *this letter.*

I paused before I signed off, wondering if I should follow his lead. Sean always signed "Yours," which could be taken several ways. Of course, he wasn't really mine. That wasn't what this was about.

Sean and I had a very long, very interesting conversation last summer about the boy-girl thing. And I was pleased in the end how we managed to agree to be friends. Even though Sean had asked me out while I was in California, I think he realized that a long-distance relationship of that kind really wasn't possible. Not at our age.

So the way I signed my letters must not encourage him toward anything but continuing the correspondence the way we'd started. When it came right down to it, I was enjoying this sort of friendship with a guy. Sean had never been pushy, and I liked the fact that he seemed to want me to decide things, too.

The age difference was a minor factor in all this. In five years it wouldn't matter, though. I'd be nineteen going on twenty and he'd be twenty-one. For now, things were best the way they were.

I slid Goofey, my cat, off my lap and settled him gently onto the window seat, where the two of us curled up together. Reading, writing, list making, and praying—all this was most readily carried out when I was cocooned away in my window-seat alcove. A world apart.

I signed my letter "Your friend" and addressed the envelope. Then I ran all the way down to the mailbox, beating the late pickup by only a few seconds.

Back at home, I gathered up two loads of my laundry and headed downstairs. Laundry was one of my weekday chores, so I'd designated Monday as my washday.

I thought of Andie slaving over her washing machine as a future mother, churning out one load of wash after another. All those children . . .

"Holly!" called Stan from the family room.

I peeked my head around the corner. "That's my name, don't wear it out!"

"Grow up," he muttered.

"What do you want?"

"Uh . . . just wondered. What's with Andie running for freshman class president?"

"It's a free country, you know."

"But isn't it a little out of character for her?" He looked like a toad, all scrunched up on the floor in front of the sofa behind the coffee table, cracking pecans.

I stared. "What are you doing?"

"Mom's baking, and I'm helping out."

"Oh." This was a first.

"So . . . what's up with Andie?" He was holding the nutcracker in midair.

"Is there an echo in here?" I looked around. "For your information, Andie's emerging from her junior-high shell."

He sighed. "Then what's she doing talking to a bunch of upperclassmen?"

"She has an important agenda, that's what." I disappeared behind the laundry room door. It would be only a few seconds before Stan burst in here, making demands.

"Well," Stan said, barging right in, "your friend's making herself way too visible."

I tossed the whites into the washing machine and started the water. "Yeah, well, none of us would be normal if we didn't change a little as we mature. Isn't that what Mom's always saying—your dad, too—that we have to be flexible in order to grow up?"

He glared at me. It was obvious he didn't want solid answers. "Andie's getting way too popular for her own good."

"You're just jealous."

He cocked his blond head. "Jealous of what?"

"You know . . ."

He blew air through his lips in disgust. "Hey, guess what Zye Greene thinks?" he said, surprising me with his sudden reference to Marcia's brother.

"Who cares what Zye-in-your-eye thinks? Don't waste your breath!"

Stan frowned and ran his fingers through his hair. "He liked her," he said in a half whisper. "He—"

"That's hard to believe. If he liked her so much, why was he such a jerk today?" I interrupted and poured the liquid detergent over the laundry and shut the lid. "Now, if you'll excuse me, I have homework coming out of my ears."

I shoved past him.

"Holly, wait!" He grabbed my shirttail. "Do you think she's . . . uh, getting in a little over her head?"

I had no idea what this brousin of mine was mumbling. "Look, if you want to catch all the latest on your ex-girlfriend, why don't you just give her a call?"

He actually slumped against the furnace. "You don't get it, do you?"

"You're right, I don't." And with that I headed upstairs.

Later, while I was eyebrow-deep in algebra, Andie called. Only I didn't talk to her. I asked Mom to tell her I'd see her tomorrow at school. Hopefully she'd understand. This homework thing was unreal.

♥ ♥ ♥

The next morning in homeroom, after announcements, the freshman class was dismissed and we poured into the school auditorium. There were kids with posters and banners everywhere. And Andie came in carrying a large flag that read *Andie's a Dandy!*

Did she come up with the clever slogan on her own? I finally got Andie's attention and squeezed past three kids to the empty seat next to her.

"This is going to be so cool." She held the homemade flag on her lap, wriggling with anticipation. "See what we made?" she said, showing me the flag.

I glanced at the flag, guessing who "we" was and deciding not to comment. I wanted this moment to be special between us. Squelching the desire to probe, I settled back and waited for the assembly to begin.

Andie looked rather peachy—I mean her cheeks. I didn't want to stare, but it seemed she was wearing more makeup than usual. And a sharp new outfit: designer jeans and a black sweater jacket over a white shirt.

"Hey, fabulous clothes," I said, touching the sleeve of her new sweater.

"Dad finally broke down and let me buy something new just for today." She was wired up. Even had on new perfume.

"Lucky you," I said, smiling.

"I called you last night . . . to tell you about it."

"Sorry," I said. "I had tons of homework."

"That's what your mom said." There was a ring of accusation in her voice.

Then two boys behind us started the clapping as the high-school principal, Mr. Crane, stood up to the podium. For a moment I felt a twinge of sadness for my old school. My junior-high days—the good old days—before algebra and homework to the hilt.

Mr. Crane got things rolling. And soon Amy-Liz was on her feet. "I would like to nominate Andrea Martinez for freshman class president."

Explosive applause. And whistling.

Andie stood and waved to her fans with absolute style. She beamed her thanks, and I watched my dearest friend as she seemed to metamorphose before my eyes. Andie's poise and confidence surprised me.

I pinched myself to make sure I wasn't dreaming, and then a girl three rows away stood up and made the nomination for Jeff Kinney. I turned my attention away from Andie, who was talking with kids behind us, pretty much ignoring me. The sights and sounds muddled together, and I noticed Amy-Liz standing up again, proudly nominating Jared for vice president.

Andie kept bumping into me, like she didn't even know I was there. She was so caught up in the moment—bustling in and out of her seat, chatting with everyone around her. The worst part happened right on the heels of the assembly. I wanted to hug

Andie and give her my support—tell her how thrilled I was at the response of the students. But she and I somehow became separated in the crush of students while exiting the auditorium.

To make matters worse, Paula and Kayla were waiting in the hallway. I could see them just ahead of me. A lump jammed in my throat as my best friend literally ran to the twins with the swell of the crowd at her back.

By the time I was able to forge through the flood, Andie and the Miller twins had vanished.

Chapter 15

With tears threatening to spill over, I headed for the girls' rest room and into one of the stalls. I dabbed some toilet paper at my eyes.

What right had Paula and Kayla to intercept Andie and snatch her away from me? We were all friends, for pete's sake!

Frantic feelings, similar to the ones I'd had on the first day of high school, enveloped me. I stood inside the bathroom stall, clinging to my books, fighting back tears.

That's when I heard Andie's voice trickle into the rest room, followed by the laughter of Paula and Kayla. The three of them were having a fabulous time while I hid, my face all streaked with tears.

Andie began to replay the class meeting for the twins' benefit. I could almost see them touching up their hair and makeup as Andie chattered on. "I couldn't believe how everyone clapped when Amy-Liz nominated me."

"Oh, I can believe it," Paula said, pouring it on. "You're going to make a wonderful class president."

Kayla spoke up. "Why did you wait so long to call us last

night? We were absolutely thrilled to drop everything and come help with your banners and flags."

Paula continued. "It's really unfortunate about Holly. After all, she was your first choice."

"Right," Andie said. "Before school ever started she promised to be my campaign manager, and now this."

I frowned, feeling caged in. No one was making any sense! What did she mean—"now this"?

"Do you think Holly's using her homework as an excuse?" Kayla said.

Andie was silent.

Paula cut in. "I don't think she would do that. But then, Andie knows her better than we do."

"Does *anyone* know what's going on with Holly Meredith this year?" Kayla asked. "She's certainly not herself, if you know what I mean."

"Yeah," Andie was finally talking. "I hate to say it, but I think she's jealous about the election thing. To tell you the truth, I think she's ticked because she isn't running for student council herself."

I despised what I was hearing and wanted to shout, "You're wrong—all of you!" but I remained silent, hoping the three of them would leave. The sooner, the better.

Angrily I stared at the graffiti scribbled on the door in front of my eyes, wishing I could block the sound of senseless chatter from my friends.

When Andie and the twins finally left, I reached for the latch. It was jammed!

"Hey, let me out!" I called.

There were snickers, unrecognizable ones. Then a scurry to the door, and silence.

I leaped up on the toilet seat and looked out over the door. No one was around. A message in red lipstick danced across the mirror. Freshman Frenzy!

I groaned and had to crawl out of the stall on my hands and knees. Quickly, I brushed myself off and washed my hands. Checking my hair, I realized that the perm was weakening a bit—getting more manageable every day. In fact, I was sure that by tomorrow I could wear my hair down instead of covering it with a baseball cap. Thank goodness for small miracles!

I knew the bell for second hour was about to ring, so I hurried to get myself together emotionally. Could I manage my second-period class—choir—without breaking down again? I cleared my throat and tried to hum as I pushed the door open and raced to my locker. Who could sing at a time like this?

I ran all the way up the stairs to the choir room, and just as I was rounding the corner, I spied Marcia Greene walking alongside Tina Frazer and her dog, Taffy.

"Marcia, Tina . . . hey!" I called.

"It's Holly," Tina said, smiling.

"How'd you know?" I said.

Tina laughed. "I depend on my hearing to identify people. That . . . and smells."

"Well, then, it's a good thing I showered this morning," I teased.

Marcia seemed happy to see me. But Tina was the one doing the talking. "Are you headed for choir?" Tina asked.

"Sure am." Glancing at Marcia, I volunteered to take Tina to choir.

Marcia smiled pleasantly. "That'd be great, Holly. Thanks." I held my right arm out for Tina, the way I'd seen Marcia do. Tina wove her left arm into mine and we headed down the hall. "How's school so far?" I asked.

"Oh, it's the best," she said. "And I love choir."

"Me too. Especially four-part harmony," I commented. "Just wait'll we get into Christmas music."

"I can't wait." Tina's face shone with joy. "May I sit with you?"

"That'd be great." I thought about the prospect of having a blind choral partner.

"I promise not to sing off-key. I really do have a good ear." She laughed softly, and I opened the door to the music room.

The bell rang just as we found two seats together in the alto section. Two rows away, Andie was accompanied on either side by Paula and Kayla. It was obvious to me she didn't want me to join them. Not a single chair in sight.

I focused my attention on the director and the new a cappella madrigal in our folders. And on Tina Frazer—a girl with a spirit of peace. Blindness was not a hindrance to her well-being. I sensed it in the way she spoke to me. The way she carried herself. The way she sat tall in her choir chair. Confidence was her middle name.

Once again, I felt ashamed.

♥ ♥ ♥

After school there were posters popping up everywhere. Zillions of them. The *Andie's a Dandy* slogan showed up on bright red banners mounted high on the walls. Above the row of freshman lockers. High on the arched doors leading to the gymnasium. In the girls' locker room downstairs. I'd even noticed one in the shower during seventh-hour PE.

Andie and the Miller twins had probably posted them during lunch. I was sure they would use the excuse that I was nowhere to be found, which was true. Evidently they hadn't waited for me.

Feeling deserted, I'd run off to the Soda Straw three blocks away for a burger and a strawberry shake. A place to think, to get lost in the crowd. While there, I'd made a list of pros and cons, deciding whether or not I actually had time to be assigned to Tina. An intriguing person—and a magnetic personality. Even if I had wanted to resist, my curiosity drew me to her.

Yet, interesting as Tina was, she made no demands on me.

Which was perfectly refreshing in contrast to the way things were turning out between Andie and me. I couldn't even do my homework—and refuse to answer the phone for once in my life—without Andie jumping to all sorts of conclusions. And the Miller-twin thing was really getting out of hand. Why, they were running everything. Andie's campaign included.

So . . . I guess the bottom line was that I just felt left out. But there was someone for me—a girl with a laugh and a sparkle who had a way of brightening up the world around her. Tina.

♥ ♥ ♥

The bus ride home was not only lonely, it was tiresome. Noisy too. With so many high-school students taking the city bus, it seemed as though we'd never get to Downhill Court. And try as I might, I couldn't stop thinking about the fact that Andie wasn't there.

I thought back to the morning assembly. Andie, in all her glory, had accepted the rousing applause gracefully yet eagerly. My heavyhearted feelings returned as I remembered Amy-Liz standing and nominating my closest friend. Not a pretty picture. I should've been the one standing up, proudly nominating Andie Martinez. Sure, I was probably blowing things out of proportion, but I couldn't do things any other way.

When I arrived home, Mom had a plate of snickerdoodles waiting in the kitchen. "How was your day, Holly-Heart?"

"The worst."

She glanced at me. "Want to talk about it?"

"Not now." I reached for two cookies. "Probably never."

She frowned, going back to the sink, where she washed the cookie sheets and the mixing bowl. I went to the refrigerator and poured a tall glass of milk. Nothing in the world goes better with snickerdoodles than a cold glass of milk. Nothing, except maybe your friends hanging out with you, sharing your favorite snack.

I knocked that thought out of my consciousness. "Mom," I asked, "did you have lots of friends in school . . . or only one?"

She turned to look at me for a second, then dried her hands. "I was always one for having a few close friends, I guess." Mom stayed near the sink, leaning against the counter. "I can count on one hand the best friends I had in school."

I took a long drink of milk.

"Why do you ask?" I figured that was coming. Mom knew me well. She and I could pretty much predict each other's moods, as well as thoughts.

"Just wondered," I muttered into my milk.

She wouldn't let it go at that; I was sure of it. And she didn't. "It's not easy moving into a new era of your life, honey." With those gentle words, she got me talking.

"But it's so cruel out there," I said. "I think I've been spoiled, you know?" I hated it when squeaks came instead of my normal voice. A dead giveaway to loss of emotional control.

But Mom was cool. She acted like I was totally together. "Some people have many good, close friends—they'd probably refer to a casual acquaintance as a very dear friend. Your stepdad is like that. He's an extrovert—has oodles of friends."

I smiled, thinking of Uncle Jack's charming ways. "I know what you mean. But what about my personality? Why'd I have to get stuck being an introvert?"

Mom's eyebrows arched slightly. "I wouldn't call you an introvert, exactly. None of us is simply one thing or another. There are many combinations and blends of personality traits."

"Then what about Uncle Jack? You just said he—"

"Your stepdad seems to be rather gregarious out in public," she explained, "and also when interacting with you kids. But there are times when he likes to be quiet and relax with absolutely no one around."

"Not even you?" This was a surprise.

She smiled. "Not even me."

I sighed. "So, then, what am I?"

Mom came over to the bar and sat on a stool. Her timing was perfect. I wasn't threatened by her being close now. In fact, I needed her near. She began again softly. "Years ago, when you were a toddler, I read a book about this very thing. I wasn't a Christian back then, but I understood in some small way that God had created each of us with a myriad of characteristics which, together, make-up our personalities."

I listened, fascinated. Never had I heard Mom talk about this.

"You have a high-spirited temperament, Holly," she continued. "But you are also loyal and patient. Often you suffer in silence instead of lashing out."

"Unless it involves my family," I said, remembering how I fought to visit Daddy the summer before last.

Mom agreed. "Ever notice how you enjoy spending time in your room, writing in your journal . . . contemplating life?"

I nodded. "It feels good being alone sometimes."

"Well, some people derive energy from being alone. Others need to be around people in order to feel charged up—alive."

I was starting to get the picture. "I think Andie's one of those people types," I said without thinking.

"So is your father."

"Carrie too?" I asked.

She nodded. "And Stephie, although I haven't completely figured her out yet." Mom chuckled.

"What happens when two friends have opposite personalities?" I figured Mom knew what I was really getting at.

"I think that's probably a good sign. Some of the best friendships of history came out of personality contrasts."

"Give me an example." I was dying to know.

"Well, one comes to mind without trying too hard—David and

Jonathan," she said. "David was an outgoing, gregarious warrior, and Jonathan was a loyal, behind-the-scenes kind of guy."

I was beginning to see that maybe Andie and I just needed some time apart. Maybe if she hung around the Miller twins long enough, she'd get tired and come home. To me.

Mom continued, "Sometimes, though—and you may already know this—people drift apart during the high-school years. It has much to do with growing up—finding who you are. That's not to say that your closest friends won't always be special to you; they will, but many times your circle of friends begins to widen from mid- and late-teens on. It's a normal outgrowth of maturity."

What a blow! Mom had just implied that if I were mature enough, I'd be moving ahead with my life, with or without Andie. How could she say such a thing? I mulled things over in silence.

"Holly?" She leaned over and touched my hair.

I didn't want to hurt her. My negative reaction would have to stay well hidden. "I think it's time to write in my journal," I said, carrying my glass over to the sink. "My energy is fading, if you know what I mean."

She nodded, catching on.

I ran up the stairs and exploded into my bedroom. So much for suffering in silence!

Chapter 16

After supper, when my homework was finished and Mom had signed all my paper work for school, I made campaign buttons for Billy. An athletic student from way back in grade school, Billy was excited to include student politics in his life. Being the freshman class treasurer would be a nice addition to his high-school resumé.

Stan sauntered through the kitchen at one point, stopped, and peered over my shoulder at the campaign buttons. "Who in the world would wear those?" he said, then left.

I ignored his snide remark, wondering how I'd survive if he started dishing out freshman initiation. Initiation had been referred to as many things, some names worse than others, but the word was out—there would never be another year like this one. Already it was beginning. I knew they'd never be satisfied with merely locking *one* freshman in a bathroom stall. No way.

Mark, Phil, Carrie, and Stephie emerged from the family room and hung around to watch me work. When the boys finally wandered off to do homework at Uncle Jack's nudging, I waited for Carrie and Stephie to do the same.

"Don't you two have something to do?" I asked.

"We never get homework," Carrie said.

"Wish I were back in grade school," I muttered.

The girls were eager to help. I could tell by the anguished looks on their little faces. And being the wise big sister, I knew they'd never stop pleading until I gave them each a pair of scissors. "Make sure you cut perfect circles so the labels will fit into the plastic button holders."

"We will—we know how to cut," Carrie insisted.

"Yeah, we're pros," Stephie said.

Mom, observing the situation, grinned at me. "How are things going with Andie's campaign?"

I really didn't want to talk about that. "She's doing okay, I guess. The students went wild at our class meeting this morning."

"Oh?" Mom raised her eyebrows, showing definite interest. "Is that because my Holly-Heart has been busy pulling things together for her?"

"If you mean have I been out there organizing Andie's election, the answer is no."

Carrie and Stephie stared at me. "Ew, she's mad," I heard Stephie whisper.

"You bet I am!"

Stephie inched away from the bar and blinked her long eyelashes.

Mom frowned. "Holly, please."

I looked at the youngest of our blended family. "Sorry," I whispered. Then, turning to Mom, I cut loose. "Honestly? Andie's making me crazy. She starts out literally begging me to help her, appoints me as her campaign chairman and all that, and pleads with me to write her speech."

Mom looked puzzled. "Then what?"

"She gets all bent out of shape because I didn't talk to her last night. Remember when she called? I was doing my algebra."

Mom nodded, watching me intently.

"Then today, she has the nerve to act like I don't exist." I paused, catching my breath. "You should've heard Andie and the Miller twins going off about me."

"How'd that happen?" Mom leaned on the kitchen bar.

"Well, they sauntered into the rest room and started shooting off all these theories they had about me. It was so bizarre."

"And where were you?" asked Mom.

"Locked in one of the stalls," I said, explaining that some hotsy-totsy upperclassmen had chosen that moment to crank up the wheels of initiation.

"You're angry, Holly."

Mom was right, but I couldn't speak. Not now.

She sighed. "Is that why you're helping Billy and not Andie?"

Tears welled up and I fought them back.

Carrie and Stephie were hard at work making perfect circles. They seemed disinterested, which was a relief. Mom, however, motioned me out of the kitchen. "Little squeakers have big ears," she whispered as we headed for the living room.

On the way, I glanced back at the girls. "You asked about Andie. Well, that's what's happening."

Mom sat on the sofa. She seemed eager to talk to me in private. "I wonder," she said, "have you thought about all of this from Andie's perspective?"

I leaned forward on the rocker. "I've tried. Maybe not very hard, though."

"Is it possible that you've been acting a bit selfishly in all of this?"

I leaned against the rocker, thinking back over the past few days. I'd been possessive of Andie, disagreeable, too. No wonder Andie felt the way she did. Still, I couldn't relinquish my anger.

The rocker creaked rhythmically as Mom stared at me.

"Why don't you pray about this?" she suggested at last.

I could feel my heels digging in. Stubbornly, I shrugged. "Maybe later."

Mom picked up a magazine, concern still imprinted on her face. I headed for the kitchen to finish up Billy's campaign buttons.

Later, when everything was cleaned up, I went to my room. I knew if I wrote in my journal before calling Andie, it would take some of the fire out of my words. Something an introvert would probably do.

I located my journal in the bottom drawer of my dresser. Then, since it was almost dark outside, I sat at my desk.

Tuesday, September 10: I wish I knew what was happening between Andie and me. She's so strange these days—which is something she said about me earlier today as I innocently eavesdropped on her.

All this talk about Paula and Kayla promoting Andie is really bugging me. They're sophomores! I still can see Andie rushing to them after the class meeting this morning. It was actually cruel! I mean, there I was, sitting right beside her, and she didn't even have the courtesy to turn around and share her exhilaration. How could she do this to me?

I stopped and scanned the page, rereading my entry. Was I overreacting?

I continued to write.

Mom and I had a talk today after school. She gave me some insight into my own personality. I've been enlightened. (Ha!) But I'm going to check out some library books and thoroughly analyze myself anyway.

Mom says I should be praying about my disagreeable self. That hurts.

I closed my journal and set it aside. Leaning back in my chair, I stared at my lavender bedroom. Things were starting to look a bit dusty.

Funny. When you've spent practically your whole life in the same room, everything around you feels solid. The same way the most comfortable relationships feel. I thought of Andie. Paula too. Was I ready to let them go—move forward—to broaden my circle of friends?

Life without my two best friends . . . Sure sounded like a good title for a sad book. Maybe I'd write something like that someday. And when I was all grown-up, and the pain of this week had long since dimmed—when I needed a point of reference—I would return to this journal and reread the trauma of the first horrible week of my freshman year.

The entries concerning Andie and me, the way I felt wounded over being left out, all of it, would refresh my memory. Maybe the book would be for teen girls. Yeah, that's what I would do. Someday . . .

I got up and put my journal away. Then I went to the hall and leaned over the long banister. The house was quiet. Maybe, just maybe, the portable phone was free. It was time for a heart-to-heart talk with Andie.

Chapter 17

Andie picked up on the third ring.

"Hey," I said, hesitantly. "Guess who?"

"I'm busy," she said.

"Homework?"

"You could say that." There were giggles in the background.

My heart was in my throat. "You're working on your campaign, right?"

"Kinda."

I waited, hoping she'd invite me over. When she didn't, I felt dizzy, like I was going to black out.

"You still there, Holly?"

"Uh . . . I guess so."

"What's wrong?" she asked amidst a backdrop of fun and friends.

"I just called to tell you how happy I am about today."

"Well, if I win, it's no thanks to you. You haven't done much of anything."

The anger rose in me. Mom had said that I often simmered in silence. But right now I felt like a volcano about to erupt.

"You don't have time for me anymore." Her words were like ice. "Your homework and other things, like making campaign buttons for Billy Hill, are much more important these days, right?"

How does she know about the buttons for Billy? I wondered.

She kept going, and finally I couldn't take it any longer. "Just stop, Andie. Stop right now," I hollered into the phone. "I've had it with you and those secret meetings you never invite me to. If you want to do everything on your own without help from me, then fine. And while you're at it, go ahead and write your own campaign speech!" There, I'd said it.

And then it happened. Without a single word of protest, without Andie pleading with me to rethink things, I heard the sound that echoed in my memory for days to come.

Click. She'd hung up the phone!

I beeped off the cordless phone and curled up on my bed. Goofey must've sensed my sadness. He came padding over and jumped onto the bed. Gently, I put my head against his soft body and let his purring soothe me.

Crying, I began to pray. "Oh, Lord, what's wrong with me? Is Mom right? Am I the one who made things go all wrong with Andie?" I sobbed into my pillow. "Please help me. I feel so sad. My best friend just turned her back on me. She didn't even argue with me at the end. What does it mean, Lord?"

I fell asleep with Goofey beside me.

♥ ♥ ♥

Around midnight, I realized Mom had come in and tried to tuck me in. There was only one problem with that, and it had nothing to do with falling asleep without my pajamas. Far worse—I hadn't finished my homework.

Drowsy, but awake enough to know it was now or never, I dragged myself out of bed. Not being a morning person would spell disaster for a foggy thinker if I left it until 6:00 A.M.!

So I began, working my algebra problems and then conjugating French verbs till nearly one o'clock. The fact that I'd already slept for several hours actually helped expedite things mentally, and by the time I was satisfied with my work, I was more than wide awake.

Reaching for my Marty Leigh mystery book, I stayed up for another thirty minutes, once again relishing the idea of being awake while the entire household snoozed away.

A week ago I'd done the same thing. Stayed up till the wee hours. Thank goodness my hair disaster was nearly over. I could cross off the frizzies on my list of prayer requests. And maybe, just maybe, Mom would agree to let me get my hair cut professionally, with layers to frame my face. What a great look that would be. Besides, I was honestly tired of long hair—it is too immature-looking for a freshman in high school!

Just before I turned out the lights, I undid my French braid, surveying the situation. Yep. This weekend I would make an appointment at the beauty salon and see what could be done. Meanwhile, a good shampoo, a gentle blow-dry, and the hot styling brush was all I would need to create a glamorous high-school look for tomorrow. As glamorous as any freshman who'd ever darkened the halls of Dressel Hills High.

With that thought, I sprang into bed.

FRESHMAN FRENZY

Chapter 18

I couldn't remember ever getting the kind of stares I got while walking to my locker the next day. Even Mr. Irving complimented me on my hair as I strolled into homeroom. Even so, I still wanted to get a shorter, layered cut.

Between classes, the halls buzzed with kids campaigning for each other. I, however, steered clear of Andie and her throng, which, surprisingly enough, now included Jared and Amy-Liz. I figured they'd be quite a clique if all of them got elected to student council.

To keep my mind off the sting in my heart, I busied myself with other things. Like taking good notes in all my classes and listening carefully to Jeff Kinney's campaign promises.

He strolled up to me unexpectedly during lunch period. Actually, it was before I even went to lunch. I was rummaging around in my locker when he stopped by, more friendly than ever. "Hey, Holly. How's it going?" His eyes scanned my hair.

"Okay." I smiled, glad to have my hair down again and feeling like a zillion bucks—hair-wise. "Hey, sounds like you've got some great plans for the year."

"Yeah, all the soda you can drink on Fridays." His eyes held my gaze only for a moment, then awkwardly shifted away.

"That's a lot," I said, questioning him. "Who's paying for it?"

He turned squirmy on me and said he had to meet someone for lunch. "Don't forget—don't be a ninny . . ."

And he was off. Voting for Jeff Kinney was probably the dumbest thing a freshman could ever do. I was convinced the kid had no substance. Probably no access to lots of soda, either. I don't know why that occurred to me, but I had a strange feeling about his shifty eyes.

I decided to do some checking, starting with Mark Jones, Jeff's main sidekick. I waited at his locker.

"Hey," Mark said enthusiastically when he spotted me. "Your hair looks great."

"Thanks."

"You're going to vote for Jeff, right?" He flicked through his combination and opened his locker.

"Haven't decided," I said.

He turned and looked at me. "Well, you're not one of those bottled-water-only girls, are you?"

I laughed. "Not me, I love a good root beer."

"So what's the problem?" He folded his arms across his chest, moving closer. Uncomfortably close.

I realized then that he was flirting. I stepped back.

"I'm thinking of having a party next weekend and wondered if Jeff might be able to get me a deal on some soda." This wasn't a lie at all; I had seriously thought of throwing a party. A two-person party. For Tina and me.

Mark shook his head. "Out of the question. Jeff's dad is on company business."

"Oh," I said, picking up on something else. Something quite strange. Not only was Jeff Kinney unable to make eye contact and keep it, his best friend seemed to be having the same problem.

"Well, catch you later," he said.

I hurried to the cafeteria and got in the hot-lunch line. While waiting for a patty melt, I spotted Tina sitting back near the windows—the section designated by the seniors as their turf. I wondered if Tina knew she was trespassing. But then I remembered Taffy accompanied her everywhere. No way would Zye Greene or any other senior mess with a guide dog.

I paid for my lunch and headed toward Tina, passing right by Andie, who sat chattering at a table with the Miller twins, Jared, and Amy-Liz. None of them seemed to notice. And I refused to care.

Cautiously, I approached the blind girl's table. "Hey, Tina," I said, holding my tray. "Mind if I join you?"

"Oh, Holly, it's you." She slid over. "Of course, have a seat."

I glanced down at Taffy, who was snoozing. "Your dog's having a nice nap."

"I could use one myself," she said. There was that charming laughter again. "Of course, no one would ever have to know, right? If I didn't close my eyes, I mean."

"That's an advantage to being blind, I suppose." I hoped my comment didn't sound too ridiculous.

Leaning back against the chair, I enjoyed the sun on my back. I was trying too hard—needed to be myself. But more than anything, I needed a friend.

"There are many benefits to being blind," Tina said, catching me off guard. "Most people wouldn't believe it, but I can actually hear better than a sighted person."

"Really? I thought your keen sense of hearing must have come from having to compensate for not seeing." I'd read that somewhere.

"Well, it definitely came in handy today." She leaned toward me. "I can give you some handy information. That is, if you're interested in not voting for Jeff Kinney."

Now I was curious. "Like what?"

Tina's face burst into an enormous grin. "Jeff's father is not a soda dealer, not even close."

"You're kidding!"

"He's a doctor," she stated.

"Are you sure?"

"Absolutely." She was still smiling. "Like I said, my hearing is one of my keenest senses."

I couldn't help myself. I danced in my seat. "This is too good to be true."

"So . . . who's going to start spreading the truth about him?" she asked.

"I, for one." Then I caught myself. Why was I so happy? Andie's election could possibly rest on whether or not I spread the word. If I really wanted to hurt her—get back at her—I'd keep Tina's secret to myself. Let Jeff win the vote.

Silence sliced the air.

"Something wrong, Holly?"

This girl was amazing. "Do you have a sixth sense or something?" I stared at her.

"Some people say that, but . . ." She paused for a moment. "Well, it's a long story. I wrote about it once. You're a writer, too, aren't you?"

"Marcia told you?"

She nodded. "But there's something she didn't tell me," Tina said.

Even though I knew Tina couldn't see me with her eyes, I felt as though she could see into my heart somehow. "What?" I managed to say. "What didn't Marcia tell you?"

Her words came softly. "That you need a friend."

I swallowed the lump in my throat. "That's not all," I said, feeling more confident. "I've decided to be your student aide. Part-time, full-time . . . whatever. I'll be at your beck and call."

"Who needs an aide?" Tina joked. "But if you want to hang with me, that'll be cool."

She was the cool one!

Chapter 19

On the way to the principal's office, Andie and the Miller twins bumped into us. Well, not really collided or anything, but they noticed me walking with Tina. And they were scowling!

Andie and company were polite enough not to say anything rude, but if looks are the unspoken expression of the soul, I knew exactly what they were thinking.

"Hey, everyone," I said, remembering how Andie had hung up on me last night. Her eyes grew bigger with each step Tina and I took together. She was staring at Tina!

"Uh . . . hey yourself," Andie answered, and I noticed her braces. She must have gotten them yesterday and never told me. Andie fumbled in her backpack, probably an excuse so she wouldn't have to look at me.

Paula started to come over, but Kayla grabbed her arm and pulled her back, and the group abruptly turned and walked away. Instantly, I felt sad for Tina. Glad too. Glad that Tina hadn't seen what I'd just witnessed. She was right; there *were* advantages to being blind.

Tina whispered, "Aren't you going to tell your friends about

Jeff's dad being a doctor . . . not a soda-pop guy? How about that false campaign promise?"

"Later," I said. But in my heart, I wasn't so sure.

Not anymore.

♥ ♥ ♥

After my visit with the principal, I got Tina and Taffy settled into pre-algebra class. Then, with a note in hand signed by the principal to inform my teachers of my new status as student aide, I hurried off to fifth period.

Mr. Irving stood behind his desk and greeted me in French as I came in. Quickly, I gave an appropriate response, thankful that I'd conjugated those verbs late last night.

He scanned the note I handed to him from the principal. "What a terrific thing to do, Holly," he said. I knew by the tone of his voice he meant it.

Unfortunately, my former friends, namely Andie, Paula, and Kayla, didn't seem to think my becoming an aide for a blind student was so terrific. I mean, as close as Andie and I had been for all our growing-up years, I never dreamed she'd behave this way. Oh, it wasn't an overt sort of thing. She wasn't coming up and saying nasty things to my face. No, Andie was more subtle about prejudice.

Prejudice?

I froze. Was that what this was about?

After class I stuffed my school books, as well as my library books on personality types, into my locker while Tina waited patiently for me. Being Hispanic, Andie knew full well the pain of prejudice. It had been fresh on her mind two days ago—the day we watched Ryan Davis, the biggest racist jerk around—from the cafeteria window. Had she forgotten so soon?

My brain clicked off the events of the day. On the one hand, I was leaning toward telling Andie—all the freshmen— the truth about Jeff's father. Jeff Kinney's campaign promise was bogus—there would never be any free soda. It was Jeff's attempt to bribe his way onto student council.

Was it fair to let him get by with lying? Besides, what kind of class president would Jeff make if he based his votes on deceit?

On the other hand, the truth could set Andie on the winning track, sail her right through to the victory she longed for. Still, part of me insisted on holding back the secret.

Justice!

Chapter 20

I kept the news about Jeff's lie quiet through Saturday, which was the fabulous day I *finally* got the kind of haircut I now really wanted. And at an upscale salon this time!

I kept the secret about Jeff and his "soda promise" through most of the whole next week, too.

Things went fairly smoothly. Class quizzes, homework—stuff like that. Tina, however, was the one bump in the road. She kept bringing it up—the "pop" secret. Had I told anyone yet?

Every day she asked me, until I finally set her straight. We were sitting on the school steps waiting for her ride the following Wednesday, the day before campaign speeches were scheduled.

"Why haven't you told anyone?" Tina asked. She sounded fed up. With me. "Andie deserves to know the truth."

"I'm not having this conversation," I said.

Tina's eyelids fluttered. "Why not? What are you waiting for?"

"I have my reasons."

She gasped. "I can't believe you'd let revenge get in the way, Holly. What kind of friend are you?"

I felt like she'd punched me in the stomach. "What?" I whispered.

"You're a Christian, right?"

I wasn't dumb enough to ask how she knew. Christians are supposed to be obvious—stick out in the world. I groaned. "Guess I'm not a very good one."

She was silent. "Well, it's never easy."

I jerked my head to look at her. How did she know, unless . . . "You're a Christian, too."

She smiled. "Since I was nine."

"Wow." I leaned my elbows on my books, thrilled with this news. "So that makes us sisters—in the family of God."

"You're right." Tina seemed pleased to hear me describe the two of us as family.

A Ford minivan pulled up to the curb. "I'll call you later, okay?" I held out my arm.

Tina held on to me as we walked down the steps. Before she got in the van, she introduced me to her mother. "Mom, this is Holly Meredith, my new friend. And Holly," Tina continued, turning to me, "this is my mother, Judith Frazer."

"Hello, Holly." The well-groomed, middle-aged woman smiled. "It's lovely to meet you."

"Nice meeting you, too," I said.

I observed the gentle way Tina's mom treated Tina and Taffy. "Well, are we ready to go?" she asked.

I closed the van door, lingering for a moment. Tina's window slid down. "Don't study too hard," she said.

"Look who's talking."

"Bye, Holly," she called as the van pulled away.

I stood there for the longest time, staring after them. Tina had somehow known that I was getting even with Andie by keeping Jeff's secret about the soda. But how? This baffled me totally.

I headed back inside to get my books out of my locker, dragging my feet as I went. The past few days had been rough—I'd stayed up too late doing homework. The lack of sleep was catching up with me.

As I rounded the corner to go to my locker, I stumbled into someone. Looking up, I saw that it was Andie. She was alone— without her usual twin attendants.

"Oh, sorry." I stepped back. "Didn't see you."

"No, it's my fault," she insisted. The light from outside flashed off her new braces.

I turned to go just as I saw Ryan Davis coming toward us. His hands were behind his back and there was a peculiar glint in his eye. "Hey, girls," he called to us.

The hairs on the back of my neck stood up. I sensed something. Impending danger?

Instinct, my mom called it. *"Always pay attention to that sensation,"* she'd warned.

I should've run for it when I had the chance.

Ryan whistled, and out of nowhere came three other guys, all upperclassmen, including Zye Greene. They grabbed me by the arms.

Zye picked up Andie and swung her over his shoulder. "Freshman frenzy!" he hollered gleefully.

"No! No!" Andie yelled. "Put me down!"

"Let me go!" I screamed as they pulled me out the front doors and down the long cement steps toward the flagpole.

"Cute freshmen don't get by without initiation as long as I'm around," Ryan Davis said in my ear.

I wanted to slap him. I pushed and shoved, trying to get free. But I was powerless against the two guys who began tying me to the flagpole.

I could feel them tying Andie up, too.

"You'll be sorry!" she yelled as the boys worked the knots and made them tight. Too tight.

When the deed was done, the despicable upperclassmen fled. I groaned. Here we were, stuck in front of the high school, our arms tied behind a flagpole with clothesline. Holly and Andie—former best friends—tied up together in the worst initiation stunt so far.

"Can you wiggle your hands?" I strained my neck, trying to see Andie behind me.

"Barely," she muttered.

"They must've learned some super-holding boy-scout knots or something," I wailed.

"You're right." She was kicking and thrashing around as though her life depended on it.

I heard the city bus blow out puffs of exhaust as it made the turn away from the school. "There goes my ride!"

Andie moaned. "Mine too. That's why I was rushing and nearly ran into you before." Her voice cracked with desperation. "This is humiliating . . . and disgusting."

"And the worst of it is, tomorrow's the day we cast our votes for student council."

"What?" She began to laugh. That mid-range laugh with an eerie staccato bounce. "Here we are, tied to a flagpole, and you're talking about ballot boxes? C'mon, Holly, you've got to be kidding."

I thought about what she'd just said. About other things, too. The way she'd booted me out of her cozy campaign hoopla. The frivolous phone comments she'd made over the past week—and hanging up on me.

"We're not very good friends anymore, are we?" I said.

"Well, it's not my fault."

"Look, Andie. I'm not pointing fingers. It's just that . . . well, we used to share our secrets. All of them."

"Secrets are childish," she said. "Face it, we're growing up, past the stage of Loyalty Papers and best friends and all that dumb stuff. It's better to have lots of friends; at least for me it is."

All that dumb stuff . . .

Her words stung me. What Andie was saying fit right into

what Mom had told me about extroverts. When they grew up, they required lots of friends. Not just one.

I stuck my neck out and came close to confiding in her. "I'm trying to branch out, make new friends," I managed to say. "But it's not as easy for people like me."

"Are we talking about Tina now?" She sounded more hesitant than brash.

"Blind isn't bad, you know."

"Who said it was?"

"Well, the way you and the Miller twins acted," I said, not really wanting to bring it up. "I was actually glad Tina couldn't see the three of you."

Andie sighed. "You probably won't believe this, but I really felt lousy about it later. I mean, it hasn't been so long ago—remember last summer and the lowdown comments Ryan Davis made about me? I know how it feels to be treated poorly when you're . . . uh . . . different."

She was backpedaling. "Forgive me, Holly?" she said.

"Always." And I meant it.

Suddenly Andie began to cry. Soft, whimpering sounds. "My hands feel really numb," she said. "I'm scared we're going to be stuck here all night."

"Maybe we should stop trying to loosen the cord. Maybe the guys made knots that get tighter when you struggle." I wiggled my fingers. "I'm not sure, but I think my fingers are tingling. They feel really weird."

"Oh, Holly," Andie cried, "what if the blood circulation goes out of our hands? What if our hands have to be amputated?"

"There goes my writing career," I moaned, joining her in the drama.

"And what about me? I'm the accompanist for show choir this year."

"C'mon, Andie. Get a grip. We have to relax." I felt overwhelmed. "Maybe if we yell, the janitor or the principal will hear us."

"Good idea." And she started hollering at the top of her lungs. So did I.

I'd never seen Andie so freaked. Usually she was the calm one under stress.

When we were exhausted from yelling, I suggested that we pray. "I'll start."

Andie agreed. "Why didn't we think of this first?"

"Dear Lord," I began, "please send someone to help us so we won't have to spend the night out here."

"Amen to someone finding us," she prayed.

We quieted down somewhat, although Andie was still moaning. At last I began to talk. "I've been holding out on you about something, Andie. I need to tell you the truth about Jeff Kinney."

"What truth?"

There was no way out now. I had to tell her. Maybe this initiation was supposed to happen to us. Maybe we were supposed to get strung up to the flagpole.

Together.

Chapter 21

"So are you going to tell me or not?" Andie demanded.

I struggled with my fabulous secret.

"Holly?"

"All right, I'll tell you," I said. "Tina overheard something last week." I paused, thinking how this moment could possibly change the course of the entire school year. Possibly the course of Andie's and my future relationship. "Tina heard Mark Jones telling some girl about Jeff's dad," I continued.

"Whoa! Slow down," Andie insisted. "I don't get what you're saying."

I repeated the circumstances again. Slowly. Then I revealed the truth. "Jeff's dad is not a soda-pop dealer."

"Huh?"

"His dad is a doctor, for pete's sake."

"Are you sure?"

"Isn't it obvious? I mean, if he's a doctor, he's not a pop dealer."

She fidgeted. "What if he's both?"

I hadn't thought of that. "I think we should call Mr. Kinney and check things out."

"Tonight?" she said, out of breath.

"As soon as someone frees us from this flagpole nightmare."

She yelled some more. Louder this time.

"Let's yell 'fire,'" I suggested. "People pay attention to that."

"Hey, you're right."

So we yelled "Fire! Fire!" until we were hoarse.

Finally Mr. Crane and two other teachers poked their heads out a window. "Where's the fire?" the principal called to us. He was serious.

"Right here," Andie shouted. "I've got rope burns on my wrists." Andie was in rare form.

After the principal left the window, I said to Andie, "Looks like we survived part of freshman initiation, or whatever Zye Greene called it."

"Freshman frenzy," Andie grunted.

"Well, if this is all there is to it—"

"Don't be too sure," Andie scoffed. "Knowing Zye and Ryan, there's probably more to come."

"I hope not. I've had my share."

Mr. Crane came with a scissors and cut us free. "Are you girls all right?" He looked concerned. "Who did this to you?"

"We'd better not say," Andie spoke up. "Seniors hate freshmen, you know."

"Thanks for rescuing us," I said. "We were getting worried there for a while."

"I can see that," he said, eyeing Andie's wrists. "You'd better soak your wrists in Epsom salts when you get home."

She nodded. "We need to make a phone call first."

"That's fine. Follow me." And the two of us hurried into the building and gathered up Andie's books and things, which were still strewn around the hallway.

I borrowed the office phone book and located the number for Jeff Kinney's father. Sure enough—Edward Kinney, MD.

Andie was still rubbing her wrists when I dialed the phone. "What're you going to say?" she whispered.

"Just listen to the pro."

The receptionist sounded pleasant enough. "Doctor Kinney's office."

"Hello, I'm a friend of Jeff Kinney," I said. "Is this his father's office?"

"Yes."

"Well, I was wondering if I could check on something."

"Certainly. How may I help you?"

I took a deep breath, hoping this wouldn't sound too ridiculous. "Jeff's telling everyone at school that his dad's a soda dealer, but you just said this is a doctor's office."

"That's right."

"Then are you saying Dr. Kinney won't be bringing free soft drinks to school every Friday for the rest of the school year?"

The receptionist began to laugh. "Well, I think I'd be one of the first to know about it, since I'm Dr. Kinney's wife—Jeff's mom."

I explained about the campaign promises. "I guess Jeff really wants to be class president this year."

"Class president?" she echoed.

"Didn't you know?"

She wasn't laughing now. "I will definitely talk to Jeff tonight. And what did you say your name was, hon?"

"I didn't say." And I hung up.

Andie was about to burst. "You're too cool, Holly. Wait'll I tell everyone about this."

"Hey, you'll win tomorrow—no problem." Part of me still missed the old Andie. The old us. But most of all, I missed the secret. The secret that might've saved us—kept Andie all for myself. Kept her from being linked up with the student council clique.

Andie beamed. "How can I ever thank you?" I thought she was going to hug me, but she didn't. Her smile said it all. "Well, we better get going. It's a long walk home."

We walked together for three blocks. Andie did most of the talking. She was wired about the prospect of her position on the student council.

Me? I was having a hard time not dwelling on the past. Our past—Andie's and mine. But Mom's words echoed in my brain. *"Sometimes people drift apart during high school . . ."*

"So, where do you see yourself in ten years?" I asked.

She didn't waste a second responding. "Hopefully, married to a terrific Christian guy. Someone who wants a big family."

I should've known. "And what about all the experience you'll get on the student council? How will that fit into your life?"

"Hey, I didn't agree to an interview yet. Wait till I get voted in." She giggled gleefully. "Oh . . . about student council. I'll definitely use my experience later in life. I want lots of kids, remember? And right here in Dressel Hills."

I nodded.

Andie continued. "Being class president means you have to learn to delegate power—you know, assign jobs. My high-school experience will fit right in with my future; you can bet on that."

I smiled. Andie was so sure of herself. I liked that.

"What about friends? When you get super popular, will you remember who your first friends were?"

Andie grabbed my arm. "I'll never forget you, Holly. Never."

I grinned. "Just remember who got you elected freshman class president."

"Don't worry," she said as we headed in different directions. I hoped it was just a short parting of the ways. Maybe, in time, we'd have our close bond again. Maybe not. Either way, I had fabulous memories . . . and hope for the future. And a widening circle of friends. Sort of.

♥ ♥ ♥

After supper I made at least twenty phone calls, getting the word out about Jeff Kinney—and no free soda! Everyone I talked to promised to vote for Andie.

Later, I called Tina. "Got any plans this weekend?"

"Not really. Why?"

"How would you like to have supper at my house Friday?"

"I'd love to," she said. "But let me ask Mom first."

When she came back, she said it was fine.

"Great. Maybe we can write some poetry together," I suggested.

"Or we could read some of our stories to each other," she said, referring to her Braille machine.

"Good idea." Tina didn't know I had zillions of notebooks full of stories and poems and things. Thoughts about life, generally and specifically. Shoot, this girl probably didn't know what she was getting herself into.

"I heard you got initiated today," she said.

"So did Andie. We were tied to the flagpole."

"Together?"

"It was bizarre at first, but then she and I started talking. We talked a lot. And I told her about Jeff."

"It's about time."

"I know." I felt ashamed again.

"Glad you did, Holly. I was praying for you."

I wasn't used to hearing that a friend was praying. Well, except for Danny Myers.

"I'd better get going," Tina said. "See you tomorrow."

"No, you won't," I teased. "You'll smell me tomorrow. Better watch out—I might be wearing different perfume."

"Hey, you wouldn't do that to me, would you?" With that, we burst into giggles and hung up.

After my homework was done, I made two very cool posters to wave during tomorrow's assembly. One for Tina, and one for me.

Chapter 22

The next morning while I waited for Carrie to get out of the bathroom—she was taking longer than ever these days—I wrote in my journal.

Thursday, September 19: Today Andie gives her campaign speech. She's first, then Jeff Kinney. I can't wait to see what he does when I hold up my poster. It says: No Friday Pop—Jeff's Pop's a Doc!

Everyone knows by now that Jeff lied about having free soda at school. Thanks to all the phone calls Andie and I made last night. The way I see it, she's destined for class president. Jared and Amy-Liz will probably make it, too. They've been campaigning like crazy. And Billy's going to be a great class treasurer if he gets elected.

Sometimes I wish I had run for office. But then I think about Tina. When it comes right down to it, I know I'd rather be helping her than getting frazzled over school politics and stuff. Besides, I really like her.

After "losing" Andie to the student council thing, I never dreamed my heart could accept someone new as a close friend . . . and so fast. Yesterday Andie said she'd never forget me. Well, I won't hold her to it, because I can see her changing. And with change comes the growing apart process—the toughest part of all. Maybe I shouldn't blame it on Andie. Maybe I'm changing, too. . . .

♥ ♥ ♥

After a bunch of homeroom preliminaries, we headed to the assembly. I sat with Tina, one row behind Billy Hill and his fans. Tina got her guide dog situated directly under her seat for the half-hour session.

"I'll tell you when to hold up your poster," I said.

Her face shone. "This is so exciting!"

"I know." But I had a fleeting thought—a lonely, sentimental feeling—floating around in my brain. And when I scanned the audience for Andie, I noticed she was sitting in the front row with Amy-Liz and Jared. Any other time I would've been there beside her. Encouraging her. Saying all the right words.

I refused to think about what used to be and turned my attention to Tina. Something intrigued me about her. Maybe it was her positive, upbeat approach to life. She was blind, yet she seemed so happy.

Just then Mr. Crane was onstage, standing at the podium. The students got quiet. Anticipation, like electricity, crackled in the air. "We have student business to conduct today." The crowd broke into wild applause.

When things settled down again, the principal continued with his introductions.

At last Andie stood in front of us. She wore her new outfit. I listened intently to her opening remarks. Honestly, I couldn't remember ever seeing her in a position of leadership like this. I wracked my brain trying to recall a time . . .

Then I heard my name!

"At this time, I would like to thank Holly Meredith for her support and encouragement. Tina Frazer was a great help, too.

Several sophomore friends of mine, including Paula and Kayla Miller, were responsible for running my campaign. . . ."

The fact that she'd mentioned my name—and first, before the twins—soothed my sore heart.

"I will not make promises that I cannot keep," Andie was saying. "The thing I will do, however, is lead my class to the best of my ability. And with your help—each of you in this room—I will represent your needs, listen to your problems, and do my best to come up with solutions. Thank you for your vote of confidence—I'll see you at the polls!"

Wow, I was impressed. Andie's speech didn't sound anything like what the Miller twins might've written. And the more I thought about it, I knew Andie hadn't written it, either.

"Great speech," I said to Tina, who was also on her feet clapping.

"Not bad for a first timer?" she said, a strange smile on her face.

I had no idea what she meant. "First timer?"

"Your friend called me last night and offered me ten bucks to write her speech," Tina said. "It was easier than I thought."

"Andie *hired* you to write it?" I shouldn't have been surprised. Andie was unpredictable. That part of her hadn't changed one bit.

Andie walked down the steps, heading confidently toward her seat. Just once, I wished she'd glance up and see me clapping for her, cheering for her. . . .

We took our seats and waited to hear Jeff Kinney's speech. I couldn't imagine that he hadn't heard what we'd been spreading around about him. Bottom line: He was not an honest guy.

"Hold up your poster," I whispered to Tina.

Lots of other students were waving gimmicky posters as Jeff Kinney approached the stage, shuffling his papers.

The auditorium was still. Jeff stood at the podium and coughed. I felt embarrassed for him, wondering what he could possibly say to save face. "Fellow classmates, teachers, and Mr. Crane," he began.

Oh, brother, he's pouring it on, I thought.

"Today I stand before you to stand behind you, to tell you something I know nothing about."

Snickering rippled through the audience.

"Now . . . to get things straight right from here on out," he continued, "my dad's not going to be able to supply free soda on Fridays as previously promised. He will, however, offer free flu shots to any student this winter. Thanks for your support."

By now, Jeff's face had turned a bright red. And as he made his way off the stage, only a few of his close friends applauded. It was an awkward moment for everyone, and I touched Tina's elbow and told her to put her poster away.

We listened to the other candidates' speeches, and at the end I decided that Andie's was best. "It was perfect," I told Tina. "You wrote a fabulous campaign speech."

"Thanks," she said, leaning over to whisper to her guide dog. I carried both the posters as we headed up the aisle, toward the hallway doors.

During lunch, Tina and I went to study hall, where the ballot boxes were set up. I helped her find the square she wanted to check. When she was finished, I waited for her to fold her ballot. Carefully, she felt for the opening on the ballot box and dropped the paper in.

♥ ♥ ♥

I had an email message from Sean when I arrived home. I couldn't wait to read it.

Hey, Holly,

Well, how do you feel about writing to a bald guy?

Seriously, I did it. I shaved my head! Most all the guys in Mr. Fremont's class did, too. It's weird what some people will do to encourage a friend.

I thought about Sean's words. And I thought about Andie. I hadn't shaved my head or anything drastic, but I had done something. Something to assure her a desired goal.

Mom had said flexibility was a big part of growing up. Was that happening? Was I growing up?

I stared at the computer screen. Sean was a perfect example of true maturity. I couldn't wait to write him back, so I clicked on Reply and began typing away.

Chapter 23

The next morning Mr. Crane's voice came over the intercom with election results. "Andrea Martinez has been voted in as president of the freshman class, Jared Wilkins was elected vice president, Amy-Liz Thompson will be the new secretary for the class, and Billy Hill is the treasurer. Congratulations to each of these fine students."

The hall at lunchtime was crowded with well-wishers, streamers, balloons, and confetti. I hurried to pick up Tina and Taffy in study hall, then we made our way through the tangle of humanity.

"Do you mind if we stop by Andie's locker?" I asked Tina.

"No problem," she said, reminding me of Andie.

I laughed, but I was sure she didn't hear me. Not against the backdrop of hilarious celebration. When we found Andie, she was being swarmed by half the freshman class. At least, that's how it appeared as I waited with Tina for a chance to congratulate the winner.

Even Stan showed his face, in spite of his sophomore status.

And when he walked past me, he gave me a decent smile for a change.

Andie sparkled as she talked to her adoring fans, hugging them, thanking them, and accepting their enthusiastic remarks. And from my vantage point, I surprised myself by not feeling so left out.

I was actually part of it all. I'd helped make this moment happen for Andie, and I was glad.

Nobody could move, it was so crowded. But I waited patiently, and then it happened. Andie glanced up, and her eyes caught mine. "Holly! Holly-Heart, get yourself over here," she called.

"C'mon," I said to Tina, guiding her to Andie. The mass of devotees parted like the Red Sea as we came. Then Andie hugged me hard.

"You did it," I said. "Congratulations!"

"*We* did it," Andie said, not letting go of me. "Thanks for everything." I knew what she meant. So did Tina. And long after the throng of kids had gone, Andie, Tina, and I hung around talking.

When the Miller twins finally caught up with the three of us, we were sitting in the cafeteria, well within the seniors' silly boundary line.

"Congrats," Paula said.

"We heard the news," Kayla said.

"Isn't she fabulous?" I said about Andie.

The twins agreed. Tina too. We sat there reliving the events of the past two days, and I never once felt a twinge of pain. Sure, my circle of friends had begun to widen, but the Holly-Andie bond was as strong as ever. The only difference was it didn't encompass every inch of our lives. It didn't have to.

We were freshmen now, for pete's sake.

HOLLY'S HEART

Mystery Letters

To my HOLLY'S HEART fans

at Radiant Church:

Kelly Brinkley

Jennifer Davis

Ali Drobeck

Kris Harris

Rachel Jones

Tiffany Littleton

Amanda Neely

Colleen Nelson

Kimberly Noxon

Katie Root

Tiffany Sturgeon

Alicia Weckman

Theresa Weckman

Andrea Catalano

Melissa Davis

Megan Goerzen

Beth Horner

Brittany Littleton

Tonya Nadeau

Cheryl Nelson

Jennifer Noxon

Dani Root

Kim Stone

Stacy Tremble

Brandi Weckman

Chapter 1

I hurried off the bus and rushed into the house. "Mom, I'm home!"

"Upstairs," she called back. "Mail's in the kitchen."

Grinning, I flung my jacket over a living room chair. Mom was mighty perceptive these days. Fact was, I'd been inquiring about the mail every day this week.

I made a beeline through the dining room to the corner of the kitchen, spying the letters on the desk. My fingers flicked through the stack. Bills, junk mail, letters . . .

Miss Holly Meredith caught my eye. I studied the familiar handwriting. Clear, even strokes. California—the return address.

Perfect. The letter I was waiting for! I held the cream-colored, textured envelope close to my heart. What had Sean Hamilton written *this* time?

Slowly, I turned the envelope over, starting to open it. Then I noticed something strange. Scotch tape—two jagged pieces— stuck to the back of the envelope. Hmm. I'd been getting letters from Sean nearly every week—emails, too—since school started, and he *never* used tape to seal the envelope.

"Mom!"

"Don't yell, I'm right here," she said, coming into the kitchen.

"Where's Carrie?" I demanded.

Her blue eyes squinted almost shut. "Holly, please don't start something with your sister."

I showed her the envelope. "There's only one person in the house who'd do this."

Mom sat on a stool and leaned her elbows heavily on the island bar. "Be careful about accusing someone, Holly-Heart." She sighed. "Carrie might not have anything to do with it."

"And she might have *everything* to do with it!" I stormed out of the kitchen and down the steps to the family room, clutching the envelope. Carrie-the-Snoop, just turned ten, sat on the floor watching TV. Stephie, our eight-year-old stepsister and cousin (because Uncle Jack married Mom after his first wife—my dad's sister—died) lounged on the sectional. Both sets of eyes were totally focused on the tube.

"Okay, you two, listen up," I said. Neither of them paid attention, so I stood in front of Carrie, waving the envelope in her face.

"Hey, you're blocking my view," she hollered.

"I'll move when you explain this." I pointed to the tape on the back of the envelope.

Her mouth curled into a surly smile. "Yeah, so? I read your letter. Who cares?"

"Mom!" I dashed upstairs to the kitchen, hoping she was still there. She wasn't. Goofey, my cat, glanced up at me from his sunny square on the floor. A brown patch of fur colored the gray around one eye. I leaned down and stroked his motley fur. "My sister's a total nightmare," I complained.

Goofey agreed and gave a comforting *me-e-o-ow*.

I stood up and headed for the doorway leading to the lower level. "Okay for you, Carrie. You'll be sorry, I promise."

"See if I care. You're wasting time. Go read your love letter from Sean."

Love letter? I gulped. She must've read through the whole letter. Sean never started his letters out mushy, but sometimes at the end . . .

I fumed. How could she do this? Just when I hoped things were improving between Carrie and me. I mean, she was a preteen now. Man, if this was how life with Carrie was going to be at ten, I hated to think about her full-blown teen years!

I turned and ran two floors up to the master bedroom at the end of the hall. The door was cracked slightly. "Mom?" I whispered, trying to control my rage. At one point, both she and Uncle Jack had promised stiffer laws for snoopers. Stuff like no TV for a full week. And double kitchen duty. Threats of that sort of discipline being dished out did seem to help some. But not much.

I peeked around the door to see Mom sacked out on the bed. Her face looked pale and her eyes were a bit puffy. Was she sick?

Without disturbing her, I left the room, closing the door silently behind me. Goofey was right under my feet; I nearly tripped over him. Picking him up, I pressed my face into the back of his neck and tiptoed to my room. There, I settled down on my window seat, still holding Goofey close. He didn't protest, but when I began to open Sean's letter, Goofey slinked off my lap and sat opposite me on the padded seat, eyes glaring.

"Don't be silly," I laughed. "It's not really a love letter." I opened the envelope and began to read.

Chapter 2

October 7

Dear Holly,

As always, I enjoyed your letter. Thanks for writing back so quickly. It was interesting to hear that, as the new assistant editor for your school paper, you'll be writing your own column. My friends and I think The Summit *is a cool name for a high-school paper in a Colorado mountain town. So . . . when's your first column scheduled to appear? I definitely want a copy of my Holly's creative literary work in print.*

I stopped reading.

My Holly? Had I read correctly? I scanned the line again. Yep!

I remembered Carrie's nasty smile and flippant response to my reprimand. *Oh great. She knows about this, too!*

It took more than the usual amount of self-control to keep myself from charging downstairs and wringing her little neck. My reward for staying put—not giving in to temptation—came as the delicious autumn sun warmed my shoulders. I let myself lean back against the window on my multi-pillowed seat, savoring Sean's words.

His letter turned out to be shorter than usual. I finished reading it in a few minutes, only to reread the first several paragraphs again. Sean seemed sincerely interested in my new editorial position on the school paper. He was the kind of guy most girls would give their eyeteeth for.

If only Carrie would keep her nose out!

♥ ♥ ♥

Mom rested until Uncle Jack arrived home. I heard his footsteps on the stairs, and he headed straight for their bedroom. It was all I could do to keep from poking my head into the hall and eavesdropping. Mom seemed awfully tired lately. I hoped she wasn't coming down with a case of the fall flu.

Around here, the change of seasons wreaked havoc on us locals. The first snowfall always brought out-of-town tourists and ski bums, some from overseas. And with the start of the ski season came a variety of international flu bugs. Fortunately, I hadn't succumbed to any of them yet.

A few minutes passed, and I was aware of Uncle Jack hurriedly leaving the house with Stan, Phil, and Mark, my three brousins—cousins-turned-stepbrothers. Something was up.

In less than thirty minutes, they returned with pizza and soda for everyone. I guess Mom wasn't well enough to cook supper. She was even too sick to come down and sit at the table with us. Rats! I needed her input tonight when I brought up Carrie's snooping violation.

Not so patiently I waited until after Uncle Jack's prayer. Carrie eyeballed me, looking profoundly sheepish. It was time.

"Uncle Jack," I began. "I thought you should know . . . Carrie opened my mail today."

My stepdad's slice of pizza halted midway between his plate and his mouth. His eyes shifted to Carrie, several place settings away. "I thought we had this problem worked out months ago."

I spoke up. "And that's not all. She's acting all hotsy-totsy about it, too." I felt like a tattling third grader instead of a freshman in high school.

"Have you forgotten the consequences for this kind of behavior?" he asked, still gazing at Carrie.

Yes!

"I . . . uh . . ." Carrie sputtered.

"You must never open someone else's mail—snail mail or email," he continued. "Including your older sister's."

Carrie acted cool about the reprimand, but her cocky attitude was squelched quickly when the sentencing came.

"No TV or phone privileges for a week," Uncle Jack stated. "Starting tonight."

"No phone?" she wailed.

Uncle Jack resumed eating his pizza. When he'd chewed and swallowed, he took a long drink of soda. "Now"—and here, he leaned forward slightly—"your mother is resting quietly, Carrie, so don't get any ideas about going to her with your whining."

I'd never heard Uncle Jack come down so hard on Carrie, or on anyone, for that matter. Something was definitely bothering him. And I was fairly sure it had nothing to do with Carrie's snooping.

"Is Mom sick?" I ventured.

"She's going to need a good amount of rest," he said guardedly.

"Can I go up and see her?" Stephie asked.

Uncle Jack nodded. "Later, when she wakes up."

Stephie's eyes filled with tears. "Is *this* mommy gonna die, too?"

Uncle Jack pushed his chair back and went to his youngest daughter. "Mommy's not that sick," he reassured her.

Phil, eleven, and Mark, nine, looked concerned as their dad

hoisted Stephie up and out of her chair and carried her into the living room. The rest of us tried not to watch. Stephie, after all, was the baby of the family. Possibly Uncle Jack's favorite, if such a thing could be. She was the image of her deceased mother, my aunt Marla, who had been my all-time favorite relative.

I tried to ignore the hard lump in my throat. And the strange, fluttery feeling in my stomach—a confusing mixture of hunger and worry. We all ate in silence while Stephie sniffled in the living room in Uncle Jack's arms.

Finally, after we finished pigging out, Stan, the oldest of the Meredith-Patterson clan, suggested we clear the table.

"But it's not my turn," Carrie insisted.

"C'mon, Carrie," I said. "Stop fussing and help."

"You stay out of it!" she shot back.

Stan grabbed her arm and guided her gingerly out to the kitchen. "Look, little girl, do I have to *make* you wanna help?"

"I'm not little," she wailed. "And I'm telling." She made a face. "Uncle Jack!"

Mark cupped his hand over her mouth. "Didn't you hear what Dad just said about letting Mom rest?"

"He's *your* dad, not mine!" With that, she pulled away from both Stan and Mark, plowed through the dining room, and nearly knocked a pile of paper plates out of Phil's hands.

That was my cue to exit the kitchen. I'd had it with Carrie's lousy attitude. What my flesh-and-blood sister needed was a good heart-to-heart talk. Starting with her ridiculous notion about Uncle Jack's place in our family.

Chapter 3

I didn't bother to knock—I barged right into Carrie's room. Determined, I closed the door behind me. "We have to talk."

"Says who?" she sneered.

I sat down on her bed, praying silently for the right words. "Look, I know you're mad at me because of the letter."

"You're dangy-dong right I am. You didn't have to go and tell on me."

"That's true; I didn't," I replied softly. "But you can't seem to conquer your snooping addiction. What kind of big sister would I be if I didn't intervene?"

She crossed her arms over her chest and exhaled loudly. "Stop talking so grown-up, Holly. You think you're such a big shot because you're in high school. Well, I'll tell you what kind of sister you really are."

"Carrie, keep your voice down."

She screwed up her face. "I wish you'd just go away and leave me alone."

We sat there, staring at each other. Finally I turned away, facing her bulletin board. A small black-and-white picture of our dad was stuck on the board with a white thumbtack. He'd autographed it for her last Christmas when we'd gone to California for a visit. *Robert Meredith,* the scribbled letters ran across the bottom.

"What are you staring at?" Carrie demanded.

I turned to her. "You're angry at Daddy, aren't you?"

"Why shouldn't I be?" she spouted. "He left us, didn't he? Went off to California without us. Divorced Mom. Left us kids behind." The tears spilled down her face. "All those years he belonged here."

I understood her pain. Oh, how I knew . . .

Yet I'd dealt with it—worked things out with myself about the divorce. With God's help. Daddy's too. But I knew exactly how Carrie was feeling. The whole Daddy thing had started for me six years ago. The questioning . . . the wondering . . . those wretched feelings of worthlessness . . . the rejection.

And now, as I looked into Carrie's face, I could see the hideous thing rearing its head in my preadolescent sister. "Carrie," I whispered, reaching for her hand. "Let me tell you about Daddy . . . and Mom."

Carrie listened through a veil of tears and occasional sobs. It surprised me that she was experiencing this stuff now. Lots of young girls experienced the emotional ups and downs of the prepuberty roller coaster. For some, it started at age nine. Shoot, I'd worried myself nearly sick in seventh grade wondering when I'd ever become a "real" woman. And now here I was, helping my little sister cope with what appeared to be full-blown hormonal upheaval.

"It's not your fault about the divorce," I explained gently. Mom had told me the same thing years ago. "Our parents weren't Christians back then. Things were a little crazy, from what Mom says. She wasn't as submissive as Daddy thought she should be, and Daddy had his heart set on a career instead of his family."

"How'd you find out all this stuff?" she asked.

"Little bits at a time. Every so often I'd sit Mom down and

ask her questions. And after my second visit to California last Christmas, I started to feel more comfortable with Daddy."

She pouted, looking down at the floor. "He likes you best."

"Why do you think that?"

"I just do."

"Well, I can tell you one thing. Daddy really wanted you to come along last summer. Remember when Andie and I flew out there together? He was really disappointed."

Her face brightened a bit. "Are you sure?"

"Perfectly sure."

She stood up and walked over to the bulletin board. "I wish I knew him better."

"Maybe you will someday. But till then, be thankful that he's become a Christian. Oh, and something else." I paused, studying the girl who was in so many ways a miniature me. "Please try to be thankful about Uncle Jack."

She shrugged.

"C'mon, Carrie, you know how wonderful he is to Mom. Honestly, he's the best thing that could've happened to this poor, messed-up family."

"But . . . he's only a stepdad," she insisted.

"Only? He's the *best* stepdad ever."

Carrie looked at me, startled. "You really think so?"

"Give him a chance. You'll see."

She wrinkled her nose. "That's easy for you to say. You're not on restriction."

"It's only a week. Besides, you can't blame Uncle Jack for that."

She pulled on her long blond ponytail. "A week without the phone is an eternity."

"You'll survive." I got up and gave her a hug. The anger between us had pretty much fizzled. "Still friends?"

"Do I have a choice?" She twirled her ponytail around her finger, the way I used to when I was little. I headed for the hall.

Back in my room, I sorted through a zillion homework papers, especially the miserable algebra assignment for the weekend. I couldn't stop thinking of Sean's letter and his astonishing words. Thank goodness Carrie hadn't mentioned anything in her usual snippy manner. More than anything, I hoped she'd keep Sean's interest in me quiet from Mom.

Poor Mom. She'd spent the whole afternoon and now the evening in her room. Did I dare peek in?

I muddled through my math homework, carelessly going from one insignificant set of problems to another. What good would algebra do me in the future? I wanted to be a writer, for pete's sake!

Thirty minutes passed while I fussed over a mere two problems.

The phone rang. Stan yelled up the stairs, "Holly, it's Andie."

"I'll get it up here." I headed out to the hall phone, hoping to keep my comments from floating down the hall to Mom's ears. That is, if she was awake.

"Hey," Andie said when I answered. "I'm writing a letter to the assistant editor of *The Summit*." She laughed into the phone. "That's you, remember?"

"What's going on?"

"Just wanted to keep you on your editorial toes, you know. Wanted to come up with a really off-the-wall letter for you to answer in your new column."

It was my turn to laugh. "Look, I'm not playing Dear Abby, if that's what you think."

"Have you thought up a cool name for your column yet?" she asked.

"At the moment I'm trying to think up some cool answers for my rotten algebra homework."

"On a Friday night—are you nuts?"

"Why not?"

Andie snickered. "Join the ranks of the procrastinators of the world. Wait till late *Sunday* night."

"Not me; I'd flunk for sure." We talked about *The Summit* some more and then how glad she was about not taking a foreign language. "I think you're making a big mistake," I said. "French class is fabulous."

"If you say so." I could hear her whispering in the background.

"Who're you talking to?" I asked.

"Somebody wants to know if you're interested in him," she said, trying to keep from laughing.

"Andie, this is *so* junior high. C'mon!"

"Just answer one question. Are you tied up with anyone right now?"

"Uh, not really."

"What about Sean?" she asked. "You two still writing?"

The way she said it made me wonder if she was hoping I'd say no. "Uh, this is a little personal, don'tcha think?"

More whispering.

"Andie, who are you talking to? Who's over there?"

Loud, hilarious laughter. Andie's . . . and some guy's.

"Andie, talk to me," I demanded.

Several more seconds of stupidity passed. Finally I couldn't stand it anymore and hung up.

Funniest thing. I didn't care two hoots about the guy at Andie's house inquiring about me. Nope, didn't care one bit. Sean Hamilton and I were very good friends. And that's all that mattered to me.

Chapter 4

I slammed my algebra book shut and went down the hall.

Mom was awake and in the master bathroom. I could see the light coming from the crack under the door as I peeked around her antique pine dresser. The faucet was on and swishing sounds came from the sink. She was either washing her face or brushing her teeth. A good sign.

I decided not to wait around for her, and I headed downstairs to make a cup of cocoa. Phil and Stephie showed up just as I plopped a handful of miniature marshmallows in my hot chocolate.

"Where's mine?" Phil sniffed the sweet aroma.

I pushed his head away from my after-supper treat. "You're not helpless." I pointed toward the mug tree on the kitchen counter. "Make your own."

Stephie muttered something and ran back downstairs to join Uncle Jack and the remaining family members. Phil, however, hung around, acting like he wanted to talk. He sat at the bar, still eyeing my cup of cocoa. "Was seventh grade cool?" Phil asked.

I smiled. "Not as cool as ninth."

"So . . . what's it like, in your opinion?"

I stirred the marshmallows, watching them melt into foamy white suds. "You've got a whole school year to worry about it."

"Maybe not." He scratched his head. "The counselor gave me another test today."

"What kind of test?"

"Just an assessment test to see if I'm too smart for my britches, like Mom says."

I smirked at his comment. "So your teachers must think you're gifted or something."

He nodded enthusiastically. "You're lookin' at the first eleven-year-old genius at Dressel Hills Middle School. I'll be skipping a grade soon—going into the seventh-grade TAG program."

"Talented and gifted—you?" This was the first *I'd* heard this.

Phil got up and swaggered around the kitchen. He grabbed a cup off the mug tree and turned on the faucet, gloating all the while. "Betcha can't guess what my best subject is?" He shot me an impish grin. "Actually, I'm brilliant in all subjects, but, hey, I wouldn't be surprised if they hired me out as a tutor in—"

"Spare me," I groaned. I'd had enough of his crowing and strutting. Especially after I'd struggled away my entire Friday night on homework.

"Give up?" he taunted.

I shrugged uncaringly.

"Math. I'm a marvel," he exclaimed. "Algebra, geometry, you name it."

I nearly choked at his arrogance, not to mention the frustration over my own recent algebraic nightmare. "Pride goes before destruction . . ." I said, quoting the proverb.

Phil opened his mouth for a comeback, but Mom came into the kitchen just then. She looked rested, refreshed. "Where *is* everyone?" she asked.

"Downstairs in the family room." I slid off the barstool and went to her. "Feeling better, Mom?"

She nodded, returning my hug. "Much better."

"Do you want some peppermint tea with honey?" I asked. "I'll make it for you."

"Sounds good, thanks." She sat down at the bar as I slid Phil's cup of cocoa out of the microwave to make room.

"I can see who rates around here," Phil said to Mom. "Holly wouldn't cook for *me*."

I suppressed a laugh. "You'll get over it."

Mom ignored our bantering and smoothed her blond hair. "Well, Phil," she said, "I've been hearing some terrific things about you."

Yeah, yeah, I thought. *Do we have to rehash this?*

Phil was all too happy to give her the rundown on his latest test scores and teacher remarks. I stirred the honey into Mom's cup and quietly exited the room. It was time to answer someone's letter—someone very special. Whether Andie liked it or not.

♥ ♥ ♥

Normally Jared Wilkins and Amy-Liz Thompson—his current girlfriend—sat toward the back of the classroom and off to one side in algebra. Always together. Today they sat on opposite sides of the room. I gave their present classroom positions only a fleeting thought, then tore into my notebook, hunting down the pathetic homework I'd toiled and fretted over during my entire weekend.

Andie Martinez slid into the desk behind me. "Did you get your homework done?"

"I guess you could call it done. Did you?"

"Late last night," she admitted. "Couldn't let it spoil my week-end, you know." I remembered her comment about procrastinators. She'd practiced what she preached.

Billy Hill hurried in, grabbed a seat across from Andie, and took out a pencil. Andie leaned over and whispered something to him. I could hear their voices buzzing behind me.

A few seconds later Mrs. Franklin, our resident math wizard, made her debut. Andie kept whispering with Billy, but I ignored them. Mrs. Franklin was getting her things situated and I watched intently, scrutinizing her every move. What sort of woman—a married, civilized woman—would want to teach high-school algebra? What motivated her to impose nightmarish assignments on students? And for money, no less?

I tore out a sheet of lined paper and jotted down some of her obvious characteristics. Who knows—this true-to-life description might fit into one of my stories. Or maybe even my editorial column someday.

Mrs. Franklin

1. Too aloof
2. Pinched up in the face (from creating too many excruciating math problems?)
3. No jewelry—not even a wedding band (is she Amish?)
4. No makeup (sure could use some!)

I ran my hand through my hair, eager to turn in my homework and have the worst hour of the entire day behind me. Third hour . . . forty-five agonizing minutes to go.

At the risk of drawing attention to myself, I began gathering up homework papers from students in my row. Jared grinned when I glanced his way. "That's it, take charge, Holly-Heart," he said.

His comment didn't strike me as odd at the time. He'd never been one to comment publicly on things or call me by my nickname in front of other students, at least not in high school, but

I thought he was just flirting. It was second nature with him. As much a part of his personality as my compulsion to write.

I collected several more students' papers, then headed down the opposite row. When I came to Billy's desk, he handed his homework to me. Funny thing, though. His face blotched red, and he glanced away.

I'd never known Billy to be shy around me. We'd become friends back in seventh grade when he helped me set up certain things—and people—at my thirteenth birthday party. Later, he started showing up at youth activities at my church with Danny Myers, another friend.

Billy and I were just good friends. There was nothing else between us. Andie, however, had another spin on the subject. And she told me so while I stashed my books in my locker after algebra. "Billy's crazy about you."

"He's what?"

Andie grinned, leaning back against the lockers. "He wants to know if you'll go out with him."

I was dumbfounded. "How do you know?"

"He was at my house Friday night," she confessed. "He made me call you."

"Billy did?"

She grinned. "Isn't it cool?"

"What's Paula Miller think? I mean, isn't she Billy's girl-friend?"

She waved her hand. "It's October—we're well into the school year. People start looking around, getting antsy about now."

"Oh, I get it. You're trying to talk me into this Billy thing, right?" I closed my locker door and pressed the combination lock in place.

"Not exactly." She tossed her dark curls and looked away. Billy was coming down the hall. His face turned radish-red when he spotted me with Andie. Having a crush on someone changes your outlook—good friends or not.

"Look, Andie, I don't want to hurt anyone," I whispered. "But I'm not interested in anything more than friendship."

She turned quickly, looking at me with penetrating brown eyes. "Will you listen? Billy's not just any guy."

"Don't you think *I* know that? He and I—we're friends. I'd just like to keep it that way."

She followed me to the cafeteria, and after we went through the hot-lunch line and found a table, the conversation got started all over again. "Open your eyes," Andie said, gazing around at the crowd of kids chowing down. "There are new guy horizons everywhere you look. Take your pick."

I wondered what warped romance novel she'd been reading. "Get a life." I reached for my milk carton.

She sighed. "I'm *living* in the real world. You . . . you're hiding out with your fantasies."

"Excuse me?"

"Letter writing is a total waste. Sean Hamilton can't take the place of a real, live guy."

I scoffed. "That's what you think. You just don't know Sean well enough. He's far better than any of the guys around here."

"Thank goodness for that."

"Andie, that's rude, really rude."

She stopped eating. "And so are you . . . turning Billy down like this." And with that she got up, leaving her tray behind.

"Finally, peace and quiet," I mumbled to myself, wondering what the hype about a flesh-and-blood guy was all about. Andie was the one who needed to wake up to reality.

Me? I was perfectly content to live in my—how did she put it?—"fantasy world." A letter-writing friendship with a great guy sure beat the stupidity of playing musical chairs, high-school style.

MYSTERY LETTERS

Chapter 5

After school I went to see Marcia Greene, student editor for *The Summit*. Her brother, Zye, the senior class president, and his sidekick, Ryan Davis, were hanging around outside the door. I avoided eye contact with the two of them. Freshman initiation was still too fresh in my memory!

"Hey, Holly," Ryan said, following me into the classroom. "Had anything new published?"

"Nope."

"Aren't you working on some big novel or something?" He was pushing, and I was mad.

"You don't know what you're talking about." It was my stall tactic. I *was* working on an outline for a novella, but it was certainly none of his beeswax.

Ever since I'd met Ryan Davis last summer, I found him to be repulsive. Plainly put, he bugged me. Maybe it was because he kept asking about my one and only published piece, "Love Times Two," like I was some celebrity or something. I'd sold the short story to a teen magazine the summer after seventh grade. Pure luck . . . and a lot of hard work.

Actually, Stan had been the one to spill the beans about my

only byline, because Ryan was also interested in getting published. But from my perspective, Ryan Davis didn't seem like the literary type. A good writer needed to be racially accepting—completely unbiased. Ryan, however, was prejudiced. And I resented that about him.

"So . . . nothing new?" he continued. "What about that new column of yours? That counts, doesn't it?"

I didn't exactly want to stand here talking to this known jerk about my most recent effort for the school paper. He was fishing for personal info, and I felt uncomfortable. Quickly, I went to talk to Marcia. Out of the corner of my eye, I noticed Ryan leave with Zye. Good, now I could relax.

Marcia's desk was piled with papers and what looked like art roughs from students. She glanced up from her work, eyes shining. "Glad you came, Holly. Mrs. Ross gave me the go-ahead to approve some last-minute changes."

Mrs. Ross, formerly Miss W, was now my high-school English teacher. The good-natured woman was also in charge of overseeing the school paper. Because she had always been my favorite teacher in junior high, I was thrilled that she'd opted to teach high-school English this year.

I pulled up a chair, peering at Marcia's desk. "What's our deadline? Are we running behind?"

"Actually, pretty close to schedule." She glanced at the calendar. "Today's Monday the fourteenth. Less than ten days before this mess goes to the printer." She pushed her glasses up and studied me. "Can you get your column to me by next Monday?"

"Sure. But I haven't thought of a name for it yet."

"No problem." She stuck her pencil behind one ear. "We can brainstorm tomorrow—first thing if you like. Oh, by the way, your box is crammed with letters." She pointed to a wall of wooden cubicles, which were the mailboxes for appointed personnel. One had my name on it.

Quickly, I abandoned my notebook and books on the chair

and went to investigate. Marcia was right. There were lots of letters. Several with familiar handwriting—Andie's, for one. "I'll sort through these tonight," I said.

"Be sure and check out the back of that long business envelope," Marcia said, smiling.

I found the envelope she was referring to and observed the weird acrostic on the back. It spelled out the five journalistic *W*'s—who, what, when, where, and why. "What's this about?"

"Guess you'll have to read the contents. Let me know if it seems to be from anyone interesting."

"Yeah, right. Interesting . . ." I thought of Sean just then. Right now, he was the most interesting person on the face of the earth to me.

Reaching for my notebook, I opened it to the section marked *The Summit.* When I did, my assignment from algebra floated out. I leaned down under the chair and reached for it. I'd written Mrs. Franklin's name in the upper left-hand corner. Hmm . . . How and when could I incorporate the perfect description I'd written of her into my column?

I found the algebra section of my notebook and secured the boring assignment, hunting for the wacky description of the salaried math wizard—the list I'd written during third period.

Checking through several homework pages and quizzes, I found nothing. I frowned. Where was it?

I searched through my algebra book. Surely I'd put it inside the book, safe from nosy eyes. But no, not there, either.

Worry bit at my thoughts. Had the paper gotten mixed in with student homework papers? I remembered gathering them up, row by row. Trying to be helpful in that class was all I could offer. Alas, trying to actually do algebra was getting me absolutely nowhere.

I exited the student newspaper office and dashed through the hall to the algebra classroom where I suffered daily. Slowly I peeked inside. The teacher's desk was vacant. Perfect!

Without breathing, I hurried into the room and glanced around, making sure no one was hiding under a desk. I flipped through a few papers on the top of the long, wide desk. Cautiously, I opened the top right drawer. Inside I found a group of test papers. Unfortunately, they were for students in fourth hour.

My heart sank. I closed the drawer and left. "Where *is* that paper?" I mumbled to myself all the way to my locker.

Danny Myers waved to me in the hall, but I barely saw him.

Amy-Liz flagged me down. "Hey, are you in a trance?"

"Huh?"

"Holly? You okay?" She frowned.

"Not really."

"What's wrong?" She walked with me to my locker.

"I'll let you know tomorrow after third hour."

She held on to my locker door, leaning close. "Look, if you ever need to . . . uh, want to talk about a guy, well, I'm here."

I was stunned. Where was *this* coming from? "What guy?"

"Holly, it's okay. I know what's going on with Billy," she whispered, touching my arm. "And believe me, I think I know what you're going through."

"You do?" I eeked out. I probably sounded totally dense, and at the moment, I felt that way, too. Here she was going on about guys and the misery they involved, and I was worried about my academic future.

Chapter 6

When I got home, I didn't even bother calling Andie to find out what Amy-Liz meant by "what's going on with Billy." It was absolutely pointless. Besides, Amy-Liz had no idea that Billy had asked Andie if I was interested. Did she?

Of course, guy-news always traveled fast. At least in small ski towns like Dressel Hills. People talked about what they heard. That's just how it was.

So maybe Amy-Liz *had* heard that I'd turned Billy Hill down via Andie, the self-appointed mediator. If only Billy had approached me himself. I could've leveled with him gently. But, of course, guys never did sensible things like that. Not around here.

♥ ♥ ♥

At supper Mom and Uncle Jack lauded Phil's amazing test scores. In fact, the entire meal was filled with talk of my younger brousin. I couldn't wait for it to end.

"Just think," Stephie spouted, "our brother's a genius."

"Sure as shootin'," Uncle Jack replied, looking proud.

Then and there I came to the realization that I could never bring myself to ask my parents for help with homework. Not as long as Phil's accomplishments took center stage. Some might call it jealousy, but I knew the truth. Sibling rivalry didn't set well with me. Especially when the sibling was younger.

After kitchen cleanup, I settled down to another evening alone in my room, wracking my brain. More algebra homework. Not just one page—three! I thought I'd die. Die and never be fully appreciated for the good effort I'd made—trying to keep my proverbial head above water. But no. I was sinking fast. And six-week deficiency reports were coming out in four days—Friday.

I slept very little that night. And when sleep did come, it was accompanied by fragmented dreams. Either I or someone close to me was searching for a paper. Searching frantically, and not finding it.

I awakened, too frazzled to go back to sleep, and remembered the strange envelope with the five *W*'s listed on the back. I was wobbly, but I managed to turn on the light beside my bed, drag myself out of the covers, and walk the length of my room. On my desk, I found my backpack and rummaged through till I found the stack of letters.

I carried the weird one back to bed with me. There, in the wee hours, I opened the long, thin envelope.

Dear Holly,

You must be aware of the journalistic "5 W's," right? Well, I would like to begin with the first W—that's WHO, in case you forgot. So . . . WHO are you, really? Oh yeah, I know your name. But WHAT about the nickname, Holly-Heart? WHO gave you such a nickname and WHAT does it mean? WHEN can I expect your answer? And WHERE will the answer be in your column? (Top and center, lower middle, or heaven forbid . . . the tail end.) You choose.

Oh yes. Certainly there must be a reason WHY such an unusual nickname. I will await your reply.

> *Signed—WHO am I?*

"Why me?" I gasped. Laughing, I fell back into my pillows. The letter was just what I needed to get my mind off the lost paper. I fell into a deep sleep, without a single dream.

♥ ♥ ♥

Mrs. Too-aloof-pinched-faced-Franklin did a number on me the next day when she passed back our homework. Mine looked like it was bleeding. Zillions of red ink marks were all over and . . .

Gasp!

Something was stapled to the last page. My list! And there was a note on it in the teacher's own hand. *Please see me after class today.*

Gulp!

Only one sane thought grabbed me: *Help me, dear Lord.*

All through class—fifty minutes of fear—I trembled. And when it came time for the bell, I remained at my desk, waiting for everyone to clear out. It took forever, though, because some kid kept hanging around asking Mrs. Franklin idiotic questions. Stuff even *I* knew the answers to. And algebraically speaking, that was saying a lot.

Finally he left, and my teacher sat at her desk. I figured it was my cue to stand up and walk up there—to hear the words I'd feared the most. That she had no choice but to fail me out-right. I'd scoffed and scorned her very personage. I'd described her to a T. . . .

"Holly," she began, "about your grade . . ."

Here it comes, I thought. *I'm doomed.*

"Is there something I might do to help you?" she asked.

I nearly choked. "Something?" I whispered.

She nodded. "What is there about algebra you don't under-stand?"

"Everything," I admitted. "Absolutely everything."

She tapped her unpolished nails on the desk. "I see. And are you paying attention in class?"

Here we go, I thought. *Now comes the lecture about writing descriptive lists instead of listening.*

She waited silently.

I took a deep breath. "Uh . . . I try to pay attention, but not much of it makes sense." I waited for her reply and to be cast out.

"Are you college-bound?" she asked unexpectedly.

"I hope so."

Her face suddenly pinched up tighter than before. "And what is it you hope to embrace as your major field of study?"

"English and journalism." I felt my knees shaking. What might she do with this information? Have me kicked off the school paper, perhaps? Mrs. Ross would be heartbroken, and so would I.

"Then you'll be needing a passing grade in my class, won't you?" she said with finality. The conversation was coming to a close. Hallelujah.

"Yes, ma'am," I said. "And do you have any suggestions for how I might do that?" I nearly choked on my own words. Shoot, I was starting to sound just like her.

"A tutor would be in order" came her reply. She rustled through a small black notebook on her desk. "I may have just the person for you."

I wondered who on earth could knock algebraic sense into this poor mass of intellect I called my brain. Who?

"Here we are," she said. "Jot down this number: 555-4323."

"Uh, excuse me, Mrs. Franklin, but that's *my* number!"

She picked up her notebook again, studying it. "Well, there must be some mistake. I don't quite understand."

She surveyed me with a forced smile that added to the severity of her face. "Your last name is Meredith, correct?"

I had no idea what she was getting at. "Yes, ma'am."

"Well, then, this is very strange. The name given here is Philip Patterson."

No! I nearly shouted the word. Instead, I clutched my throat. Not Phil, my disgustingly smart little brousin. Not him!

Mrs. Franklin looked up. "Is there a problem?"

"Uh . . . no, not really, er . . . yes, I believe there must be some mistake. You see, that name—the name you just said—happens to be my eleven-year-old stepbrother's."

"Oh, I see." The slightest twinge of a smile threatened to crease her wrinkled face. Threatened to reveal the truth. Some might call it poetic justice—after what I'd written about her. I couldn't help but think as I left the classroom that Mrs. Franklin was probably having a hard time keeping her stern face straight about now.

I gathered up my things and headed to my locker . . . in a fog. How had Phil's name shown up on Mrs. Franklin's tutoring list? How? I thought back to the conversation last night at supper. I had tuned out much of it on purpose. Why? Because I was sick of the hoopla at home over Phil. And now this. What could I do? There was no way on earth I'd succumb to having my stepbrother tutor me. *Pas mon frère!*

I decided to work harder. Maybe even twist Andie's arm about helping me. Anything else would be better. That's when I spotted Billy. He'd seen me and made his usual attempt at glancing away, almost shyly. So weird for a guy who used to be able to talk to me about anything.

I thought about going over and discussing my algebra dilemma. But, no, that wouldn't be fair. Besides, he might get the wrong idea.

"Holly," a voice called to me.

I turned around to see Andie flying down the hall. I expected her to stop and talk and go to lunch with me. "Hey, where're you going?" I asked.

"Got to warn Jared about tomorrow," she said. "Didja hear about a pop quiz in algebra?"

Yikes! "Tomorrow?"

"Yeah, Franklin told her second hour about it but forgot to tell us. So I assume it'll be a major surprise."

I groaned. "Oh, great, just what I *don't* need."

"What? Are you still having trouble?"

"You could say that. Want to help me?"

Andie burst out laughing. "Do I look like I can explain X plus the unknown factor equals Y? Do I?"

"But what about the quiz? What's it on?" I pleaded.

"Beats me, but it's going to count as *one-third* of our grade. I heard that for sure."

Help, somebody help!

"What's Jared doing today after school?" I asked.

She shook her head. "No way, huh-uh! You're not hanging out with him."

"But if he can make heads and tails out of it for me, why not? I mean, it's just for help with algebra."

Andie's eyes grew serious. "Jared's vulnerable right now. Read my lips. He's been dumped—ego bruised."

"By Amy-Liz?"

Andie nodded. "None other than."

"Whoa, Charlie!" Amazing news.

"I know. It does take courage—as you know."

"All too well." I closed my locker. "Well, guess I'm winging it. Shoot, I can't decide what I should do first—pray or study."

"Try both," Andie said with a wave and a grin.

"Yeah." I headed for the cafeteria alone.

Chapter 7

While standing in the hot-lunch line, I spotted Marcia Greene. She saw me, too. "Holly, I thought you were dropping by *The Summit* office this morning."

I'd forgotten. "Oh, sorry. Uh, I had this thing in algebra."

"Can we talk during lunch?" she asked. "Maybe we can come up with a title for your column."

"Yeah, maybe. Sometimes when you're doing something else—like eating—ideas come more easily." While we ate hot dogs and chili, we brainstormed. Jared and Danny came over and helped. Billy, too; rather reticently, however. Jared must've noticed the change in Billy's demeanor because there was a surprising surge of unspoken interest directed toward me. Jared was the all-time master flirt. I almost felt sorry for Billy, just trying to cope—to be himself around me.

Jared spoke up, "The best column titles so far are these: 'In Beat With Holly-Heart,' 'Holly Speaks Out,' and 'Dear Holly.' "

"I like 'In Beat With Holly-Heart.' What do you think?" Marcia asked me.

I remembered the anonymous letter querying me about my nickname. "Maybe I should leave off my nickname."

"But why?" Jared said. "It's so . . . you."

Billy nodded. "Everyone calls you Holly-Heart."

"They do?" This was news to me.

"The guys do, right?" Marcia asked Jared.

"Maybe not to Holly's face but yeah." And then Jared winked at me.

"Look, thanks for your help," I said, looking first at Jared and then at Billy. "But Marcia and I need to do some planning before fifth hour. *Alone.*"

Billy caught on and left, but Jared lingered. "If there's anything I can do to help, just let me know, okay?" He was pouring it on unbelievably thick. The old junior-high days came rushing back in my mind.

"Thanks, Jared. I'll let you know."

He beamed, eyes twinkling. What a goof. Jared Wilkins, it was clear, was desperate.

♥ ♥ ♥

All the studying in the world couldn't help me on Wednesday, not the way I was floundering. Andie was right. Pop quiz there was. And in spite of my frantic heavenly pleas, I flunked. Flat out.

Two days later, on Friday, Mr. Irving, my homeroom teacher, handed out six-week deficiency reports as discreetly as possible. Deficient wasn't exactly the best word to describe how I felt. I avoided Andie and all my other friends as best I could throughout the rest of the day. But just as classes were finally over and I was about to escape, I bumped into Ryan Davis as I turned the corner near the administration office.

"Hey, Holly," he said, his eyes bright and his voice too loud. "How's the column?"

"No time to talk." I glanced in all directions. "You haven't seen me—remember that." I rushed for the front doors and slipped unnoticed out of school.

I was the first of the freshmen to board the city bus. Hiding in the backseat wasn't my style, but it was the only way. The only other option was walking home, but the high school was quite a ways from my house.

Mom and Uncle Jack would have a cow over this, I was certain. *F*'s weren't acceptable in our family. God's people put their best feet forward—they were to make a practice of excellence. Mom would be howling the loudest. And I braced myself for the barrage of inquiry.

Stealthily I crept into the house, hoping to avoid an immediate confrontation from the powers that be. Wonder of wonders, Mom wasn't even home.

"She's at a doctor's appointment," Phil, the know-it-all brousin, informed me. "Simply routine, I suppose."

Phil . . .

Just looking at him gave me the heebie-jeebies. His new wire-rim glasses drooped almost off the tip of his oily nose. Really disgusting. But more than his appearance, his attitude bugged me. Thank goodness Mrs. Franklin was not inclined to phone my home and suggest to my parents that Phil tutor me. The way she'd left things, I figured it was up to me to pursue the tutoring business. Whew!

Honestly, I couldn't imagine sitting down with my greasy-faced brousin over algebra. Not for one single second.

Silently, I went to the hall closet and hung up my jacket, keeping my distance. Between glances at the kitchen, where Phil and now Carrie, Stephie, and Mark were gathering, raiding the fridge, I felt in my jeans pocket for the dreaded deficiency report. Nothing, absolutely nothing, could be worse than having an *F* incubating—and in the first six weeks of high school.

I sighed, almost wishing for the old days when I would come home from school to encounter only my blood sister, Carrie. On desperate days like this, I needed peace. Time to contemplate. Time to devise plans and strategies. There were so many kids hanging out in our kitchen these days. *Our* kitchen—Mom's, Carrie's, and mine.

Nearly one year had passed since Mom had said "I do"—on Thanksgiving Day, of all things. And in that year, we'd made an attempt at blending two families—six kids, to boot. Unfortunately, one of those kids happened to be a walking, breathing, theory-developing egghead. How *had* his name shown up on Mrs. Franklin's list of tutors? He was only a sixth grader, for pete's sake!

"Hey, Holly, there's another letter from your wannabe-boyfriend," Carrie called from the kitchen.

"Why, you!" I flounced through the kitchen to the corner desk, sending fiery darts her way. "You're not supposed to touch my mail."

"I didn't even *breathe* on it." She glanced up from her bowl of ice cream. "Do I look stupid?"

"Whoa, leading question," Mark said, laughing.

"Just keep your nose out of it," I told him.

Phil ignored us, reading *The Wall Street Journal* while woofing down bites of a club sandwich. Mark, however, persisted. "Carrie's sick of being on restriction," he teased. "Every time the phone rings, she salivates."

Stephie let out a hyena shriek. "Big double woo!"

"Hush," I said, threatening both Mark and Stephie with my pointer finger. *Big double woo!* I wished Stan were home; then he could handle this, since most of the kids cluttering up the kitchen were *his* annoying little siblings.

Stephie wouldn't stop giggling, driving me crazy.

I lost it. "Stephie, puh-leeze!"

She stopped long enough to sneer. "Who died and made you boss?"

"Okay, fine. Have it your way," I said, throwing my hands up. "If this kitchen's still a mess when Mom gets home, I'll tell her exactly who's responsible."

"Hey, don't forget what Sean wrote in his last letter," Carrie jeered. "You know, how he said—"

I clapped my hand over her sassy little mouth. "That's enough."

"What? What?" Stephie was jumping around. "What did your boyfriend say?"

"Never mind." I squinted my eyes at both Carrie and Stephie the way Mom does when she means business. "And you both know better than to call him my boyfriend."

I wasn't kidding, and Carrie knew it. She squirmed away from my grasp. "I'm outta here," she said. "Homework calls."

Phil chimed in as Carrie and Stephie made their exit. "Like Mark said, Carrie's sick of being on restriction." He folded the paper and placed it in front of him. Then, without pushing up his glasses, he cast his gaze on me.

"So you *were* listening," I said, baffled at his ability to concentrate on multiple levels.

He nodded without blinking. "Mind-boggling, isn't it?"

I didn't want to admit it. Not now, when things were going so rotten for me.

"It's a lonely road," he blurted. "People don't understand a kid like me." I might've actually felt a tad sorry about my response, except the whiz-geek finished his remarks by saying, "At least my place in history is invulnerable."

Invulnerable? Spare me.

I clutched the letter from Sean Hamilton. Thank goodness for a few sane males left in the world.

Instead of going upstairs to my room, I left the kitchen and my dazed brousin and went outside. The porch swing looked inviting and quiet enough for reading letters . . . and making plans. Plans such as how and when to spring my six-week report on Mom and Uncle Jack.

But first, I needed a reprieve. Sean's letter was just that. An escape from my dismal life.

Chapter 8

Dear Holly,

Hey! Your letter arrived in only two days. The mail between Colorado and California is getting speedier.

Sounds like things are going great for you so far your freshman year.

Yeah, I thought, *wouldn't he be surprised?*

I've been helping organize a new program for middle schoolers at my church. I'm on the youth board now, along with everything else. We're starting something really cool every other Friday night beginning next weekend. It's called Power House, and I'll be hanging out with sixth through eighth graders.

Does your church group zero in on younger teens? If so, I'd like to hear about it. Maybe get some ideas.

Anyway, how's your column writing coming along? Do you like reading the letters from students? Any interesting stuff?

I wanted to send him an email message about the mysterious letter writer with a fondness for *W*'s. I planned to include it in my very first column. Maybe because it was so quirky.

I finished reading the letter, smiling at the way Sean wrapped things up.

> *When are you coming out to visit your dad again? Christmas, maybe? I miss you a lot, Holly.*
>
> > *Yours, Sean*
> >
> > *PS: Mr. Fremont, my calculus teacher, is almost finished with his chemo treatments. He and I had a soda after school yesterday. We talked about God again. He's so open to spiritual things. Terminal illness has a way of doing that, I suppose.*
> >
> > > *Yours, S.H.*

I refolded the letter and placed it back in the envelope. So much of what Sean had written stuck in my brain—his involvement with the youth group, his ongoing interest in my writing, and his strong Christian witness. But something else hit home, something I'd totally spaced out before. He was taking calculus—an advanced form of mathematics.

Would Sean consider tutoring me by email? I knew long-distance calls were out of the question. But, yeah . . . email was perfect. *Maybe Mom would even let me IM him.*

In my excitement, I moved too quickly and nearly fell off the porch swing. My cat wasn't as lucky—Goofey flew onto the wooden floor, whining his dissatisfaction.

"Sorry, baby." I leaned down to pick him up.

Me-e-e-ow! He was obviously peeved. Being thrust out of a cozy spot was no fun.

I carried Goofey into the house, kissing his fat kitty head, all the while thinking of my latest plan to salvage my algebra grade. Sean as my tutor would be fabulous. Now, if I could just get my mind focused enough to write my *Dear Holly* column for the school paper. I'd decided to leave off the nickname Holly-Heart and go with something less gimmicky. Something direct.

Heading upstairs, I remembered Andie's words to me a week ago. She'd wholeheartedly suggested that I join the procrastinators of the world. Well, with this being Friday night and Marcia Greene wanting my column polished and ready to go by Monday—I'd say this was as good a procrastination stunt as any.

I chose to sit at my computer to write, even though my comfortable window seat beckoned. Goofey blinked his eyes at me from the pillowed perch, pleading for some additional cuddle time.

"Sorry, not now, baby." I reached over and nuzzled his fat neck. "Maybe later." Goofey curled his tail around his front paws and settled down for a contented snooze. End of discussion.

The first letter I picked out of the stack was Andie's. It was the off-the-wall letter she'd told me about. The one to keep me on my editorial toes . . .

I nearly choked at the salutation.

Dear Holly-Heart, great imparter of human wisdom,
Can you believe it? My locker is so messy I couldn't find my algebra homework. I mean, this is a HUGE problem. Remember how disgusting my locker always looked in junior high?
People say, "Less stuff means less mess," but where do I start? I mean, it's too embarrassing for the freshman class president to set up a garage sale in front of her locker.
Help me, Holly! (You're so-o-o organized.)
Signed,
Andie Martinez
PS: Please don't edit this letter, if you know what I mean.

I couldn't help myself. I laughed out loud, waking Goofey up once again. After a quick apology to my fussy feline, I began writing my answer. A best friend's letter to the editor had to get chosen for publication. It was expected, and I knew Andie would be more than hurt if I failed her.

Picking up a pencil, I gave her my best editorial reply, keeping personal comments to a minimum.

> *Dear Andie,*
>
> *There are a zillion ways for a person to create a sense of order in her life. Begin by simply marching up to your locker with a sense of determination. (You want to clean up and throw out, right?)*
>
> *Start by labeling three large plastic bags—Give Away, Trash, and Garage Sale (thought you were kidding?). Now comes the easy part. Remove things from your locker one by one.*
>
> *If you don't want or need it and it's useless, toss it. If someone else could use it and you don't want it, put it in the Give Away bag. If you think you can make some bucks on it, but you don't want it, well, there's your first garage-sale item.*
>
> *Remember, the hardest part is opening your locker—be sure to duck!*
>
> > *Happy organizing,*
> > *Holly*

I reread my answer. It was okay. Might need a little rewriting, but for a first draft, not bad.

Reaching for the stack of letters, I pulled out the weird business envelope next. Now for a real challenge. This writer, whoever he/she was, wanted personal answers. Hmm, let's see . . . What should I write?

I flexed my fingers and began typing.

Dear Who Am I?:

 First of all, my nickname is off-limits to strangers. Secondly, my mother gave it to me because I was born on Valentine's Day. And last but not least, you're nosy!

       Sincerely, Holly

 PS: Oh—you'll receive this answer when I'm good and ready. And WHERE will it be in my column? WHO says I'm even going to publish it?!

I reread my clever letter and—having second thoughts—I decided *not* publishing it was the best answer for the Who-person.

Chapter 9

I cuddled with Goofey as promised. I needed to kill some time until my parents arrived home. Hopefully Uncle Jack would get here first. Of the two, he was less inclined to freak out over my lousy math report. But that wasn't saying much. Uncle Jack wasn't a full-blown perfectionist, but he was adamant about his kids doing well in school.

My birth father was the same way, if I remember correctly. It's hard to recall those long-ago days. I'm just thankful to have the kind of relationship I have with him now. It was tough going for years—the silent years—when Daddy kept in touch with Carrie or me only through birthday and Christmas cards.

"Holly," Stan called from downstairs. The oldest Patterson sibling had arrived.

I hurried to the top of the stairs. "It's about time you're home."

He waved a paper in his hand on the landing below. "Lose something?"

Yikes! I ran downstairs, reaching for the paper, hoping it wasn't what I thought. "Give it to me," I demanded.

He held it higher. "Man, are you in for it big," he taunted, playing keep-away. "And I mean big." After repeated pleading on my part, Stan relinquished the deficiency report.

"Where'd you find this?" I caught my breath.

He pointed to the living room. "Right there on the floor in plain view."

I groaned. It must've fallen out of my pocket when I carried Goofey inside.

"Guess who's gonna be grounded next," Stan sang as he shuffled through the dining room to the kitchen.

I followed him. "You don't know that."

"Dream on, Meredith."

"Don't call me that!"

"It's your name, isn't it?" He poured a tall glass of milk, mocking me.

"Hey, save some milk for Goofey," I said, trying to divert the conversation.

"Goofey *Meredith*? You bet!"

I wanted to scream. This stepsibling was the worst.

"So . . . when do you plan to break the news to the chain of command?" Stan scoffed.

"Don't be disrespectful to our parents."

He slapped some turkey slices on a piece of bread, then squirted mustard all over before putting the sandwich together. He raised one eyebrow. "You *are* going to tell them, aren't you?"

"None of your business." I stomped out of the room.

Upstairs, I headed for the hall phone. Andie was someone I could call and dump on. Maybe even get a little sympathy, too. At least she'd offer a little understanding.

"Martinez residence," she answered.

"Hey, why so formal?"

"Oh, you know. It's proper."

I got the strong feeling her mom was in close proximity. "Can you talk?"

"Uh . . . sure."

"Depending on what it is, right?"

"You got it." I could just imagine Andie grinning into the phone.

"So . . . what's going on?" I asked.

"Oh, not much. You?"

"To tell the truth, I'm seeing purple about now," I complained. "Your former boyfriend and my present brousin is driving me nuts."

"Uh-oh, what'd Stanley Patterson do now?"

"He found my *deficiency* report," I said, reluctantly at first. "Bottom line: If he tells Mom and Uncle Jack about it before I do, I'll deprive him of his old age."

"Wait a minute," she interrupted. "Did you say deficiency report?"

"I wondered if you were paying attention."

"Oh, good, so it's really not that."

"Worse," I confessed. "I'm flunking algebra, and Mrs. Franklin is suggesting a tutor." I didn't tell her who, of course.

"Flunking? That's rough."

"Do you know any tutors my age?"

"Well, yeah . . . I think so."

"Please don't suggest Billy. Not because he isn't smart enough; it's just not fair, you know, the way he—"

"But wait, Holly. Maybe Billy wouldn't be such a bad idea."

I could almost hear the matchmaking ideas buzzing in her brain. "You're supposed to be on *my* side," I said.

"It's just that Billy would be so fabulous for you—if I can use your word."

"Billy?"

"Think about it. Billy's right here—in Dressel Hills."

Oh, not this again, I thought. "Look, I don't need another lecture about long-distance relationships, okay? That's up to me to decide."

"Why can't you see the light, Holly? Besides, Billy's really hurt."

"Why? I don't get it . . . I mean, what's changed?" I said. "I think he's great . . . as a friend. Just like always."

"To tell you the truth, I promised to help him," she finally admitted.

"Don't kid around. C'mon!"

There was unbearable silence on the line. Andie snapped to it at last. "Well, I think I hear my mom calling. It's almost supper and I have to help. See ya."

"Okay." I hung up the phone, feeling worse than ever.

Chapter 10

By the time both Mom and Uncle Jack were home, it was sup-pertime. No one, at least none of us kids, had taken the initiative to prepare anything.

"I'll cook," Uncle Jack volunteered. He rubbed his hands together as though doing so might start a roaring campfire.

I laughed. "This isn't the Boy Scouts." I reached for the largest pot in the house. "I'll cook tonight. How's spaghetti?"

"That's my Holly-Heart," Mom said, smiling weakly. She leaned against the kitchen counter. For the first time, I noticed how gaunt her face looked.

"Mom, are you okay?" I asked.

"Don't be silly." She seemed apologetic. Uncle Jack went over and put his arm around her, leading her into the living room. Now I was worried. Wasn't it a week ago we had pizza because Mom was too tired to make supper?

This just wasn't Mom. Not the hardworking mother who'd been a paralegal all those years to support Carrie and me after Daddy left.

I sprinkled salt into the water and turned the burner on high. Then I filled Goofey's dish with his favorite liver and tuna cat food and refilled his milk dish. A glance toward the living room filled me in on Mom's status. She was resting her head on Uncle Jack's shoulder. A good sign for not-so-newlyweds, I guess. Only thing, Uncle Jack was reading the paper, not stroking her hair and saying sweet nothings. So what was I to think? Was Mom sick or just tired?

Not only was I worried about Mom, I was apprehensive about when to share the horrors of my six-week report. I certainly didn't want to make her feel worse. But if I didn't tell, would Stan jump the gun? What if I didn't tell at all? Who would sign on the parental line?

Maybe after supper and devotions I could get Uncle Jack off by himself. Besides, I needed to find out what he thought about an electronic tutor. Namely Sean Hamilton.

♥ ♥ ♥

My spaghetti dinner turned out fine; so did devotions. Sorta. We sat around the living room in a haphazard circle. Uncle Jack read several Bible passages. One verse really touched me. Second Corinthians 12:9—"My grace is sufficient for you, for my power is made perfect in weakness."

Wow! Did that mean God was going to give me grace to bear the hardships of algebra? Was He also going to make a way to escape? No, that was another verse.

My grace is sufficient. I had to cling to that promise. I was a child of God. I was entitled to make this verse mine.

Later, Uncle Jack asked if any of us had something to pray about. Carrie's hand shot up, and I wondered what she was going to say. "We need to pray for Sean in California," she said, avoiding my glare.

"Oh?" Uncle Jack said. "Why is that?"

I held my breath. What would she say?

"Well, it's like this," she began. "He's been writing to Holly, you know, and—"

"Carrie," Mom interjected, "is this really something to be discussed in front of the family?"

Hooray for Mom!

Carrie frowned.

"Is this a prayer request or not?" Uncle Jack continued where Mom left off.

"Well, yeah, *I* think it is." Carrie's face wore an impish, triumphant look.

I cast a stern eye on my younger sister. She dropped it immediately. "Uh . . . never mind," she stammered.

Uncle Jack ran his fingers through his wavy brown hair, looking a bit confused. "Anyone else?"

Phil's hand went up. "Pray that I'll fit in with the rest of the seventh graders at my school. This Monday I'm getting bumped out of sixth grade."

This was no prayer request. The little know-it-all was showing off. What nerve—announcing his skip to seventh grade like this.

"Well, congratulations, son," Uncle Jack said, getting caught up in the whole thing. If Mom hadn't prompted him back on course, our family prayers might've gotten preempted by Phil's tales of accomplishment.

After we took turns praying around the circle—I prayed for Mom in general terms since I didn't know if she'd fallen prey to the flu or what—I followed Uncle Jack around the house. Discreetly as possible, of course. I hoped, and silently prayed, that I'd have a chance to discuss my algebra plight with him. The way things were going, though, it looked like I'd be stuck worrying the whole weekend. Why? Because Phil had become the focus of Uncle Jack's attention. Not that it was so bad, but it left me out in the cold. Way out.

One look at Mom, sprawled out comfortably on the couch, and I knew she wasn't up to being told. *F*'s stood for failure.

I certainly felt like one tonight. Especially pitted against the atmosphere of genius pervading the house.

My grace is sufficient for you . . .

"Please, send down your grace, Lord," I prayed as I headed for my room. Here I was, facing another Friday night of solitude.

My *Dear Holly* column was basically written, and I had hardly any other homework to do. Except algebra. That would have to wait.

I turned on my CD player and found my yellow spiral notebook. Its pages held the first novel I'd ever attempted to write. It would be a novella—a mini novel. I nestled down with my cat on my window seat, pushing out my worries as I began to round off a scene in the second chapter. That done, I reread what I'd written, then erased several words and chose stronger verbs and fewer adjectives. This time, when I read it, I was satisfied.

Over an hour had gone by when I reached for a Marty Leigh mystery and began to read. I figured if I was going to be a great writer, I had to read the best authors. Ms. Leigh certainly fit that description.

Unfortunately, in the book I chose—in the very first chapter— the main character had an aversion to math. Nope, this would never do. Too close to home, so I closed the book.

Frustrated, I went to my bottom dresser drawer and pulled out my journal.

Friday night, October 18: I hope to talk to Uncle Jack first thing tomorrow . . . give him the news that I'm flunking algebra. It won't be easy, but nothing like this ever is. Then, before he has a chance to freak out, I'll tell him my plan to ask Sean to be my tutor. Or . . . maybe I could tell him about my tutor plan BEFORE I say anything about the deficiency report. Yeah, that's better.

Hey, perfect! God's grace is beginning to work for me. Now, if I can just make it through tomorrow.

Chapter 11

Saturday I got up, showered, and dressed long before any other kids in the house were up. I fixed my hair, too. I wanted to look as though I was in complete control of my senses when I sprang the long-distance tutoring idea on Uncle Jack.

Mom was stirring up a bowl of waffle batter when I sailed into the kitchen. "Morning, angel." Her voice sounded sweet, strong.

"Feeling better?" I asked, stealing a glance at Uncle Jack, who was spooning sugar into his coffee.

"Much," Mom answered, looking preoccupied.

Uncle Jack glanced up. "A good night's sleep changes everyone's outlook. Right, hon?"

She turned, smiling across the room.

Perfect, I thought. *Mom's rested up . . . Uncle Jack's had his first cup of coffee . . .*

I dragged a barstool across the floor and sat at the corner of the island, kitty-corner from Uncle Jack. "Got a minute?"

Uncle Jack winked at me. "For you, sweet toast, I've got all day. What's up?"

"I have a fabulous idea . . . to pull up my algebra grade."

"I'm all for pulling up grades." He nodded, listening.

"Well, since mine's a little low, and since my friend Sean Hamilton is taking calculus, well . . . I just thought maybe I could correspond with him about my homework and stuff. Maybe IM him."

"How low a grade are we talking?" he asked.

Rats! I had no choice but to turn over the deficiency report. This conversation was going backward. I sighed.

"C'mon, out with the whole truth," Uncle Jack said, his smile fading fast. Mom came and peered over his shoulder.

Doomsday!

True to form, Mom was the first to react after she saw the report. "My goodness, Holly, you've never had an *F!*"

"I know. And I feel rotten about it. That's why I want to get help."

"You could have asked your mother or me for help," Uncle Jack was saying.

"Why did you wait till you were failing to tell us about this?" Mom asked.

Questions, questions. I felt like an idiotic lump. In fact, I had a strong desire to limp out of the room. Away from all this pressure. Show them how lousy they were making me feel.

"Holly?" Mom persisted.

"I've been trying to raise my grade, really. But the problem is, I don't understand algebra. It's like a *foreign* foreign language." I had to say that, because I was making *A*'s in my French class. "Besides, I didn't want to bother you with my schoolwork. I didn't think it was fair." I didn't want to look like a dodo bird next to my super-intelligent brousin, either.

Phil and Mark trooped into the kitchen, still wearing their pajamas. Hair askew, they headed for Mom's mixing bowl. "I'm starved," Mark said. He threatened to poke his finger in the batter.

"When's breakfast?" Phil asked.

Mom rushed over to the counter and shooed the boys away, continuing her Saturday morning ritual. Without looking over her shoulder, she spoke to the wall. "Well, something's got to be done about this, Holly."

Phil's ears perked up. "Is this about grades?"

Uncle Jack held up his hand. "No concern of yours. You boys go and wash up."

"But, Dad," Phil continued, "If it's math we're talking about, I can help Holly. I know I can."

Gulp!

Uncle Jack kept talking to me, as though he hadn't heard Phil's comment. "I really think getting Sean involved is a mistake. He's a junior this year, right?"

I nodded.

"And he's taking calculus?"

"He's really smart," I pleaded my case. "He's headed for pre-med . . . wants to be a doctor."

"Which means he's probably loaded up with homework of his own," Uncle Jack argued.

Phil stood by, as if waiting for a lull in the conversation. "I'm on the school district's tutor list," he volunteered. "My teacher signed me up to help math students. I'll get extra credit for it."

I held my breath. Hoping . . . no, *praying* that Uncle Jack wouldn't consider such a ridiculous idea.

"You're a tutor?" A proud smile burst upon Uncle Jack's face, and he grabbed Phil's arm and hugged him. "Well, what do you know. When did all this happen?"

Phil grinned. "About two weeks ago. Except I haven't been assigned to anyone yet."

Yeah, and over my dead body will you get extra credit from me, I thought, refusing to look at the geeky little Einstein.

"Well, maybe it's time for your first assignment," I heard Uncle Jack say. "Your mom or I could help Holly, but it would be much better—great experience—coming from you."

I bit my lip. "Please, no, Uncle Jack." I wanted to say more. Something like, what have I done to deserve this? Phil smirked mischievously behind his father's back.

I felt the urge to choke him. Phil was making a fool of me!

"I can find someone else—honest, I can," I pleaded.

"Oh, now, let's not get melodramatic about this, Holly," Uncle Jack teased.

Didn't he realize how upset I was?

"How would *you* like to be tutored by . . . by . . ." I couldn't finish. Phil was enjoying this whole nightmarish scene. I couldn't stomach it. Or him.

Unfortunately Uncle Jack wasn't registering my complaint. Not even close. He got up and went over to Mom and nibbled on her ear. "What do you think, hon? Should we let my son tutor your daughter?" It was like they had something secretive going on between them.

Mom plugged in the waffle iron. "Why not? Give it a try—say, two weeks. See how they work together."

My heart sank to my tennies. Work together—with Philip Patterson, smart-alecky brousin and big-time troublemaker? There was major potential here, all right.

Potential for a nuclear explosion!

Chapter 12

Bad news travels fast. In small mountain towns, in major cities—doesn't matter. If there's something bad to be said about someone, you can bet someone's willing to talk about it. So I was reminded in my meeting with Marcia Greene first thing Monday.

Instead of discussing the upcoming paper, Marcia brought up the algebra thing—and my new student instructor. "Word has it you're being tutored by a younger sibling." It sounded like something straight off CNN.

"And?" I said.

Marcia frowned. "There's more?"

"Well, I sure hope not," I muttered. "I'll never live this one down—a freshman flunky with her eleven-year-old brousin for a tutor."

"Brousin?" Marcia looked very confused.

I shook my head. "Never mind; it's a long story."

I showed her the nutty letter from "Who Am I?"

She read it quickly. "This guy's a loony tune."

"If you think his letter's strange, you should read my reply."

She nearly doubled over as she read my answer. "This is really great stuff, Holly." She read it once more. "I say we publish it."

"Fat chance getting Mrs. Ross to agree."

"You might be surprised. What do you say?" She waited for my answer while her fingers drummed lightly on the desk.

"Uh . . . I don't know," I hedged.

"C'mon, it shows off your uncommonly creative talents." She shuffled through my pages of responses to first several student letters. "This *Dear Holly* column is going to be a big hit. I can't wait till the November issue screams off the press."

I was thinking about the weird writer again. "Are you sure you want to run that 'Who Am I?' letter with my response?"

"No doubt in my mind. You're good, Holly. Let's get the column off to a wild and fantastic start."

"Fabulous," I said, not sure I meant it.

💜 💜 💜

In a few hours, most of Dressel Hills had heard some version of my academic plight. But the most messed-up paraphrase came from my sister Carrie.

"You've got to be kidding," I told her at home. "You repeated something that stupid?"

Carrie didn't mind rehashing totally twisted accounts of my personal life. She seemed to live and breathe for such things—especially now that she was ten. "Well, the way I heard it, you pleaded with Phil to help you with your algebra," she said. "And since he needed the extra credit, he caved in and agreed."

"That's ridiculous, and you know it."

"Well, I didn't actually witness what happened last Saturday. It's really your word against everyone else's." Carrie tossed her nearly waist-length blond hair in defiance.

"Wrong again," I muttered, heading for the dining room.

My eleven-year-old tutor was perched in the chair where Uncle Jack always sat during meals, awaiting our first session.

Believe me, if Mom and several other members of the family hadn't been in close range, I'd have smashed my algebra book over his pointed little egghead!

Phil waited till I sat down to speak. "To begin with," he said, all hoity-toity, "I think you probably need to review some basic arithmetic."

Arithmetic? Who is he kidding?

"Look, for your information, I can add, subtract, multiply, and divide just fine." I restrained myself, eyeing Mom every so often as she sat in the living room sipping peppermint tea.

"A quick review can't hurt," Phil persisted.

"Can't help, either," I argued. "Not when it's *algebra* I don't understand."

"Okay, have it your way." He actually stopped diagnosing my math problems.

I opened to last week's homework pages. "Here's what I have to do over. Mrs. Franklin said so." By throwing around my teacher's name, I hoped Phil would stop acting like such an obnoxious boss. Because, in the long run, *she* was the person really in charge of all this tutoring business. I curled my toes, remembering the weird scene in Mrs. Franklin's class today after school. Phil had come to meet her—and to be coached about my homework problems—while I sat there in total humiliation.

Hearing Phil articulate on the same intellectual level as Mrs. Franklin made me feel . . . well, inadequate. That feeling, however, disappeared the second we set foot in the house. Here at home, I was not going to be intimidated by my little brousin's IQ. He had a lot to learn when it came to dealing with a big sister, and like it or not, I was going to have the last word.

The two of us hung on as long as possible, but when it came to working on actual problems, I couldn't take his arrogance. Sure, he was bright, and yes, he understood all this mathematical hodgepodge—but that sneer! And those cocky, superior grins. His attitude angered me—made me resent what he was trying to do. So our first tutoring session fizzled after about fifteen minutes.

"I have an idea," Phil said as I stood up to go to my room. "Why don't you just ask for help when you get stuck? I'll be right here doing a memory experiment."

I pounced on his verbal niceties. "And I'll be making reservations for intergalactic travel," I huffed, then dashed up the stairs.

"Holly!" Mom called. "Come down here."

I stopped at the top of the stairs. "Mom, he's driving me crazy."

"Let's talk," she said, standing firm.

I shuffled back down and sat on the bottom step, pouting. "It's not working. He's impossible."

Phil blinked his eyes like a lizard. One of his most disgusting attempting-to-appear-innocent routines. "We can't give up on the first day," he said.

"Oh yeah? Watch me."

Mom put her hand on my shoulder. "The two of you need time to adjust. I think after several more sessions, things could fall into place. Holly-Heart, won't you give it another try?" She was trying so hard to smooth out the rough edges. Mom was a true peacemaker.

Lizard Phil blinked again, his eyelids coming down like shutters. Made me livid.

I stood up. "Not now. I've had it for today."

Once again I left the room, taking the stairs two at a time. Goofey ran up after me and clawed at my bedroom door. I endured his stubborn meowing for several seconds, then let him in.

"Life's the pits." I tossed my algebra book on my four-poster bed and pulled out my journal. If I didn't unload my feelings soon, I knew I would explode.

*Monday, October 21: I don't know what to do! Having
my stepbrother as a math tutor is absolutely horrible. It's
worse than I thought! I wish I could get past his puffed-up
demeanor.*

*It's true, I need help—Mrs. Franklin won't let me forget
that fact. Besides that, I almost lost it today when Phil started
conversing with her like he was applying for a teacher's aide
position or something. It's tough keeping my cool when what I
really want to do is wring his little neck!*

*Praying is what I need to do right now. But it's not like
I haven't been talking to God. I have. Being patient isn't
always easy. And the grace—where's the grace?*

*Sometimes I think I'm a lousy Christian. Especially when
I lose my temper and blow up at my own family members.*

*Surely Jesus never went off on one of His own brothers.
I'm trying to be loving . . . and failing. Lord, help me. Please.*

Chapter 13

Tuesday morning before school, a note was stuck on my locker. I surveyed the area, checking to see if anyone was observing— someone who might've planted the note. In the sea of student humanity, no one stood out as looking suspicious.

Marcia Greene and her brother, Zye, and his tagalong, Ryan, were heading down the hall. I figured they didn't count, and everyone else was pretty much minding his own business.

I opened my locker and leaned inside a bit, shielding the note from prying eyes. Quickly, I opened it and began to read.

Dear Holly,

So you're going to publish my letter—and your response to it—in the next issue of The Summit. *WHERE do you think my words will appear in your column? And WHAT did I do to deserve such an honor? (Heh, heh.)*

Certainly, I'll be eager to see if you answered all my questions—the 5 W's are so important to good journalism. Oh yes, and 1 H (HOW). Don't forget!

HOW did you get to be so pretty?

Signed: WHO am I?

PS: WHY did you cut your beautiful hair?

I crumpled up the note and threw it into my locker. Whoever this was . . . he was out there.

Gathering up my books for the morning classes, I closed my locker and headed for my first-hour class. Government.

Jared Wilkins was waiting for me just inside the door. "I'm real sorry to hear what's going on at home," he began. "A girl like you shouldn't have to put up with a little brother for a—"

"Save it, Wilkins." I pushed past him and found a seat close to the front of the classroom.

"Holly, what's wrong?" I heard him say. "I can help you. I'm pulling an *A* right now in algebra." He sat behind me, ranting about his incredible tutoring abilities.

"Too bad everyone in Dressel Hills has to mind *my* business," I mumbled into my backpack, searching for the textbook.

Jared touched my shoulder, and reluctantly I turned around. He flashed his dazzling smile. "I'm offering my services, Holly. No strings attached."

A first, I thought, pulling a smirk.

"Seriously," he continued, "if you want help with algebra, I'm here for you."

"Thanks, but no thanks."

"Well, I don't believe for one minute that you're okay with having a fledgling brother tutor you."

"I'll survive." The class was filling up, and I didn't care to pursue the conversation further. I turned back around, facing the front.

Jared tried to push the issue, but I refused to budge in his direction. I opened the textbook, grateful to be pulling top grades in *this* class.

♥ ♥ ♥

When the bell rang at the end of first hour, I noticed Billy and Andie together in the back of the room. "Yo, Holly!" Andie called. "Come here a sec."

Jared was attempting to get my attention again. I ignored him and hurried to see what Andie wanted. "Hey," I said, looking first at Andie, then at Billy.

"Hey, Holly," Billy's voice was hardly more than a whisper. Laryngitis, maybe?

"I'll leave now," Andie said, grinning at me. "Billy wants to talk to you." And with that, she left.

The little sneak.

I stood there, feeling awkward. Billy coughed a little. "Got a cold?" I asked, trying to break the ice.

"Not really." He looked uncomfortable, right down to his sneakers.

"Look, did Andie put you up to this?" I asked.

He shrugged. "I wouldn't say that."

"Then what *would* you say? I mean, about Andie. Is she trying to get you to do something for her—about me, I mean?" I was remembering that she bristled every time I mentioned Sean. The long-distance letter-writing thing really bugged her.

"Don't blame Andie." Billy looked me square in the face. "I really wanted to talk to you, uh, about some . . . some other stuff."

I was getting antsy. We only had five minutes for passing periods between classes. If we were late, there was a pink slip. Three pink slips equaled after-school detention. With a temporary *F* in algebra, I couldn't afford even the tiniest flaw on my high-school record.

I glanced at the wall clock. "Okay, we can talk sometime. When?"

"After school?"

"Where?"

"Soda Straw okay?" he asked.

I almost asked why, but decided I was sounding like the nut who'd written the weird letters.

Then it hit me, and I probably stared at him. Could Billy

Hill be the letter writer? I mean, he was obviously infatuated or whatever. But would Billy really do something that dumb? I couldn't imagine it, but I was sure I could devise a plan to test my suspicions.

I eyed the clock. "We better get going. See you after school." I rushed off to choir.

The risers were filling up when I arrived. Andie was perched on the piano bench, waiting for Mrs. Duncan, the director. Andie's face lit up when she saw me.

I slid onto the piano bench and gave her a nudge. "Hey," I whispered, "what are you trying to do? With Billy, I mean."

"Nothing."

"Think again," I said. "You're doing something weird—and using Billy in the process. I just know it."

Andie offered a frown. "I can't believe you think that."

"Truth hurts."

Mrs. Duncan arrived, carrying her burlap shoulder bag crammed with music. I hurried to my place on the risers, next to the Miller twins—Paula and Kayla, sophomores.

"You're tardy," Paula said smugly, and I smirked at her choice of words. Paula and Kayla both had a strange way with the English language.

"Not actually late," I countered. "Just close."

Paula rolled her eyes. She was obviously ticked at me. And I was sure it had nothing to do with tardiness. More than likely Billy Hill.

"Look, Paula, if you think I'm moving in on the guy you like, you're wrong."

She was silent.

"But . . ." I hesitated, thinking ahead. "I think you should know that he and I plan to meet somewhere to talk after school. It's Billy's idea," I explained, in no uncertain terms. Paula, after all, was a good friend; it had taken a long time for us to get to a decent level of rapport. I wasn't going to let Billy's present insanity interfere. Besides, I wanted Paula to know I wasn't sneaking around behind her back.

"It's really none of my concern," Paula replied. "What Billy does with his leisure time is entirely optional."

Sounded like Paula and Billy might actually be history. No wonder Andie was pushing Billy toward me. It was perfect from her standpoint. Get Holly to fall for Billy and . . . *au revoir* to Sean.

But why was Andie so set on the demise of Sean's and my friendship? I made a mental note to ask her.

Mrs. Duncan located her director's copies of several songs; then she took the podium. "Sorry about the delay," she said, adjusting her glasses. "Now . . . will the section leaders please pass these songs around?" She held up three of my favorites. One was from the musical *Cats,* titled, "Jellicle Songs for Jellicle Cats."

We rehearsed parts on the first piece, then put the harmonies together. Paula, however, was barely singing. At least, not in her usual robust manner. I could tell she wasn't just a little ticked over this thing with Billy. Of course, she would never admit it. Not in a zillion years.

♥ ♥ ♥

I tried to honey-coat things over after choir by offering to sit with Paula at lunch. She had other plans. "Kayla and I are eating together today, but thanks." She glanced at her twin, who was gathering up the sheet music. The two of them were dressed exactly alike in matching jeans and red shirts. It struck me as highly unusual since they'd been working so hard to establish their separate identities. Then Paula turned to me unexpectedly. "Did you get the letter I wrote, you know, for the editorial column?"

"I haven't checked my mail yet today, but I will." Then another idea came to me. "Did you sign your name to your letter?"

"Well, why not?" she said in a huff. "Of course I did. I don't have anything to hide."

I nodded. "I didn't mean to imply that, Paula. It's just that I keep getting these strange letters from someone who never signs off with a real name."

"Really?" Her eyes grew wide. "Who would do that?"

"That's what I'm trying to find out," I explained, suddenly thinking of the perfect plan. "By the way, do you think you would recognize Billy's handwriting?"

"Billy's?" She stiffened. "You think Billy's writing weird letters to the school paper?" She looked completely aghast.

"I didn't say that, did I?" It was getting close to the third-hour bell.

"No, but—"

"Would you be willing to at least take a look at one of the letters?" I asked.

"Well, I guess"—then a smile spread across her face—"if you'd be willing to do something for me."

"Anything," I said as we headed for the hallway.

"Promise you won't meet Billy after school?"

"What?" I studied her. What a strange request.

"Please?" she said, accompanied by a pained expression.

I sighed. Paula wasn't being devious. The girl was hurt—grasping at straws to keep her guy.

"Just plain stand him up," she said. "Deal?"

This was unbelievable. "Uh, okay, you win," I said, realizing how much I needed her help. "Meet me at my locker before lunch. I'll show you the letter then."

Paula's face broke into a sunshine smile. Things seemed much better for her. But what about me? What would I tell Billy? I couldn't just not show up.

Could I?

Chapter 14

Paula appeared at my locker immediately after fourth hour. I smoothed out the scrunched-up letter and she read it. "The handwriting isn't familiar to me, but that doesn't mean it's not Billy."

I was puzzled. "Why can't you be sure?"

She pushed her brunette hair behind her ears. "Billy can write with *both* hands. He's ambidextrous." She smiled as though it were some inside information, between just the two of them.

"Hmm, I never knew." I surveyed the letter. "Could it be that Billy is also two-faced?" I had to say that—had to test her loyalty.

Paula's eyebrows lurched up. "Two-faced? Not on your life."

I closed my locker door and Paula turned to go. "Wait, there's one more thing. You can't mention any of this to Billy, okay?"

She nodded. "Sure."

"And something else. I'll tell Billy that I won't be meeting him today . . . and the reason why."

Her face turned ashen. "No, please don't. It would be a big mistake to tell him you and I talked."

"Why? Because then he'd know exactly how you *still* feel about him? Want to know what I think? I think you're crazy about him."

She shook her head. "It's not important anymore, honest." Seemed to me she was pleading.

"So . . . what really happened between you two?" I probably shouldn't have stuck my nose in, but I was dying to know.

"Let's leave well enough alone," she said.

I could tell by the sad look in her eyes that the parting of ways hadn't been her idea. Which had me even more worried. Did it have something to do with Billy's silly crush on me?

Paula and I headed in opposite directions. Inside the cafeteria I felt torn up—really sorry. Especially for Paula. And now also for Billy. He'd had a difficult time getting up the nerve to ask me to meet him at the Soda Straw. And now I wouldn't be going at all. I'd made a deal with Paula, and I wouldn't think of breaking it.

Andie waved me over to her table, smack-dab in the middle of zillions of people. When I sat down and started eating, she jumped all over me. "Are you out of your mind, Holly?"

This line was beginning to wear thin. "What now?" I wailed.

"I saw you talking to Paula." She tilted her head toward the hallway. "Don't you know you'll mess things up between you and Billy if he sees the two of you hanging out?"

"I really don't care what Billy thinks."

She sighed and shook her head at her tray. "Don't you see? Billy's gun-shy."

"What's that supposed to mean?"

"You know, it's taken him all this time to have the courage to—"

"Wait a minute," I interrupted. "*All* this time? What are we talking here, a week—ten days?"

She threw her hands up, looking completely disgusted. "I'd think you'd catch on after a while. I mean, c'mon!"

She was actually frantic. So . . . why was Andie acting so strange?

"Look, I think we need to talk about something," I said. "It's about Sean."

"Hamilton?"

I nodded. "Why are you so worried about him?"

Andie's dark eyes clouded. "You're making fun of me."

I touched her shoulder. "Don't be so sensitive."

She was quiet for a moment. Then the words "I'm afraid" slipped out of her mouth.

This was bizarre. "Afraid of what?"

"Of losing you—us," she muttered. "And don't laugh."

Again I was baffled. "You think I'm going to lose my head over Sean Hamilton? Is that it?"

She picked at her food. "Could be. After all, I did meet him last summer, remember? He's a real gem, as my mom would say."

"But aren't you jumping to conclusions? I'm not even allowed to date for another four months, for pete's sake."

"But," she protested, "you can't tell me he's not thinking and probably praying—if I know Sean—about God's will for his life. Same as you, right?"

"Of course." I reached for my chicken sandwich. "But you don't have to worry *now* about that."

"You'll be going off to college in a few years."

"That's my goal." I knew she'd ruled out going, but I kept hoping maybe she'd change her mind.

"So, no matter what, we'll end up apart." She leaned her elbow on the tray, staring at me. "We really only have a short time left, you know." She sounded awfully gloomy. Almost as depressed as I'd been last month.

"Andie, you're sounding morbid. Will you quit?"

"Well, at least now you know the truth. I've been the one

encouraging Billy, have been all along, hoping for a way to keep you here in Dressel Hills," she confessed. "Because if the two of you actually get together—and get married eventually, after college—Billy would probably bring his bride back home to Dressel Hills."

"There's no guarantee. You can't know what Billy or I would do after graduation—*separately*!" I said. "People move around; things change. Just because I might marry a hometown boy doesn't mean I'd live forever in this town—or even in Colorado. You should know that. Besides, what if you end up marrying a guy from somewhere else?"

"I can't see that happening." She sighed. "Oh, it's all so scary—the unknown—when you think about it."

I laughed, trying to lighten the mood. "Then quit thinking. It gets you in trouble."

She laughed, too, only not her cheerful, robust laughter.

My best friend was depressed over our future options, and she was also becoming paranoid. I couldn't stand it—her obsession and fear of the unknown. "You really ought to get a grip on this whole future thing, Andie," I said. "Why don't you let God handle it—mine, too, while you're at it."

"I know, I know. Just please, whatever you do, don't stand Billy up."

I shook my head. "Look, it's just this once—I have no choice."

We talked some more. And wisely, I steered the conversation away from future hopes and dreams . . . and her fears, all the way to the big math mess I was in. "So how would *you* like to be stuck with your little brother for a tutor?"

That got a sincere smile. "How's it working?"

"It's not. In fact, it's so bad I suggested we meet in a public place to avoid killing each other."

Andie twisted a curl. I should've known right then she was

cooking something up in her mind. "Are you saying you'll be hanging out at the library after school today?"

I nodded. "And if you see Billy, would you mind giving him a message?"

"Like what?"

"Tell him I'm really sorry, but I can't meet him after all."

She gasped. "You're honestly breaking your first date with the poor boy?"

"It isn't a date, and Billy's not poor."

Andie frowned. "Why *are* you standing him up?"

"It's a long story."

"Yeah, right. Paula must've gotten to you."

Suddenly, I missed Tina Frazer, my blind friend. *She* wouldn't be giving me the third degree! She was as cool as you get . . . except she'd gone back to the School for the Deaf and Blind for the semester.

Andie stared at me. "Well, did she?"

"Paula?" I was tired of being interrogated. "Let's just call it a day, okay?"

Andie made a face. "Whatever."

"Ditto for me." I was maxed out with Andie.

Chapter 15

We had an open-book test in French class, and Mr. Irving was nice enough to come around and help some of us. Next class was English, and Mrs. Ross was her very cool self, encouraging several students to submit articles for *The Summit*. I secretly wondered if I'd ever be fortunate enough to have my novella published. The way I saw it, if I could just conquer my algebra problems once and for all—figure out the unknown quantities— I'd have plenty of time to work on my book.

Hey, wait a minute! I sat straight up in my desk. *The unknown.* That's what Andie was talking about at lunch. She was afraid of it. Afraid and obsessed.

Was that my problem, too—except with algebra? Was I afraid of solving unknown factors? Maybe I was causing my own mental block. Hey, this was heavy, something a shrink might come up with. But I was still in that weird stage of life when adults expected hairbrained behavior. Actually, I was close to turning fifteen.

Ah, to be fifteen, I thought. *Or sixteen, even.* The magical midteens when freaking out should be limited to finding the perfect clothes to wear on your first date. None of this rebellious stuff with parents, or fighting with smart-alecky stepsiblings or even best friends. Nope, very soon I would be breezing easy.

Mom always said once I got past fourteen, my up-and-down emotional roller coaster would probably start to level off. I hoped she was right.

There was something else I couldn't wait for: the "Dear Holly" column, soon to be launched. It would be so fabulous to see my words in print again.

Mrs. Ross was talking to the class. "Holly, will you please distribute school papers to homerooms next week?"

I snapped out of my daze. "I'd love to."

Her round face broke into a huge grin. "I had a feeling you might." She took her place at the chalkboard, preparing to write the assignment. I thought back to seventh grade, when one of the boys had made fun of the fat under her arm. It jiggled when she wrote. But not anymore. Mrs. Ross had slimmed down considerably since she'd married our former science teacher.

"Dear class," she began, as though dictating a verbal letter. As she lectured, I thought about another letter. The one I'd crumpled up and Paula had inspected. Could it be—was it possible—that Billy was the guy behind the strange letters?

Sitting there, spacing out, I wished I could take back the promise I'd made Paula. Why had she tricked me? If only I hadn't fallen for her deal. If only . . .

"Each of you will write a scene—an imaginative scenario—based on an 'If only,' " Mrs. Ross said. It registered in my brain as I began paying attention. I was amazed at this coincidence.

Smiling, I reached for my assignment notebook and pen. *If only?* What a perfect assignment for a girl who basically lived her life around the words. Now there was another thing I couldn't wait for—the chance to sit down and begin working on Mrs. Ross's ingenious assignment.

♥ ♥ ♥

After school I found my stepbrother Phil at the library, plugged in to a book. I'd chosen the public library instead of the high-school library for obvious reasons.

"Let's hurry and get this over with," I whispered, pulling out a chair and arranging my books. Glancing at him, I realized it hadn't even registered with him that I was there. "Yoo-hoo, nerd-brain, your victim has arrived."

Phil lowered his book, his eyes staring blankly. "Victim? Where?" He looked around.

"Duh? Are you dense, or what?"

He shook himself back. "Now, where were we?"

"We weren't anywhere, at least not yet." I had the feeling I'd interrupted a fabulous read. I reached for his book. "What's the title?"

He showed me. *Search for the Unknown Species*.

"Sci-fi?"

He nodded. "A little out there, so to speak, but then again, maybe not as far as we think." A weird, half-baked expression flitted across his spectacled face. "You'd have to read it."

I put up my hands. "Uh, no thanks, not my genre."

"What *is* your fictional taste?"

"Oh, things like mysteries, suspense . . . and, of course, a little romance mixed in." After I divulged my preferences, I realized that I'd actually lowered my guard.

"Hey, this is good." He grinned goofily. "We're making a connection."

I didn't let his remark shake me up. Honestly, I felt very weird talking to Phil at all. In public anyway. Sure, he was my blood cousin and stepbrother, but hanging out with ultimate geeks was not the best way to enhance one's high-school reputation.

High-school students comprised a rare breed. I, having been thrust into high school prematurely, was beginning to see my own metamorphosis. At times, though, I didn't like what I saw.

"Uh . . . hello, Holly?" Phil leaned forward on the table,

waving his hands in my face. He was wearing a brown turtle-neck, and for an instant, I thought he looked more like a *turtle* than a tutor.

"Sorry. Guess I spaced out."

"You know," he said, "since we're opening up like this, I might as well tell you something." He looked at me as though waiting for an invitation to continue.

"We're here to work on algebra."

"First, let me point out one of your bad habits." He pushed his glasses up. No, he *slid* them up, with a lot of help from the nose grease that continuously oozed from his preadolescent pores. "You daydream too much. Way too much."

I glanced around, embarrassed. "That's none of your business." Whew, it sure seemed like I was saying or thinking those words a lot these days.

Phil must've picked up on my aggravated state. He dropped the subject of my reveries and opened my algebra book. "Let's begin, shall we?"

"Oh, puh-leeze, can we just cut the intellectual jazz and talk like normal human beings?"

"Normal? According to whom?"

I shook my head. This was hopeless. "Just explain the stupid homework."

He explained it twice. Then a third time. "Do you get it *now?*"

"I think so."

"Okay, do the problem," he said. "I'll watch."

I worked the problem, slowly . . . carefully.

Then he checked it. "Almost," he said.

"Are you kidding? It's still not right?"

Patiently, he showed me that I'd added instead of multiplying one of the sets of numbers.

I gripped my pencil. "Do you think I'll ever get this stuff?"

Again, Phil pushed up his glasses. This time, without commenting . . . and we started over on another problem.

That's how things went on Tuesday afternoon. Along about an hour into an exasperating tutoring session, Andie had the gall to show up all smiles. With Billy, no less.

"Hey." She came up and hugged me like she hadn't seen me all day. "How *are* you?"

"Okay." No way was I going to elaborate. If she'd had any brights at all, she could've sniffed out the tension between Phil and me.

Instead, Andie surveyed Phil, then the scraps of crumpled-up papers where I'd tried—and failed—to finish the problems. "Oh, I get it. You two are working here," she remarked.

"It's a tutoring session," Phil said.

"I see . . ." Andie was carrying on like she'd had no idea we'd be here. Like this had been some chance meeting. I despised the charade.

Phil spoke up. "We're really very busy now, so if you'll—"

"Assertive little soul." Andie grinned at Phil. "Spunky too."

For a second I thought she was going to rumple his hair. "Uh, Andie, can we talk later, maybe?" Truth was, I never wanted to talk to her again. Not the way she was pulling this ridiculous stunt. She knew Phil and I were going to be studying here. She *knew*. Why was she acting like this?

Andie turned to Billy. "I guess they're tied up," she said. "But you could give her a call later. Okay with you, Holly?"

A call? About what? About whatever it was that Billy wanted to talk to me about at the Soda Straw?

I looked at Billy. "Was this your idea?"

He shook his head back and forth. "Well, kinda . . . I guess."

"So in other words, *no*. Right?" I glared at Andie.

"Shh!" a group of students shushed us. Then the librarian came stalking over.

Phil sized up the situation. "Better beat it," he said to Andie and Billy.

"We'll be quiet," Andie whispered to the librarian when she motioned for her and Billy to skedaddle. Andie pulled out a chair and Billy followed suit. She pulled the algebra book her way, and when I grabbed it to intercept, she clutched it with all her might. "Let me just see it," she demanded through clenched teeth. "Billy knows this stuff. He can help Holly understand . . ."

Phil seized the book, too. "Excuse me? This is *my* responsibility."

Andie looked at Billy, as though giving him the cue to jump in. She waited, looking as if she might blow up. Billy, on the other hand, said nothing.

Then it hit me. I knew why she'd come. Billy was just supposed to waltz in here with her and take charge—show me he could tutor me just as well as, if not better than, Phil. Andie, in her delusional state, hoped that Billy and I would hit it off as tutor and student . . . then discover we liked each other. Maybe a lot. Of course that's what she'd planned. I would bet my cat on it!

Andie held on to the book for dear life. "Philip Patterson, did anyone ever tell you you're a nerdy kid?"

Phil wasn't going to let academic slurs stop him. "If the textbook splits, you'll have to purchase a new one," he stated matter-of-factly.

"That's the least of my worries," she hissed.

Suddenly Phil let go.

The book—along with Andie—went flying, knocking down one of the chairs and a stack of library books behind her. "What a little brat," she said, getting up.

I'd had it. "You . . . you are despicable!" I'd never meant something so much in my life. "How dare you talk to my . . . my . . ." For a second I didn't know what to call him.

But I recovered quickly. "Phil's not only my brousin; he's my friend. Now go, before *I* kick you out."

Phil's eyes nearly popped out. I'd defended him—to his face!

Andie glared, and Billy seemed a little disoriented. He'd never heard such words fly from my sweet lips. In fact, if I could have, I would've dreamed up a far-flung future for myself right now. Away from Dressel Hills, Colorado. And Andie, too.

Chapter 16

As if things weren't already bad enough, they instantly got worse. Andie flew out of the library. Billy, however, stayed seated and calmly surveyed the stormy situation.

Until . . . in walked Paula Miller. Talk about awkward. This was it.

My hunch was she would ignore us, pretend she hadn't seen Billy sitting across the study table from me.

But I was wrong.

She came right over, "Well, hello," she said, taking Billy into consideration as she spoke.

I was speechless. Billy wasn't. For pretty much the first time since he'd walked into the library, he spoke. "Have a seat."

Paula pulled out a chair next to me. Her perfume was sweet, like she'd just sprayed it on. "What's everyone studying?" she asked.

Phil took the opportunity to take her small talk literally and began rehashing my algebra homework. He continued while I glanced nervously at Billy, who seemed to be taking the situation in stride.

Paula, however, was sending me signals with her eyes, as

well as poking me under the table. It seemed like she was tapping out a code of some kind on my knee. Something like: You promised. You promised. . . . Of course I couldn't be sure, but it certainly seemed to fit the rhythm of the words.

When Phil finished his spiel, Billy seemed convinced that my brousin was the best tutor for me. Paula, however, didn't show any interest in that. She was seething, but her face never showed it.

"I think it's time we head home," I said, making the first move to call this nightmare meeting adjourned. Phil started gathering up the papers. And while he went to dump the balls of wadded paper in the trash, I said good-bye to Billy, who was in an obvious rush to get going.

Paula and I stood there for a moment, waiting until Billy disappeared down the stairs and out the front door. Then she cut loose. "I thought we had a, well, an understanding."

"We do, or rather . . . we did."

"Then why are you and Billy here—together?"

"I'd hate for you to think I'm making this up as I go, but I had nothing to do with Billy showing up. Just ask Andie."

"Andie?"

Phil came back and picked up the algebra book. "Ready?"

"Almost," I said. "Meet me out front." I turned to Paula. "Andie's having some trouble sorting out reality—"

"Why is it," Paula interrupted, "that you constantly blame Andie for your own errors?"

I noticed the librarian creeping up, so we scurried to the door. Once outside, it wasn't as easy to talk. Phil was waiting.

"I'll call you later, okay?" I offered.

"That won't change the fact that your word is definitely mud." Paula walked away, holding her head high. I hadn't seen her so perturbed since our earliest feuding days.

"Well," I said to Phil, "I guess it's time we catch the bus home."

We walked almost a whole block before he said anything. "You caught me off guard earlier."

"Oh?" I could sense what was coming.

"You called me your friend. It was quite shocking."

I poked him in the ribs playfully. "Don't let it go to your egghead, tutor-boy!"

♥ ♥ ♥

At home I got busy on my English assignment. I had the perfect idea. I wrote the title at the top of my paper: *If Only I Could Know the Unknown Future.* Wow, this sort of an essay would knock the socks off Mrs. Ross. Maybe I could weave some sci-fi lingo into it. Phil could help with that.

My first draft was rougher than usual. It had something to do with thinking constantly about the weird scene in the library this afternoon. I couldn't believe things had gotten so crazy. Made me wonder if Andie and I were through for good. The way I felt right now, she didn't deserve a friend like me.

Paula Miller didn't, either. She hadn't given me the benefit of the doubt, the way I would have if the tables were turned. Paula had behaved true to form—pounding away at my knee and maintaining a calm, cool face, though her searing eyes made it clear she was rattled.

And Billy? He'd acted really strange around Andie. Totally unlike himself. I felt sorry for him. Andie had obviously railroaded him into going to the library with her. Whether or not he knew I'd be there was another story.

One thing was sure: Phil and I had experienced a moment of truth. Straight out of nowhere, I'd stuck up for him. Now I knew firsthand what the saying meant—"blood is thicker than water."

Coming to this conclusion—and actually experiencing such a thing—would've been enough for one day. But, as it turned out, the phone rang after supper, and Billy was on the line.

"Hello?" I said.

"Hey, Holly. Thought I'd give you a quick call."

"Yeah?"

"Getting right to the point . . ."

Whatever that is.

"Paula called me earlier," he said. "She told me you were asking around about my handwriting. What it looks like, to be exact. So . . . what's this about?"

What had Paula said to him?

In a flash, I knew. This was her way of getting back. I'd messed up the deal with her, so she'd broken her promise to me about not telling Billy about the weird letter I'd shown her today. Some friend she was.

"Uh, Holly? You still there?"

"What did Paula tell you?"

He mumbled like he wasn't really sure what she'd said or why she'd called. I could relate to his feelings about it. After all, some people *I* knew could come across rather fuzzy on occasion, especially when they were upset.

"I really think it's probably just a big misunderstanding," I said.

"Huh?"

I almost let myself think, *Poor Billy, stuck in the middle.* But I wasn't going to do that. Billy, after all, was as cool a guy as there was in Dressel Hills. Probably one of the coolest. But, of course, he was no match for Sean. And even as I talked to Billy, trying to smooth over the ridiculous situation at hand, I was thinking of Sean Hamilton . . . out in California. Where I really wanted to be.

"Holly? Did you hear what I said?" Billy asked.

"I'm sorry. I've got a lot on my mind."

"Hey, don't worry about it. Probably nothing important, any-way."

I agreed.

"Well, I'll see ya."

"Okay," I said, forgetting that he'd wanted to meet me at the Soda Straw "to talk" a few hours earlier. After we'd hung up, I remembered.

Just now, our conversation had been a total flop. My fault. Maybe Phil was right—I *did* daydream too much.

Funny how a person could go from one extreme to the other about a brainy brousin. All in a single day.

Chapter 17

After a warm bath, I sorted through the latest stack of letters to "Dear Holly" and found Paula's letter. I had stopped to check my personal editorial cubbyhole before heading off to the library. Now it was time to catch up on some correspondence.

I opened the envelope and read Paula's cleverly written note. But she had used such big words, and I really couldn't see the point of her letter. She was congratulating me on acquiring assistant editor status at *The Summit*.

Thinking back to what had transpired between us earlier, I wondered if Paula might now be wishing she hadn't written this at all. Fact was, I'd solved one major problem—the strained relationship between Phil and me—rather spontaneously. But in doing so, I'd created two more problems. How could things get so complicated this quickly?

I patted my bed and Goofey jumped up, purring as he found a warm spot next to me. Opening my devotional book, I discovered that the Scripture for October 22—today—was 2 Corinthians 12:9—"My grace is sufficient for you, for my power is made perfect in weakness." It was the second time this verse had come to my attention this week. So . . . was God trying to tell me something?

For a moment I wondered if Uncle Jack had borrowed my teen devotional book for the family's time together the other night. But, no, I knew better. He would've asked permission.

I read the "Think It Through" section, contemplating my weakness—my anger and big mouth, in this case. I thought, too, of how God's grace could make me strong. But there was a catch. I needed to ask. Plain and simple.

I had been waiting for grace to rain down on me. As I read more of the devotional, I realized that God's grace was with me, in me—because I belonged to Jesus. What I hadn't realized before was that I needed to ask the Lord for help with my impulsive nature.

I got out of bed and knelt down. Goofey stayed put, listening in on my prayer. "Dear Lord," I began, "I'm grateful that your power is strongest when I'm weak. I know *you* know how weak I was today. Please forgive me for mouthing off to Andie and Paula and for losing my cool, too. I'll try harder next time. Your grace is enough, and I thank you for it. In Jesus' name, amen."

Getting up, I knew I'd settled some important things spiritually. I just wished I didn't have to learn things the hard way. Now . . . how to get Andie and Paula to believe me when I apologized?

♥ ♥ ♥

Two days passed, and neither Andie nor Paula would let me get close enough to atone for my sins. Oh, I tried, all right. But they were ticked. Could I blame them?

Billy offered a solution when he and I ran into each other at lunch. "Tomorrow, first thing, Andie has student council. Why don't you try to talk to her then?" His face didn't flush red while we talked this time. Something was different.

"Did Andie say anything to you . . . about, you know, the thing at the library?" I asked.

"She only said she couldn't believe you'd thrown a fit like that." He blinked twice, looking at me. "By the way, about that talk we were going to have. When do you want to meet me?"

"Maybe we'd better skip it. If that's okay with you."

"Cool." He leaned against the locker next to mine. Like he was beginning to relax around me. Like the old days before this bizarre infatuation started.

"To tell you the truth, I'm a little confused. I still get the feeling that Paula likes you. Did you two actually split up?"

He rolled his eyes. "That's another subject."

"Really?" I was dying to hear it from Billy's lips.

"I better not try to explain now." He looked me straight in the eye. "And I hope you and I won't become enemies over this."

"Over what?"

He blushed then. "Well, you know . . ."

So I was right. Billy still liked Paula a lot, even though he seemed to be struggling with some sort of feelings for me. Yet I was sure everything would work out for the best in the end.

♥ ♥ ♥

Friday, before school, I planted myself in front of the student council office door and waited for Andie. I wanted to make amends. Desperately.

Five long minutes had come and gone when Ryan Davis showed up. "Hey," he said, smiling.

"Looking for someone?" I asked, although I figured it was Zye Greene.

He stuck his hands into his pockets. "Waiting for the man. You?"

"Andie."

"Cool."

Then Jared came over, all smiles. I hoped he wouldn't mistake my cheery reaction to his being there. Actually, he was the "out" I needed. Truth was, Ryan totally bugged me. In the past, his obvious prejudice toward Andie—toward all dark-skinned people—had made me furious. A sort of righteous anger. Of course, I didn't hate him or anything. But I certainly couldn't stand his half flirty, half-witted comments here lately.

Jared stood so close I could feel his shirtsleeve against my arm. "How's the most popular editor in the school?"

"Guess again."

"C'mon, Holly-Heart, you'll be terrific," Jared gushed.

"We'll see." I was thinking about that ridiculous reply I'd written to "Who Am I?"

"When's the paper coming out?" Ryan asked.

"Monday."

Ryan's face lit up like the Fourth of July. "Great!"

"What are *you* so excited about?" Jared asked Ryan, who was still hovering near me.

"I think I'm going to be published—at last," Ryan said.

Jared shrugged like it was no big deal. "Wouldn't be the first time Mrs. Ross twisted someone's arm to write an article for the paper."

I could see these two guys weren't crazy about sharing the same turf with me. And I was relieved when the office door opened and Andie walked out. "Hey, Andie," I said, scurrying down the hall after her. "I need to talk to you."

She kept walking, not talking.

"Look, I'm trying to apologize."

Andie huffed. "I saw fire in your eyes, Meredith." She was referring to Tuesday afternoon. The day she and Phil were fighting over *my* algebra book.

"You looked absolutely hateful." She scowled. "Do you really dislike me so much? You caused a major scene!" She headed for the girls' room and darted in. Before I could get to her, she disappeared into one of the stalls.

"So what does it take to say 'I'm sorry'?" I asked, standing with my nose to her door.

Silence.

"C'mon, Andie, we can talk this out . . . we're best friends."

"Were."

I stood my ground. "Please, can't we just talk?"

"You already said that, but you know what? I think you should just forget about Billy Hill and grow up and go off to college and maybe marry your fine and fancy Sean Hamilton and get as far away from Dressel Hills as possible." She sucked air into her lungs.

"Okay, now that that's off your chest, are you finished?"

Tomblike silence.

"Andie?"

"Leave me alone," she fired back.

So I did. I checked my hair in the mirror and walked right out of the rest room.

But feelings of rejection overwhelmed me, and I almost didn't see Zye and Ryan on the opposite side of the hall. When Ryan's eyes finally caught mine, I snapped to it, hurrying down the hall past them.

"Holly-Heart." He rushed to catch up.

Shocked that he'd used my nickname, I whirled around. "Don't ever call me that."

"But it's your name, right?"

"Not exactly." I turned away from him, longing for the safety of my locker. If only I could get away from this obnoxious person. If only . . .

Just then I spied something pink and heart-shaped stuck to my locker door. "Oh great," I muttered. "What's this?"

"Looks like someone's got a secret admirer," Ryan said, still following me.

I stopped cold in the middle of the busy hallway. "Excuse

me! I don't know what you want, but if you don't mind, I'd like to be left alone."

He grinned. "Sorry there, Holly, just wanted to clear up one thing." He glanced down the hall. "Uh . . . back there, when your friend Jared said something about Mrs. Ross asking me to write an article for *The Summit*—well, she didn't ask me nothin' like that. Okay?"

I was completely unprepared for his totally foggy confession. "Whatever." I said it just to get him out of my hair.

Surprisingly, it worked. Ryan turned and headed the other way.

Quickly, I got to my locker and snatched off the . . . *valentine?* What on earth was this for?

I opened it and read the verse:

> *Roses are red,*
> *Andie is blue,*
> *I think it would help a lot*
> *If she stayed away from you!*

No signature. And besides that, the poem had been printed, not written in cursive. I studied it carefully. Nothing to go on. I glanced around the hall, hoping for a clue. This mystery-letters-and-notes thing was really getting out of hand.

♥ ♥ ♥

I was still obsessing about the mystery writer in algebra.

Bravely I showed the valentine note to Jared, who was sitting behind me again, oddly enough. He read it and handed it back. "Sounds like you and Andie really tore into things."

"That's not why I showed you this," I insisted. "Does the *printing* look familiar to you?"

He shook his head. "Nobody I know prints like that, but if you want my opinion, I think some girl probably sent it."

"Thanks for nothing." I turned around in time to see Mrs. Franklin staring at me. Looking down at my desk, I was embarrassed. What would she say about my homework today?

"Holly, may I see you after class, please?" she said.

I nodded without looking up, worried sick about another *F* grade, or worse—flunking algebra altogether. Not worried enough, though. Because, as hard as I tried, I could not keep my mind on the new assignment. I figured Phil would say I'd done it all wrong anyway when I got home, so why waste my time trying?

Instead of doing algebra problems, I doodled. Even concocted another scene for my novella, which had begun to suffer due to lack of time. My powers of concentration were focused on tutoring sessions. That, and worrying about the friends I was losing because of my bad temper.

And there were the mystery letters . . . and now an anonymous valentine poem. Who was writing them? And why?

Chapter 18

Mrs. Franklin's face showed zero emotion as I sat next to her desk. The classroom was empty, and she and I were alone again, just the two of us. I tried to bolster my bruised ego.

Glancing at my watch, I knew I'd probably be late for fourth hour. Mrs. Franklin would be more than willing to write an excuse for me, though, and probably include the reason for my tardiness on top of it.

I waited as she opened her desk drawer and found a file folder. "Here we are." She looked at me momentarily. Her face seemed almost relaxed, instead of pinched up. Was this going to be good news after all?

I was puzzled.

"Holly, your stepbrother is doing an excellent job, I do believe."

"He is?" I squeaked.

Was this a backhanded compliment? I couldn't be sure.

She pointed to my score for our last homework assignment. "You missed only five problems."

Five out of thirty.

"This is definitely an improvement," she said. "Now, I want

you to continue working with Philip for another week or so. We'll see how you're doing then."

I nodded. "Thank you." I wasn't sure why I said that. Maybe because she had intimidated me so much before today. Anyway, I felt encouraged. And more confident.

♥ ♥ ♥

After lunch I waited for Paula at her locker. She and her twin were strolling down the hall toward me. They stopped talking immediately when they saw me.

"Is this your idea of funny?" I held out the valentine to show them.

Paula sauntered to her locker, flicking through her combination. "Andie and I have had it with you, Holly" came her words. "For someone who's going to be answering letters to the editor, and—" she paused, glancing at Kayla—"and for a Christian, well, you are certainly not reflecting God's grace to the school population."

God's grace. There it was again.

I nodded. "I agree with you, Paula, and I'm here to say I'm sorry about Tuesday." I waited. She said nothing, so I continued. "I just want an answer about this valentine poem," I said, "and then I'll be on my way."

"Holly, you can't simply walk away like that." This time Kayla was doing the talking.

"I'm not trying to avoid either of you. I just think that right now Paula may not be interested in patching things up." I sighed. "By the way, have either of you met any perfect Christians?"

Paula's mouth dropped. "Well, I . . . I, we try to follow the Lord's example in all things."

I smiled. "Don't most Christians? But notice, you said *try,* and trying is exactly what I'm doing. Tuesday, I failed. Big-time. But if apologizing and trying my best to stay cool by walking away from a potential hot spot offends you, then, once again, I apologize."

I turned to go.

"Wait," Paula said.

Surprised, I froze in place. Kayla's brown eyes twinkled.

Then Paula confessed. "I wrote that stupid poem. I think we, Andie and I, went a little overboard, though."

Smiling, I was delighted with the way things were turning out.

Paula ran her hand through her hair. "I accept your apology, Holly. Now"—she pointed to the valentine—"will you forgive me for that?"

"Gladly."

The Miller twins sported matching smiles as they resumed their chattering.

I hurried down the hall, wondering if the same approach might work on Andie. The more I thought about it, the more I knew she would reject me even more if I came across too boldly.

How could I get to her without stirring up more anger? Should I have someone else, another friend, tell Andie how sorry I was? I figured Jared would be more than happy to fill the bill. And there was always Billy. Paula too. But I wanted to handle this mess myself. After all, I'd started it. So I needed to finish it . . . with God's grace.

Leaning against the wall, I wondered how I could ever get Andie to listen to me again.

Then it hit me. I knew exactly what to do. Right after school I would start working on my plan. In fact, I would start the minute I got home.

♥ ♥ ♥

Turned out my hopes for reconciling with Andie had to wait.

I hadn't factored in the usual pressure from my tutor to get to work on the algebra homework I'd brought home.

"Give me one hour," I told him. "Then I'll be ready."

Phil grinned mischievously and set the timer on his watch. "Sixty minutes, it is."

I ran to my room, pulled out a pen, and began to write:

Dear Andie (on behalf of the "Dear Holly" column)—

    I know it's too late to get this published in the school paper this month, but could you see that Holly gets it for me anyway?

    I just had to write. You see, I have this best friend—I won't mention any names—but believe me, she's been my best friend since we were toddlers.

    Anyway, my friend and I got into this horrible fight the other day. Actually, she wasn't all that bad. I was the one who ended up saying the really horrible things. (I'm sure if my friend reads this, she'll know what I'm talking about!)

    I want you to help me tell her that I'm sorry (honestly sorry) without making her mad, because right now—actually, for several days—she hasn't wanted to have anything to do with me. Sure, I've tried to talk to her, but she's still ticked. And I don't blame her. Nobody should be called despicable. Nobody!

    I really need your advice.

                Signed: A Best Friend (I hope!)

I read what I'd written. This type of letter was my best shot. A little tricky, but it might work. I hoped so. Later on this weekend I would take time to revise it. But in the meantime, I'd be praying for Andie, that her heart would soften toward me. That she wouldn't view this attempt as stupid.

Stroking Goofey's fur, I thought how clever it would be to print out this letter using one of the cool fonts on my computer.

"Your hour is up," Phil called from downstairs. "Tutor time."

"I'll be right there," I called back.

Quickly, I concealed all evidence of the letter. Then I headed downstairs.

Phil was extra patient this session, not that he hadn't been all week. I did notice that something had changed between us. He was nicer. And not as greasy haired.

Maybe I was trying not to zero in on his negative aspects so much. Yeah, maybe that was it.

Anyway, Phil explained each of the new problems. Then he worked some of his own homework while I did my thing. Looking over at him, I remembered what Mrs. Franklin had said about Phil. "Hey, guess what my teacher told me today?"

He scratched his head. "Something about your work?"

"Nope, something about *you*."

He pushed up his glasses. "Me?"

"She said you were doing an excellent job."

A crooked smile crossed his lips. "Which means, you're catching on," he said, bouncing the compliment back to me.

"I think you're right." I leaned back in my chair. "I think I'm finally getting it."

"It helps when you have a friend for a tutor, right?"

I laughed. Phil would probably never forget what I'd said last Tuesday. That was okay. Things had worked out between us. Far better than I'd ever dreamed possible.

Mom strolled through the dining room. "Well, well, looks like the master and student are hitting it off."

I twirled my pencil, grinning at Phil.

"Maybe Holly could tutor Carrie," Mom said. "She's been having lots of trouble with long division."

I groaned.

"Might as well pass on the knowledge." Mom headed off to the kitchen.

"Pass it on," I said softly, going back to my algebra but thinking more about what I'd learned from the verse in 2 Corinthians. Maybe I'd share it with Andie. Once we got over the current hurdle and were speaking to each other again, that is.

Only time would tell. Next Monday, to be exact.

Chapter 19

Saturday a letter showed up in the mail. The mystery writer strikes again!

I scanned the page, nearly bursting with laughter. This time I was being asked the ultimate personal question. (Not will you marry me? But close.)

Dear Holly,

Because you are a sweet, kind person, I thought you wouldn't mind if I sent this to your home address. Although you have not answered any of my previous letters, I have high hopes that you might choose one of my letters for your "Dear Holly" column. Am I on the right track, thinking this way?

Perhaps you are wondering about me? (WHO is he? WHAT's his problem? WHEN will he ask me out? WHY is he writing all these letters? WHERE will it all end?) Well, that takes care of the 5 W's. Do you think it's strange—the things I write?

Spare me—this was too much!

From what I've heard of your work, you are a talented writer, possibly headed for greatness. HOW do I know this?

I pay attention when Mrs. Ross happens to be name-dropping in class. I enjoy her literature classes a lot. And I also like hearing about one of her star students. You!

Hmm . . . literature with Mrs. Ross. Interesting. *This guy's definitely an upperclassman,* I decided.

I hope you will meet me for a long, get-better-acquainted chat. The pen-and-paper method is getting old. I'm hoping to have a better idea of how you feel about me on Monday when I read your column—that is, IF you selected my letter to be published.

> *Another secret admirer,*
> *WHO am I?*

Thank goodness, there was no PS this time. Shoot, the main body of the letter was filled with enough nutty things to fill a fruitcake. Yet I tried to fit the puzzle pieces together as I reread the letter.

Then something hit me. Those words: *Another secret admirer.*

They were like an echo in my brain. Sometime this week . . . in school . . . in the hallway . . . somewhere very recently, someone had referred to the pink valentine note as coming from a secret admirer. Who was it?

Think, I told myself. *Think!*

Then it came to me. I swallowed hard, trying not to choke on the realization. Could the person who'd said those words be the same one who had written them?

Yikes! I freaked out in front of my cat. And Goofey arched his back in protest.

Wait a minute. This guy said he wanted to meet me in person.

Just then, a sense of relief came over me as I realized, thankfully, the weird writer could *not* be Ryan Davis. After all, I'd already met him—several times.

♥ ♥ ♥

Sunday was a real disaster.

Andie wouldn't even let me sit with her in Sunday school. The Miller twins were aghast. So was Jared. She got up and moved when I squeezed through her row toward the vacant seat next to her. Our teacher raised her eyebrows but probably assumed it was just a mere adolescent struggle. Mere, of course, by no means described Andie's rage.

I sat down alone and soon was surrounded by Paula and Kayla. "I wouldn't be surprised if Andie's totally embarrassed next week at this time," Kayla offered.

Her comment didn't make me feel any better. Andie, however, needed time to chill out. Unfortunately, I assumed her time was up for such nonsense. Counting today, which of course hadn't completely transpired yet, it had already been five days since the library fiasco. Hadn't I been punished enough? But I would not lose my cool and tell her so. Nope, my letter to her would have to suffice. Tomorrow!

During class I caught Billy watching me. And there sat Jared—girlfriendless. What an unusual turn of events. Amy-Liz, however, didn't seem upset by it. She'd done the dumping. She was sitting between Joy and Shauna near the front of the class. Jared's eyes weren't on Amy-Liz, though. They were twinkling at guess who. Would this boy ever grow up?

Danny Myers, on the other hand, was way too mature for his own good. Any girls who were even remotely interested decided to play it cool when they found out how serious and severe he was. Kayla Miller included.

Stan, of course, didn't count. He was just a brousin and not so proud of it. Funny, I'd thought last November, before Mom and

Uncle Jack married, that Stan and I might be close stepsiblings some day, but when it came right down to it, Phil was the one who'd won my heart. Phil and little Stephie—when she wasn't snooping in my room.

And that was pretty much the extent of the guys my age. Like I'd told Andie last week, there was no future for me here in Dressel Hills. At least, no romantic future. But as upset as that comment had made Andie, it was positively true.

Then I wondered . . . could Andie's behavior be an outgrowth of two things? My angry words to her and my stubbornness about Sean Hamilton and his letters?

I wanted to turn around and look at her. Study her face, see how she was sitting. Arms crossed, a scowl . . . what?

Usually my best friend was an open book. Today, however, I couldn't read her so well, probably because she was directly behind me. Tomorrow, though, I would be watching her. Very closely. Somehow, I must see her expression when she read my mystery letter to her.

And what a kick it would be if I could observe the "Who Am I?" guy when he saw his words in print. That was impossible, though, because I had no idea who he was.

Chapter 20

It was unusual for Stan to ride the bus to school. But Monday morning, my oldest brousin surprised me and walked to the bus stop, even sat with me.

"What's the occasion?" I asked.

"Can't a guy ride to school with his little sis?"

"Little? I'm almost as tall as you."

He shrugged. "Well, you know."

"No other reason?" I was fishing. But Stan was no dummy. He knew.

"Okay, so today's kinda special," he admitted. "You're a celebrity, right? Everyone's going to be reading the latest feature column in the school paper. Who knows? Your name might become a household word."

"Maybe . . . if students like what they read."

He glanced at me. "Having second thoughts?"

"It's just that some weirdo is writing personal stuff to me." I told him about the mystery letters.

"Any clues who's sending them?" he asked.

"At first, I wondered if it was that guy you hung around with last summer—Ryan Davis."

Stan laughed. "Why would Ryan want to write you anonymous letters?"

"Well, he *does* want to be published. *The Summit* would be an easy way, maybe."

Stan ran his fingers through his blond hair. "Still, I can't believe he'd stoop to something like that."

"There's more," I said. "The mystery writer wants to have a long talk with me. He said he was tired of the pen-and-paper method of communicating."

"Ryan's never been shy before. I doubt he'd say something like that."

"Have you ever read any of his stories?" I asked.

"A few."

"Any good?"

Stan shifted his books. "For one thing, he writes a lot different than he talks."

"Well, believe it or not, Marcia actually liked the first letter I got from the weirdo and decided to run it, along with my crazy response. So if it *is* Ryan's letter, he ought to be pleased."

When we pulled up in front of the high school, Stan was still thinking out loud. "Hey, wait a minute!" He stood up, holding on to the seat. "Come to think of it, Ryan was asking questions about you."

"Really?" I got out of my seat. "When?"

"About two weeks ago, I think."

"Well, that's when the letters first started."

Stan looked surprised. "You sure?"

"Positive. How could I forget? I mean—those letters—they were so freaky."

Stan headed for the front of the bus. I followed. Then, I couldn't believe it—he actually walked me up the steps and into the school. Definitely a first.

Even Billy Hill noticed. Jared too.

"Where're you headed?" Stan asked as we took our time weaving in and out of students.

"English, of course. I'm dying to see how my column looks."

"Okay, I'll see you later." Stan stopped and waved. "Good luck, or break a leg, or whatever."

I chuckled. Why was Stan going overboard, being so nice to me? And what did he know about Ryan that he wasn't telling?

I dashed into the English classroom, which doubled as the newspaper office. Mrs. Ross and several other students were counting out papers for the various homerooms.

I had seen the layouts before they'd gone to press but not the final copies. Eagerly I pulled a paper off the stack and opened to the third page—prominent right side.

There it was—"DEAR HOLLY." The first column of my entire life. The heading was snazzy, printed in a stylish font—almost a literary-romantic look. I scanned the whole thing, rereading the mystery letter, which was followed by my reply.

"Man, if this *is* Ryan's letter, I'm doomed," I blurted out. I could see it now. I'd be the laughingstock of the upperclassmen. Not that I cared; it was just so humiliating.

So how could I know Ryan was the culprit for sure? Should I confront him? Would he even admit it?

Mrs. Ross was peeking over my shoulder. "Holly? You look upset. You should be pleased. You've done a marvelous job. I had to laugh out loud at the interesting letter from that mysterious writer."

"I'm glad you liked it." I closed the paper. "Everyone did a fabulous job. And thanks for your help, too, Mrs. Ross."

Marcia Greene and several others who'd written articles came up to congratulate me. I thanked them and volunteered to take *The Summit* around to the senior class homerooms.

Perfect. I would drop the papers off in the various classrooms and hang around when I came to Ryan's homeroom—while he read the paper. If he carried on and showed everyone the letter, I would know I'd solved the mystery. If not, I was back to square one.

There was only one problem with my plan. I had no idea which homeroom Ryan Davis happened to be in. Maybe Stan knew, so I scurried down the hall to his locker.

When I arrived in the vicinity of his locker, I realized that Stan had already gone. Rats! Who else would know?

I stopped in the middle of a swarm of kids to wrack my brain. Then I knew who to ask. Marcia Greene's brother, Zye, was good friends with Ryan. Surely Marcia would know something.

I made a beeline back to Mrs. Ross's classroom, still carrying the pile of newspapers.

"Marcia just left," Mrs. Ross said when I inquired. She eyed the stack of papers in my arms. "I thought you'd gone to deliver those."

"I was, but . . ." No time for explanations. "Guess I better get going," I said over my shoulder.

"Better hurry—there's a pep rally for homecoming first thing after homeroom this morning," she reminded me.

I'd forgotten. If I didn't hurry, I wouldn't get a chance to observe Ryan Davis reading the paper. Then all this thinking and planning would be for nothing.

Instead of trying to track down Marcia or her brother, I headed straight for the school office. The secretary would know about students' homeroom locations. Perfect.

I raced upstairs, lugging the papers. Too many kids were crowding the stairwell. Still hurrying, I tripped on the next to the top step. The papers flew down, scattering every which way.

A few polite boys stopped to help, but when the bell rang for homeroom, I found myself quite alone. Out of breath and racing against time, I scurried around like a frantic little mouse gathering up the loose papers. If I hadn't had a specific mission—a serious goal—this scenario would've seemed almost funny.

At last, I restacked the papers and trudged back up the steps. So much for celebrity status. Stan was wrong. I was actually a lowly freshman peon. I couldn't even deliver papers.

Frustrated, I marched, huffing and puffing, toward a designated homeroom. I didn't even knock, just headed in and placed the papers on one of the student's desks and left.

The plan I'd concocted involved standing outside each of the senior homerooms and peering in inconspicuously, searching for Ryan, hoping to observe his expression. Unfortunately, I couldn't find him anywhere. I craned my neck back and forth, trying to spot him at each classroom.

He simply wasn't there.

Discouraged, I dashed down the hall to the stairs and headed back to English. "I need an excuse for class," I said to Mrs. Ross, who was sitting prim and proper at her desk. "I had a little accident with the newspapers, and now I'm late."

She smiled, disregarding her homeroom students, and pulled out the appropriate form, filled it out, and signed her name. Then, before I left, she mentioned something about a guy bringing me a letter. "I believe it might be from a secret admirer," she said with a smile.

Mrs. Ross pulled out the top desk drawer. "Here you are, dear." Some of the kids in her homeroom snickered.

"Thanks." I ignored the whispers flying around me, feeling my suspicions rise. My curiosity won out, as always, and I opened the envelope as I hurried to my locker.

Dear Holly,

Congratulations! You must be totally jazzed about your new column. I know I am happy for you.

This sure didn't sound anything like the mystery writer. I read on.

*I'd like to work things out between us, Holly-Heart. Remember
last year, before things changed so radically? Think back . . .*

*Please, won't you give me another chance? I promise I
won't mess things up this time.*

> *Always and forever,*
> *Your #1 Secret Admirer.*

This letter was no mystery—it was from Jared Wilkins. Had
to be!

*PS: By the way, I heard about those letters you've been get-
ting. Paula said she read one of them, and she's right; they're
NOT from Billy. If you want to know who wrote them, meet
me in front of the cafeteria. I'll be the one smiling.*

Why, you . . . ! I thought. Jared would do anything to get my
undivided attention—even pretend to have information on the
mystery writer. What a rat. But would I fall for yet another plot
masterminded by the master of flirtation himself?

I was about to mentally nix the idea as ridiculous when, just
as I rounded the corner—within a few yards of my homeroom—
Ryan Davis appeared. "Holly, you're just the person I've been
looking for."

"I am?"

"You did a grand job of putting together that column of
yours. Even Zye was impressed. He's the senior class president,
you know."

"Yeah, I know." I looked around to see the pep squad coming toward us. "Are you headed for the assembly?"

"I'm in charge of the sound system."

"Oh." I kept waiting for him to mention his letter in the column. "Did you get a chance to read *The Summit* yet?"

"Sure did. It's great. You have a way with words."

"Hey, thanks." I glanced toward Mr. Irving's classroom. "I'm late for homeroom. Better get going."

"See ya." He turned to go.

"Thanks again." *Thank heavens, you're not the mystery writer,* I thought as he left.

I hurried to my homeroom, and several kids clapped when I stepped foot into the room. "Three cheers for Holly!" Mr. Irving said in French.

I gave him my signed form and then hurried to my desk, my face turning red.

"Holly," Mr. Irving was talking above the noise of the students. "We're all wondering about that interesting letter in your column. Will you tell us who wrote it?"

"Oh—the 'Who Am I?' guy?" I replied. "Well, I'm sure no one will believe this, Mr. Irving, but I honestly don't know."

Groans came from around the room. Even Amy-Liz looked disappointed. And Jared? Well, I refused to look in his direction. Nope, Jared had pulled another fast one. And for all I knew, *he'd* written the stupid letters.

Chapter 21

After the pep rally I headed for the girls' rest room.

Paula and Kayla were redoing their hair in front of the mirrors, helping each other like sisters do. "Holly, hey," Kayla said, looking over at me.

"What an exceptionally good column," Paula cheered. "Accolades to the writer."

"Thanks." I plopped my backpack on the ledge below the mirror.

Paula stopped brushing her twin's hair and strolled over and started fooling with mine. "Did you ever find out who wrote that strange letter?"

"I really thought I had this mess figured out, but I honestly have no idea," I said. "Any thoughts from either of you?"

Kayla shook her head.

I pulled out the latest letter. "This one is not a mystery to me. It's got Jared's name all over it."

Paula and Kayla surrounded me, reading it. In seconds, both girls were laughing. "What'll we do with that boy?" Kayla said.

"That's what I want to know. Do you think he might know who's writing letters to me?"

"You could take the chance and show up at lunchtime and find out," Kayla suggested.

Paula grinned. "But Holly doesn't want to get anything started again with Jared, right?"

"Who would?" Kayla scoffed. "He's lonely for one reason— because Amy-Liz got wise to what he's about."

"But what if he's truly changed?" Paula asked. She'd always had a soft spot in her heart for the guy.

Kayla commented, "How is that possible?"

"People do change sometimes," Paula replied.

I looked at her reflection in the mirror. "You're kidding, I hope."

Paula smirked back.

"Andie says you've got a guy friend in California," Kayla said. "Does that mean Dressel Hills boys are out of the picture?"

"Oh, Sean and I are just good friends . . . but that doesn't change anything for the guys here. For now at least, I'm happy with things as they are," I replied.

Paula whipped out a lip gloss. "Surely you wouldn't pass up a chance to go out with some of Colorado's most dashing males. Remember, you'll be fifteen soon."

"In February," I reminded her. "Mom says I can go on a real date then."

"You'll snub *our* guys here?" Paula asked.

"Surely you won't abandon them," Kayla echoed.

I frowned. "You two sound like Andie. Did she put you up to this?"

A mischievous expression crossed Paula's face.

I shook my head. "Andie's gotten to you, hasn't she?"

Kayla touched her soft curls. "Gotten to me?"

"Yeah, because Andie's after me to quit writing to Sean. She has her reasons. Pretty pathetic if you ask me."

"That's interesting." Paula put away the lip gloss.

I laughed. "C'mon, you guys. I know you've already had this conversation with Andie. She's filled you in on her latest goal. Sounds like paranoia, but you know how Andie is sometimes."

They nodded.

"No matter what she or anyone else says, I'm going to stay in touch with Sean. He's so cool you wouldn't believe it." The three of us headed for the door.

"Well, to give up a chance with Jared, he certainly must be extra special," Paula said, trying to be serious. That's when I chased her down the hall.

♥ ♥ ♥

After government class I rushed to Andie's locker. I wanted to deliver my own version of mystery—the letter I'd written Friday night. I smashed the envelope into the air vent of her locker and skittered away.

Down the hall, I stood behind an open door, holding the school paper open in front of me, hiding. I felt the muscles in my shoulders tense as I waited. How would Andie react to my letter?

And, then . . . there she was. Andie headed straight to her locker and opened it with a jerk. My letter was waiting at the bottom of her messy locker. She leaned over and picked it up, her face scrunched into a bewildered look.

Watching her like a hawk, I peered around the paper as she stood reading my letter.

I held my breath.

What would happen? Would she crumple it up . . . toss it away?

Then, surprise, surprise. Andie did a strange thing. She called out to me. Called my name loudly. "I know you're watching from somewhere, Holly. Get yourself over here!"

"What on earth?" I muttered to myself. And go, I did.

"You silly," she said, hugging me. "What sort of letter is this?"

"A nutty one."

"You can say that again." She was giggling. When she calmed down, Andie said she was sorry, too. "I shouldn't have called your stepbrazen a brat."

"*Brousin*," I said.

"Huh?"

"Forget it; I get the idea." I laughed.

"So how's the tutoring going?"

I used her skinny locker mirror to primp. "I'm actually learning some math, finally."

Then a peculiar look crossed her face. "And, uh . . . how're things with Sean?"

"We correspond pretty often. Why?"

"Just wondered." I turned to look at her. Now she had a squirrelly sort of grin. "Guess I've been a jerk about that, too."

"That's okay."

"What a waste of emotional energy," she admitted. "Even if we do go separate ways in the future, we'll always keep in touch, right? No matter what."

"Always."

She closed her door and hoisted her books over to her left arm. "Uh-oh." She stared down the hall. "Guess who . . ."

I turned to see Zye Greene and Ryan Davis.

"It's the Double-X Files," she muttered.

"Aliens at school?" We laughed.

"Something like that," she whispered. "Hey, did you hear? Ryan might be coming to our church youth group."

"You're kidding. Really?"

"Danny Myers invited him. Danny is trying to evangelize the entire Dressel Hills population, I think."

"That's good, isn't it?" Suddenly I felt sick inside. I'd treated Ryan poorly. Just because I didn't agree with his racial prejudice was no reason to reject him as a person. A person who was most likely struggling like the rest of us—probably searching for truth. Bold Danny had the right idea, whether Andie approved of it or not.

Now Ryan and Zye were coming our way.

"I wonder what they want," I said.

"Well, I'm outta here," Andie said, turning to leave. "I'm not hanging around to find out."

I stood there for a minute. It was time I stopped being so rude to these guys. Sure they were upperclassmen, and yep, they'd humiliated Andie and me during freshman initiation, but they were human beings. Jesus had come to save them, too.

Zye stopped a few yards away to talk to another guy, and Ryan spotted Stan, who was fumbling around at his locker. The two of them stood there talking like old friends. Once, Stan glanced over at me, looking a little sheepish.

I headed for second hour, wondering what was going on. Were Ryan and Stan hanging out again? And if so, why hadn't Stan told me this morning on the bus? Things were absolutely confusing.

♥ ♥ ♥

During choir Andie and I sat together for the a cappella songs. We were forming a unified front against Jared Wilkins, who kept looking my way, trying to get my attention. By the time class started, I'd filled Andie in on his mystery note.

"Don't do it," she strongly urged. "Do *not* meet him for lunch. He doesn't know a thing; I can almost guarantee it."

"Paula says we can't be sure," I teased.

Andie opened the music folder, ignoring my comment. "There

has to be a better way, you know, to find out who's been writing those letters."

"Will you help me?"

"Super sleuths to the rescue!" she said, laughing. Knowing she had agreed to join forces with me made the solving all the more intriguing. We would get to the bottom of all this. One way or another!

Chapter 22

In algebra class Mrs. Franklin passed our homework back to us. I did a double take at mine. There was a big, red *A*, almost the way a grade school teacher would write it, high on the top of my paper. I'd missed only one problem.

After class I showed Andie. "Check it out."

"Well, congratulations. The girl not only writes, she does math," she joked.

We were headed down the hall when I noticed Ryan. He was standing in front of my locker, blocking it.

Andie took charge. "Excuse us, please!"

Ryan didn't budge. He was looking at me like he wanted to talk.

"Oh, I get it," Andie said. "You want some privacy." She backed away, and Ryan smiled.

"Hey, wait up," I called to her. Then, slowly turning, I looked at Ryan. "Mind if I open my locker?"

He stepped aside. "You know," he began, "I think you should keep writing . . . a lot. You're very good."

"Thanks." I thought he'd already said that earlier.

"Everyone's talking about that one letter, uh, that mystery dude."

I reached for my English notebook. "Yeah." I laughed. "Even my homeroom teacher asked me about it."

"So, like . . . who is it? Do you know?"

"Beats me. But I intend to find out."

Ryan scratched his chin. "I bet I know someone who could help you with that."

I shut my locker. "Who?"

Ryan ran his fingers through his mousy brown hair. "You're lookin' at him."

"You?"

"Hey," he said, holding up his hands. "It started out as a joke—Zye's idea. But the more I thought about it, the more I liked it. Writing secret letters to a pretty editor. A real kick."

I still couldn't believe it. "Stan told me there was no way it was you."

His eyebrows arched. "He said that?"

"Not exactly, but—"

"Well, Stan was the one who helped set it up," he blurted. "He gave me your home address and all."

"He did what?"

Ryan nodded. "Someone else helped, too. Someone who says he and you were close friends once."

"Don't tell me. Jared?"

"Looks like you've got at least two guys paying close attention these days." He started walking with me.

Sean's the only one who really matters, I thought.

"You're not mad, are you? I mean, it's not so bad, is it, getting letters like that—from a secret admirer?"

I refused to lead him on. Wouldn't be fair. By his smile and the way it looked like he was going to walk me all the way to fourth-hour class, it seemed as though he liked me.

Ryan began to explain. "For the past few weeks, I've wished

I could do something to change your mind about me. I was a bigoted jerk about your friend Andie. Nobody can help who their parents are. Or their skin color."

Was he apologizing for his prejudice?

He kept talking. "Another one of your friends has been talking to me about going to church. We've even discussed the creation of man and how we're each made in the image of God. Wow, that struck me as real cool."

My mind was still reeling. "Danny knows what he's talking about."

"You got that right. The guy knows the Bible upside-down . . . inside out." Ryan's eyes were shining. "Danny knows something else, too."

I didn't need to ask. It probably had something to do with Danny and me—how we'd been pretty close when I was back in seventh grade.

"I'll say this," Ryan continued, "whoever the guy in California is—the dude you're writing to—well, he should be counting his blessings. 'Cause the guys back home are feeling shut out."

"That's nice of you," I replied, deciding not to tell him it was none of his business about Sean.

Out of the corner of my eye, I saw Jared and Stan hanging back, trying not to be seen. I turned and waved, and they fled.

I wanted to finish my conversation with Ryan before encountering the likes of either my brousin or my former first crush.

"More than anything," I said, leveling with Ryan, "I'm glad you said what you did before about racial hatred. It's a frightful, destructive thing, not only for the victim, but also for the person doing the hating. I'm glad you've had a change of heart, Ryan."

The bell rang.

"You're quite a girl," Ryan said. He turned to leave.

Something in me wanted to tell him I would actually miss

reading his creatively weird letters. But I watched him go in silence.

I wondered, as I took my seat in my next class, if I, too, had been prejudiced. Thinking back, I realized I'd sized up Ryan based on my emotions at the time. Shoot, I'd tuned him out last summer because of a pimple.

Sure, he'd shown despicable signs of racial prejudice, but what had I done to help him? It had never crossed my mind that I should invite him to church or have a serious talk with him about God's plan for mankind.

I had messed up.

♥ ♥ ♥

I met Jared before lunch. After quickly filling him in, telling him I already knew who my mystery writer was, I excused myself and went to the library. There, I found a quiet place. Alone.

Without being noticed, I pulled my tiny New Testament out of my backpack and found 2 Corinthians 12:9: "My grace is sufficient for you, for my power is made perfect in weakness."

Thank you, Lord, I prayed from my heart. *Thanks for your grace. Please help me always remember what Ryan said today. Show me how I can help others. Not just my Christian friends, but others, too. Amen.*

I pulled out my spiral notebook and began writing to Sean. He was anxious to hear about the success of my column. I'd have to remember to scan a copy of *The Summit* to email to him.

And there was something else very important, too. I wanted to share the Bible verse in Corinthians with him—the one that had made all the difference for me.

HOLLY'S HEART

For HOLLY'S HEART *fans*
everywhere, and especially—

Holly Allen
Holly Bradham
Holly Breuer
Holly Ferguson
Holly Holdren
Holly Loritts
Holly Pinkham
Holly Tang
Holly Weymouth
Hollie Zaborski

Chapter 1

Not every girl finds out exactly one month before her fifteenth birthday that her mom's going to have a baby. But that's what happened at my house.

During Sunday dinner on January 14, somewhere between meat loaf passing and potato mashing, my stepdad sprang the news on us. By us, I mean my ten-year-old birth sister, Carrie, and our four stepsiblings, who were also our blood cousins. Their dad, my uncle Jack, married Mom after Dad's sister, Aunt Marla, died.

Anyway, Stan, sixteen; Phil, eleven; Mark, ten; and the present baby of the family—Stephanie, age eight—and Carrie and I had totally different reactions to the bundle-from-heaven alert.

"This is so-o cool!" Carrie said. "If it's a baby girl, I'm gonna start practicing my baby-sitting skills right away."

Mark crossed his eyes. "It better not be a girl. We've got enough females around here!"

"Three girls and three boys," Carrie reminded him. "We're even Steven."

Stephie sat next to Carrie, pouting, probably not entirely because of Mark's comment. After all, she did hold the "baby spot" in our blended family, and by her frown I figured she wasn't ready to relinquish it anytime soon.

"If it's a boy," Phil said, "I'll be teaching him to figure square roots long before he can walk."

Uncle Jack leaned his head back and laughed. "Who knows?" he said. "Maybe we *will* have another genius in the house."

Stan didn't say much. Neither did I. As far as I was concerned, this baby news was bad news. The house was already crammed to capacity with six kids. There was absolutely no room for another body around here, pint-sized or not!

Mom's eyes shone as she laced her fingers through Uncle Jack's, right there on top of the table. For pete's sake, they were acting like newlyweds. After all, it had already been over a year since they'd said "I do" and the Meredith-Patterson merger had begun. Four kids of his, two of hers, and soon there'd be one more . . . of theirs. What were they trying to do—show up the Brady Bunch?

Fork in hand, I poked at my green beans. Why would Mom want to start over with a baby at her age? Weren't there already zillions of chores to keep her busy, including the never-ending mountain of laundry?

Six kids plus two adults were plenty. Sometimes too many. *Eight is enough,* I thought.

Besides, I needed space and plenty of time to write. Next thing, Mom would have me tied down with baby-sitting after school. My writing project, a half-finished novella, would definitely suffer. And where would that put my future writing career?

I sighed, bolstering myself with the thought that I still had some time to get used to the idea. Life would remain the same for a good while longer. After all, babies took nine months to cook. I sighed, determined to grab every available minute between now and that not-so-blessed event.

Carrie pushed her plate back and leaned forward in her chair, looking at Mom. "When's the baby due?"

Uncle Jack regarded Mom, who must've taken his stare to mean she should do the talking. "Our new little one"—and here she gazed into Uncle Jack's eyes—"is due on April twenty-fifth."

"April?" I blurted. "That soon?"

Carrie glared at me. I ignored her, trying to grasp Mom's statement, all the while doing a quick mental calculation. "That means you must be about six months along."

Uncle Jack nodded, eyes bright. He leaned over and kissed Mom's cheek. "We've already started picking out names." He began listing combinations of first and middle names for all of us to hear and approve or disapprove of.

I kept my head down, staring at my plate, trying hard to block out the sound of his voice and the two of them in general, lovebirds that they were. It was plain to see how delighted they were. But what about the rest of us? Wasn't this a family matter? They should've called a family meeting—to vote on things. Our opinion counted for something, didn't it?

I felt numb.

"Holly-Heart," Mom said, her eyes penetrating me. "Everything okay?"

I shrugged. "I guess." No sense causing a scene. I'd have to work this out for myself. Still, I wondered why they'd waited so long to announce the surprising news.

Mom had appeared normal all these months. Oh sure, she'd gained a few pounds and worn those flowing tops over her stretch jeans, but that seemed to reflect her more casual style since quitting her job at the law firm. Surely she hadn't tried to hide her condition. Had she?

While we ate dessert, I thought back over the past months, searching for clues in my mind. Then it hit me. Memories of frozen dinners and occasional order-out pizzas. Unexplained doctor visits . . . Oh yes, and there was the night I'd made spaghetti because Mom was too tired to cook.

Now I remembered. Back in October, when I was getting those bizarre mystery letters, Mom had camped out in her bedroom. A lot. Every day she had seemed exhausted. I'd even wondered if she might have the flu.

And Christmas? By then, things seemed perfectly fine. Mom had resumed her normal routine around the house, decorating for the holidays and sending out zillions of cards and notes. We'd had dinner guests off and on throughout December. People like Uncle Jack's co-workers and employees from his consulting firm. There were relaxed evenings spent caroling with church friends, but all during that time Mom had never said anything about a baby.

Until now.

Shocking as it was, my almost-middle-aged mother was going to have another child. I should've been happy, but as much as I loved her, I couldn't muster up a speck of excitement.

The truth was, I wished she had confided in me. The way she always did when she was a single mom . . . before Uncle Jack moved to Dressel Hills and married her.

On second thought, though, even sharing a secret like that with Mom wouldn't have made much difference. Not this kind of news. Bottom line: I didn't want another brother or sister.

Not now, not ever.

Chapter 2

It was a gray Monday morning. No sunshine—not a single mountain peak could be seen from my window seat, where I peered out into the fog. A thick, dismal haze had enveloped our Colorado ski village.

I was gray, too. Inside.

During breakfast, while Mom exhibited her sunny cheerfulness, my somber mood persisted. The grayness lingered with me all day, and by the end of seventh hour—swim class—I was exhausted.

While I dried off, my best friend, Andie Martinez, buzzed over to me. "You're not yourself today. You sick?"

I forced a smile. "I'm okay."

Andie followed me to my PE locker. "C'mon, Holly-Heart, something's bugging you." She grabbed my arm and held on. "I know you!"

With my free hand, I reached for my clothes. "Thanks for your concern, but I don't want to talk about it."

"Hey, whoa—I'm your best friend, remember?"

Nodding, I turned to look at her, wondering if I dared share my ridiculous family secret.

"What's wrong?" Her dark eyes reflected intense interest. "What is it?"

I shook my head, thinking how absurd it would sound if I told her. "Don't ask," I muttered. It was probably the worst possible thing I could've said. From past experience, I knew that a few curt words never discouraged someone as persistent as Andie. Not dying-to-know-every-ounce-of-your-life Andie. Nope. My comment would simply egg her on.

"Aw," she pleaded, "just give one little hint."

I buttoned my jeans. "It's not worth discussing, really."

She cocked her head. "Well, it certainly must be worth brooding over." She exhaled loudly. "Your chin's been dragging on the floor all day."

I chuckled at her comment. Andie was like that. She'd pull out all the stops, say whatever she had to, to get me to succumb to her pleading.

"I'll be fine." I turned toward the mirror, brush in hand.

Andie followed close behind. "I can't believe you'd shut out your lifelong best friend like this, Holly Meredith."

I brushed through my hair, wondering how long before she'd bug me to death and I'd finally tell her that my mom was pregnant.

Andie was so desperate to crack my secret, she even solicited help from another friend of ours, Amy-Liz Thompson, who'd just stepped out of the shower. "Hey, Amy!" she called to her. "Come help me talk sense to this girl."

Amy-Liz shivered in her towel, blue eyes wide. "Why, what's going on?"

"Look at her," Andie said to Amy-Liz, pointing at me. "Is this the face of a happy, well-adjusted freshman?"

"Spare me," I groaned. Her theatrical outbursts were too much.

Amy-Liz began to giggle. "Holly looks fine to me."

"But check out her eyes," Andie said. "Don't you see the disappointment, the pain, the—"

I intervened. "Go ahead and dry off," I instructed Amy-Liz. "I'm sure Andie'll get over this sooner or later."

Andie faked a heart attack, holding her hands to her chest. "Holly, you can't do this to me. I'm here for you. It's you and me. . . ." She paused to breathe. "No, seriously, we need to talk. I know you're not okay. I can feel it!"

"I think you better get dressed," I told her. "Unless, of course, you wanna walk home."

Andie checked her watch. "Oh no, the bus! I'll miss the bus," she moaned. "Why didn't you say something?"

"If you hurry, you can make it." I sat down, doing the loyal, best-friend thing—waiting for her.

On the way home, the bus stopped in front of the Explore Bookstore on Aspen Street, which was the main drag in our tiny town. While passengers exited and new ones boarded, I stared at the window of my favorite bookstore. It looked like . . . yep, sure was!

"Hey, Andie! Is that what I think it is?" I strained to see the large poster displayed in the bookstore window. "Isn't that the new Marty Leigh book cover? It sure looks like her latest mystery novel, *Tricia's Secret Journey*. Hmm, it must be coming out soon." I squinted to see the date on the ad. "Wow, it's next weekend— fabulous! It'll hit the stores this Saturday."

"That's nice," she mumbled.

I turned to look at her. "What's wrong with you?"

"I'm not wild about mysteries," she replied. "You should know that."

"Well, I can't wait to get my hands on it." I looked back at the store window as the bus pulled away. "Marty Leigh's books are fabulous. I mean, you actually feel like you're there—in the book—living the story with the characters."

Andie made a low, disinterested grunt. "Give me romance

novels any day, anytime. Historical, fantasy, contemporary—doesn't matter, just so it's pure romance."

I slumped down, leaning my head back against the rail behind the seat, thinking. "In the romance novels you read, how old do you like the main characters to be?"

She thought for a second. "Old enough to fall in love. Why?"

"Just wondered." I was thinking about the marital romance going on between my mom and Uncle Jack. Sure, they were old enough to be in love and married and all—but way too old to be starting a new family.

"Excuse me, Holly. You're doing it again," Andie said.

"Doing what?"

"Spacing out." Andie touched my hand. "I'm here for you. Whatever it is, whatever is bothering you—trust me, I can help."

The bus turned right, heading for Downhill Court, my street. A light snow had begun to fall. The flakes swirled and floated down, their silvery whiteness turning to gray in the fast-approaching dusk. Cars in driveways looked gray as we passed. Yards and houses. Sidewalks too. Everything was gray. Everything.

Trust me, I can help. Andie's words echoed in my mind.

But could she? After all, Andie's mom had given birth to twin boys four years ago, when Andie was twelve. I supposed if anyone could possibly understand how I felt, it would be my best friend.

Suddenly she stood up, and I noticed the bus was heading toward my stop. "I'm getting off here with you. Like it or not."

I didn't argue. If she wanted to come over, fine. I just hoped Mom would be resting. Or out running errands.

Anything to keep Andie from discovering the truth.

The two of us crossed the residential street one block away from my house, and as we walked, I decided I would whisk her up to my room as soon as we got into the house. Because, knowing Carrie, she'd start talking baby stuff right under Andie's nose.

I was not ready to discuss the baby thing. I had to be cautious and avoid it.

Chapter 3

My free hand turned the doorknob. I poked my head inside the front door, wary of any activity that might call attention to the family secret.

"What are you doing?" Andie asked, nudging me forward. "You're not grounded, are you? Is that what's bugging you?"

While she babbled behind me on the porch, I scanned the living room. Vacant.

Good.

Inching myself past the door, I glanced at the dining room. Coast clear.

I breathed a sigh of relief. "C'mon in."

Andie looked at me cockeyed as I took her jacket and hung it in the hall closet. From where I stood, I could see Carrie, Stephie, Phil, and Mark standing with their backs to us out in the kitchen. They were all leaning forward, studying something on the center island. I could only guess what they were looking at so intently. Probably baby furniture in a catalog.

Not wanting to investigate, I steered Andie away. "C'mon, let's go to my room." She cast a quizzical look my way, and we scampered up the stairs.

My bedroom was the second room on the left, the first being the bathroom. Carrie and Stephie shared the room straight off from the landing, and true to form, their music was blaring. Instantly, I wondered if having a baby in the house might—at least for the first few months—quiet things down a bit. Only a serious writer would think of such a thing, I guess.

Andie and I hurried into my room and closed the door. Goofey, my cat, was sunning himself on the window seat. One lazy eyelid lifted nonchalantly, then closed. I chuckled at his passive approach to hellos. "That was Goofey's welcome to you, in case you didn't know," I told Andie.

She snorted, not amused. "For some reason, cats hate me. I don't know why. They just do."

"Aw," I defended her, "that's not true. Goofey doesn't hate you. He knows you . . . after all these years. Nah, he's just being a big, fat cat, minding his own business. Aren't you, baby?"

Goofey raised his round, furry head and began to lick his paw, completely ignoring us.

"Better watch who you call fat," Andie said, laughing as we flung ourselves on my canopy bed. I pushed my shoes off and got comfortable.

"Goofey's used to the truth about his size, aren't you, boy?" I leaned my head around the bedpost, sneaking a peek at him.

Andie watched me, and I could tell she was trying to be discreet in her scrutiny. "Holly?"

"Uh-huh?"

"Why don't you tell me the truth?"

I leaned up on my elbow. "About what?"

"You've been acting really weird today."

I was silent. *Should I tell her or not?*

Goofey leaped down off the window seat and came across the room, sniffing our stocking feet. Then he jumped up onto the bed, parading past us like he owned the place.

"Goofey," I said. "For pete's sake, can't you see we're talking?"

I reached out and pulled his shaggy gray-and-brown body over next to me.

"I think your cat's trying to tell you something," Andie said.

"Yeah? Like what?"

"Like to spill your soul out to your best friend. Cats—er, animals—sense things like that."

Man, was she grasping at straws. I stroked Goofey's fur, contemplating my life. "It's just that things are way out of control these days. I feel like I'm about to drown in a sea of people."

Andie's eyebrows arched. "Huh?"

"It's not like I don't want to tell you about it, it's just . . ." I paused. "I don't know if I can make anyone understand what I'm feeling." I covered my face with my hands. "I'm so ashamed. . . . I really should be happy. I—"

"Holly, don't worry about all that. None of those *shoulds* are important," she assured me. "The important thing is that you have someone to talk to. Someone to confide in."

"I know." I leaned back on the bed. "You're a very good friend, and I'm thankful we have each other—especially at times like this." I was actually going to tell her; I was that close. But someone knocked on my door.

"Coming!" I got up to see who was there.

It was Mom, wearing a brand-new maternity outfit. It displayed her rounded stomach quite well. I kept the door from opening too wide. "What do you think?" she asked, twirling halfway around. "It's my coming-out dress."

"It's, uh, nice." I closed the door quickly.

"Holly?" she called. "There's more. I want to show you the slacks—you can trade out the skirt for a more casual look."

Andie got off the bed, looking bewildered. "Why'd you close the door on your mom?"

I wagged my pointer finger close to my mouth.

"Holly-Heart? What's going on?" Mom asked through the door.

"Uh, it's nothing," I replied, feeling ridiculous about carrying on a conversation this way. "Can you show me later? I'm . . . uh, sorta busy right now."

There was an awkward pause. Even through the closed door, I could tell her feelings were hurt. Finally she said through the door, "Well, honey, when you have a minute . . . okay?"

I held my breath. What would Mom say next?

"That'll work," I said quickly, hoping she'd head down the hall to the master bedroom. Maybe put on her old jeans and one of those loose, flowing tops. An encounter with my pregnant mother was not the way I'd envisioned sharing the news with Andie. Not even close.

Leaning my head against the door, I listened for Mom's footsteps. When I heard the familiar crack of her ankle, I knew she was on her way.

I stood there in the middle of my room, looking at Andie, wondering what she thought of all this. Of course, I didn't have to wait long to find out.

"I don't get it," she scolded. "Sounds like your mom's got a new outfit and you won't even look at it. What's the matter with you?"

"I'm sure it seemed disrespectful, but there's so much more to it than meets the eye."

Andie scrunched up her face. "I have no idea what you're talking about." She sat back down on the bed. "Why don't you spell it all out for me, starting with what you were saying right before your mom knocked on the door."

"Why? What was I saying?"

"It's not what you said but what you were about to say." Andie was so good at this. Knowing when I was close to caving in with desired info. That's what happens when you grow up best friends.

I didn't blame her for wanting to know. Shoot, I'd kept my mouth shut long enough. I pulled on my hair, which was no longer waist length. I'd had it cut to midback before the beginning of high school last September. Taking a deep breath, I turned to Andie. "I know this'll shock you, and believe me, *I'm* still in shock, but maybe you can help me."

Andie's eyes were saucers. "What . . . what on earth are you saying?"

I sighed, mustering up the strength to tell my secret. "My mom's expecting a baby."

There. The words were out. They were floating around my bedroom even now as Andie stared at me.

Chapter 4

Andie's head lurched forward. "You're kidding. Your mom's pregnant?"

"Even as we speak."

"Oh, Holly." She fell back on my bed, making it shake a bit. "I thought you were going to say something horrendous."

"And this isn't?"

Andie sat up abruptly. "Get a grip, girl."

"But my mom's nearly forty and she's having another kid." I insisted, "That's horrendous . . . and scary."

Andie didn't buy it. "Healthy women can have babies way past forty these days." She studied me. "What's *really* bugging you?"

"I just told you."

"No, I mean, why is this such a hard thing for you?"

"I really thought you'd understand." Tears clouded my vision.

"Hey, look on the bright side: You might actually enjoy having a baby sister or brother." She grinned. "I remember when Dad brought Mom home from the hospital with the twins. Oh, they were so-o tiny and cute."

She was putting me to shame. Still, I listened.

"Even now, in their sometimes rowdy four-year-old stage, Chris and Jon will come to my room, dragging their teddy bears, and crawl up on my bed, pleading for a story."

"That's nice," I said softly. "But there are only five of you at your house."

"Five, eight, twenty . . . what's it matter if you all love each other? Families are forever."

"Yeah . . . forever and ever," I muttered.

"Snap out of it," she demanded. "I don't know what I'd do without my little brothers. I mean, if they hadn't been born—man, I'd be a lonely, only child!"

I could see that telling my secret to Andie had been a big mistake. Not only did she not understand my feelings, she sounded like she was taking sides against me.

Suddenly Andie got up and opened the bedroom door, poking her head into the hallway.

"What're you doing?" I asked.

She grinned. "I want to congratulate your mom."

I hauled myself off the bed. Andie was showing me up significantly. The least I could do was go out and stand next to her while she offered her congratulatory remarks.

"Why, thank you, Andie," Mom was saying. "Maybe you and Holly can baby-sit sometime."

"Oh, I'd like that," she said. "I love babies." I tuned her out when she started saying how soft and sweet little ones were. I shouldn't have been surprised; after all, Andie had prided herself in telling everyone how she wanted a large family of her own someday. It was a fact of life with Andie Martinez.

♥ ♥ ♥

Much later, after supper dishes were put away and my homework was finished, I wrote in my journal.

*Monday night, January 15: It's not a happy sight. I mean
Mom parading around, wearing bona-fide maternity clothes.
Now that I know she's expecting, she even looks pregnant!*

*I don't care what Andie says, it's not right for Mom and
Uncle Jack to live in their own private world—planning secret
things like babies and all—apart from the rest of the family.
Don't they realize what bringing another child into the world
is going to entail?*

I stopped writing and thought of zillions of reasons why a
family of our size—and parental age—shouldn't be added to. Had
Uncle Jack and Mom taken everything into consideration?

I picked up my pen and continued.

*It's unfortunate that Andie and I don't see eye-to-eye. She's
thrilled—literally. I can't believe how she carried on today
with Mom, discussing the special aspects of having a baby
around. Shoot, I was embarrassed at the way she gushed.*

*When it comes right down to it, the thing that bothers me
most is the timing. Mom and Uncle Jack waited till almost
the last minute to announce this. I mean, it would've been
nice to have had seven or eight months to get used to such
a monumental change. But no. We weren't even given fair
warning.*

I bit on the end of my pen, wondering if, on top of everything else, I'd have to give up my room to create a nursery. This
room would be the logical place—just a few steps away from the
master bedroom. But now wasn't the time to be thinking logic,
was it? Logic had flown out the window back sometime in July,
probably while I was out in California visiting my dad.

Resentment welled up in me as I thought of Uncle Jack and
Mom discussing the possibility of having a baby together. Tears
made two paths down my face, and I cried out to God. "It's not

fair!" I prayed. "And I don't know what to do about it, Lord. Please, help me deal with this." I sobbed into my pillow. "I'm not doing a good job of it. I feel so deserted—by Mom, especially."

I stopped praying and lifted my head off the damp pillow. There it was. I'd just voiced it to God—the truth Andie was pleading for.

Rejection.

I felt left out. The way I'd felt after Daddy divorced Mom all those years ago. That's what was bugging me, but I couldn't help what I was experiencing. Things like divorce left open wounds. About the time I thought my gash was scabbed over, beginning to heal, something like this was tearing it open—bringing all the insecurities back.

♥ ♥ ♥

Later that evening, Uncle Jack called a family meeting. My first thought was that it was a bit late to confer with everyone now. The baby was already on its way. Of course, it was a nasty, sarcastic thought, and I tried to suppress it.

The living room was draped with people. Stan sprawled out on the couch as usual; Phil and Mark sat near the coffee table, counting strings of bubble gum. Carrie and Stephie had dragged their beanbags down from their bedroom and were clumped together in the middle of the room, whispering. Mom sat in the rocking chair with hands folded on her stomach, emphasizing its roundness. Uncle Jack carried one of the straight-backed chairs in from the dining room and planted it next to her.

I chose the farthest corner of the room, where a tall Ficus tree sheltered me as I sat cross-legged on the floor. Goofey purred in my lap as I stroked his thick fur.

"Tonight, let's begin with questions," Uncle Jack said. "Carrie and Stephie, in particular, have been curious about how babies grow inside a woman's body." He gave a fatherly glance at the girls sitting near his feet. "I think now is a good time to talk about all of that as a family."

I put my head down, staring at Goofey's adorable kitty ears and nose. *How ridiculous,* I thought. *Why is Uncle Jack doing the birds and bees thing? Doesn't he know we already know this stuff?*

Stephie's hand shot up. "When can we feel the baby kicking in Mommy's tummy?"

Mom spoke up. "The baby doesn't kick all the time. Sometimes she is asleep."

She? Mom thought the new baby was a girl. Did she know for sure?

Mark asked, "But if the baby's a boy, can Phil and I help name him?"

Uncle Jack chuckled. "We don't know yet whether the baby's a boy or a girl, but we can all help choose a name."

Now he includes us, I thought. *Now that it's too late. . . .*

Carrie twisted her long blond ponytail. "What if the baby turns out to be twins? What then?"

My stomach churned at the thought.

Mom laughed. Then Uncle Jack spoke up. "The ultrasound showed only one baby growing inside Mommy, but if there miraculously happens to be two, well, I'm sure we'll manage somehow. Won't we, honey?"

Mom nodded, a twinkle in her eye. She didn't seem opposed to the idea at all! I, however, was appalled. Surely God—in His mercy and love—wouldn't let something like *twins* happen to us.

After everyone else was finished asking questions, I managed to voice my greatest concern. "Where's the nursery going to be?"

Mom and Uncle Jack looked at each other. The way their eyes caught made me even more worried. They'd already discussed moving me out of my room, I was sure of it.

"We haven't completely decided all the details," Mom said hesitantly. "For the first few weeks, the baby will sleep in a bassinet in our room."

Uncle Jack reached for Mom's hand. "We've thought of various options, including putting all three of you girls in our master bedroom and taking the room Carrie and Stephie have now for ours."

"Which would leave my room for the nursery?" I sputtered.

"That's only one possibility, Holly," Mom said softly. "We still have time to plan."

I wasn't totally ignorant. The option they'd just voiced was the most viable choice. For them.

I fumed as I thought about moving out of my room. Of being stuck in the same bedroom with two little sisters—and snooping ones, at that.

How could Mom even think of doing this to me?

Chapter 5

I spent most of my Tuesday morning in a daze—hardly remembered anything that happened in either government class or algebra. Choir was a blur, too, although I did remember working on our songs for All-State choir auditions, which were coming up in a few months.

The nursery scenario kept cropping up, though, pounding my brain like the rhythmic wail of a newborn baby. To think that Mom and Uncle Jack would actually tear me away from my fabulous room—the room Daddy had planned for me. It was unthinkable that Mom would allow Uncle Jack to voice such a thing.

The house at 207 Downhill Court housed my roots, my very life. A girl of almost fifteen years ought to have some say in where she laid her head at night—not to mention where she wrote her stories and kept a written record of her life.

My future writing career might be completely thrown off course if I were uprooted and forced to be in the same room—master suite or not—with Carrie and Stephie. It was outright injustice.

During lunch I poured out my heart to Andie. Even though

she didn't think the overall baby thing was anything to lose sleep over, she was sympathetic to the pain of giving up my room.

"My parents would never have done that to me, and we had *two* new babies at our house," she said.

Paula and Kayla Miller, our twin girl friends, had been listening. But when they spoke up, it was obvious they weren't exactly on my side, either.

"Perhaps you're getting yourself worked up over nothing," Paula suggested.

Kayla nodded. "Once the baby comes, you might surprise yourself and be willing to share your room. Who knows?"

"I doubt it," I replied. "How would you like to go home to the sounds and smells of a newborn while you're trying to write a novel or figure out the latest mumbo-jumbo algebra problem?"

Paula's ears perked up. "Did I hear you correctly? Did you say you're writing a novel?"

I shrugged. "Well, it's not actually a full-blown one. It's more like a novella—you know, a mini-novel."

Andie whipped out her pocket dictionary, an English class requirement, and read, "A novella is a short novel."

"Okay, Miss Know-It-All." Reaching for the dictionary, I read the definition for myself. "Yeah, I guess Webster's right—that's what I'm writing."

Andie slipped the tiny dictionary into her shoulder bag. "Okay, that's settled." She propped her elbows on the table, leaning over next to me. "So . . . when do we get to read your masterpiece?"

"Maybe never."

"C'mon, Holly, you know you need a second opinion," Andie said. "We're precisely the ones to give it."

Paula and Kayla were nodding their heads. "What could it hurt?" Kayla said. "We wouldn't think of being hard on you. We give our solemn promise."

Paula picked up her sandwich, inspecting it as she spoke.

"Maybe the manuscript will turn out to be absolutely perfect, and then, when we tell you so, you'll decide to dedicate your first published book to us."

"Hey, I like that," Andie chimed in. "Will you please dedicate your book to your best friends?"

I giggled. "You guys are too much."

"Well, if you won't let us read it, will you at least tell us the story line?" Paula asked.

Andie whispered, "Is it a romance?"

Paula and Kayla leaned in, waiting for my response.

"Definitely, it's a romance. But I can't tell you anything more."

"Aw . . ." Andie groaned. "Don't keep us in the dark like this."

"Why not?" I said. "Are you worried that I'll be old and gray before I ever find a publisher? That you'll have to wait forever to read it?"

"No way," Paula said. "You're a good writer, Holly-Heart. I'm positive you'll land a publisher."

Kayla smiled. "Want to know what I always read first when the school paper comes out?" Paula and Andie were nodding their heads in agreement. "It's the 'Dear Holly' column. I simply adore the way you answer those letters."

"You're very clever," Paula said. "No editor in his right mind would abandon the opportunity to work with such a talented young author."

"Girls, girls," I said, blushing. "Enough."

We ate in silence for a few moments, then Paula brought up the fact that Marty Leigh's next novel was coming out soon. "Did you see the poster in the window at Explore Bookstore?" she asked.

Andie answered for me. "Boy, did she ever. You should've seen Holly hanging out the window, drooling all over the side of the bus."

"Not quite." I laughed. "But I am counting the hours till Saturday."

"So are we," the Miller twins chorused in unison, which didn't happen often, but when it did, we always got a kick out of it.

"Speaking of Marty Leigh," Paula said, "did I tell you about the cool letter I received from her?"

"You actually wrote to Marty Leigh?" I was in shock.

Kayla grinned. "I wanted to, but Paula had more courage. So she wrote for both of us."

"I'll bring the letter tomorrow—actually, it's a newsletter high-lighting the next books in her series, but she also sent a personal reply in her own handwriting!"

Now I was leaning forward. "You asked her questions?"

"My letter to her was almost like an interview by mail," Paula replied. "I couldn't believe it—she went through them one by one and responded to every question. It was astonishing."

"Wow, you're not kidding," I said. "Do you have any idea how many fan letters she must get every month?"

"Probably tons," Kayla said.

Andie was eating quietly, obviously not interested. Of course, if Marty Leigh's mysteries had included romance, she would've been hooked.

"Tell me some of the questions you asked her," I said, dying to know.

"Well, Kayla inquired about her favorite foods, hobbies, things like that, but I asked how she got started writing."

I was all ears. "What did she say about that—how she got started?"

"Her grandfather was a journalist," Paula continued. "She's quite certain that she inherited his love for the printed word."

"Wow," I said. "When did she first get published?"

"I asked her that," Paula said. "She said she'd had a short story published in a regional newspaper when she was only thirteen."

"Hey, just like Holly-Heart," Andie piped up. "Remember that cute story you wrote?"

Of course I remembered. It was my very first byline, and in the very teen magazine Marty Leigh had helped to launch, too. You never forget fabulous stuff like that.

"What was the title again?" Kayla asked.

" 'Love Times Two,' " I said. "About two girls liking the same guy."

"It was fiction but actually based on the true story of Holly and me—and our crushes on Jared Wilkins," Andie reminded them.

"Thank goodness those days are long gone," I said.

"But Jared's still in love with you," Paula blurted.

I shook my head. "So he thinks. Please, don't remind me."

Andie played with the gold chain at her neck. "How's Sean Hamilton these days? You two still writing?"

Andie hadn't asked about him for several weeks. I figured she had at last come to grips with my long-distance friendship.

"Oh, Sean's great," I said. "In fact, he's coming to ski here next month—maybe Valentine's week."

"Woo-hoo!" Andie cheered. "Just in time for Holly's fifteenth birthday and her first real date."

"That's right," I said, grinning. "I'm saving my first date for Sean."

Andie was pretending to play a violin under her chin. "Aw, how sweet," she sang.

I didn't comment. The girl had romancitis!

"Is he coming alone?" Paula asked.

"He's bringing a group of kids from his church youth group— they call themselves Power House. The group's just for sixth through eighth graders, and Sean's one of the youth leaders."

"He sounds like a great guy," Kayla said.

"He is," Andie said, probably referring to last summer, when she met Sean for the first time. "Hey, maybe our youth group should join them when they come. We could have a snow party."

Paula smiled, displaying her perfect teeth. "Maybe we should let Holly decide about that."

Andie and Kayla stifled their laughter.

"Oh, c'mon," I said, "there'll be plenty of time for me to visit with Sean." I gathered up the trash at our table.

"Uh-oh," Andie said, "sounds like they've got this visit all planned."

I felt my cheeks blush. Sean and I had discussed his trip here—in fact, we'd sent several letters' worth of plans—emails, too. He was beginning to share more freely about his feelings for me. I, on the other hand, was careful not to seem too eager. Sean, after all, was older by almost two years.

I wanted God's perfect plan for me as far as the boy I dated—and most of all, the man I would ultimately marry.

Andie got up with her tray just as Stan, my brousin—cousin-turned-stepbrother—and two other guys walked past our table. Kayla glanced up, following Stan with her eyes. I wondered about it.

Two years ago, when the Miller twins first moved to Dressel Hills, Kayla had confided in me about Stan. She'd had this major crush on him back in Pennsylvania, where the Millers had lived in close proximity to Uncle Jack's family, long before Aunt Marla passed away.

After the funeral, months later, Kayla's father encouraged his friend and prospective business partner, Uncle Jack, to move to Colorado for a fresh start. Kayla was thrilled to discover that Stan was attending the same school in Dressel Hills.

For the longest time, I thought she'd given up on Stan. But just now, the way her eyes lit up when he passed by, I had a feeling she wasn't exactly over him. I decided not to say anything, though. Kayla was supersensitive.

Quickly, the Miller twins and I gathered up our trays and carried them to the kitchen, where Andie was waiting.

"Have you told Sean about your mom yet?" Andie asked.

"You mean about the baby?" I frowned. "Where in the world did that thought come from?"

Andie tapped the top of her dark, curly head. "I was just wondering. Sean seemed like a kid-crazy sort of guy when we were out in California, remember?"

She didn't have to remind me. Sean's married brother had two kids. In fact, Sean wrote often about his niece and nephew.

"I'm sure I'll be telling him soon," I found myself saying, wishing Andie hadn't brought up the topic just as we were heading off for fifth hour. I'd had a tough enough time concentrating during my morning classes. I couldn't afford to space out during French. The new dialogues were getting harder and longer this semester, and our teacher, Mr. Irving, wasn't as lenient about prompting us these days.

Le bébé. French for *the baby.* I'd have to get used to the baby idea eventually. Maybe saying and writing the words in another language would help.

Then again . . . maybe not.

Chapter 6

After school I headed for the public library several blocks from the high school. I hadn't been able to focus on my writing since last Sunday, when the baby news had been heralded at dinner. I was eager to get going on my project again.

Among the rows of tall bookshelves and long study tables, I began to work on my novella. *Okay, fine,* I thought, getting serious about chapter eight of my book. Only four chapters to go. When the first semi-polished draft was finished, I would go back and fill in, delete, tighten, and refine. Who knows, maybe I'd get brave and try to find a publisher. Mrs. Ross, my English teacher, had mentioned certain publishers who wanted only works by young people. Maybe I should talk with her further.

Unfortunately, I was going to have to deal with a new baby brother or sister in the next few months, and that could hinder me from completing the book. Maybe, if I was lucky, I'd finish it by the time I was twenty-something. By then, though, those publishers searching for young authors wouldn't want to see my work. Nope. I'd be too old for them and probably not old enough for the other book publishers. *Sigh.*

I jumped right in where chapter seven left off. My main character, Julianna, had just received a letter from her boyfriend, Christopher. As I wrote the lines, I thought of Sean. In no way did I want this story to be about him and me, fictionalized or not. I scratched out what I'd written and started over.

Thirty minutes later I stopped writing and was tempted to reread what I'd written. A mistake for me—deadly, actually—in terms of slowing me down and putting my mind in the editing mode. My creative side would get bogged down; I'd lose my flow. But my curiosity won out, and I went back and read each word, scrutinizing the whole.

None of it, however, was working. I was a perfectionist when it came to writing. So, discouraged and not looking forward to those inevitable baby discussions at home, I decided to stay right here and switch gears. I decided to write a letter to Sean, even though Mom would be wondering where I was. We had this after-school phone rule at our house. If any of us was going to be gone longer than one hour after school, Mom expected to be informed.

I'm not sure why I didn't get up right then and call home. Something in me lashed out in defiance. I ignored my better judgment and stayed put.

It was time Sean heard from me about the latest turn of events at the Meredith-Patterson residence. Actually, I wouldn't have been too surprised if he'd already heard the news. Sean attended the same church as Daddy, and Daddy's mother, my grandma Meredith, still kept in touch with Mom. No doubt, Mom had phoned my grandparents with her news.

I took a clean piece of notebook paper out of my three-ring binder and began to write.

Tuesday, January 16
Dear Sean,

Hey! How're you doing? I've been wanting to write for a couple days. Bet you're having great weather there. It's cold and snowy here, but what can you expect this close to the continental divide?

My algebra grades are up now, but I still have to work hard at keeping them there. Sometimes I wonder how this kind of math is ever going to help me as a writer. That is, IF I ever get published again. Maybe I'll need to know algebra when it comes time for me to double-check my royalty statements someday. Ha!

Not long ago I read about five well-known authors and how they worked. One said that getting published the first time was relatively easy, but the second and third time he really had to work at it. I can't help but wonder how I ever landed that first story with Marty Leigh's cool teen magazine. Right now, if I didn't have the published story to prove it, I'd probably doubt it ever happened.

By the way, my favorite author's next mystery is due out this Saturday. I know you aren't interested in books for teen girls, but my friends Kayla and Paula Miller and I are going to be the first ones at the bookstore when it opens! Andie, on the other hand, says she's sleeping in—she couldn't care less about mysteries.

I stopped writing, wondering how I should tell Sean about Mom's baby. There wasn't any creative way to say it, I decided, so I picked up my pen and flat-out informed him.

I wouldn't be surprised if maybe Daddy's already heard this news, so you might know about it, too. My mom's expecting a baby at the end of April. It's not all that surprising, really, and I should've guessed Mom would want more kids, but when reality hits you in the face, you have to be ready to pack up and move out of your bedroom. Yep, most likely I'll have to give up my private domain.

Can you believe it? How would you feel if this were happening to you? But then, there are only two of you in your family, and now, since your brother's much older and married with his own family, you probably feel like an only child. Right?

Writing this, I stopped and thought of Andie and the many times she'd remarked about what great fun a big family would be. A lot she had to learn. Big families were okay, but when eight people were crammed into a house built for four, even with a new addition, the result was sheer frustration.

Mom and Uncle Jack, however, never seemed to notice how stressful life at 207 Downhill Court had become. Is that what happened when people fell in love? They blocked out the negative parts of their life altogether?

I finished off the letter to Sean, trying very hard not to sound like a whiny, spoiled brat. Packing my schoolbag, I headed for the library doors.

♥ ♥ ♥

At home, Mom was sitting on the living room couch trying her best to follow crocheting instructions for a yellow baby sweater and booties to match. Carrie and Stephie were helping her roll the brightly colored yarn into a smooth, round ball.

"You're late," Mom said as I flung my coat onto a hook in the hall closet. "And you didn't call."

"Lost track of time."

"We have an understanding in this house, Holly-Heart." She looked at me with accusing eyes. "That rule has been a long-standing one. You know better."

"Sorry." I took off for the kitchen, not waiting for her response.

"Excuse me, young lady." Mom only used those words when she was upset. "I'm not finished with you."

I crept backward through the dining room and into the living room. Carrie was covering her mouth with her hand. Stephie, too, smirked, watching my every move.

"Pull up a chair," Mom said to me. "Let's talk."

"Not in front of them," I sneered, shooting darts at the would-be roommates of my not-so-distant future.

"Holly Suzanne Meredith!" barked Mom.

Quickly, I sat down in the rocker. "I'm sorry."

"If you don't follow rules, you know there is always a consequence."

I nodded. "I'll try to do better next time."

Carrie opened her mouth. "If there is a next time!"

Mom shushed my sister and turned to me. "This is serious business."

"Well, I think it's time we cancel out some of those little kid rules," I pled my cause. "I'm a freshman now."

"Rules help families run more smoothly," she said, obviously not eager to lay down her defense. "I'm willing to compromise, perhaps, but not do away with the rule completely. Letting me know your whereabouts after school hours is still essential, even during your high-school years."

"Can't we talk about it, at least?"

"Your stepdad will be home for supper; we can discuss it then." End of discussion, she'd evidently decided, and she went back to her precious crochet hook and baby project.

"I'd rather not talk about this in front of the whole tribe," I spouted.

Mom's head shot up. "Tribe? Since when do you refer to your family that way? Holly, what's gotten into you?"

"I learned it in government class," I said glibly. "A tribe consists of more than one family with common characteristics and interests, although in our case I'm not so sure." With that, I got up and walked out of the room.

I could still hear Mom calling for me to "come back here—right now, young lady" as I slammed my bedroom door.

Chapter 7

Slamming doors and spewing annoying words always got me in hot water. And I mean hot. Uncle Jack didn't take too kindly to one of us sassing his bride of fourteen months. Mom, who was known to take occasional outbursts in her stride, had come down on me harder than ever.

Shoot, if I didn't do some fast-talking—as in sincerely apologizing—I would be grounded from now to Valentine's Day. Of course, I was smart enough to admit that I was wrong; Mom was right. Still, I chafed at their correction—their unified front.

"Your mother says you want to modify the calling rule," Uncle Jack said as we settled into the downstairs family room for the intimate meeting. The rest of the family had been shooed away—upstairs. Mom and Uncle Jack sat on the sectional, halfway across the room from me. I observed them from the bottom step, where I'd chosen to sit, keeping a safe distance.

I got the ball rolling. "After school, I think I should be allowed to have two hours of freedom. To go to the library or do whatever. That would be perfect," I said, hoping I sounded polite enough to wage a victory.

Mom spoke up. "It's the 'do whatever' that has me concerned."

She sighed. "How do I know you won't be hanging out at the mall?"

"What's so wrong with that?"

"Holly," Uncle Jack reprimanded me. "Watch your attitude."

"But all my friends are allowed to do whatever they want after school. For as long as they want."

"*All* your friends?" Mom asked.

"Well, you know," I said. "I was just trying to make a point. Sorry."

Uncle Jack frowned suddenly. "No, I don't believe you are sorry, and until you can discuss things respectfully, your mother and I won't be interested in any sort of compromise."

Rats, I blew it. I pulled myself up off the step. Being lectured to—no fun. Things around here sure weren't anything close to the old days, before Uncle Jack had come along.

To be honest, I was sick of the super-private world he and Mom had created for themselves. Honeymooners? Lovebirds? Who cared! Their plans no longer seemed to include me. Maybe I was jealous; could that be it? Anyway, I seethed all the way up to my bedroom.

On Wednesday Paula brought her letter from Marty Leigh to school. I went wild with excitement, and Paula let me make a copy of it during lunch. Reading and rereading the letter was the high point of my entire week.

Unfortunately, the days flew by without another opportunity to talk about the after-school phoning rule with either Mom or Uncle Jack. Maybe it was just as well. Mom's head was somewhere in a blue or pink cloud called baby land, and Uncle Jack was just as preoccupied with his work.

First thing Saturday I met Paula and Kayla at the bookstore on Aspen Street. Bright anticipation shone from their eyes. "Holly!" they called to me. The girls were dressed in their typical weekend attire of blue jeans and warm sweaters. Their trendy ski jackets were new, Christmas presents probably.

"Looks like there's no line," I said, glad to see the twins.

"I can't believe we're the only Marty Leigh fans in town," Paula said.

"All the better, my dears," I chanted. "We want to be sure to get some pre-signed copies, right?" I peeked in the frosty window. "Hey, look! There's a brand-new floor display loaded with books—it must've just arrived."

"I know. I came by yesterday after school," Paula said, "and the display was nowhere in sight."

I shivered with excitement and from the cold. "This is going to be so cool." Glancing at my watch, I knew we wouldn't have to wait much longer to actually hold the books in our hands.

"I wish Marty Leigh would make more public appearances," I said.

"High-profile authors usually only hit the big cities, don't they?" Paula suggested.

I laughed. "Dressel Hills doesn't exactly qualify for city status, but she was here the summer before last."

A familiar face greeted us with an enthusiastic smile as the store manager unlocked the doors. "Good morning, young ladies," he said. "I have a feeling you might be interested in my latest shipment. Am I correct?"

"Never more so," Paula said as we scooted inside and dashed to the Young Adult section.

Kayla was first to find a book with the author's autograph. "Here's one with Marty's full name and a special greeting."

Paula and I crowded around her. "Oh, I hope there're more," I said, snatching up several from the display and finding the title page. "Fabulous! At least three books are signed."

We stood there scrutinizing the cover and then flipped to the back and read the summary. Each of us held the treasured new books in our hands at last.

The book was about a girl named Tricia who'd decided she wanted to get to know her estranged father better and had initiated a joint-custody petition to the courts.

"This isn't a mystery," I said. "At least, it doesn't seem like one."

"Keep reading," Kayla said.

"Why doesn't Ms. Leigh come out with two or three books at a time?" Paula lamented. "Do you have any idea how fast I read these? Honestly, I cannot put them down!"

"Personally, I devour them," Kayla said. "They're addictive but in a good sort of way."

I nodded. "I can only hope to write like her someday, with page-turning suspense and chapter cliff-hangers to die for."

The twins exchanged secretive glances, grinning at each other. Paula reassured me that if I continued practicing my writing, I might offer Ms. Leigh some great competition someday.

Someday, I thought as I waited at the cash register.

Someday, if there weren't a screaming half sister or brother to anticipate, who'd eventually grow into toddlerhood with even louder noises and, heaven forbid, into a school-aged snooper like Carrie and Stephie.

Someday might never come. Unless . . .

I reread the summary on the back of the book, my mind spinning nearly out of control. It said right here that Tricia Joellyn Engle, the main character, needed space—a break from her mother and sisters. Why else would she go through all the trouble of pleading to live with her dad part of the year? Did Tricia really want to get to know her dad better? Or did she just need some breathing room?

Joint custody, I thought. *Hmm, is this an option for me?*

Daydreaming, I thought of the warm beach sand, the pounding

waves, the natural, peaceful setting of Daddy's beach house in Southern California. What better option could an aspiring young author have as a place to live and work?

The store manager's voice broke into my thoughts. "Will that be cash today?"

I dug into my wallet. "Here you are. And thanks!"

"Thank you," he replied.

Kayla and Paula suggested we hit The World's Best Donut Shop before heading home. "But I'm dying to get home and read," I said, hugging my book.

"You have all weekend for that." Paula took my arm and nudged me forward down the snowy sidewalk. "Besides, we have a surprise for you."

"A surprise?" I went willingly, of course. Curiosity ruled my life. "Aren't you going to give me a hint?" We were within sniffing distance of the pastry shop.

"No hints," Kayla said. "Just put on your best smile."

"Uh-oh. This isn't about a guy, is it?"

Paula blocked my view into the shop. "Come along," she teased. "You won't regret it."

"I better not," I said. Sean Hamilton came to my mind, and I wished he might be sitting in a booth waiting for me.

Now, *that* would be a fabulous surprise!

Chapter 8

But the boy waiting for me wasn't Sean. It was Jared.

"What's *he* doing here?" I whispered as we opened the door to the pastry shop.

Kayla said it first. "Just act happy."

"Yes, please look as if you're thrilled to see him," Paula said softly, then led the way.

We hurried across the room to a table set near a window. Window boxes filled with fake red geraniums framed the sill inside. Why did Paula and Kayla think coming here and finding Jared waiting for us was such a great surprise? I played along, though, and pasted a smile on my face.

"Hey, Jared." I slid into the booth across from him.

"Holly-Heart, I'm glad you came," he said as Kayla and Paula divided up and sat on opposite sides of the table, Paula next to Jared.

Why is he here? I wondered.

There was no flirting involved—surprise, surprise. Jared pulled no punches, either; he got right to the subject at hand, although I had no idea that what he had to say would turn out to be so incredibly fascinating.

"Have I ever told you about my uncle in Chicago?" he asked.

I shook my head. "I don't think so. Why?"

He ran a hand through his thick brown hair. "My uncle just bought a small press—a publishing company—and believe it or not, he's looking for quality writing from young authors. I'm talking kids around our age."

I sat up instantly. "Really?"

Jared's eyes lit up. "Andie says you're working on a short story or something."

"Word gets around," I muttered.

"Well, my uncle's the publisher, like I said, and he's putting together an anthology—compiling short stories by lots of different teen authors."

I took a deep breath. *Can this be true?*

"Holly, are you okay?" he said.

"I'm fine. It's just so . . . so . . ." I reached for the pastry list at the edge of the table and began to fan myself. "It's just that I can hardly believe it. Are you sure about all this?"

Jared reached into his jeans pocket and pulled out a letter. He handed it to me. "Here, read it yourself." I could feel his gaze on me as I read silently. "I'm planning to submit a story— well, it's a little longer than a short story," he said. "Are *you* interested, too?"

Kayla and Paula smiled encouragingly, waiting for my reply.

I folded the letter. "Are you kidding? I've been living for this moment all my life. To be published in a book, a real book!"

Jared glanced at Paula. "Thanks for bringing Holly here." His grin made his blue eyes twinkle.

I poked Kayla. "So you guys set this up with Jared? You knew about it?"

"Well, aren't you glad?" she said.

"This is the best surprise I've had in years." I opened my wallet. "Who wants a doughnut? I'm buying."

Jared resisted my offer, but I managed to pull it off anyway. Kayla and Paula were nearly clucking with delight. They even opened their bookstore bags and showed Jared the new Marty Leigh book.

"Be careful, don't get any chocolate on it," Paula warned.

Jared listened as the three of us chattered about how wonderful we thought Ms. Leigh's writing was. "Not better than some of the male authors I've read," he scoffed.

"But if you've never read a Marty Leigh mystery, how could you possibly know?" I interjected. "She grabs you in the first paragraph. Here, let me give you an example."

I wiped my sticky fingers, then licked the worst ones in anticipation of holding the brand-new book. "Oh, rats, wait here—I'll be right back." Quickly, I headed for the ladies' room, where I washed the stickiness off my hands.

When I got back, Paula and Kayla were informing Jared in no uncertain terms that Marty Leigh was the contemporary queen of teen novels. "There's no one better, trust me," Kayla said. "And I've read tons of books."

"Well, if she's so great, let's hear some of this wonderful writing," Jared said, baiting me as I sat down. "Are your hands clean enough to touch the golden pages?"

I playfully slapped the book at him. "Okay, now you judge for yourself." I began to read. Out of the corner of my eye, I could see Jared leaning forward, listening. After three paragraphs, I stopped.

"Whoa, don't quit now," he said, playacting. "Keep going! I think . . . I feel it . . . it's happening . . . oh no, I'm being sucked into the story!"

Paula punched his arm. "Act your age."

"No kidding," I said, closing the book and studying Jared.

"I suspect what is lacking here is a mature, female mentality. Obviously."

Jared groaned. "It's not that I don't think the author is good—she is, but . . . I just tend to think that men have a better grasp of the English language."

"Oh, puh-leeze," I said.

We finished our doughnuts as we continued to talk. "I'll let you know where to send your manuscript," Jared said before we left.

"The entire manuscript?" I asked. "Your uncle wants the whole thing?"

"Don't worry, mine's not finished yet, either."

I slung my purse over my shoulder. "So how long do I have?"

"The cutoff date is March something, and then they'll make the decisions in April. I'll have to check and let you know."

"That should be perfect," I said, thinking that if I hurried I'd have plenty of time to write and rewrite my novella before the Meredith-Patterson offspring arrived.

"April's the birth month for Holly's baby brother or sister," Paula commented as we walked outside together.

"Yeah, Stan told me," Jared said. "Big surprise, huh?"

I wrinkled my nose. "Whoop-de-do."

"So you don't approve?" he probed.

"At my mom's age it seems very weird."

The city bus was heading toward us. "Sounds like you're not too thrilled," he said.

"You can say that again."

Paula took my side. "Think how you'd feel having to move out of your room to make space for a nursery."

"You'll have to do that?" Jared asked.

"Let's put it this way: It's been discussed as an option," I said. "But I have a few options of my own."

"Like what?" Kayla asked.

"I have to think things through first," I replied rather secretively, although I hadn't intended to encourage curiosity on their part.

"Hey, don't get some wild idea about moving away to California or somewhere," Jared said almost desperately. "Your friends need you here."

His words thoroughly shocked me. Not the friends part, but what he'd said about California. How could he have possibly known what I was thinking?

I stared at him. Jared Wilkins had been my first crush, or whatever it was I'd suffered through back in my seventh-grade days. Anyway, here he was, somehow connecting with me. Almost pleading for me to stay.

The brakes screeched as the lumbering bus came to a crunching stop in the snow. We all scurried down the sidewalk in the frosty air and boarded it.

Jared scooted in beside me, behind the Miller twins. For a split second, the thought that they had set this up—this seating arrangement, this entire bus ride home—crossed my mind. Had they?

"You're not really thinking of going to live with your dad, are you?" Jared asked softly.

I felt brave suddenly, so I tested the waters. "Why not? He's my real father."

"That's true, but what about the rest of your family?"

"Mom has Uncle Jack, if that's what you mean."

Jared was silent, hands stuffed into his jacket pockets.

"There isn't room in the house for me anymore," I surprised myself by blurting out.

Kayla and Paula turned around, aghast. Paula spoke up. "That can't be true, Holly. What about that addition your uncle had built onto the back of the house over a year ago?"

"It only added two more bedrooms, and those are filled up

with brousins—Stan, Phil, and Mark. Even if it's a boy, there's no way Mom will put a newborn that far away from her at night."

"But maybe when the kid's older," Jared suggested. "Stan wouldn't mind sharing his room with a little brother. I wouldn't."

"You?" I was shocked. "You're not into little kids, are you?"

"Hey, what's the big deal? Kids are kids."

It was a male thing to say. Truth was, guys had no idea what they were talking about when it came to babies—or toddlers, for that matter. Sean was the exception, however.

He knew exactly what it took to make a little kid happy. I'd seen him in action, and I was convinced he'd be a good father someday. No way could Stan or Jared ever begin to match that kind of behavior.

"Hang in there, Holly," Jared said as the bus turned toward my street. "No need to freak out and do something impulsive you might regret."

"How do you know I'd regret moving to California?"

Again, the twins turned around wearing stunned expressions. "Relax," I said to them. "Jared's the one freaking out."

"Guess again," Paula said.

"All right," I admitted. "But don't you dare breathe a word of this. Not even to Andie. I have some phone calls to make before I decide anything."

Jared's body slumped down in the seat next to me. He was actually hurt at the thought of my leaving.

I stood up, ready to exit the bus, but Jared wouldn't budge. "Don't do anything today, Holly. In fact, why don't you wait a few days before you call your dad?" He'd done it again. He'd said out loud what I was already planning.

"Jared, for pete's sake, will you move your legs?" I stood there, waiting for him, blocked in my seat.

Reluctantly, he slid out of the seat, standing up to allow me to pass. "I'll call you later, and don't say not to."

"We'll call you, too," the twins said together.

I smiled at the unison comment. "Bye!"

"Thanks for the doughnuts," called Paula.

"Yeah, thanks, Holly soon-to-be-author," shouted Kayla just before the door closed behind me.

I should've felt terrific as I crossed the street and began the brisk walk home. Only one block to go, with thick flakes of snow falling faster and faster. With the new Marty Leigh mystery snug in my purse, the sweet taste of doughnut in my mouth, and the prospect of being published, I attempted to cheer myself.

Surely a phone call to California would make me feel better. Hearing Daddy's voice always did that. So did staying at his big, luxurious beach house.

Yep, my plan for joint custody was absolutely perfect. Now, what would my dad think of it?

Chapter 9

I waited till after lunch to call Daddy. Mom and Uncle Jack had gone downstairs to look at a department store catalog of baby furniture. All the kids were outside playing in the snow, even Stan.

Going to the kitchen, I picked up the portable phone and carried it to the living room. Quickly, I pressed the numbers, remembering to include the area code.

Busy signal.

Rats, I thought. Just when I'd found a tranquil moment on my end, Daddy or Saundra, his wife, was tying up the phone.

I waited a few minutes, then tried again. Still busy. Frustrated, I got up to return the phone to the kitchen.

Just then the front picture window broke—*crash-crinkle-smash*—sending glass flying through the air. A snowball shot through the dining room and landed near the kitchen island, yards away.

Uncle Jack appeared in a flash. "What was that?"

"Someone broke the window," I said. And suddenly I realized that if I hadn't been trying to get through to California the second time, I might've been hit by the snowball or cut by the shattered glass.

By now, Stan and the boys were on the front deck, inspecting the damage. Carrie and Stephie crept up the front walk, looking worried.

"Man, you're in for it now," Mark said, poking Phil.

"I didn't mean to hit the window," Phil said, quickly apologizing.

"No one ever does," little Stephie chimed in, her eyes big as saucers.

Uncle Jack took the incident in stride, not losing his cool. He was like that—calm and collected in the face of problems. "We'll have to get a replacement for the window," he said, instructing Phil to run inside and get a dustpan and broom.

"What about a heavy blanket with some duct tape?" Stan suggested. "Wouldn't that help block out the cold?"

Mom appeared at the door, a baby catalog in her hands. "A blanket wouldn't be secure enough," she said. "Not these days."

I figured she meant it wouldn't be safe. Someone—a cat burglar or whatever—could easily pull a blanket down and come into the house while we were sleeping. Rob us blind.

Uncle Jack was a sensible man. After all, he had a wife with a baby on the way, not to mention six kids. He would protect us and make the house secure for the night.

"We'll head downtown right now and see what can be done," Uncle Jack said. "Stan, run and find my measuring tape in the tool cabinet."

Stan scurried off to the garage. Phil returned with the broom and began sweeping the shards of glass off the redwood deck.

"Be very careful," Mom warned as Phil swept. "I don't want any of you ending up in the ER."

Carrie pulled Stephie back, away from the glassy mess. "C'mon, let's finish making our snowman," she said.

"We weren't the ones throwing snowballs," Stephie assured Mom over her shoulder.

Mom smiled and nodded her head. "Go have fun."

Stan returned with the retractable measuring tape, helping Uncle Jack with the measurements.

Mom's expression showed concern as I shivered, watching. "Why don't you come in and get warm, Holly?" she said.

I didn't want to be inside with her alone—I didn't trust myself. I might say something I'd regret later.

"I'll be okay," I said, not surprised when she left for a moment and came back holding my coat and a knit ski hat.

"Here." She handed them out the door.

I had no choice but to obey. Uncle Jack wouldn't stand for open rebellion at this juncture. Besides, he had his hands full at the moment.

Turning, I looked out over the front lawn, which was covered with several inches of powdery snow. Stephie was patting the head on the snowman, packing the snow down. Colorado snow didn't have much moisture content, and most of the time, we used buckets filled with water to help make our snowballs and snowmen. Wet snows usually came in the early spring. Those were the best for snow forts and snowmen.

"Come help us," Carrie called to me.

"Okay, just a minute." I ran inside to get some waterproof mittens. The phone rang while I was rummaging around in the hall closet, searching. "I'll get it," I called to Mom, who was still surveying the scene of the accident.

Hurrying to the kitchen phone, I picked it up. "Hello?"

"Holly-Heart, it's good to hear your voice." It was Daddy. "How's my number-one girl?"

"Hey," I said, pleased to hear from him. "I tried to call you earlier." I leaned around the corner of the kitchen, checking to see if Mom could hear my end of the conversation.

"Oh, really?" he said. "That's interesting, I believe we may have been trying to call you around the same time."

"How's Saundra?" I asked. "And Tyler?" Tyler was my stepbrother, Saundra's son.

"Fine, fine, everyone's doing well here. And you? How's Carrie?"

I chuckled. "She's outside making a snowman."

"Sounds like she's having fun. With her stepsister, no doubt."

"Yeah." I felt funny about springing the custody thing on him now, within earshot of Mom. This wasn't the time.

"So . . . were you calling about something in particular?" he asked.

"Well, I really want to talk to you . . ."

There was awkward silence between us. Then he spoke. "You don't feel free to talk?"

"Not really."

"I understand," he said. "Well, when it's convenient, why don't you call me collect? You have my office number, don't you?"

"It's in my wallet."

"I'll be around the house tomorrow and in and out of the office on Monday, so keep trying if you don't get me right away."

"Okay."

I thought he was about to hang up, but then he said, "Sean Hamilton's brother mentioned something interesting to me yesterday at work." I knew Sean's older brother worked with Daddy. In fact, he'd been one of the ones who'd first talked to Daddy about God.

"I think I know what you're going to say." I crept toward the dining room to check on Mom's whereabouts. It seemed she'd gone upstairs. Maybe to lie down.

"Your mother's going to have another child." He said it frankly, almost without feeling, as though it were just another financial fact or sales projection.

"Yeah, in April. And that's kind of why I wanted to talk to you." I'd found my opportunity. Mom was safely upstairs; Uncle Jack was still outside with the rest of the family. "Do you think I could come out there for a while?"

"Now? During the school year?"

"Well, maybe not right away, but soon?"

He paused for a moment. "Are you asking if you can come here to live, Holly-Heart?"

"I . . . I guess I am." It was strange. Now that the words were out, I wasn't so sure. "For part of the year, at least."

"Is everything okay there? I mean, are you happy?"

"Well, no, not really."

"Is this something your mother and I need to discuss?"

I wasn't going to get Mom involved. "That's not necessary. Besides, Mom's busy these days. I wouldn't want to upset her."

"I see." He sighed. "Is this idea partly because of the new baby? Is that why you want to come out?"

"It got me thinking, I guess you could say."

"Are you and your mother getting along all right?"

Now it was my turn to exhale. "We aren't fighting, if that's what you mean. We just don't . . . we don't really ever talk the way we used to. And . . . and she kept her pregnancy a secret from me all this time." In some ways, I felt better sharing this with him. But in another way, I felt like I was betraying my family here.

"A secret, you say?"

"Right." No way was I going to complain about the cozy marriage Mom had settled into with Uncle Jack. There was no reason to mention my feelings about any of that. Daddy was a Christian now, and he and Saundra were doing okay, too. The old days of fantasizing about Daddy and Mom getting back together were past. Besides, the fantasy was just that—a fantasy.

"Well, I'm wondering if things won't change for you once the new baby arrives. You're one big happy family now."

Yeah, right, I thought. *Guess he's not wild about my moving out there.*

"I wish you'd let me come," I said softly, feeling hurt.

"Let you? I'd love to have you. Don't you know that, Holly? But things like this aren't decided in an instant of anger, or whatever it is you're feeling, dear. Why don't you think about it . . . pray about it, too, and we'll talk later."

He's putting me off.

"I won't change my mind," I vowed.

"Please think it over?" he said.

"I'll tell Carrie you said hi."

"Yes, do that. Good-bye now."

Usually I would say "I love you," but the words didn't feel natural today. Not at all.

I hung up, heavyhearted. Daddy had seemed hesitant on the phone. He hadn't responded the way I thought he might. I was more than disappointed. His lukewarm response had thrown a wrench into all my plans.

I'd have to find another way to convince him.

Soon.

Chapter 10

All day Saturday I kept my conversation with Jared about his publisher uncle a secret from Mom and Uncle Jack. In many ways, I wanted to savor the information—keep it to myself. Not out of revenge, though. Well, then again, maybe it was.

I purposely showered and dried my hair early in the evening so I'd have uninterrupted time to read my new book.

Tricia's Secret Journey had grabbed me on the first page and wouldn't let me go. Even when Kayla called, I could hardly pull myself away from it.

"Hey, Kayla. What's up?"

"Remember, Paula and I told you we'd call?"

"Right."

"So what's going on with you? Are you really thinking of moving to California?"

"Nothing's decided yet."

"Oh, Holly, we don't want to go through this moving thing again with you." She was referring to last year, when Uncle Jack had announced he was moving us to Denver. Depressing days for all of us.

"This won't be traumatic, I promise. If I can get my dad to consent to it, you'll be happy for me. Won't you?"

"You've talked to your dad already?" She sounded frantic.

"A few hours ago."

"And? What's he think about it?"

I sighed. "I'd rather not say."

"So it didn't go well? Is that what you mean?"

"Look, Kayla, I really shouldn't be discussing this with anyone. Do you understand?"

"Sure, but don't worry about us spreading it around," she said. "You have our word of honor."

"Thanks." I was dying to get back to my book.

"Oh, Holly, something else. This has nothing to do with you and your dad. I was just wondering if you know . . . well, that is, I thought you might have an idea if . . ." She stopped.

"What is it, Kayla? What're you asking me?"

"I'm sorry, it's just so hard. I hope your stepbrother isn't anywhere nearby. Is he?"

I glanced around, even leaned over the stair railing and looked down. "Nope. It's all clear."

"Okay, here goes," she said. "Does Stan have a girlfriend?"

"Stan?" I giggled. "I was right. You're still crazy about him."

"Oh, Holly, please, please, don't breathe a word of this to anyone. Especially not—"

"You don't have to worry about that," I reassured her. "As for girlfriends, Andie was his last, and of course, they stopped hanging out last summer."

"I'm so relieved."

"Relax, Kayla. You don't have anything to worry about."

"Well, I better get going. My mom wants to use the phone."

"Okay, well, tell Paula hey for me."

"I will. See you at church tomorrow."

"Yep. Bye."

Bingo! Kayla wanted Stan to ask her out. Now, instead of dying to get back to my book, I was thinking of ways to "help" my brousin get the message. Without telling him in so many words, of course. Kayla would have my neck. I'd have to be very discreet.

But once my thoughts about getting Kayla and Stan together faded, I curled up in bed with my book. I found myself absolutely absorbed with the main character, Tricia Joellyn. She was so much like me, had most of the same problems in life, and more than anything wanted to get away from her present family and live with her dad for a while. And the amazing thing was that Tricia's dad wasn't all that enthusiastic about her joint custody idea, either. Just like Daddy. In fact, the reason why Tricia called an attorney after the initial talk with her dad was the very reason I'd secretly considered making a phone call to the law firm where my mom had worked as a paralegal before she got remarried.

My reason? I felt rejected, and I wanted my father to know I was serious. Getting an attorney involved didn't have to mean I was becoming hostile. I certainly hoped Mom or Uncle Jack wouldn't see it that way.

Monday, I would make the call from a pay phone during lunch. No one would ever have to know.

Chapter 11

Jared came right in and sat down beside me in Sunday school the next day—like he owned me or something. Danny Myers sure didn't like it. At least, that's how it looked from where I sat, catching his annoyed expression.

Actually, Danny seemed rather forsaken these days without a girlfriend—namely, Kayla. Being the studious sophomore that he was, I had figured he didn't care much about the boy-girl thing anymore. But evidently I was wrong.

"Hanging in there?" Jared whispered to me.

"Why shouldn't I be?"

"I'm talking about the California thing."

I looked him square in the eyes. "I *know* what you're talking about, Jared."

He must've gotten the message that I didn't want to discuss it. Not here, in front of everyone. Abruptly, he changed the subject. "How's your story coming?"

"Haven't written another word."

He looked surprised. "I thought you wanted to get published . . . again."

"I do, it's just . . . well, everything's happening at once."

Our teacher came in then, and Jared said no more about either matter. Still, I felt strange sitting next to him, knowing that Sean would be coming to see me. We'd be having our first real date in just over three weeks!

♥ ♥ ♥

On Monday, Paula and Kayla surrounded me at my locker first thing. They were worried about my custody plans. Both of them.

"Look, it's not like I'm divorcing my mom or anything," I explained.

"Who's not divorcing who?" It was Andie.

Stunned, I turned around. The twins were silent, too.

"Well, excu-use me, I can tell when I've stumbled into unwanted territory." She spun away on her heel.

"Andie! Come back!" I called to her.

And she did. In a flash. "What's going on?"

Of course, I had to tell her. There was no way around it. I couldn't shut out my very best friend forever. So I quickly summarized the state I was in, leaving out the secret phone call I planned to make during lunch.

"This is craziness," Andie yelped. "I can't believe you'd go to such measures—to get attention, no less."

"You're wrong," I snapped. "That's not what this is about."

"Could've fooled me." She rolled her eyes at the twins, who were doing everything they could to support my decision by staying calm.

"Holly's going through some rough waters right now," Paula said, putting her arm around my shoulders.

Andie laughed. "Hey, welcome to life."

"She's in need of encouragement," Kayla piped up, "not . . . not—"

"Not what I have to say?" Andie asked. "Is that what you mean?"

"Calm down." I grabbed her arm the way she always did to me. "Your opinion counts, honest. Please don't freak out about this. If everything goes as planned, I'll be back here in time for the last half of summer."

"Huh?" Andie said. "You actually want to leave in the middle of the school year?"

"It's really very complicated," I said. "Besides, I don't think any of you understand what's going on with me. Read my lips, there are *eight people* living under one roof at my house. Soon to be nine. Does that mean anything to you guys?"

The twins stared at me, blinking their long eyelashes.

Andie sighed. "Like I said before, what's the big deal?"

"It's crowded at my house, and I can't think. I'm losing my privacy just when I have a chance to be a book author."

"A what?" Andie hadn't heard. "When did this happen?"

"Saturday, at the doughnut shop." I filled her in quickly about Jared's uncle. "And by the way," I said, remembering how the twins had seemingly orchestrated Jared's showing up just as we were going to get doughnuts, "I think we should talk about last Saturday . . . the bus ride home and, well . . . everything."

"What are you saying?" Paula asked.

"Don't play dumb with me. Jared asked you to arrange things, right?"

"Are we talking Jared Wilkins here?" Andie butted in.

"None other," I answered.

Paula and Kayla remained stone silent.

"C'mon, girls, I have a strong feeling about this." I stared them down.

"Jared does, too—about you," Paula spoke up.

"Oh, not this again." I remembered that Paula had thought I should talk to Jared about who was writing those mystery letters to me last fall. She'd actually believed he knew something. Of course, he did in the end, but Paula had encouraged me to have lunch with him about it.

Funny. Paula herself had been interested in Jared when they'd first moved here from Pennsylvania. Maybe she still was. . . .

"Listen, if you think Jared's so wonderful, why don't you go out with him?" I suggested. "Me? I've got myself the best guy friend in the world."

On that note, the four of us disbanded. The bell had rung for homeroom.

♥ ♥ ♥

At lunch I was able to sneak out of school, grab a burger at a fast-food place nearby, and find an available pay phone—all in less than fifty minutes.

"Hello, I'm calling to get some preliminary information," I said. *Is this what I really want to say? Preliminary information?*

I always got nervous when I had to talk to professionals. Especially strangers.

"One moment, please," the receptionist said.

Soon a paralegal came on the line. She identified herself. Instantly I recognized her as one of Mom's friends at the firm. "How may I help you?" she asked.

She'll know me in an instant, I thought. For pete's sake, she was in my mom's wedding to Uncle Jack! I almost froze, almost hung up.

I decided to count on her not recognizing my voice. "Well, I'd rather not identify myself if that's okay. I'm simply gathering information at the present time."

"I'll help as best I can" came the professional-sounding voice.

I took a deep breath. "I'm wondering how to go about arranging for a joint custody situation between myself and my divorced parents."

"Are you of age?" the woman asked.

"I'll be fifteen in twenty-three days."

"Then I believe you would have some say in what happens to you."

"What do you mean, what happens to me?"

"I'm talking about in abuse situations, a foster home is often called upon. The Department of Social Services—"

"No, no, I'm not saying any of that. I've never been abused in any way." I stopped to catch my breath. "I only want to know how difficult it would be to get my parents to change custody arrangements against their will."

I could just imagine her face. She probably wondered what rock I'd crawled out from under.

"Excuse me, miss, I don't understand. Are you telling me neither of your parents is in agreement with joint custody?"

"I'm not completely sure about my mom, but I don't think my dad's very interested."

"So your mother has full custody of you at the present time?"

"Yes."

"Then that's tricky," she replied. "I think you'd better make an appointment with one of the attorneys. And about the fees—"

"I have enough money saved up for the first visit," I said. "If it's not too expensive."

"Well, I think maybe we might be able to arrange a court-appointed attorney for you. But that would require a court hearing. Would you like someone here to set that up?"

This court talk scared me silly. "Uh . . . I'll have to think about it," I said. "I'll call you again tomorrow. Is that all right?"

"Of course."

"Thank you."

"You're very welcome" was the reply.

I returned the phone receiver to its cradle and opened the folding doors to the phone booth. The winter wind blew hard against me as I walked up the hill toward the high school. I wondered how I'd have the nerve to pull any of this off.

But I had to try. There was no giving up. I would call Daddy again.

Tonight.

Chapter 12

"Do you mind if I use the phone?" I asked Mom before supper. She was peeling a sink full of potatoes with Carrie's and Phil's help.

"Long distance?" Her eyes gave her away. She knew.

I nodded.

"To your father?"

"Yes." I could feel the tension between us.

"Now's as good a time as any," she said. "Why don't you use the phone upstairs . . . in our bedroom?"

"Can I talk to him, too?" Carrie pleaded to Mom as I hurried out of the kitchen, through the dining room, and up the stairs.

I closed the door to the master suite, feeling my heart pound with anticipation. "Daddy?" I said when he answered.

"Well, hello again. How are you?"

Formal, unnecessary greetings, I thought. *Let's get on with it.*

"I don't know for sure what to do next," I said. "I called a law firm today. Talked to a paralegal."

"You did *what?*"

"Just to get some information. Nobody here knows."

"Holly, dear, what are you doing?" He sounded upset. "I thought we agreed you were going to think about this—take some time before deciding anything—and talk to God about your feelings."

This sounded strange coming from Daddy. All those years before, he'd never cared about what God thought about anything. He'd lived his life the way he chose to. Left Mom, Carrie, and me for the big city and a big-time job. All that.

But now. Now he'd come to a place of faith in Christ. Now he prayed regularly. Like I did. Or like I used to, I should say. Lately, I wasn't on speaking terms with God much at all.

"Holly?" he said gently. "Can we talk about this?"

The lump in my throat was growing. "I don't want to stay here anymore," I said, tears spilling down my cheeks. "They're taking my room away . . . they don't care how I feel. . . ."

I couldn't go on. The ache in my throat pinched my words.

"You don't think your mother and Jack care how you feel about the baby?" Daddy prompted me. "Is that it?"

I managed to squeak out something.

"If you lived with your mother part of the year and with me the other months, how would this affect your education? Have you thought of that? And what about your sister? What would Carrie think?"

"Carrie doesn't think," I protested. "She's starting to act like . . . oh, I don't know what's happening to her."

"Now, don't be hard on your sister. You know what she's going through," he said. "You remember your own preteen years, don't you?"

"Yeah, but there's no way I'm staying here just because of her."

My statement didn't seem to shock him. "What about your mother? How would such a change affect her?"

"We've already discussed her. She's in love with Uncle Jack, with her new baby. Her life is perfect."

Daddy made no comment about that. "But your friends. Wouldn't you miss Andie? And the others?"

"Sure, I'd miss them, but it wouldn't be like I was going away forever. I'd come back for half the year and then go live with you the rest of the time. A simple rotation—it's easy."

He sighed. I actually heard him sigh! Like this was a burden or something. "How did the attorney's office advise you?"

"Listen, Daddy, if you're not in favor of this," I blubbered, "then I need to know right now. Yes or no."

"Well, I must say that I certainly don't approve of your reasons for joint custody. If you ask me, I think you're acting rather selfishly."

"*I'm* selfish? Mom's selfish! She's the one destroying my life. She's the one getting everything she wants."

"Hold on, honey. I think you're overreacting, and I suggest you put your mother on the phone."

He was ordering me around! My father was ruining everything—complicating my already horribly messed-up life.

"Mom's busy," I said. "She can't talk now."

"Well, then, I'll phone her later," he said. "I wish you weren't so upset. Good-bye, Holly."

That was the end of that. Daddy had practically hung up on me!

Putting the phone back on the nightstand, I hurried around the bed toward the door. On my way out, I noticed more skeins of yarn piled up on the chair in the corner. Greens, yellows, and a pearly white. Mom was playing it safe, crocheting colors that would work for either a boy or a girl.

I stood there, daydreaming. Scarcely could I remember the day Carrie was born. I was four years old when Mom and Daddy brought her home from the hospital. Hard as I tried, though, I couldn't remember actually holding her as an infant. Oh sure, there were tons of pictures, and sometimes from studying scrapbooks I got the mistaken impression that I actually remembered the occasion or how she looked. But it was really only the pictures tricking me, making me think I remembered when I really didn't at all.

I shook off the images from the past and headed to my room, frantic. Daddy was going to call Mom and blow the whistle on me. How could he? If he loved me at all, he'd go along with my idea. Wouldn't he?

Stephie was across the hall, playing over and over the same miserable song that she loved. Without saying a word, I tiptoed over to her room and closed her door.

"Hey!" she hollered. The door flew open. "What do you think you're doing?"

"I have to write something," I said, towering over her.

"Well, I'm not stopping you."

"No, but your music is. So either turn it off or shut your door." I made a move toward her, and she misread me and started yelling for Mom.

I grabbed her by the shoulders. "Stop it right now, Stephie. Mom's busy."

Truth was, I didn't want to recite any part of my phone call to Mom. In fact, I wished I'd never called Daddy in the first place.

"I'm telling," Stephie yelled, and for an instant, I saw the worst part of myself in her. The way I'd been acting for the past week or so. Ever since the baby news.

"Fine," I said. "Go ahead, yell and scream. Act like a spoiled brat. See if I care."

That shut her up. She turned around, flounced back to her bedroom, and slammed the door.

Relieved, I raced to my room and closed my own door.

I knew I had about forty-five minutes before supper. Forty-five precious minutes. I needed to make tracks; there was no getting around it. If I didn't hurry and finish this story, I'd lose my golden opportunity, as Daddy used to say.

Picking up my pen, I began to write.

Five words later, I was twirling the pen. Stuck.

What will I do if Daddy refuses me? I'd be on thin ice. And all the while, Mom was planning for her new baby, while Uncle Jack was bursting his buttons with pride.

I tried to push myself, force myself to write more, but it was no use. Moods were a problem with me. Either I was revved up, ready to write, or I wasn't. Today it wasn't coming. Not at all.

Maybe today's writer's block was a good thing, because the phone rang, and when I answered it, I heard Jared saying, "Hey, Holly-Heart. Are you okay?" Like he cared or something.

I would've positively died if Mom had announced that Jared was on the phone, calling to me for everyone in the house to hear.

"I'm fine, thanks. How are you?" I asked.

"You don't have to be so polite with me."

This was weird. Was Paula right? Did Jared still care? I couldn't imagine in my wildest dreams dating him for real this time. Not now, not ever.

"Why are you calling?" I asked.

"Can't a friend check up on another friend?"

"I don't get it."

He didn't answer.

"C'mon, Jared, you don't have to play games with me. Why'd you really call?"

He cleared his throat. Was he nervous? "I can't forget you, Holly-Heart. I just can't."

"That's what you say to all the girls," I retorted. "I know you."

"You *do* know me. That's why I can talk to you. That's why I'm telling you that if you push this custody change, I'll never speak to you again."

I snickered. "Hey, that wouldn't be so bad."

"Give a guy a break." I knew I'd hurt him. But he'd hurt me. Bad. Last year and then again last fall at the start of school. He and Amy-Liz Thompson . . . seeing them together. Now, *that* hurt.

"I'm real sorry about this, Jared. But I don't think there's any hope for us. Ever."

"You sound so sure."

"I am. But thanks for calling. And if I do end up going to live with my dad, I hope you won't clam up on me. You won't, will you?"

A long pause.

"Jared?"

"I can't believe you'd want to leave us all behind, Holly-Heart. Doesn't Dressel Hills mean anything to you anymore?"

He'd hit my soft spot. I loved this ski town. My roots were here. Always and forever. Still, it didn't hurt to branch out—see the world. That's what Andie kept saying all last summer.

"Sure I'd miss Dressel Hills," I managed to say. "You know how I feel about my friends. And you, too, Jared. We've been good friends awhile now. Nothing can change our past. But the future . . . well, the future's coming up fast. I don't want to deal with what's happening here."

"I think maybe you've hit the nail on the head," he said.

"Huh?"

"You know what I think, Holly? You're running from your problems. Why don't you ask God to help you handle things?" He paused for a moment, then said, "I've been doing that a lot lately. It really helps."

"I know." But I hadn't prayed in almost a week.

"Well, I'd better go. Don't be mad at me for calling. Promise?"

I smiled. "I'm not mad. We're friends, right? Good-bye, Jared."

"Not good-bye," he said softly into the phone. "How about—see ya later? That's much better."

My heart sank as I hung up the phone. What was Jared Wilkins doing to me? Again.

Chapter 13

5:05 A.M.

I read the glowing numbers on the bedside digital clock. I'd awakened before the alarm.

Tuesday morning—another day of school. Lazily, I swung my legs out over the side of the bed and sat there, rubbing my eyes.

Yawning, I tried not to think about my conversation with Daddy. He hadn't called back to talk to Mom. Thank goodness. On the other hand, anticipating his call to her would slowly drive me insane. I could only hope that he'd had a change of heart and wasn't going to get Mom involved from his end. Man, that would be so awkward. Thorny, in fact.

I went to my window seat and knelt down to pray. "Dear Lord," I began, "it seems like a long time since I've talked to you about what's going on in my life. I know you've helped me many times before, and I'm thankful.

"Lately everyone's recommended that I come to you with my hopes for joint custody. So here I am, wishing I could say something positive about my life, but unfortunately I can't. Not right now, at least.

"Things are worse than crazy. I've got this baby brother or sister coming along soon. But you know all about that. Anyway, I need help with how I feel toward this kid who's not even born yet. I resent Mom and Uncle Jack, too, for not including me— not sharing the fact with me early on, when they first found out. Things aren't the way they used to be with Mom and me. We used to be so close. Unbelievably so."

Goofey nuzzled against me. I held him gently while I continued my prayer: "I wish this idea I have about living with Daddy half the year wouldn't be such a big deal to him—or to Mom when I tell her about it. Why can't things be more simple, the way I view them? I don't want to hurt anyone; I just need a break."

I stopped praying. Someone was tapping on my door.

"Come in," I said, still kneeling.

"Morning, Holly." Mom studied me with loving eyes. "I'm sorry to disturb you. You were praying, weren't you?"

"Just finished."

"We could talk later if you like." She moved back toward the door, as though she were going to exit.

"Uh, no, that's okay."

She tied the belt on her terry-cloth bathrobe more snugly. Feeling uneasy, I motioned for her to sit on my bed. She went and sat down, then patted the spot beside her.

"I don't want to cause additional problems between us," Mom began, glancing down as if she was hesitant to speak. "Things have been awfully tense lately. Honestly, I don't know where to begin."

I sat next to her, watching her face. *What's she trying to say?*

Without warning, Mom's eyes were bright with tears. "This is one of the hardest things I've encountered in a long time."

"What is it, Mom? Are you okay?"

"Someone said . . . well, I must confess that I heard this

straight from a friend. You're thinking of going to live with your father . . . you've contacted an attorney's office."

I thought of the paralegal I'd spoken to on the phone. "I should've known she'd recognize my voice," I muttered.

Mom's eyes held a strange hurt, almost a disbelief. "Such a thoughtless thing to do, Holly. I'm surprised at you—inquiring about joint custody behind my back."

I steeled myself. "Lots of kids with split families go back and forth between their divorced parents. What's so wrong with that?"

"That isn't something I would have agreed to."

"Maybe not back when you and Daddy split up, but now . . . now I'm almost fifteen. I should be able to decide certain things. It . . . uh, might help us, you and me, if I lived with Daddy for a while."

"I wish you would've talked to me about it first." She reached for my hand. "It's because of the baby, isn't it? You're angry with me."

I glanced over at Goofey, who was curled into a tight ball on my window seat. "Bottom line, I hate the thought of losing my own space—this room. Stan has a huge room all to himself. So should I."

Mom listened.

I continued. "Daddy built this house for us—you, Carrie, and me. He designed the house with his kids in mind. How could I ever begin to let you take my room and turn it into a . . ." I sputtered angrily at the thought. "Into a nursery for your baby?"

She responded softly, almost sadly. "Holly, do you really think we're scheming to take away your room? It's only one of the options we have in mind."

"I need time to write." I ignored what she'd just said. "I have an incredible opportunity to become a published book author. This year! But I need my space, and I have to be able to think and write without—"

"Why didn't you tell us?" she interrupted. "When did you find out? How . . . what's this all about?"

I told her about the initial conversation with Jared.

Mom literally beamed. "What good news! Oh, I'm so excited for you."

"Do you understand better now?" I said, using the writing project as an excuse for being upset. Of course, that wasn't entirely true.

"You should have told us immediately," she said, "when you first heard about the publisher."

And I wish you'd told me about the baby when you first found out, I thought, biting my tongue. That was the number-one reason I was so ticked.

She let go of my hand. "I really wish you hadn't gone behind our backs and called the law office."

"It might seem like I did that, but I didn't, not entirely. I talked to Daddy about it. Last night when I called him."

She gasped. "You mentioned this to your father?"

"He'll let me come live there. I'm sure of it," I said with a confidence I didn't really feel. "I'll have a large, private bedroom suite and study area. It's perfect, don't you see? Besides, Daddy can have his attorney look into it. No hassles for you and Uncle Jack."

Mom's face fell. "I'm not an unfit mother, Holly," she whispered. "No court in the land would change custody based on a whim."

I was fired up. "They would if I took the stand and testified. Not against you or Uncle Jack but just to say where I wanted to live. How I feel about it. Judges are leaning more and more in favor of kids these days." I sighed. "What is in the best interest of Holly Suzanne Meredith? Have you thought of it that way?"

"For heaven's sake, you sound like a spoiled . . ."

"Go ahead, say it. I'm a spoiled brat."

"Where are you getting such ridiculous, selfish ideas?"

I didn't dare tell her I'd stayed up late reading *Tricia's Secret Journey*. Most of my ideas had come from Marty Leigh's shrewd and conniving characters.

"Where on earth?" she demanded.

Mom had just lashed out at me. Now I had to turn the tables on her. Stick up for what I believed in. "Why shouldn't living with my father part of the time be an option for me? Why?"

She shook her head. "Please, Holly. Don't push this."

"But what if adding another kid to this household destroys my entire future as a writer?" I insisted. "What about that?"

She eased off the bed slowly. "You're not making sense."

"I know the feeling," I mumbled under my breath. "By the way, when can we discuss the phone-calling rule?"

"Maybe we won't need to." There was a strange, icy edge to her words. "If you're moving out, why would you need to call home after school?" With that, she burst into tears and left the room.

I could hear Uncle Jack's gentle voice at the end of the hall as she went to him for comfort, no doubt.

Whew, was I in trouble now!

Chapter 14

I kept running into Jared Wilkins all day at school. Although I felt responsible for breaking Mom's heart, I felt confident enough in myself to remind Jared again that we were nothing more than friends.

I complained to my friends about him during lunch. "When will he ever get it through his head? He and I . . . we're through."

Andie, Paula, and Kayla listened, sympathizing with me.

"You know Jared: If he's not with someone, he always wants to be," Andie reminded us. "This will pass as soon as he finds his next victim."

The twins laughed. "She's right," Paula said.

"Well, I hope so." I opened my carton of chocolate milk.

"So . . . what's everyone think about the new Marty Leigh book?" I asked.

Andie snorted. "*Everybody's* not reading that book!"

I grinned. "You're right, and what a mistake. You're totally missing out."

Kayla nodded. "I love how she wraps everything up in the end. It's really amazingly satisfying and truly wonderful."

"Don't tell me what happens," I said, dying to know, but eager to read it for myself.

Paula fluffed her hair, frowning. "I have a feeling I know exactly where you got your ideas about living with your dad."

"What do you mean?" I was playing dumb.

"You know—the joint custody thing in the book," Paula said. "It was Tricia's idea first, long before it was yours. I'm right, and you know it."

I thought back to last Saturday at the bookstore, when I'd read the back of the book. Paula was right; I had gotten the idea from the book.

I sighed dramatically. "Look at it this way—maybe it was meant to be. Maybe I was supposed to read *Tricia's Secret Journey* at this stage in my life."

"Oh, please! Surely you aren't saying it was planned by God," Andie said. "I think you're stirring up trouble for your mom and dad. They've already been through a divorce; why do you have to start something stupid like this?"

"My wishes and desires are not stupid!"

Andie stared at me. "I hardly know you anymore, Holly-Heart. It's like your personality has been altered somehow."

"Really? Is that what you think?" I stared back at her, then at the twins. "Do *all* of you think this?"

"Well, I wouldn't go so far as to agree with a personality change," Paula spoke up. "But I do think you should wait, give your mom a chance to have her baby, and then decide. It's the kind thing to do."

Kayla was nodding her approval. "I agree with Paula. Why not wait and see how things go after the baby comes?"

"Seems logical to me," Andie said.

I took a long drink of chocolate milk. "Then, none of you are on my side?"

"What do you mean?" Paula asked. "This has nothing to do with taking sides."

"Seems like it," I muttered into my milk carton.

"Well, why don't you come to youth group tonight? You missed last week," Paula said.

"Yeah, we'll save you a seat," Kayla offered. "Okay?"

I gave in to their suggestion, realizing once again that they really *did* care. No one was siding against me. Not really.

♥ ♥ ♥

We had a substitute teacher in French class, and she hadn't the slightest idea how to either speak or write the language. So she gave us free study time.

Gratefully, I used the fifty minutes to work on my novella. Perfect. I had decided to wait until the very end of the book to think of a fabulous title, but the more I wrote, the more I realized that a good title was essential to the entire structure of the story.

That's what I'll do tonight, I thought. *After youth group.*

I would create a sensational title. Titles, after all, caught book editors' attention first. I certainly didn't want to lose the opportunity to impress Jared's uncle, the publisher.

Speaking of Jared, he was waiting for me after French class. "Hey, I found out the deadline for our manuscripts." He fell into step with me.

"Really? When is it?"

"March 15."

"That's good. Mom's delivery date is still over a month away." Perfect timing. "I'll have my story finished long before that time."

If all goes well at home, I thought.

"So how's it coming—the writing, I mean?" he asked.

"Really great. What about yours?"

"Cool." He flashed a heart-stopping grin. "Thanks for asking."

"It was just a simple question," I told him. "Don't read anything into it."

"Aw, Holly, stop being so defensive."

"I think it's time for me to go." I turned to leave. No sense hanging around. Jared was still driving me crazy.

"Wait, uh, Holly. Would it be okay if I walked you to your locker?"

I studied him. This guy never, I mean *never,* gave up!

"C'mon, it's no big deal," he assured me. "Just a friendly gesture."

"Oh, all right. Come on." He had to hurry to keep up—it didn't turn out to be the romantic hall stroll he might've anticipated. Basically, Jared ran behind me all the way to my locker. It was ridiculous what I was doing to him, but I had my reasons. No way was he going to get the wrong idea about me . . . us.

♥ ♥ ♥

After school I needed to head straight home. Uncle Jack had told me in no uncertain terms during breakfast that I was on restriction. Not surprising. I'd dished out some pretty nasty stuff to Mom this morning, thanks to my lousy attitude.

Mentally, I abandoned the power struggle over the after-school phoning rule and hurried to the bus stop. The rule wasn't worth the fight. Besides, I had a hunch there might be some mail waiting for me, so I didn't mind going right home.

My hunch was correct. Sean's letter lay on top of the pile of mail on the corner desk in the kitchen. Mom had probably placed it there so I'd see it right away. Funny, she never held a grudge. Never.

Quickly, I opened the envelope and leaned on the island in the middle of the kitchen, reading the letter.

Saturday, January 20
Dear Holly,

I'm afraid I have some bad news. Remember the group of middle schoolers I told you about—Power House? Well, there have been a few problems with some of the younger kids— parental permission, finances, etc.—and it looks as though we are not coming to Dressel Hills to ski as planned.

At the present time, the adult leaders are leaning toward going to San Diego for the weekend of February 16.

I'm sorry about this turn of events, Holly. I had no idea our personal plans would have to be altered like this. I really wanted a chance to celebrate your birthday with you, even if it was going to be two days late.

More than anything, I hope there will be many other opportunities to see each other.

The words on the page faded, blurred in a flood of tears. *More than anything . . . other opportunities . . . not coming . . .*

I ran, sobbing, to my room.

"Something's wrong with Holly," I heard Carrie say as I closed my bedroom door. I wanted to lock it—shut the whole world out. Crying my eyes out was all I could do.

Poor Goofey, helpless to know how to comfort me, meowed out of concern and pushed his furry back up against me as I lay on the bed.

Minutes later someone tapped on my door. "Holly?" It was Mom. "Is there anything I can do?"

I couldn't speak for the tears.

"Holly-Heart?"

This was one time—one of the very few times in my life—I desperately needed to be left alone. Ordinarily, when I was sad or depressed, I wanted someone to pursue me, help me through my pain, even if I insisted I didn't. I was weird that way.

At this moment, however, I needed time to cry. Time to feel

sorry for myself. Sean wasn't coming to Colorado after all. Our plans, all of them, had melted away with this letter.

No one else—*no one*—could possibly understand what I was feeling. Any coaxing or offering of sympathy would be useless.

"Holly?" Mom called again.

"I can't talk now," I managed to say, hoping with all my heart she'd believe me and leave me alone.

"Okay, honey," she replied, "but I'm just down the hall if you need me."

Need me. Of course I needed her. Maybe not at this instant, but later, if I ever got over this horrible disappointment. Mom was my mainstay, my rock-solid support in life—the one I'd always counted on, the only one who'd never let me down.

But now, the way things stood between us . . . how could I possibly expect kind words from her after the heart-wrenching things I'd said this morning?

Holding the letter, I reread Sean's words. He wouldn't be coming for my fifteenth birthday. That meant there'd be no snow party with the Dressel Hills youth group. No first date with the one and only Sean Hamilton.

So much for bragging and blabbing about my California guy friend. If only I'd kept my big mouth shut.

Chapter 15

For the second week in a row, I couldn't bring myself to attend youth group. Andie and the Miller twins might've thought I'd deceived them by saying I was coming. I hoped not, because I had fully intended to go when we discussed it at lunch.

But now . . . with my eyes swollen and my cheeks red from crying, well, it was totally pointless.

I stayed home and worked on coming up with a title for my novella. *Nothing But the Heart* was one of my stronger title options. I knew it might not be the one I would end up with, but as a working title it spurred me on.

Miraculously, with Stan and the rest of the kids out of the house at church clubs, I was able to write two more good chapters. I surprised myself. Usually when I was in a gray mood like tonight, nothing, absolutely nothing, flowed when it came to writing. Sometimes, though, my writing was therapy. Tonight, it was just that—keeping my mind off the big disappointment.

When I went to the kitchen for some pop, Uncle Jack and I avoided each other. Mom didn't dodge me but seemed a little distant. Maybe she was hurt. Knowing Mom, she would survive. She always did.

As for me, things were piling up emotionally, like the steady snowfall outside. First the baby news, the custody issues, then Sean's letter. What next?

My shoulders drooped as I headed back upstairs to edit my chapters.

Less than five minutes later Mom was at my door, knocking gently, almost hesitantly. "Your stepfather and I would like to see you for a minute." She stated it so formally, I wondered if there was going to be additional discipline heaped upon me for the way I'd behaved this morning. Maybe going without phone calls and having to come straight home from school today wasn't enough for my stepdad.

I dropped everything and left my room.

When I arrived, Uncle Jack was sitting at the dining room table, having a slice of frozen yogurt pie. Mom pulled out a chair next to him, and I, wanting a cushion of space between myself and the powers-that-be, sat at the far end of the table.

Uncle Jack glanced at Mom before he began. "Your father called here this afternoon, Holly . . . and spoke to your mother briefly."

I felt my throat constrict, go instantly dry.

"Your father's talking lawyers, court hearings, the works." He studied me with serious eyes. "You've created quite a stir in the family."

I was secretly pleased. Daddy was coming through for me, after all these years!

Mom started to sniffle, reaching into her pocket for a tissue. I hoped she wouldn't cut loose and really start boohooing. But, at this advanced stage of her pregnancy, who was to know.

"As you can see," Uncle Jack continued, "your mother is taking every bit of this very hard, kiddo." He let his fork hang off the edge of his plate. "As for me, I'd like to see this difficulty worked out for the best of everyone concerned."

"What about my best interests?" I blurted. "Isn't that what the judge will look at?"

Mom sighed, folding her hands on the table. "We're hoping it won't go that far. We'd like to be able to work things out with you."

"Me?" I coughed. "I'm the one feeling pushed out. You need my room for your nursery; I need the chance to breathe again. Daddy has the space for me to do that."

"We're in shock," Mom said through a veil of tears. "How can we . . . I . . . let you go? You're my first child, Holly-Heart. I love you so. . . ." Her voice trailed off, intermingled with tears.

"What's so wrong with splitting my time between Colorado and California?" I wailed.

"What's wrong is your attitude." Uncle Jack was getting up now. He began to walk back and forth, rubbing his hands together like he was stirring up his thoughts. "You aren't working with us—you're fighting us. Fighting everything we're trying to do for you."

"How can you say that?" I shot back.

"Think about it," he said softly.

I drew a deep breath. "Oh, I know, this must be about that stupid rule—that after-school phoning rule. You think I should just comply with it, even though I'm older now. Lots older than when Mom first created it. I never complained about it all those years before."

Uncle Jack stood behind Mom's chair, massaging her shoulders gently as she cried. "I don't think we're getting anywhere with this." He looked over at me, concern in his eyes. "I want you to promise me one thing, Holly. Your father is in agreement with this, too."

What is he going to say?

"We—all of us—want you to spend time praying about the joint custody decision. We'll be praying, too."

Mom was literally sobbing. Uncle Jack leaned down and

whispered, "I think it would be best if you'd rest now, honey." He kissed her on the top of her head. "We surely don't want anything to happen. Not now."

Mom got up with Uncle Jack's help, leaving in tears from the dining room. I was outraged. Uncle Jack had just implied that I might be causing problems for Mom—for her pregnancy. How could he say that?

I would never do anything to cause Mom to lose . . . to lose the baby, I thought. *Never!*

The anger pounded in me. I stared at the man who was my uncle and stepdad rolled up in one. It was all I could do to control myself. Holding in my frustration only brought indignant tears. They fell unchecked.

"You think I've planned this—set all this up—to make Mom have trouble with her pregnancy?" I said, my words pouring out with a vengeance. "Is that what you think?"

He looked at me with bewildered eyes, standing there silently.

"You know me better than that!" I shouted. And with that, I flew out of the room and up the stairs.

EIGHT IS ENOUGH

Chapter 16

The next week was a blur of gloom. At least for me. Everyone else in the house seemed to be involved in some baby activity or another.

An unspoken wall of tension remained between Uncle Jack and me. Mom kept to herself, however. I was beginning to wonder if she'd ever get used to the fact that I wanted to split my time between her and Daddy. Usually, Mom took things in stride. But when it came to heart matters such as these, I guess Mom simply couldn't pull herself out of the doldrums.

I didn't get around to calling the attorney's office back. The way I saw it, if Daddy was actually willing to consider the possibility, I'd rather use his private family attorney than have the state appoint one for me here. As for proceeding with the legal side of things, I wasn't sure what I was waiting for. Maybe the fact that everyone had insisted I pray about it. Maybe that was what was holding me back.

But I hadn't obeyed. All week I avoided the prayer issue, even neglected my personal devotions. Deep within myself, I recognized my problem. I was stubborn and unwilling to let God work in me. I wanted things my way or not at all. Yet I was too headstrong to change my course.

Carrie was the one who got me charged up about things again. I was cleaning my room after school when she knocked on my door.

"Hi," she said, wide-eyed. Her hair was in a long ponytail; the way I used to wear mine. "I heard you want outta here."

"Oh, really?" So Mom had finally gotten around to informing the rest of the family. I closed the door behind her, allowing Carrie into my private domain.

"I think it stinks," she said, and before I could comment, she began to cry.

"Carrie, what's wrong?" I went over to where she stood in front of my dresser, burying her head in her hands. Stunned, I wrapped my arms around her. "It's okay, you don't have to cry."

But cry she did. Not just a little, either. Heartbreaking sobs poured from her. "Don't leave, Holly . . . please, don't go away. . . ."

I felt my own eyes watering—that's how incredibly crushed Carrie sounded. Waiting for her to calm down, I finally spoke. "I hope you don't think I want to go away because of you." The thought had occurred to me while she was bawling. I didn't want Carrie to think that I was abandoning her just because she was turning into a snooty little so-and-so.

"Mom said you need some space—to get away from here for a while," she blubbered. "I don't see what's so bad about living here."

I tried to explain. "It's not just the space. It's other things, too."

She looked up at me suddenly, her tearful eyes demanding answers. "Like what other things? What could possibly be so awful about living here?"

"I didn't say it was awful."

"You know how much Mom . . . how much I love you."

"And I love you, too." I hugged her.

"But just not Mom, is that it?"

"Of course not, silly. That's not it at all." I was groping for words. Everything I wanted to say to her sounded trite inside my head.

"Then is it about the baby?" she asked, wiping her eyes.

I waited a few seconds before responding. "Yes, the baby's a big problem for me."

She didn't understand. I knew by the incredulous look on her face. "How can you say that?"

I shook my head. It was no use. "I can't explain it."

"You're jealous, then, that must be it."

I hated her for saying that. Everyone was saying it. Even Andie. "Why should I be jealous of an unborn baby, for pete's sake?"

She stared at me, determination in her eyes. "It's written all over your face."

I chuckled. "You're sounding more like Mom every day."

"So that's it, huh? You have nothing to say for yourself."

At that moment, I wanted to escort her—no, I wanted to *throw* her out of my room. The haughty little brat! "I don't need a lecture from you." I went to the door and opened it wide.

"Someone should talk sense into you. You're making our mother sick, Holly. Why don't you think about someone else besides yourself for a change?" In a huff, she bounced out of the room.

♥ ♥ ♥

It was impossible to work on my novella that night. Algebra came first, of course, and later, I attempted to add another chapter to my book. Nothing came. The words were scrambled up in my brain, so how could I expect to sort them out on paper?

Along about ten o'clock, I gave up and went to bed. My sleep was erratic and filled with weird dreams. Even Goofey was restless and finally left his cozy spot on my bed for the peaceful solitude of the window seat.

♥ ♥ ♥

The next morning I felt lousy when the shrill sound of the alarm awakened me. I stumbled into the bathroom and reached for the shower knobs, hoping the warm water would soothe my tired body and spirit.

While I let the water run against my back, I thought of Kayla's questions about Stan—a mild relief from the true frustrations of my life. What could *I* do to tactfully inform my brousin of Kayla's ongoing crush? Why were guys so dense, anyway?

One thing led to another, and soon I was mulling over Jared Wilkins. Again. Why did it seem I never quite got the guy out of my head? I mean, once my birthday passed, I was as good as Sean's girlfriend.

These days, I could honestly say I never thought about Jared in that same way. If what Amy-Liz had told me months ago was true—that she broke up with him because he couldn't stop talking about me—well, that was hard to believe. Even if that really was the reason, I had a hard time bringing myself to consider Jared as more than just a good friend. Funny thing, we *were* that—good friends. In fact, probably closer friends, at least at the present time, than when he and I both liked each other. Amazing, but true.

What would Sean think if he knew I was thinking about Jared this way? What would my future husband, whoever he was, think if he knew how emotionally caught up I was in both Jared and Sean?

I couldn't determine how, or from what submerged brain cells the idea came, but suddenly the disturbing notion was there—certainly uninvited, perfectly crazy.

Sean Hamilton wanted to end our friendship—that's why he'd written the letter. Could it be true—was my intuition correct? Was his excuse about the Power House group not being able to come to ski merely a convenient way for Sean to say good-bye?

Briskly, I dried off, anxious to reread his letter. But by doing so, I felt only more rejected, reading things between the lines that may or may not have really been there. I was more frustrated than ever and fussed over my hair for no reason. It was easy to manage now that the too-frizzy spiral perm had finally relaxed. Except for the shorter length, I actually liked my hair. Sean had written that he liked it, too, after receiving a recent photo from me. He'd gone on and on about how pretty I looked.

But even better, you're pretty on the inside, which is far more important to me. He'd written that, and I'd believed him. But now? Now he wasn't coming to Dressel Hills at all and was making no effort to reschedule another time. What did he expect me to think?

♥ ♥ ♥

Mom didn't show up for breakfast, so we kids did our fending routine and managed just fine. Basically, Stan and I saw to it that everyone bowed their heads for prayer and ate a well-rounded breakfast before heading off to our separate schools.

I couldn't help thinking about the playpen or high chair soon to be making its appearance in the kitchen. Babies didn't stay little long. They grew up rapidly, threw applesauce and oatmeal all over the floor, and made big messes.

When breakfast and cleanup were over, I hurried to the bus stop, eager to see my school friends. All of them—Jared included.

Chapter 17

Jared was as charming as ever when he stopped by my locker before lunch. He wore a shirt that brought out the blue in his eyes. And, for a change, I actually listened as he told two jokes, one right after the other.

"You're in rare form today," I commented as we walked toward the school cafeteria.

"Hey, I like what I'm hearing." He turned to look at me with a smile.

I refused to allow things to get out of hand between us. That's why I headed straight for the table where Andie, the Miller twins, and I usually sat at lunchtime. I had to be careful. It wouldn't be fair to soak up Jared's obvious interest just to divert my own thoughts and change my mood. I wouldn't use him that way.

"What's the latest about living in California?" Andie asked as she, Paula, and Kayla converged on us.

"I'm waiting to make my decision," I stated.

Paula smiled. "Waiting till after your mom has her baby?"

"Not that long," I replied, not telling her that I'd been advised to pray about my choice. But I still hadn't.

"What will be the determining factor?" Kayla asked.

I glanced around at each of them, feeling suddenly over-whelmed with their presence. "Can we drop this for now?" I gave them a weak smile. "I have a lot to think about."

Jared was first to agree. "Yeah, let's give Holly some breath-ing room."

Andie caught my eye and gave her wordless warning. I knew she didn't want me going soft on Jared.

Then he brought up the subject of a Valentine ski party. "Pas-tor Rob's been talking a lot about it. What do you guys think?"

I held my breath as Andie jumped in on the conversation. She didn't know—no one knew—about Sean's letter or that he'd canceled his trip.

"Well, Holly's guy friend is coming from California with a bunch of middle-school kids. What do you say we include them?" Andie said.

"Fine with me." Paula studied me with a question mark in her eyes, probably wondering why I didn't respond.

"That's cool," Jared said, but his expression gave him away. He didn't really think Sean's coming was cool at all.

"Great!" Andie continued. "What do you think, Holly-Heart?" She looked right at me.

"Maybe next year." I decided to level with them. "Sean and his youth group are going to San Diego instead."

Andie gasped. "No," she cried. "Oh, Holly." She reached over and grabbed my hand. "You must be totally devastated."

I forced a smile. "Not exactly."

"Yes, you are," she insisted. I knew it was all a show for Jared's sake.

"Really, it's okay." I pleaded with my eyes for her to drop the subject. But she kept it up. That is, until I picked up my tray and left the table.

I wasn't surprised; Jared got up, too, following close behind as I headed for the kitchen to return my tray. "Are you okay with this . . . this cancellation?" he asked.

He's fishing, I thought.

"There'll be other times," I said.

Andie was headed our way, plowing through a group of students, frantically trying to get to me. I don't know why she didn't trust me. Didn't she know I wouldn't fall for Jared's sweet talk just because Sean wasn't coming?

"Oh, Holly," she called, displaying a desperate look. "Walk with me to my locker." She completely ignored Jared, who stood beside me. "Come on!"

"Excuse me," I called to Jared over my shoulder.

"See you after school," I heard him say as we hurried down the hall.

"What're you doing, Andie?" I demanded. "I can take care of myself."

Andie snorted. "Didn't look like it to me."

We were coming up on her locker. A group of upperclassmen were hanging out nearby. Three of them glanced at us as though we were slime. What else was new? This was high school, after all.

"Smile!" Andie called to them, only to receive the cold shoulder and some loud, disparaging howls of laughter. At times like this, I wished I were homeschooled.

Not Andie. She loved social challenges. "C'mon, you can force a smile for us lowly freshmen," she shot back.

"Andie, please," I whispered. "Cut it out." This time I was the one grabbing her arm and hauling her away to my locker.

"What are you doing?" she asked.

"Saving you from yourself." I kept going, dragging her along.

Reluctantly, she followed me to my locker. I made her hold my books while I searched in my purse for Sean's letter. "Here," I said, finding it. "Read this and tell me what you think." I pushed the letter into her face.

"I can't read it that close," she complained, piled up with my books.

I stepped back, still holding the letter as she began to scan it. "So . . . what do you think?"

She shrugged. "About what? He's not coming; it's that simple."

"But . . . do you think he's really hoping to avoid me?"

Andie frowned and shook her head. "I don't get that from reading this, why?"

I sighed. "Once more—read it again."

She did. "Nope. It's not curtains for Sean Hamilton."

"You're absolutely positive?"

"What are you worried about, Holly?"

"Just a feeling I have."

"Well, your feeling's wrong." She handed back my books. "Did you write him back?"

"Not yet."

"You'll be getting another letter from him. You'll see."

Going on Andie's instincts, I felt okay about answering Sean's letter, which I did during French class. Most of the class was studying for a test scheduled for tomorrow. I figured I could review my dialogues that night. Easy.

Surprisingly, I felt better once the letter was written. Not because I'd written in an upbeat manner, but because my best friend thought I was mistaken about why Sean wasn't coming. To tell the truth, hoping she was right was one less burden to carry around. The mental and emotional load was still weighing me down. And now I had another burden to add: Mom's ultrasound results. Also scheduled for tomorrow.

Tomorrow, on the first day of February—the beginning of my birthday month—the doctor would probably be able to determine whether Mom's baby was a boy or a girl. On top of that, if the ultrasound pictures were clear, Uncle Jack was going to play a video of it for the family. Like he thought we were actually interested.

Personally, I couldn't imagine spending tomorrow evening viewing such a thing—an unborn baby floating around inside my mother's stomach. The very same baby who was upsetting my entire life!

Chapter 18

After school that day, both Andie and Jared were waiting at my locker. Andie's scowl gave her away—she wasn't thrilled that he'd shown up again. She totally dominated the conversation. In fact, there was no time for Jared to say what was on his mind before we had to leave to catch the bus.

"Okay if I call you?" Jared asked as the three of us headed down the hall.

"Of course," I said, smiling. "I'll look forward to it."

Andie looked like she nearly died on the spot, but she was polite enough not to make a rude remark. Jared said good-bye to both of us and hurried off in the opposite direction to the library.

"About Jared," Andie said as she and I waited at the bus stop. "You're leading him on."

"I'm only being polite," I assured her. "There's nothing to worry about."

"C'mon, you know what'll happen."

"What? What can happen if I don't want to go out with him?"

She was silent. But only for a few seconds. "So . . . are you really going to push for the custody thing?"

"It's the best thing in the world for me."

"For you? Since when does your family's life revolve around one person?" She'd launched off on one of her pet peeves. "Families are a community effort—they're forever, and don't you forget it."

"I didn't say they weren't, but if I remember correctly, we've already had this conversation. If you don't mind, could we please just drop it?" I'd had it with her know-it-all attitude.

"Well, excu-use me. If I can't talk sense to you, Holly, who can?"

I kept my mouth shut even though I knew she was baiting me. The atmosphere was heavy with conflict, ripe for a fight. Besides that, Andie's biggest hang-up lately was irrational worry over the future. In other words, what would happen to us—our friendship, our close bond—after high school, college, and beyond? The question had plagued both of us in recent months.

"So . . . aren't we talking now?" she asked.

"I see the bus." That's all I could say without getting into a word war.

"Okay, fine. No more talk of California or joint custody," she volunteered. "I promise."

"And what about Jared?"

She shook her head. "Do whatever you want about him."

"Really?" I said, elated. "Did I hear you correctly? You're actually giving me permission to live my life without consulting you every five minutes?"

Andie ignored my ranting and boarded the bus.

Case closed. At last!

♥ ♥ ♥

I couldn't wait to get back to *Tricia's Secret Journey*. But first I worked through my French homework on the bus.

Back home, Carrie and Stephie had already claimed the dining room table, spreading their homework every which way. Phil was using the kitchen island for his space. Mark was outside playing in the snow, and Stan still wasn't home from school. As best as I could calculate, Stan had ten more minutes before he should be calling home. The after-school calling rule remained in force. Even for male sophomores.

Mom was resting quietly in her room. Uncle Jack was still downtown at his consulting firm. No one else was upstairs. Fabulous—everyone in the house was occupied at the same time. I curled up beside Goofey and opened my book.

As always, Marty Leigh's writing pulled me into the familiar fiction world I loved. Tricia Joellyn had succeeded in getting the joint custody issue resolved and was now living six months out of the year with her dad and stepmom. Naturally, she'd discovered a mystery while there.

Yes! The suspenseful part, I thought.

I had actually begun to wonder why this book was classified as a mystery. But here it was, in the incredibly suspenseful last third of the book. Tricia had uncovered a long-kept family secret—there was a twin sister she'd never known. The girls had been separated at birth. Somewhere out in the vast world, Tricia's twin lived with another set of parents—adoptive parents. A girl with Tricia's face. But where?

I was so engrossed in the plot, I never even heard my name being called. Stan had come home, evidently bringing someone with him, or so Carrie was saying as she opened my bedroom door. "I've been calling you, Holly."

"Uh, sorry." I marked my page with my finger, still absorbed in the book.

"Someone's downstairs to see you," she said. "One of your girl friends."

Reluctantly, I searched for a bookmark and closed the book,

wondering what girl friend of mine would be coming home with Stan.

I heard Kayla Miller's bright, cheerful laughter. She'd managed to get Stan's attention, it seemed. Without my help. This was fascinating.

I headed downstairs. "Hey, Kayla," I greeted her as I came into the living room. "What's up?"

Kayla's eyes sparkled. "Stan's going to be my project partner."

Stan had already begun to unroll some wide sketching paper across the living room floor. "We're making a timeline for world history class," he informed me.

I grinned at Kayla. "Really?"

She nodded. "We chose the Middle Ages. It's due next week."

"Cool." I was dying to know who'd asked whom but didn't want to embarrass Kayla.

It turned out Stan escorted Kayla home after supper. They took the city bus since he hadn't had his license long enough to drive with an underage passenger—not one who wasn't related to him. I observed the way the two of them interacted comfortably in front of Mom and Uncle Jack and the rest of the family at the table. They were a good match. Kayla had been right all along.

I was putting the last plate in the dishwasher when Jared called. "Hello?" I said, getting it on the first ring so there'd be no competition in the house.

"Hey," Jared said. "I wish we could've talked earlier. After school."

I laughed. "We're talking now."

"Guess you're right." He paused, like he was getting up the nerve to ask me something. "Uh, Holly, I've been doing a lot of thinking—mostly praying, though."

Strange, hearing Jared Wilkins talk this way.

"I think God's telling me that you shouldn't continue pursuing the joint custody thing," he said.

"Telling *you*." I chuckled. "Who is this talking, really?"

He didn't laugh. "I'm serious, Holly." He didn't go on and on trying to persuade me. His words were brief and to the point. This approach was refreshing after having put up with Andie's constant nagging on the subject. She never could just make her point and then stop. With her, it was all about overkill.

I wanted to hear more. "You think God's telling you this . . . for me?"

"You sound surprised," he said. "I thought you'd be getting the same sort of spiritual direction."

"What do you mean?"

He didn't answer for a moment. "You're praying about this, aren't you?"

I was caught. What could I say? I felt humiliated. Here was Jared, praying about *my* future circumstances.

"Holly?"

I took a deep breath. "To be honest with you, I haven't prayed about joint custody. Not really."

"Something so life altering, and—"

"This is *my* business," I interrupted.

"I can see that." He said it firmly, almost sternly. "Well, I guess I don't have anything more to say to you. Other than I'm praying you'll do things God's way." Jared said good-bye and hung up.

I was baffled by his words. If I hadn't known better, I would've thought he'd conferred with Danny Myers, the most spiritual guy in our entire youth group. Had someone coached Jared on what to say just now?

Surely not. And Andie thought *I* was the one undergoing a temperament change. Whew, this was unbelievable.

I couldn't wait to tell someone. Anyone!

Chapter 19

The following evening, Uncle Jack was rounding everyone up. Time to watch Mom's baby swim around in her tummy. I couldn't believe I was actually going to sit through this event.

Mom settled down in her favorite spot in the family room downstairs—on the far end of the sectional. The arm was wide and comfortable there, and she propped several throw pillows behind her back.

Stan, Phil, Mark, Carrie, and Stephie sat cross-legged on the floor in front of the TV screen, eager for the show to begin. I, however, perched on the edge of the sectional at the opposite end from Mom and Uncle Jack. The way I figured, a noncommittal attitude was best for a night like this.

"Show us our new baby," Carrie called as Uncle Jack picked up the remote. His enthusiastic smile gave his excitement away.

Not a word had been said at supper about whether the baby was a boy or a girl. Top-secret info. Maybe Uncle Jack, being the unorthodox kind of guy he was, really and truly wanted this to be a memorable moment for the family.

"We should have a meeting after the video, to name the baby," Mark said.

Uncle Jack looked Mom's way. "What do you say, honey? Good idea?"

She nodded, pushing a loose strand of hair out of her face. "I'm open to any and all suggestions. Within reason, of course." Since we had several comedians in the family, she probably felt she had to say that.

"You're on, Mark. Great idea," Uncle Jack said, to which Mark and Phil gave each other high fives.

Must be a boy, I thought. *They probably already know. . . .* Of course, someone to carry on the Patterson name. Not that Uncle Jack needed another son! But Mom—she'd probably be thrilled. She'd never given birth to a boy.

"Okay, kill the lights," Uncle Jack said, nestling back into the sectional next to Mom.

The video began.

Reluctantly, I watched as a shadowy, almost ethereal image was projected on the screen. My eyes scanned the ultrasound picture. Then I saw it—the baby, curled up in a snug position. Sucking its thumb.

Uncle Jack began to narrate as we watched. "Each of us grows from one tiny cell, smaller than a grain of sand, to a full-grown baby of about seven or eight pounds."

"How long is a baby when it's ready to be born?" Stephie asked in the darkness.

"Around twenty or twenty-one inches," Mom replied. "You and Holly were both a little over twenty-one inches at birth."

"Will *this* baby be that long?" Phil asked.

Who cared about lengths and pounds? What was this kid, anyway—male or female? Wasn't that what this viewing session was all about?

Uncle Jack kept talking about the way babies grow and prepare for birth. I knew all this stuff. Eventually, though, I found myself paying closer attention, looking for evidence to indicate that Mom's baby might be a boy.

Stephie was the least shy one in the bunch. "I can't see any-thing," she said. There were several snickers in the darkness.

Uncle Jack explained about ultrasounds—how it wasn't always easy to tell if the baby was a girl or a boy. "They have to be turned just right," he explained. He was cool that way. I mean, I didn't know many fathers—er, uncles-turned-stepdads—who could handle this subject so delicately. Anyway, Stephie seemed satisfied.

Uncle Jack continued to watch from his cozy spot with Mom. Then he began to quote some verses from Psalm 139. The ones that always made me shiver when I realized how much God had loved me, even before I was ever born. " 'For you created my inmost being; you knit me together in my mother's womb. I praise you because I am fearfully and wonderfully made. . . . ' "

Wonderfully made . . . this little child . . .

"The baby's a girl," I blurted without thinking.

"Holly's right," Uncle Jack said. "We're going to have another little girl."

I held my breath, watching. My soon-to-be little sister—tiny hands and feet, fingers and toes—perfectly formed. The more I watched, the more I had to fight back the tears. What a horrible big sister I had been, treating this precious, God-ordained life with disdain. With resentment.

In the dim light of the video, I stole a glance at Mom and Uncle Jack. Happy newlyweds, anticipating the birth of their firstborn child together. What heartbreaking sadness each of them had endured. Lonely, grievous times. Now they had each other. And all of us.

Eight isn't enough, I thought. Not when you have plenty of love to go around. Mom and Uncle Jack certainly did. That was, and had been, clear all along. I'd been too stubborn, too caught up in my selfish plans, to see the truth.

Jared was right. God's way was best. Always.

I studied my siblings—the tops of their heads silhouetted

against the bright screen in front of me—as they sat watching, spellbound, on the floor. We were a family, all eight of us. In April this little child growing safely inside Mom would make us nine.

I could hardly contain myself. "We should name her April," I said as the video ended. "It's the perfect name."

I caught a glimpse of Mom's smile as Stan turned on the lights. "April's a lovely name," she said. "In fact, I wrote it down just yesterday as a possibility."

Our baby-naming meeting had officially begun. Carrie and Stephie had several ideas, but in the end the name April stuck. Phil and Mark tried to get Mom to consider names like Jo or Dale for the baby's middle name, but those got vetoed quickly. In the end, all of us agreed that April Michelle went very well with Patterson.

April Michelle. Our new little family member was greatly loved. Already!

"Is there anything else we should talk about?" asked Uncle Jack, looking at me.

I nodded. And for the first time, I asked the question that had been burning in me for days. "I've been wondering why you and Mom waited so long to tell us about the new baby."

Mom leaned forward. "We wanted to be absolutely sure every-thing was going well," she began. "You see, back in October, I almost lost our baby."

I gasped.

Uncle Jack continued. "Do you remember all those nights of frozen pizzas when Mom stayed upstairs in bed?"

I remembered all right. I'd worried that Mom had the flu or something. But this? Almost losing baby April. The thought brought tears to my eyes.

"That's why we waited," Mom assured me. "Until we knew for sure."

Stephie and Carrie asked a few more questions. "Are we having a baby shower?" Carrie asked.

"Probably not," Mom said, smiling. "You usually only get a shower for the first baby."

"When are we going shopping for baby furniture?" asked Stephie.

Mom laughed, reaching for the catalog on the coffee table. "We ordered everything almost two weeks ago. Have a look."

Stephie and Carrie scooted over to inspect the white baby crib, dresser, and changing table to match. "Oh, you played it safe," Carrie observed. "This was before you knew we were having a sister."

"That's right," Mom said. "We didn't want to have something too fussy or too tailored."

The next question was on the tip of my tongue—where were they going to put the furniture?—but Uncle Jack announced that we were all going out for ice cream. "Your mother's been craving some peppermint ice cream all day."

I giggled. "What about some peppermint tea and honey?"

"Cravings have a way of changing during pregnancy." Mom laughed as Uncle Jack winked at her.

I could hardly wait for some time alone with the two of them. There was so much I needed to say. *I'm sorry* was only the half of it.

Chapter 20

After school the next day, I worked on the last two chapters of my novella. It was amazing what could be accomplished in a short time, especially when the writer wasn't caught up in stressful life battles. Feeling confident, I knew I would finish *Nothing But the Heart* in plenty of time to submit it.

Before going to bed, I wrote in my journal. Time to catch up the private record of my life.

Friday, February 2: I finally got things out in the open with Mom and Uncle Jack last night. After that incredible ultrasound video, well, things totally changed for me—the way I view things around here, at least.

First off, I apologized for the crummy way I'd treated Mom and Uncle Jack. I even offered to share my bedroom with baby April whenever they were ready to set up the crib.

Of course, I have no idea how all that'll work out, but I figure by the time I graduate from high school and head off to college (about three-and-a-half years from now), my baby sister will already be a toddler. How hard could it possibly be sharing my beautiful, spacious room with someone named April Michelle?

Oh . . . the joint custody issue is pretty much solved by the fact that I no longer sense a conspiracy between Mom and Uncle Jack. There had been one reason, and only one, why Mom hadn't told her special secret. Fear of miscarriage. Knowing what I know now, her decision makes perfect sense. I plan to call Daddy tomorrow and fill him in on my decision. After talking to God, I know what I should do.

Last night, at the end of our talk, Uncle Jack said something really fabulous. Some cool quote from a philosopher guy named Kierkegaard. I really like it, especially in light of my recent blunder. I hope I never forget the lesson. The quote goes like this: "Life must be understood backward. But that makes one forget the other saying: That it must be lived— forward."

Everything, right down to the anger and belligerence that prompted me to call an attorney's office and to get Daddy all upset, EVERYTHING is clear to me now. I fully understand my life—this segment of it, at least.

Jared and I had a long talk today at lunch. We ate by ourselves until Andie and the Miller twins showed up and tried to rescue me. They were mistaken, of course; I didn't need rescuing at all. Jared and I are friends. Good friends and nothing more. Someone else holds a special place in my heart. Someone who's never given me any reason to distrust him. Someone who's seeking God for guidance about his own personal future. And for mine.

I sort of doubt whether Jared heard God telling him I should drop the joint custody issue. But his comments got me thinking more about prayer, and I'm happy to say that I'm keeping the heavenly lines of communication open again. I missed talking to my number-one BEST friend.

I put my pen down and closed my journal. Reaching for my Bible, I turned to Psalm 139—the Scripture Uncle Jack had recited to us while we watched our baby sister float inside Mom's stomach. "For you created my inmost being; you knit me together in my mother's womb."

This verse was awesome. The more I thought about it, the more I realized something powerful. This same Creator-God who knew me and made me also knew my future. He knew what would happen between Sean Hamilton and me. He knew whether or not I'd have a first real date on or after my fifteenth birthday. He also knew if or whom I'd marry, if I'd have children—all that kind of important stuff.

I had desperately needed a lesson in trust. To learn to trust God's plans for my life—the way Mom had entrusted her unborn child to the care of the heavenly Father.

"Thank you, Lord," I prayed, "for loving this family of eight enough to give us a bonus baby. And thanks for helping me accept your perfect plan. Amen."

HOLLY'S HEART

It's a Girl Thing

For my delightful fans
Mindy and Katie Dow.

IT'S A GIRL THING

Chapter 1

Opening my eyes, I sat up in bed and stretched. A fabulous sensation zipped through me, something like the adrenaline rush you get when you know beyond any doubt that something incredible is about to happen. I could feel the excitement in my bones—wrapped right around my nerve endings.

Hours later, at school, I stopped at Andrea Martinez's locker to tell her about my jazzed feeling. Andie reacted a bit nonchalantly, and I should've expected as much. My best friend's not a morning person. Who is?

Anyway, she got bossy on me. "Take a deep breath, Holly. You'll get over it."

"But you know how it is when there's anticipation electrifying the air," I said.

Andie shrugged and touched her dark curls, obviously not wildly interested. "Maybe you've got it in your mind that we might have placed at district choir competitions. But don't go getting your hopes up about Washington, D.C. Lots of choral groups make it this far."

She was right. Still, I couldn't help the feeling . . . and the hoping, holding out for a trip to nationals—at our nation's capital. What a way to top off our freshman year!

If the Dressel Hills High School Show Choir made it to state finals—and we would find out this week—and then went on to win at regionals, the way I figured it, we'd have a fabulous chance at nationals. And after that, maybe the international choir competitions in Europe!

Andie took her time gathering up her usual Monday morning assortment of books and a three-ring binder. I waited for her, trying to control the thrills I felt prancing up my spine. We could be going to state . . . this Friday!

When her backpack was finally jammed full, the homeroom bell rang. I said my overly enthusiastic good-byes. "See ya second hour," I called over my shoulder before merging with the student congestion. Second hour was choir.

Andie nodded and headed in the opposite direction, toward Miss Shaw's homeroom, Room 210. I still found it hard to accept our homeroom setup; Andie and I were in different rooms. Here it was almost the end of March, nearly halfway through the second semester of my freshman year. By now I should've been accustomed to separate homerooms. But Andie and I had never been split up before.

She had, of course, handled the situation well—actually was very cool about it. I was the one having to adapt.

Amy-Liz Thompson, a friend from our church youth group, fell into step with me, and we allowed ourselves to be carried along with the throng of Dressel Hills High School students.

"It's a good thing I'm not as short as Andie," she shouted over the roar. Her wavy, honey blond hair floated away from her face. "I'd sink and drown for sure."

"No kidding." That's when I grabbed her elbow and pulled her out of the current. Exit: Room 202.

Jared Wilkins showed up, all smiles, just as we made the turn into Mr. Irving's homeroom. I heard Amy-Liz groan softly, and she promptly followed me, sliding into the desk ahead of mine.

"Don't worry about Jared," I whispered. "I think he's starting to grow up."

"If you say so." She pulled a notebook out of her backpack. Naturally, she didn't believe a word of it.

Just then Stan, my ornery brousin—cousin-turned-step-brother—poked his head into the room, motioning to me. "Holly," he called softly.

"What's this about?" I muttered, getting out of my seat and going to the doorway.

Stan was a sophomore, a bit tall for his age, and almost as blond as I was. But he had an ever-growing chip on his shoulder, and I wondered how long it would be before he exhibited it today.

"Look, Holly, I need you to go straight home after school." His voice sounded confident and sure, like I was going to fall for whatever he said.

"Why should I?"

"Don't ask, just do it," he shot back.

I sighed. Stan was sixteen now and the oldest of our blended family. More than anything, he liked to throw his weight around. Especially with me. And it wasn't just my imagination, either. Even Andie and some of my other friends had noticed how Stan seemed to enjoy picking on me.

"I suppose you want me to cover for you," I retorted. "Mom's counting on *you* today, isn't she?"

"C'mon, Holly, just this once." He wasn't asking or pleading. Nope. He was plain cocky.

"So something's come up, right?" I said, his attitude making me upset. "You need me to help out."

His eyebrows floated to his forehead, accompanied by a frown. "Why do you have to be so difficult all the time?" I knew right then that he did not want me to view the situation as a problem that only I could solve for him. He glanced around, probably hoping he wasn't causing a scene.

I sighed. "All the time, huh? Well, thanks for that enlightening comment." I was not going to allow Stan to talk to me this way, not here, at the entrance to my homeroom—a place that was supposed to be a sanctuary, a place secure even from haughty stepbrothers. "You came here wanting a favor, and this is how you act? Well, forget it!" I turned on my heel and marched away— back to my seat and Amy-Liz's curious expression.

"He's totally impossible," I said when I was seated.

"Brothers can be," Amy-Liz replied.

I grinned. My friend was the lucky one. She had no male siblings to drive her crazy. No siblings at all. "What do *you* know about brothers?"

"You're always complaining about yours, that's what!" Amy-Liz laughed, but I could see she was dead serious.

"I am?"

Amy shook her head. "As a matter of fact, you complain about Stan a lot. I actually get the feeling that you can't stand him."

"Can't stand Stan," I whispered, trying not to laugh. I thought about it and was ready to say something back—something to defend my position—but Mr. Irving walked into the classroom just then.

I had to settle down and switch my thoughts to academia. It was time for morning announcements even though I had zillions more comments for Amy-Liz—things to verify the fact that Stan Patterson was *so* a rotten brousin.

Chapter 2

I never had the chance to give Amy-Liz the earful I intended. My government class notes somehow got misplaced, and by the time I located them in my binder and frantically reviewed them for a quiz, it was time for first hour.

The government quiz was child's play, but the homework assignment looked like a nightmare in the making. I jotted down the notes, hoping there wouldn't be tons of this sort of homework dished out all day. It was only first hour, for pete's sake!

After government I hurried to choir, hoping we'd have choir competition results from Mrs. Duncan, our director. She made her cheerful entrance, a flurry of navy and white, and my hopes soared.

Her stylish canvas shoulder bag was brimful, as usual. She promptly headed to the piano and began discussing several musical scores with Andie, our accompanist.

It seemed to me that Andie was eager to get to work, because I noticed her fingers wiggling on the piano bench on either side of her. But she listened intently as Mrs. Duncan pointed out various musical phrases. Andie had been doing some radical improvisation at the piano, somewhat hamming it up for the class, while we'd waited for our teacher to show up. Now, though, Andie was focused. And surely as anxious as all of us to know the outcome from district competitions.

I fidgeted, sitting next to Paula and Kayla Miller, my twin girl friends. "I'm dying to know if we made it," I whispered to Paula.

She nodded. "I certainly hope we did. We sounded absolutely wonderful, didn't you think so?"

"I guess it's hard to tell for sure if you're not out in the audience," I said.

Kayla pulled out her compact and peeked at the tiny mirror. "Mrs. Duncan wants to go to Europe as much as the rest of us," she said.

I grinned. Did we really have a chance?

The quiet click of Kayla's compact seemed to signal the end of the director's discussion with Andie. Mrs. Duncan walked purposefully to the music stand, adjusted it for the correct height, and took the podium.

For a moment she surveyed each of the choral sections: soprano, alto, tenor, and bass. Then, with a broad smile, she told us the competition results. "Are all of you ready to perform . . . again?" Her hands gripped the sides of the music stand.

"Yes!" we cheered.

"All right, then, we have some work to do." She gave Andie a nod and raised her hands, and with a gentle sweep of her right hand, we stood in unison, ready to practice our pieces from memory.

I was almost too giddy to sing. We were actually going to Denver for state competitions!

Partway through the first madrigal, I stepped forward—slightly out of my row—and grinned at Jared Wilkins and Danny Myers just to the right of me, in the boys' section. Jared gave me a not-so-subtle thumbs-up, and Danny, standing next to him, beamed back at me.

Quickly, I turned my attention to Mrs. Duncan's directing, even though I was pretty sure I could sing the entire choral repertoire in my sleep.

♥ ♥ ♥

As it turned out, I did go straight home after school. Not to help Stan, though. I wanted to send an email to Sean Hamilton, my friend in California.

I'd met Sean, who was now a high-school junior, two Christmases ago, while visiting my dad and stepmom. During the course of many months of correspondence, he had become quite a close friend. In fact, if I dared to admit it to myself, I really liked Sean. Even more than Jared Wilkins, who had been my very first major crush. Actually, I liked him more than any boy I'd ever known.

Sean had a sensible way about him that most younger guys seemed to lack. He was a reliable, true friend and a strong Christian who had agreed to pray with me long-distance on several occasions. And he loved kids—maybe because he was already an uncle.

But there was more between us than just friendship, I was beginning to discover. For instance, when he signed off that he missed me or asked when I was coming again to visit my father—those sorts of words made my heart flip-flop. And two weeks ago, when Sean called and we'd talked for nearly twenty minutes, I found myself floundering a bit, almost at a loss for words, which never, ever happens!

Mom was okay with his phoning me; she figured we had a good, firm friendship through our letters and email. She'd even had the chance to meet him once herself. Besides, I was fifteen now—fifteen years old as of Valentine's Day. The reason for my unique nickname, Holly-Heart.

Anyway, I couldn't wait to write Sean about our choir winning at districts.

Hey, Sean!

I'm so excited. Remember I told you about some of the choral music we were practicing, trying to memorize and polish the songs in time for the district competition? Well, guess what? We'll be going to Denver this Friday afternoon for state competitions. That's right—we took first place at districts. Can you believe it? (I hardly can myself!) If we make it at state, Mrs. Duncan thinks we have a good chance at regionals, which will be held in Topeka, Kansas. Ever been there?

I went on to tell him about some of the baby-related plans my family had been making. Mom was getting more and more eager as the weeks rolled by, and quite uncomfortable, as well. Baby April—we knew it was a girl because of the ultrasound— was due April 25.

The crib and chest of drawers fit perfectly in my bedroom, which is a large room to begin with. I don't know when I've been so excited about something, unless maybe show choir and the competitions coming up. Of course, that'll only last a short time. Little April will be my sister forever!

I'll write the second I know if we place this time. Okay?

Sorry this is so short, but I have gobs of government homework—mostly reading and answering essay-type questions. How about you? Is second semester going well? I hope so.

> *Write soon.*
> *Your friend,*
> *Holly*

PS: How's your calculus teacher doing now that his chemotherapy is finished? Is his hair growing back yet? Is yours?

Last September, Sean and a bunch of the guys in his class had joined ranks to offer support for their teacher, who had cancer. They'd actually shaved their heads!

As far as I was concerned, it was a noble thing to do. But that was the kind of guy Sean Hamilton was. Maybe that's why I liked him.

I clicked Send, and my message flew into cyberspace to Sean's laptop in California. Fabulous!

♥ ♥ ♥

By the time Stan got home, I'd almost forgotten how bossy he'd been at school. Besides, this was one of the quieter afternoons in the Meredith-Patterson household. Carrie and Stephie hung out in their shared bedroom, listening to their favorite songs while Phil and Mark did homework on the dining room table. Surprisingly enough, everything was under control.

Mom, however, would want an explanation from Stan as to why he'd transferred sibling power to me while she was away from the house.

"You better tell her," I said later. "If she finds out, you'll be in big trouble."

Stan swaggered around the kitchen, searching the cupboards for snack food. "I'll handle it," he muttered.

I figured Stan would probably forget about it, hoping Mom wouldn't find out. He was like that sometimes, irresponsible about the truth.

"I think you had better get used to hanging out here after school," I told him. "Our baby sister's gonna need lots of attention."

He snorted. "Don't look at me. I'm not changing diapers—none of that stuff."

What a macho guy he thought he was. "Having a baby around might do you some good," I replied.

"It's a girl thing," he shot back. "And don't you forget it!"

"Well, I can see you'll make a fabulous father someday."

It was a retaliatory remark, and I could tell by his face that he recognized it as such. Fuel for the fire.

Stan snatched up a large box of pretzels, wearing a determined frown. He marched to the door leading to the family room downstairs. This was not to be the end of round one. Not even close.

IT'S A GIRL THING

Chapter 3

After supper Mom was settling into her comfortable Boston rocker when Stan sauntered into the living room. He glanced at me, his head giving a jerk toward the kitchen—my cue to get lost.

As I left the room, I heard him telling Mom about an unexpected intramural game that had come up after school. I was curious to know if he'd get in trouble, so I hung around the area between the dining room and the kitchen, listening.

Uncle Jack came downstairs then, headed to the living room, and sat on the couch near Mom. I could see the three of them from my vantage point and was about to indulge myself in a bit of delicious eavesdropping when Carrie caught me.

"What's going on?" she whispered.

"Nothing."

She scowled. "C'mon, I'm old enough to know things."

"You're only ten," I replied.

"I'm a preteen!" Her eyes flashed impertinence. "So . . . what's Stan in trouble for?"

I wasn't going to let my mouthy little sister blow her top at me. Turning away, I headed downstairs to the family room, where Stephie and the younger boys were channel surfing in front of the TV.

Carrie followed. "It's about you coming home and baby-sitting us instead of Stan, isn't it?"

My lips were sealed. How did she always seem to know?

"Why aren't you talking to me?" she demanded.

I turned and looked at my one-and-only birth sibling. "You don't get it, do you? I just told you it's none of your business. You're acting like a spoiled brat."

"I'm not a brat—I'm nearly a teenager! Start showing some respect."

I shook my head. "You're hopeless."

"She sure is!" Mark hollered.

"No, she's not!" loyal Stephie shouted back.

And before I could stop it, a full-blown shouting match was under way.

Uncle Jack called down the steps, and when the noise continued, he showed up, looking peeved. "Your mother and I are trying to have a quiet conversation upstairs," he said calmly. "Do you think it might be possible to watch TV without raising the roof?" He smiled unexpectedly. "Very soon, there's going to be a baby in this house, and the five of you"—and here he included me—"may need to rethink your interactive skills."

"It's not my fault," I spoke up.

"You're the oldest in the room, Holly." That's all he said before turning to leave, as though my age made me in charge.

Carrie moved her lips at me, mimicking our stepdad's words, and I charged at her.

"Help!" she yelled. "Holly's gonna—"

I mashed my hand over her mouth. And then I felt it. Her tongue, warm and wet, pushed through her lips into my hand.

"Eew!" I yelled, jumping away. "Don't do that!" Which brought Uncle Jack right back downstairs.

This time he wasn't as cordial. He was tired. The wrinkle lines around his eyes were more evident than usual. He was working hard these days. His consulting firm had become so busy that he and the Miller twins' dad were hiring on several more employees for the Dressel Hills-based company, as well as the Denver branch. With a new baby on the way, Uncle Jack was even more stressed, especially because Mom had experienced some problems early in her pregnancy.

"Must you be yelling tonight?" he asked.

"I'm sorry," I said quickly, making no excuses as I wiped Carrie's tongue print off my palm.

"And the rest of you?" He looked at Carrie now, and Phil and Mark.

"I was quiet," Stephie piped up.

He nodded. "Let's try and keep it to a dull roar, okay?"

"This is the last time you'll have to tell us, Daddy," Stephie volunteered. "We promise."

Uncle Jack laughed softly, rumpling her chestnut hair. "It better be."

I decided to remove myself from the room. Being the oldest sibling in the lower level of the house was dangerous. Besides, homework was a good excuse to leave.

Phil and Mark had located a reality show now, and Carrie was inching her way over to investigate it.

Stephie, however, carried Goofey, our cat, upstairs behind me. She followed me all the way to my room. "Here's your Goofey boy," she said, putting him down gently.

"Thanks." I hoped she wouldn't want to hang around and talk.

But she did. She closed my door behind her and plopped down on my window seat. "I wish you'd come home and baby-sit us every day after school," she began.

"Really?"

"Uh-huh." She played with Goofey's tail.

"Why?"

"Because Stan's way too bossy."

I smiled. Nothing new.

"Well, we're all going to have to work together from now on—and especially once our new baby sister comes."

Stephie rolled her eyes. "It'll be tough."

"I know." I went over and sat beside her. "You won't be the baby of the family anymore. Right?"

"I'm being bumped."

"You sure are, but won't it be fun to have a real live baby-doll around?" I was groping for the right words. What did I know about this? Shoot, I had been four when my little sister came along—not eight, like Stephie. By the time a kid reached her age, she had every right to assume that her spot on the birth-order ladder was fixed.

"Do you think Mommy will let me hold her baby?" she asked, her round face full of anticipation.

"I'm sure Mommy will show you how. But you might have to sit down the first couple of times . . . you know, to get the feel of a squirmy bundle."

She giggled about that, and when she was satisfied that Goofey was snuggled down for the night, she left the room.

I set to work reading my chapter for government, hoping I'd remember all the facts when it came time to write the long end-of-unit answers. It was a struggle but not as hard as algebra had been last semester.

Later, I went downstairs for a bowl of strawberry ice cream—my reward for finishing homework in less than two hours.

Stan, however, was snootier than ever. He dished up his own ice cream and made a big deal about taking it into the dining room, probably hoping to make me think he was abandoning me on purpose.

I, on the other hand, greeted his abandonment with sheer delight. *Fine,* I thought as I sat at the kitchen bar alone. *Act like the jerk you are.*

And he did. Right up to the moment I said good-night. "Mom wants both of us to come home right away tomorrow after school," he stated snidely.

"Whatever." The word slipped out a bit sarcastically, but I didn't care. Stan had wormed his way out of parental discipline once again.

How he managed to pull this one off, I'd never know!

Chapter 4

Friday, when Jared asked me to sit with him on the bus ride to Denver, I agreed.

Andie, the Miller twins, and Amy-Liz took my decision in stride and sat across from us. Anyone could see that Jared was not the flirt he once was. Actually, the guy was metamorphosing, like most of the other freshmen in our class.

I found it easy to talk to him, the way it had always been with Sean in California. And we had a lot in common, too. Both of us were still waiting to hear back about the manuscripts we'd sent to a small publisher—Jared's entrepreneur uncle, who was eager to work with young authors like us.

"Heard anything yet?" I asked, feeling completely comfortable now about sitting beside Jared Wilkins.

He ran his hand through a shock of thick brown hair. "Only that they've narrowed down the manuscripts to be considered to seven or eight."

"Really?" This was amazing. "Betcha don't know which ones made the cut."

"My uncle won't tell me anything. I guess it wouldn't be fair, you know, since I'm related . . . and since you're my friend."

Jared smiled his glorious grin, making his blue eyes dance. "You *are* my friend, aren't you?"

I glanced over at Andie and Paula. They were playing a card game, wrapped up in their own little world. Good! I wasn't wild about someone listening in right now. Not with Jared starting to talk personal stuff.

Nodding, I said that I was. "And you know what?"

He turned toward me, and for a moment I thought the old, flirtatious Jared might return. But I was wrong. After all, I'd opened the door wide for whatever smooth-talking reply he might want to offer.

I took a deep breath. "It's a fabulous feeling . . . you and me, uh, the way we are now."

He chuckled softly. "I couldn't have said it better myself." And that was that.

We talked about story lines for our own individual projects, and by the time we arrived in Denver, Jared and I were actually discussing the possibility of collaborating on a bigger project. Someday.

Andie couldn't believe it when I told her about it in the ladies' room a while later. "This is so-o cool! You're actually getting along with Jared without the mushy stuff."

"I wondered what you'd think," I replied, grinning. Andie had this thing about my becoming friends with lots of Dressel Hills boys, since she still wasn't all that crazy about my long-distance relationship with Sean.

Paula and Kayla listened without saying a word, and I wondered if they weren't still a bit leery about Jared. After all, in the past he'd done a fabulous job of fooling every single one of us into thinking he was absolutely crazy over us.

But things were different now—for me, at least. I didn't feel vulnerable anymore. Mostly because of Sean. And Jared knew it, which made all the difference in the world.

I primped and fussed over my hair, which was growing out

from its first and only real cutting—back in September, the day before school started. And the perm was perfect now, too—relaxed but not limp. I only wished it might've behaved this way right from the beginning. But that was another story.

"C'mon, Holly-Heart," Andie said, gathering up my brush and comb and stuffing them into my purse. "This is a choir competition, not a fashion show."

"I know, I know."

"So forget the hair." She pulled me away from the mirror.

I studied her short, bouncy curls. Maybe someday I'd get brave and have my long hair really whacked off. With that thought, I followed Andie and the other girls out the door and down the hall to the practice room.

Everyone seemed jittery. Not Mrs. Duncan, however. She was confident, poised—ready to go. "Let's knock the judges' socks off," she said, sporting a winning smile.

That got us revved up a bit, and then when we went through our vocalization warm-ups, I could feel the enthusiasm in the air as we worked to make our unison sound strong and clear, like one voice. The spirit of camaraderie and oneness was powerful. Like an electrical current.

Was it even remotely possible for us to place at this level?

We were certainly dressed for the occasion, wearing our Sunday best. For a change, Danny Myers fit right in. He was always dressing up for school and other everyday things, but that was his style. And thinking about metamorphosing, I had a sneaking suspicion that he was changing, too.

♥ ♥ ♥

The auditorium where we were scheduled to sing was bright with overhead lighting and a wall of windows on one side. The judges—two women and two men—sat about a third of the way back, their postures severe and precise, an indication of how scrutinizing they would probably be. Only one of them, the woman on the far left, even so much as cracked a smile.

We filed onto the stage from behind the curtains, taking the risers without a single one of us tripping or falling. When we were all standing with attention-perfect postures, Mrs. Duncan lifted her arms, offering an encouraging smile, then gave us a one-measure cue, and we began. Even as we sang, I sensed that things were going well.

The judges never took their eyes off us. Not once. And when they did glance down to write and calculate our points, we had already finished singing our first madrigal.

By the time we'd performed the required competition pieces, I felt emotionally drained. All of us had expended so much energy putting out a great sound that we were more than ready to chow down.

Back on the bus, Mrs. Duncan announced that we were going to stop off for supper. Everyone cheered.

Somehow or other, Danny ended up sitting across from me at the restaurant. There had been a time, not so long ago, when he'd had the audacity to admonish me about my eating habits. He'd amazed me by quoting several Proverbs, humiliating me in front of my church friends—all because I'd ordered a giant helping of French fries after having devoured a strawberry sundae with three scoops of ice cream.

Today, however, he said nothing when I smothered my order of fries with ketchup and salt and prepared to eat the Whoppin' Burger complete with pickles, tomatoes, and extra cheese.

What made the difference? I figured it was the maturation process. The tongue-lashing over my cravings for ice cream and fries had come in the autumn of my eighth-grade year. Danny, now a sophomore, was coming of age. At last!

"So . . . how do you think we did today?" I said between bites.

Danny leaned back and sighed. "To tell you the truth, I doubt that we've ever sounded better."

"Really?" Andie chimed in. "That good?"

"Well, it's not quite the same as our youth choir at church," he said. And I knew what he meant. The spiritual unity was missing. Still, lots of us were Christians in the choir, which counted for something. And on top of that, we'd worked hard polishing our repertoire the past few months in preparation for the competition.

Mrs. Duncan came around to chat at each table. Danny asked her opinion on how the choir sounded. Her face lit up. "I can't ever remember a group sounding so terrific. Honestly, this year's show choir is really tops."

"Do you think we have a shot at the international competitions in Vienna?" I asked.

"It's hard to say. I'm very sure the competition will become more intense as we move up the ladder, but if you kids keep singing as well as you did today—the sky's the limit!"

We must have really believed her, because when the final tally was announced the following Monday, none of us was too surprised to hear that the Dressel Hills Show Choir had taken first place once again!

♥ ♥ ♥

"We're going to Kansas," I told Mom after school on Monday.

"When?" Her arms were wrapped around her protruding stomach as she sat in a sunny spot on her side of the bed.

"Next Saturday and Sunday."

"Well, I hope you won't be gone when the baby decides to make her appearance." She looked a tad worried.

"Do you think there's a possibility of that?"

"Holly-Heart, I don't want to spoil your opportunity to sing with the choir," she said, encouraging me to come around and sit near her. "But I'll be needing your help here with the other children when I go to the hospital."

"What about Uncle Jack? Can't he help?"

She smiled. "Your stepdad wants to be present for the birth of our baby."

I wondered about that. Hadn't he already witnessed a real, live birth? After all, he was the father of four other children.

But the more I thought about it, the more I realized that Uncle Jack would definitely want to witness the miracle of this child's birth, as well.

"What about Stan? Can't he help out here if you go into labor while I'm gone?"

Her forehead shifted up, creating lines. Lines that probably meant she didn't think my brousin could handle the task, or worse, she didn't think he would cooperate enough to pull it off. More than likely, the latter was true.

"Stan's not as eager to assist with the younger children, if you know what I mean," she was saying.

"Right," I fired back. "Isn't it just a little too obvious?"

"Now, don't go jumping to conclusions. Stan has his reasons." She paused, then continued. "Your brother's making his way through some very advanced high-school classes these days."

Sounded to me like she was sticking up for him. "C'mon, Mom, don't you see? He'll use any excuse he can."

She was silent for a moment, looking tired and radiant at the same time. Her golden blond hair hung in soft waves around her face, creating an almost ethereal impression.

But I wasn't dense. I could see she didn't need her oldest daughter giving her grief about household chores and the possibility of having to baby-sit during her labor.

My mother was pushing forty and not as energetic as she had been years before, when she carried Carrie and me to full term. Besides, she'd suffered a miscarriage back when I was in grade school, before she and Daddy got divorced. I wanted to go gentle on her. "It's just that Stan expects me to pick up the pieces for him all the time . . . you know, sort of be his backup."

Mom nodded. "I understand how you must feel."

"I really don't enjoy being Plan B," I said, but in this case, I didn't relish the idea of being Plan A, either. Especially if it meant jeopardizing my plans for choir.

"Is there a good chance the baby will come early?" I said softly, afraid the very question might stir her up, get her thinking about it.

She reached for my hand. "I don't think we have anything to worry about. Many prayers have been going up for our baby, so we can both relax."

I gave Mom a kiss on her cheek. Everything was under control in the baby department. Mom would be just fine.

What a relief. I was going to Kansas next weekend!

Chapter 5

There were no signs of false labor, premature labor, or any other kind of labor as Mom waved to me from the living room window early the following Saturday morning. But thanks to the new cell phone I'd just received for my birthday, I was sure to hear the moment anything happened.

Uncle Jack backed the family van out of the driveway, and we headed to the school parking lot, near downtown. The city school district had come up with the revenue for a chartered bus, maybe because Dressel Hills High had never placed in anything cultural. Oh sure, there were always trophies for football and track, but we'd never won one in the arts.

I had a fabulous feeling about all of this. Our show choir was about to put Dressel Hills, Colorado, on the map!

We boarded the bus while it was still dark. I waved good-bye to Uncle Jack, who stood tall and proud along with the other parents. I was surprised there was no media coverage of the event. This was definitely a first.

♥ ♥ ♥

By three o'clock in the afternoon, Central Time, we had

arrived in Topeka, Kansas, warmed up, and were ready to out-perform ourselves. The trip had taken less than ten hours, with no stops for lunch or anything else—we'd brought snacks and sack lunches with us, and the bus had rest room facilities. .

Most of us had snoozed off and on, so no one was really too wiped out from the trip. Except maybe the driver. Anyway, we did our best when it came time to hit the practice room. Mrs. Duncan, grinning broadly, gave us a pep talk before it was our turn to sing.

"We're this far, aren't we? Is this great or what?" Her hazel-brown eyes twinkled as she looked out at all of us, perched on the risers. "Anybody here not ready to show the world who's the best high-school choir around?"

I smiled at her comment and stood up with the others when she gave the familiar motion. We worked through several inter-pretative spots from "Alleluia" by American composer Randall Thompson. Man, did I love this piece—I sang my heart out. Paula and Kayla did, too. In fact, as I glanced around, everyone seemed jazzed up about where we were and what we were about to do.

After the competition we found the nearest fast-food place and pigged out. Once again, Danny Myers ended up sitting at the same table with me. He seemed more mellow than I'd ever remembered him. And as he talked, I noticed the preachy edge was missing from his voice.

"What's with Danny?" I asked Andie later that night. We were staying at a Comfort Inn near Interstate 70—four girls to a room. Paula and Kayla were my other two roommates.

"Danny?" Andie stared at me. "Are you trying to tell us some-thing?" She glanced at the Miller twins, who, by now, were listening intently.

"Yeah, Danny. He's different . . . I think," I said.

"Well, you must want to be a preacher's wife," Andie said.

"Which really is fine with me. At least you won't be going off to California and getting married."

"Oh, Andie, please! Who said anything about marriage?" I opened my suitcase and pulled out my pajamas.

"Danny's definitely waiting for the right girl to come along," Kayla spoke up. "He says he's not going to date; he's going to wait for God to bring the right mate to him."

I thought about that. "Hey, I like that."

Paula dug around in her suitcase and pulled out a slim paperback. She waved it in my face. "Here, take a look at this. I think this could be where Danny first heard about his approach to finding a wife."

"Really?" I turned the book over and read the back. "This sounds really interesting."

Andie came over and peered at the book. "Maybe you've just found some food for thought."

I looked at her. "Huh?"

"You know, the next time Danny shows up at your table, you two could discuss this—common ground for conversation."

"Now you're teasing me." I handed the book back to Paula.

"No, really. I mean it, Holly. The guy's really tuned in to what he believes is the best way to discover God's plan for a life mate—simply wait." Andie wasn't joking at all. "It sounds unbelievable, I know, but I guess we'll just have to read it for ourselves."

"Where'd Danny get the book?" I asked.

"The church library has it," she said.

"So . . . how soon will you be finished reading it?" I asked Paula.

"I'm on the next-to-last chapter." She pulled on her terry-cloth robe. "If I finish it before we get home, I'll let you take a look at it." She showed me where she was in the book. Then, while

Kayla, Andie, and I engaged in girl talk, Paula went to read in the corner of the hotel room nearest the table lamp.

I couldn't help glancing over at her every few minutes. The book intrigued me. I couldn't wait to read it, too.

♥ ♥ ♥

The next day we were approaching the outskirts of Junction City, Kansas, on our way back to Colorado when Paula handed the book to me. I was so eager to start it that when Jared came and asked me if I wanted to talk, I declined. Politely, of course.

"Do you mind?" I said apologetically.

He spied the book in my hands and shrugged. "Well, if that's what you're reading, fine."

"You've read it?"

He grinned. "It's really . . . uh, different, but great." And before he left to go back to his seat, he said, "When you finish it, let's talk, okay?"

"Sure." I hadn't realized how riveting a nonfiction book could be. I didn't want to put it down! The concepts made perfect, good sense. And they were based on biblical principles—romance God's way.

Andie tried to get my attention several times. When I looked up, she was frowning. "Didn't you hear the announcement?"

"What announcement?" I looked around. Choir members were raising their hands for something.

"They're doing a head count for the McDonald's in Salina. Do you want a burger or something else?"

"What are the choices?" I asked.

She told me it was either burgers with the works—no special orders since we were only going to stop for a few minutes—or grilled chicken sandwiches.

"Better tell Mrs. Duncan you were spacing out," Andie admonished.

I trudged up to the front of the bus and gave my burger

order. When I returned, the book on God's will for a mate was nowhere to be seen.

"Andie!"

"What?"

"Where's the book?"

"Which one?"

"C'mon, you know." I could see she'd set me up.

"Oh, this." She held it up, wearing a smirk.

"It would be nice if I could actually finish it before you start it."

She was reluctant—already had her finger stuck in the second page. "Well, I absolutely have to read the rest . . . and soon."

"Okay, I'll hurry." The truth was, I didn't want to rush through it. Now that I was actually able to date, the idea of courtship was intriguing. There were definitely times I found myself thinking about what my future would be like. Who I would marry, or if I would at all. . . .

My mom's marriage record wasn't exactly the best, obviously. She and Daddy had suffered through a separation and then divorce by the time I was eight years old. I was hardly old enough to know what was going on but old enough to know it hurt. Bad. Their divorce had left a skeptical imprint stamped in my mind, especially about the happily-ever-after kind of love.

Now, though, Mom seemed settled and happy with Jack Patterson, and they were starting a brand-new family together. The big difference, the way I saw it, was that Mom and Uncle Jack were both dedicated Christians. And they worked hard at their relationship, which was something lots of couples with kids seemed to neglect.

Anyway, I wanted my marriage to last forever. And I knew if I could follow the radical precepts in Paula's book, it just might happen for me.

Someday.

Thinking about what I'd read—about giving myself totally

to Jesus and falling in love with *Him*—made me wonder if the unique message of the book had been the reason for the change in Jared. Danny too.

Quickly, I found my place and began reading again, blocking out Andie's chatter with Paula and Kayla. Even the stopover for fast food couldn't keep my nose out of the book.

If only I had read something like this earlier. I could have saved myself the heartache of the boy-girl thing. I'd had too many emotional ups and downs over guys.

I could hardly wait to email a note to Sean. But I wouldn't be so bold as to share with him about my fabulous new discovery. Not yet, anyway.

Chapter 6

In Colby, Kansas, I turned the book over to Andie just as I spotted the city limits sign. She was thrilled and dived right into it.

On the opposite side of the bus, Paula, Kayla, and I discussed some of the alternatives to modern dating as presented in the book. Things like hanging out in groups and being platonic friends with the opposite sex. And parental involvement in the choice of a mate. Most of all, being patient as God worked out His loving plan for our lives.

"I'd give anything to skip over the crushes of my life," I admitted softly, glancing around to make sure neither Danny nor Jared was within earshot.

"I know what you mean," Paula said. "The dating game is for the birds. You get hurt because the boy might end up liking someone else after a while."

Kayla nodded her head. "That's so true."

Paula continued, "Some people say you can't find God's choice unless you date lots of people. But waiting for God's perfect timing—waiting for *Him* to bring along your life mate— makes a lot more sense."

"Spiritual sense, too," I whispered.

Andie perked up her ears. "Hey, what am I missing over there?"

"Nothing compared to that," I replied, pointing to the book in her hands.

"Oh good." And she went back to reading.

💜 💜 💜

I did finally have a chance to talk with Jared before our bus made its way over the first mountain pass west of Denver, Colorado.

"I don't know if I ever apologized for hurting you the way I did last year," Jared said at one of the stops to stretch our legs.

"Well, you did," I reminded him. "Many times."

He smiled wistfully. "I wish I'd known then what I know now about trusting the Lord for my romantic future."

"You're not the only one." We walked back toward the bus, and I felt joyful. Jared and I really were good friends now. The old boy-girl thing was gone between us. Both of us wanted God's best for the other—the way it always should've been.

Andie was saying some of the same things when she finished reading. In fact, it seemed that half the bus was buzzing about the book.

"Doesn't it beat a Marty Leigh mystery?" Paula asked.

"All to pieces," I said, realizing that I might consider reading nonfiction for a change.

Andie chuckled. "I wondered when the three of you would come to your senses about mysteries."

"They're better than those silly romance novels you read," I countered.

Andie shook her head. "You mean the romance novels I *used* to read." She glanced at the book in her lap. "Now I'm not so sure."

"Maybe someday I'll sprinkle some of these ideas into one of my novels for teen girls." Sounded like the perfect plan to me.

"Don't forget, I get the first dedication," Paula said with a smile, showing off her perfect white teeth.

"Why, because she showed you the book?" Andie retorted. "But I'm your best friend, don't forget."

"We're all best friends," I said. And I could tell by the twinkle in her eye, Andie understood.

♥ ♥ ♥

It was almost dusk when the bus pulled into the parking lot of the high school. Mrs. Duncan suggested we all head home and get a good night's rest. "You're all excused from turning in home-work assignments to all your classes tomorrow," she said.

Danny raised his hand. "When will we know if we placed?"

"No later than next Thursday."

The kids, including me, groaned. How could we wait that long?

I hugged my girl friends good-bye, promising to meet them for lunch in the school cafeteria tomorrow.

It didn't take long for me to spot our family van, but when I looked more closely, I noticed Stan was sitting in the driver's seat.

I shoved away the thought of complaining. At least I had a ride home.

As it turned out, Stan had taken time out from the Sunday evening service to come for me. No heading home or resting for me. He drove back to church, where Mom, Uncle Jack, and all the kids were sitting in the seventh pew from the front. On the left side, as usual.

We tiptoed in and sat in the back—Stan and I. Exhausted from my whirlwind weekend, I let myself slouch down in the seat a bit. Stan shot me a superior, almost parental look.

"I'm beat, okay?" I whispered.

He looked away, acting disgusted. And that's how things got started again between us.

❤   ❤   ❤

All through the following week, Stan was his non-adorable self, chewing me out whenever possible. Over the weirdest stuff, too.

For instance, Tuesday he came into my room, where I was folding some baby blankets in the crib. He scowled as he watched, then started to remind me that he was not, under any circumstances, going to feed, change, or burp Mom's new baby.

"Hey, don't tell me about it," I said.

His face flushed red. "Holly, you're taking things for granted about this baby—"

"Who isn't even born yet," I interrupted, studying him. "I can only hope that April doesn't turn out to have any of your sinister qualities."

He shook his head. "You're grasping at straws."

"Here, catch." I threw a pink plastic baby bottle at him. "It's high time you get the feel of things. Someday you'll wish you knew how to do all this wonderful baby stuff—for your own son or daughter. Or, hey, here's a concept: Maybe, just maybe, you'll want to help your wife out. What about that?"

He snorted something that I didn't quite catch. And really didn't want to.

"You know, there's nothing sissy at all about any of this," I offered.

He scratched his head, like he was trying to figure me out. "I told you, Holly. It's a girl thing." And with that, he threw the bottle back at me and left the room.

Frustrated, I hurried to my door and closed it. Ah, peace at last. And time for another journal entry. Maybe, I thought, if I wrote down my frustrations, I'd feel better.

Tuesday, April 10: The oldest brousin is hopeless, as in completely gone. I'm referring to Stan, which comes as no surprise. When I look back over the pages of this secret diary, it's obvious that the boy has dished out nothing but harassment ever since his father married my mother.

Now . . . on a lighter side. Mrs. Duncan told us today that she'll have the outcome of the competition in two more days. Andie suspects that she already knows but is waiting till our principal returns from an administrative conference before announcing the news.

Anyway, between Mom's bouts with sleepless nights (she really does think the baby might come early!) and the possibility of show choir going to Washington during spring break, I'm freaked out.

If only Stan would cool it with his ridiculous macho remarks!

Chapter 7

*Thursday, April 12: Things couldn't be better! We're fly-
ing to the nation's capital in exactly eight days—the high-
school show choir, that is.*

*Our chorus's status has finally hit the papers, and there
was an exclusive interview with Mrs. Duncan on the Dressel
Hills evening news.*

*My friends can hardly believe we're going, especially
Paula and Kayla, who have relatives in Pennsylvania. Paula's going to ask Mrs. Duncan tomorrow about getting them
in to see us sing.*

*My family? Now, that's a problem. Mom's so sure that
the baby is coming early. And Uncle Jack wants to talk to me
tonight after supper. Shoot, I can almost imagine what he's
going to say. I only hope the baby arrives before I leave!*

*To round off the fabulous things in my life, a long email
came from Sean today. He's planning to attend college days
at George Washington University, which isn't far from the
location of our competition. (I looked it up on the Internet.)
Of course, he has no idea I'm going to be there that same
weekend, but I'm sure he'll want to know. So . . . one email-
writing session coming up!*

♥ ♥ ♥

After the supper dishes were cleared away and loaded in the dishwasher, Uncle Jack sat me down in the living room. Mom had already gone upstairs to get off her feet, which seemed to be swelling, my stepdad informed me.

Stan was out with some friends, and the rest of my siblings were either tending to homework or waiting for family devotions to begin.

"I think we need to talk," Uncle Jack began softly. His wavy brown hair looked disheveled from the long day, and a five-o'clock shadow stubbled his chin. "Your mother and I are thrilled for you about the high-school choir competitions back East. There's only one little hitch."

Here it comes, I thought.

"If the baby comes early, we're going to need you here, Holly."

Mom had already said the same thing, in so many words. But hearing it from Uncle Jack made it sound terribly final.

"The choir's flying out a week from tomorrow," I told him.

The school board had decided to pitch in half of each plane ticket. The rest had come from past parent-teacher association fund-raisers.

Uncle Jack glanced at the calendar on the lamp table near the couch. "Let's see, that's Friday, April 20?"

I nodded. The baby was due exactly five days later, on April 25.

Uncle Jack scrunched his lips. "That's cutting it close."

"I'm really praying about this," I volunteered, "so if it's okay with you, let's not plan for the worst."

He chuckled good-naturedly, and I felt the heaviness lift.

Soon he was calling for the rest of the family, and instead of having devotions in the living room, we gathered in the master bedroom upstairs. That way, Mom's swollen feet and ankles could be elevated, and she could relax.

I listened to the Scripture reading but couldn't keep my mind on the story that followed. I was too deep in thought, pondering how incredible it was going to be to sing and compete against America's best ensemble groups.

Remembering Miss Hess, my choral director from junior high, I wondered how she must be feeling about the news. Surely it was a direct result of her careful training that the choir was at this present level of excellence. I decided to stop by the junior high after school tomorrow and pay her a visit.

After our prayers Mom let Carrie and Stephie talk to the baby sister in her stomach. I hurried off to my room to send a note to Sean.

Andie called in the middle of my note. Evidently Stan had arrived home, picking up the phone on the first ring. He shouted up the stairs to me, his voice sounding polite in spite of the volume, probably because Uncle Jack was sitting nearby.

I took the hall phone. "Hey, what's up?"

"Hey." Andie paused. "What's Stan doing home?"

"He lives here." I giggled.

"I know that, silly. But I thought you said he was going out with friends."

"They must be done doing whatever it was they did."

We both burst into laughter.

"Seriously," she said, "I was wondering if Stan's read that book on praying for God's choice in a mate."

"Oh . . . I get it."

"No, it's not what you're thinking," she insisted.

"You mean you don't still like my stepbrother?"

"C'mon, Holly. You should know what I mean. After reading that book and all."

"So where's the book now?"

"Paula returned it to the church library. But if you're so desperate to finish it, why don't you just buy it?" I suggested. "The Christian bookstore has it, as well as others like it."

"Great idea. I'll check things out tomorrow after school."

"Okay, but I was hoping you'd come along with me to visit Miss Hess."

"Should I see if Paula and Kayla want to go, too?"

"Perfect." So it was set—we were going to stop by and visit our old stomping grounds. And a favorite teacher.

However, not once during the course of our phone chat did I bring up my conversation with my stepdad. No sense having Andie worry about something that most likely wouldn't happen anyway.

Chapter 8

The following Monday, Sean Hamilton called long-distance. "We could meet somewhere in D.C. and have lunch." He sounded very excited.

"How long will you be there?" I asked.

"Three days . . . my plane leaves for home early Tuesday morning. You?"

"We're leaving this Friday and coming back next Wednesday."

"Great! We should be able to squeeze in some time on Monday to tour the monuments or see the Smithsonian. Okay with you?"

"Well, I think our director is scheduling a tour for the whole choir on Monday," I replied. "Maybe it would work out for you to join us."

Sean didn't hesitate. "That'd be fine." He went on to give me a cell phone number where he could be reached, and I gave him mine and the hotel number where the choir was staying.

"This'll be really terrific, Holly," he said. "I'm looking forward to seeing you again."

I could almost see Sean's face. His voice sounded like he was really happy. So was I!

♥ ♥ ♥

The visit back to the former junior-high building the next day brought with it nostalgic feelings. Andie got it started. She talked about the day the ambulance came and took Jared Wilkins away after a mishap on the ropes during timed tests in PE. Then, one after another, Paula, Kayla, and I began to recount the events of our two years in those halls of ivy.

"Does everyone remember when Danny Myers had a big crush on Holly?" Andie asked, looking at Paula and Kayla.

"I think he still does," Paula said. She fluffed her hair and grinned at me.

"Crushes come and go," I said. "But true love, now, that's what I want!"

"Remember, the most important thing is to remain simply good friends until God brings along the right person." Kayla was sounding like a quote from the book.

"But how will we know when our future husband shows up?" Andie asked, glancing at me.

"The book says to be in prayer about it, asking God to show you—to make it very clear—and the timing will be perfect, too."

"Man, it's hard to picture it happening like that when we've been programmed so differently," Kayla commented. "I mean, the media plays up dating and sex as though they're the things to do. But I know not everyone conducts their life that way."

Andie agreed. "It's like Hollywood and the music scene is trying to brainwash us into believing a lie."

By the time we arrived upstairs in Miss Hess's cozy choir room, we were all completely sold on the book's approach to romance—God's way.

"Well, hello there, girls," Miss Hess said, looking up from her desk. "What brings you here?"

"Haven't you heard the news?" Andie asked, her dark eyes shining.

"I certainly have," our former choir director replied. "I've been following the competition results very closely. You know, Mrs. Duncan and I are good friends."

"Cool," I said. "Do you and Mrs. Duncan confer with each other about music?"

She got up and went to the piano, leaning on the back of it the way she always used to. "You may not know this, but Mrs. Duncan and I worked out some of the scores for *The Sound of Music* together last year."

"You did?" I cherished this comfortable link back to seventh- and eighth-grade days. "Are you doing another musical this year?"

"I guess you could call it that. We're doing a Victorian melodrama complete with heroine, hero, and a wicked villain. It's written by our own school librarian, and right now I'm putting the final touches on the olio, which is a collection of musical performances following the actual drama."

"Wow, can we see what you're doing?" I inched toward the desk. It was the same desk I'd snooped at last year, when I was too impatient to wait for the posted list of students who had been cast in *The Sound of Music*.

Miss Hess, her clothes as stylish and colorful as ever, agreed to show us her work. "We really have quite a strong orchestra this year," she pointed out, showing us the various orchestral scores she'd handwritten.

"Whoa, this looks awesome," Andie commented.

"Yeah," I agreed. "When's the show?"

"May 10 and 11 . . . we're presenting it two consecutive nights."

"Same as last year," I said, fond memories flying back.

"Ah, the good old days," Andie teased, putting her arm around me. "I think Holly misses the spotlight."

We laughed and talked for a while longer; then I got brave and asked Miss Hess if she knew anything about Mr. Barnett, her student teacher from last year.

"Oh yes, I certainly do." She said it as though he were a special friend. "Mr. Barnett is a high-school drama coach in St. Paul, Minnesota."

"Really?" Just hearing her mention his name brought all the crazy, crushy days zooming back.

"He and I correspond occasionally," she volunteered. "I think we were very fortunate to have Mr. Barnett come here."

I didn't say another word. Not with Andie and Paula staring at me like they thought I might still have feelings for the guy. Of course, I didn't. All that was far behind me now.

"Are all of you in show choir?" asked Miss Hess.

"Yep," Andie said. "And we're loving every minute of it."

"And you must be the accompanist?" She grinned at Andie.

That's when I spoke up. "She's fabulous. You should hear her play the interlude to some of our songs." Which got Andie an invitation to show off.

She sat right down, without being begged, and played.

"Oh, I miss having you around," Miss Hess said. "Good pianists are a dime a dozen, but pianists who can actually follow a director, now, there's a dying breed."

Andie beamed, and I was proud of my friend.

We said our good-byes, and I left the building with a sad, lumpy feeling in my throat. I wondered if my friends felt the same way; all of us were quiet until we got out to the sidewalk.

"Man, I miss that place," Andie said.

"Me too." I linked arms with my girl friends.

Paula and Kayla smiled sentimental, look-alike smiles as we waited for the city bus. The bus stop was across the street and down about a half block, facing the Soda Straw, one of our favorite spots, even now that we were hot-shot freshmen.

"Do you remember when Holly dressed up like a Catholic nun and eavesdropped on Mr. Barnett and Miss Hess at the Soda Straw?" Andie said.

I groaned. "Oh please!"

"Hilarious," Paula said. "And remember how Holly's hair was hanging out of the nun's wimple?" The twins laughed and teased me even more.

Now it was my turn. "What about the promise I made to your mom there, Andie?"

"You said you'd watch over me when I went to California with you last summer," she said. "What a mess I got myself into."

"No kidding."

The bus was coming, and it was probably a good thing. Sometimes rehashing the past can dig up pain you'd rather not deal with in front of people—even your best friends.

I dropped the subject, and we turned our attention toward the choir trip and our hopes for a win at nationals.

"Even if we don't place, it's going to be a wonderful experience for everyone," Paula offered.

"My mom says so, too," said Andie.

I kept quiet, letting the others voice their feelings. It wasn't time to tell anyone about Sean's and my plans to meet. They might think I wasn't sincere when I agreed with them that romance God's way was best.

Chapter 9

My mother started having labor pains early Wednesday morning, two days before the scheduled choir trip. And a full week before she was supposed to be due!

I didn't even want to go to school, I was that upset. Here she was going to have the baby and spoil my hopes for singing at the competition. And for seeing Sean again.

Of course, this was all very selfish, the way I felt. But the frantic, hopeless feeling persisted, and by noon, I'd called the hospital twice.

Andie hovered close to my phone as I listened to the nurse on the other end. "Did your mom have her baby yet?" she whispered.

I shook my head and hung up, then scuffed my foot against the waxed floor. "Mom's definitely in labor but not even close to delivering. Can you believe this?" I moaned and stomped off to the cafeteria, Andie trailing behind.

"Are you really sure your stepdad meant you'd have to stay home from the choir competition?" she asked.

"Uncle Jack never talks in riddles. It's clear, all right. He wants to be in the delivery room when his baby is born, which means I'm needed at home."

"Oh, Holly," she wailed, "I thought you were praying about this!"

"I have been." I turned to look at her. "Have you?"

"Not actually prayed . . . no."

"Well, if you're so worried, why not?" It was a harsh thing to say, and I was immediately sorry.

"Look, the way I see it, something big has to happen in order for you to go to Washington, D.C.," she insisted.

"Such as?"

"Like maybe . . ." She thought for a moment. "Like if your mom has the baby today or even tonight, she might be home by Friday."

"Nice try." It wasn't really, but Andie seemed desperate to help. "There's another reason why Mom's got to have this baby soon . . . like today," I said as we waited in the hot-lunch line.

Andie frowned, and I knew she had no clue. "Why?"

"Because of Sean Hamilton."

"I'm confused. What about Sean?"

"Well, it just so happens that he's going to be visiting the campus at George Washington University during college days. This very weekend he's checking out the premed program." I didn't say that he and I were hoping to spend some time together. One bombshell at a time.

"Oh, so now you tell me." She reached for a fruit salad on a bed of semi-wilted lettuce.

"You're going to eat that?" I joked.

"Oh no, you don't. You don't get off that easy!"

We paid for our lunches and headed over to the area where we usually sat—as far away from the seniors as possible, but close enough to the big window to enjoy the sunny springtime.

Andie stared me down until I started explaining things. Like how I was excited to know that Sean would be in Washington,

D.C., and how I'd already talked to Mrs. Duncan about his coming along on one of the choir's tours.

"Really?" She stopped eating, her fork dangling between her
fingers. "Then you must've been fooling me about waiting for
the perfect mate."

I'd figured she might think this. "Don't you understand? Sean
and I have been friends—just friends—from the very beginning.
He and I are not romantically involved. Nothing like that."

"Yeah, right. When have I heard that before?"

"Well, it's true."

"Then why do you want to see him so badly?"

"We miss each other. What's so terrible about that?"

"Nothing, I just—"

"Look, I don't think you and I are going to see eye to eye on
this," I interrupted. "Why can't you trust me? Sean and I really
are just good friends."

She tilted her head, unconsciously questioning me from across
the table. "Would you be willing to forfeit seeing him?"

"Why . . . because of the book?"

"Well, that and because it sounds like your parents are counting on you here at home."

I sighed. "First of all, not seeing Sean has nothing to do with
waiting or not waiting for God's will, and second . . . how long
does it take to have a baby?"

♥ ♥ ♥

The answer to my question came hours later. Many hours,
unfortunately.

I was trying to get Carrie and Stephie to stop whining about
going to bed, while Mark and Phil insisted that their dad had said
they could stay up till he got home from the hospital.

"But he might not be back till midnight or later," I
explained.

"So?" Mark said.

I talked straight to my droopy-eyed brousins. "The way I see it, you two can stay up as late as you like. Just don't complain tomorrow when you have to get up early for school, all wiped out."

Man, I was really beginning to sound like somebody's parent!

Stan was no help. He hid away in his room, shutting out his family as I tried desperately to cope with the real possibility of missing out on a school trip of a lifetime. All the while attempting to keep the house running and my younger siblings on their usual schedules. I was barely holding my own.

💜 💜 💜

"Lord, please let Mom have her baby soon," I prayed, getting myself ready for bed. "It's not just because I want to go to Washington on Friday—although that would be fabulous. It's more like so I won't lose my sanity, staying here!"

I pulled on my warmest bathrobe and padded downstairs in my slippers. My younger siblings were all tucked in for the night. It was time for me to have a little talk with Stan.

There was a light shining from under his door. Good! He was still up.

"It's open," he called when I knocked.

I poked my head in just a bit. "You busy?"

"Who, me?" He laughed, and I hoped this might be easier than I'd first thought.

Honestly, I didn't want to step foot in his room—the epitome of messy. Everywhere I looked, clothes were draped over chairs, strewn around on the floor . . . even dangling off a lampshade.

"Dad won't be thrilled about this," I said, referring to the major pigsty.

"Dad's not here, is he" came the reply.

"No, but I am." I held my breath and moved past the doorway

and into the room a few inches. "Your room doesn't meet my standards, so would it be possible to meet me in the kitchen, say, in five minutes?"

He glanced at his watch, then up at me, a quizzical look on his face. "Now's fine."

It was the answer I was hoping for. I turned and left the eyesore behind. It seemed weird being the only one up in the house—except for Stan, of course. Knowing that my younger brothers and sisters were snuggled safely in their beds (after waiting up for so long, they had finally fallen asleep!), created a peculiar response in me. This emotion I didn't fully understand. Maybe it came out of a sense of responsibility—one I wasn't exactly sure I was ready to take on—or just plain being needed. A response Stan sure could use about now.

The phone rang, and I jumped to get it. "Hello?"

"Holly, it's Uncle Jack. I wanted to check in with you before you head for bed. Is everything okay there?"

Did I dare tell him about my chaotic evening with his children? Should I mention the horrid state of affairs in Stan's room? Or Stan's lousy attitude?

"Holly?" He sounded worried.

"Uh, things are fine. How's Mom?"

"It's become quite a struggle, I'm afraid. The docs are talking surgery—Caesarean section."

"Oh no."

"I'm not wild about it, either, but if it's going to mean the difference between—"

"Mom's all right, isn't she?" I blurted.

"She's fine; it's the baby we're worried about."

I cringed. I really didn't want to hear any more. Right now, the only thing I could think about was Mom. If she lost this baby, too, well . . . she just couldn't!

"Please don't worry, honey," Uncle Jack was saying.

Now he tells me, I thought.

"I'll pray," I said.

"That's good . . . please pray," he whispered.

We continued talking—about what to do if Stephie became frightened in the night or if Mark needed his inhaler . . . important stuff like that. As for me, I didn't mention the choir trip looming before me. Or the fact that his firstborn son was now standing over me, glaring.

"Please tell Mom I love her," I said.

"I sure will, and she loves you, too, Holly. We both do. And thanks for everything you and Stan are doing to help."

Stan? What was *he* doing?

I hung up after we said good-bye and felt completely at liberty to unload on my brousin. "Your father seems to think you're involved here, helping keep the home fires burning, but what he doesn't know is you're shirking your duty as a member of this family!"

I brushed past him and went to the other side of the kitchen, leaning on the sink the way Mom did sometimes when we were having a serious talk.

"What're you so high and mighty about?" he muttered.

"Mom's having trouble," I said. "She might need to have a C-section."

"That bad?"

"The doctors must think so." I paused a moment before going on. "What's really bad around here, though, is you. Don't you realize I'll probably end up missing the national choir competitions? And it's all because of you!"

"Me?" He was playing dumb, a role he knew well.

"Look, if you were half the man you think you are, you'd get off your duff and actually help out around here."

"Why? So you can go off and see your boyfriend?" he jeered.

"Sean's not my boyfriend any more than you're a responsible big brother." The words stung the air as they flew off my lips.

Stan pulled out a barstool and sat down, flashing angry eyes at me.

"Think about it—what is it you do when you're needed the most?" I said, bringing the focus of things back to him. "I'll tell you . . . you run and hide, that's what!"

Stan smirked. "I'm not into kids . . . or babies . . . right now."

Glancing around, I played into his ridiculous comment, paving the way for my own comeback. "I don't see any babies around. But there sure are a bunch of sleeping kids in this house."

He shook his head arrogantly. "You don't get it, do you? You're the girl, and I'm the guy. Girls are supposed to do this stuff."

"Since when?"

"Since the beginning of time," he said. "Since Adam tilled the soil and Eve raised the kids."

"So . . . why aren't you out plowing or planting? What're you waiting for?"

"You're carrying this too far, Holly," he retorted. It was obvious he had no logical, sane response. His deceased mother would be turning over in her grave about now.

"Someday, if God permits, and I almost pray He doesn't, you'll probably marry some nice young woman. The two of you will eventually want to have children, but that's where the picture goes blurry. The nice husband and father . . . where is *he?*"

Suddenly he got up, almost knocking over the barstool. His abrupt movement startled me. "Are you finished?" he demanded. "Because if you are, I'm going to bed."

I didn't have the nerve to continue. My message had been loud and clear. I could only hope my ignorant brousin would take it to heart.

My dream, and possibly my future, depended on it.

Chapter 10

The sound of birds awakened me the next morning. Imagine! Birds this early in Colorado high country.

I was so disoriented that I nearly forgot Mom and the baby and my dilemma about the choir trip. Glancing at the clock, I discovered that I had a good twenty minutes before the alarm was scheduled to sound off.

Instead of nestling back down under the covers, I got up and tiptoed to Mom and Uncle Jack's bedroom. No one was there—Uncle Jack had spent the night in the hospital, it appeared.

I closed the door and hurried to the phone, dialing the hospital—directly to Mom's private room.

Uncle Jack answered on the first ring. He sounded groggy, and I could almost visualize him having slept in a chair all night. Probably at Mom's bedside.

"I was going to give you a call later, but you beat me to it," he began after we exchanged greetings. "Your mother, stubborn gal that she is, was so determined to have this baby naturally. But along about three-thirty this morning, she and the docs decided it was best for the baby to be taken by surgery."

"So my sister's already born? She's here . . . and perfectly okay?"

"She certainly is," he said, pride bursting from every word. "And wait'll you see her. April Michelle is an absolute apple dumplin'—a real charmer."

"And Mom? How's Mom?"

"Kind of out of it," he explained. "She'll probably stay here over the weekend, at least. I won't be surprised if they keep her longer."

There goes the choir trip, I agonized.

"I really do wish the timing had been different," he said apologetically. "I'm counting on you, Holly-Heart."

"I know" was all I could muster.

"Well, I have a feeling there'll be other choir trips." He said it out of sympathy. Nothing else. What he didn't know was there would probably never be another moment in time like this for me. Not for the Dressel Hills High School Show Choir.

And Sean? I knew I might as well forget about seeing him again for a very long time.

"Holly? You still there?"

"Oh . . . uh-huh." I felt torn between the missed trip and the announcement about my new baby sister. "How much does April weigh?" I asked.

"Eight pounds and eleven ounces . . . she's filled out beautifully . . . and pink! I don't know when I've seen a prettier newborn baby."

"I can't wait to hold her."

"Stan will have to bring all of you up to the hospital after school."

With the mention of "school," my alarm clock went off in my room. I could hear its muffled yet shrill tones coming through the door.

"I think I'd better spread the news here," I said. "Besides, I've never had to get this many kids off to school by myself."

"What do you mean?" He sounded irked. "Isn't Stan pulling his share of the load?"

Do I dare tell on him? I sighed, trying to decide what to do.

"Holly? What's going on?"

Desperate for some adult intervention, I struggled. "I guess . . . I think things'll be okay."

"You think?"

"Oh, it's probably no big deal." I could feel myself caving in. "But Stan and I are kinda on the outs right now. He doesn't see why he should have to help so much—it's 'women's work.' "

Uncle Jack chuckled. "Stan said that?"

"In so many words."

"Well, that's going to stop, and I'll be the one to see to it."

I groaned. "Stan will never let me live this down."

"Don't you worry, kiddo. I'll handle this."

We said good-bye and I made a mad dash for the bathroom. I figured if I showered before Carrie and Stephie got up, most everything else would go smoothly.

♥ ♥ ♥

I thought wrong.

First of all, nobody wanted to get up. Secondly, I looked everywhere for the plug-in—the electric frying pan didn't work without it—but found nothing. This meant nobody would be having any protein, as in bacon or sausage, with their breakfast. Not today.

"Why don't you make waffles, like Mom does?" Carrie hollered from the nearest barstool.

"Why don't you keep your ideas to yourself?" I snapped. "We don't have time."

"Yeah, you didn't get up quick enough," Stephie said, pouting.

"Neither did you." I motioned for her to wash the toothpaste off her chin. "Today's going to be a cereal and toast day, and if anyone has a problem with it, he or she can sign up for extra chores."

Mark's eyes bugged out, and he marched out of the kitchen and into the dining room, obviously upset.

Phil adjusted his wire rims and gave me a pensive, academic stare. "Has anyone seen the *Wall Street Journal?*"

"It's probably still out on the driveway," I replied. "If you want it, go get it."

"Eew, she's mad," Stephie whispered to Carrie, showing her dimples.

I turned around, handed her a full carton of milk, and smiled as sweetly as I possibly could under the circumstances. "Not mad, sweetie, just ticked OFF!" Somehow my voice had taken on a life of its own, creating its very own crescendo.

And Stephie jumped back in response to it, spilling milk all over herself. And I mean all over.

"Hurry, somebody get some towels!" Then I began to shriek for Stan, who had not yet made his morning appearance. "Get your tail out here and help me!" It wasn't just any plea; it was a full command.

Of course, Stan didn't appear on cue. Not our too-good-to-lift-a-finger-when-most-needed eldest sibling. Nope. He sauntered into the kitchen a good three minutes later while Carrie, Stephie, and I were down on our hands and knees mopping up the floor with bath towels from upstairs—with a little help from Goofey, too.

"Mom's gonna have a cow if you don't get this milky smell out of her good towels," Carrie informed me.

"It wasn't my idea to use the best ones in the house," I shot back. "Besides, you know where the washing machine is, right?"

She got the message and whined as she carried the drippy, milky towels, all rolled up in the largest mixing bowl I could find, downstairs to the laundry room.

"Whew, what a morning," I said, trying to avoid eye contact with Stan as I stood up.

He was tiptoeing around the yucky floor, heading for the dining room with a bowl of dry cereal in hand. "We all out of milk?" he had the nerve to ask.

I didn't even justify his stupidity with an answer. The guy was a washout! As a stepbrother . . . as a human being!

Turning my attention to Stephie, I guided her back upstairs to the bathroom, where she began to undress. I drew some warm bathwater to expedite things.

"Will I be late for school?" she asked tearfully.

"Not if I can help it."

"Will you write a note for my teacher if I am?" she pleaded.

I thought about that. Did I have the right to do such a thing? "We'll see," I said, attempting to reassure her. "Maybe Daddy will come home and surprise us. I'm sure he'll be needing a warm shower and a change of clothes this morning."

She smiled. The thought of her dad showing up on a hectic school morning must've warmed her heart. I know it did mine.

And as it turned out, Uncle Jack made it home in time to kiss all of us good-bye.

"We've got us a new baby." He beamed.

I wanted to ask if maybe, just maybe, I could possibly start thinking about packing for the choir trip tomorrow—that maybe he and Stan could alternate running the family until next Wednesday, when Mrs. Duncan and our show choir flew back home to Dressel Hills.

But no, I was overcome with shyness and a bit of dread. And not wanting to confront Stan with my brain wave right in front of our dad, I kept my mouth shut and headed off to school.

Chapter 11

Andie was a whirlwind of chatter when I caught up with her in the hall. "What's the deal?" she asked, almost demanding an answer. "I mean, your mom's had her baby, so what's keeping you here?"

"It's complicated." I sighed, not wanting to rehash things.

She stared at me, wrinkling up her face. "I don't get it. What's the problem?"

"Let's just say: Be glad, be very glad, you are not Stan's girlfriend."

"Huh?" Her face wore a giant frown. "Holly, you're not making a bit of sense."

"Take it from me: He would be an unfit husband if you·and he ever ended up married. And that's all I'm saying." I turned to go.

"Whoa. What's this about?"

I glanced back at her, spouting over my shoulder, "Stan's the key. He's the reason I can't go."

"Stan?" She was running after me now. "Why him?"

"The boy's got no sense of responsibility. He refuses to help at home. I'm stuck here because I'm the only mature offspring presently able to handle things for my parents."

She stopped with me at my locker. "What if I had a little talk with Stan?"

Shaking my head, I made her vow not to breathe a word. "Don't you dare. He's already a royal pain, and if you start hammering away at the shoulds and shouldn'ts of his life, it'll just cause more trouble for me."

She reluctantly agreed. "When will you know if you're going or not?"

"As it stands this minute, it's been decided—I'm not."

"So"—her dark eyes grew wide and she twisted a curl with her pointer finger—"are you saying we have one day to turn this whole thing around?"

Leave it to Andie. I hugged her hard. Never, ever had there been a better friend.

Suddenly I remembered the promise Uncle Jack had made on the phone earlier. "I'll work on Uncle Jack," I said, "if you'll pray . . . really pray!"

"And you're positive I shouldn't say anything to Stan?"

"Absolutely." I fumbled for the cell phone in my pocket. "Sorry to cut this short, but I have to make a quick call."

"No problem," she said. "I'll catch you later."

I flipped open the phone and hit the speed dial.

"You have reached the residence of a very proud father," Uncle Jack said first thing.

"Hey, that's a nice touch." I laughed.

"Holly? Is everything all right at school?"

"Sure is." Now that I had him on the line, I didn't know how to begin or what to say.

"Something on your mind?" he asked.

I said it. Came right out and asked, "Did you talk to Stan this morning about, uh . . ." I paused, suddenly at a loss for words.

"Oh that. Yes, we intend to work things out after school, probably sometime tonight."

Tonight? Too late.

"Oh."

"Well, if that's all you called about, kiddo, I'm real anxious to get back to the hospital."

"Okay, well, bye." I hung up. Nothing had been settled. I'd have to tell Andie that things looked bleaker than ever. As far as I could see, it would take more than a miracle for me to be on the plane to Washington, D.C.

Tomorrow.

♥ ♥ ♥

I was attempting to follow one of Mom's outstanding recipes for chicken and rice when the phone rang.

Carrie caught it on the first half of the ring. "Meredith-Patterson funny farm," I heard her say from the kitchen.

"Carrie!" I reprimanded, only to witness a stream of giggles. My sister was definitely puberty-bound.

"It's for you," she called.

"Who is it?"

"Andie—she needs you." She peeked around the corner of the dining room, making a smirk.

I washed and dried my greasy hands. "I'll get it out here," I informed her and picked up the portable phone.

"How's kitchen duty?" Andie joked when I answered.

"Very funny."

"Any news?"

"About?"

"You know . . ." She was too eager for an affirmative answer.

"Well, for starters, Stan's in his room and Uncle Jack's not home yet, so there's nothing new."

"I suggest you do your laundry and start packing, just in case," she advised. "You never know what might happen."

"I can just imagine what might happen. The house could burn down and everyone will go hungry if Stan's in charge. You know, I'm actually starting to think maybe I should just stay put."

"Holly! How can you say that?"

I went to the archway between the kitchen and the dining room and poked my head in, scouring for snoopers. And sure enough, Carrie was sitting, knees squashed up to her chin, under the table—eyes wide.

"Excuse me a sec, Andie," I said, making a big deal about this even though I wasn't really that upset. I figured I ought to set a precedent since I was the only one in charge at the moment. I covered the receiver with my hand. "Carrie Meredith—out of there!"

"You sound like a mean mommy," she wailed.

"And I'll be dishing out extra chores like some moms do, too, if you don't watch your mouth."

"I'm sorry," she sputtered.

"I could use some help in the kitchen," I told her. "But give me five minutes."

She nodded compliantly and headed upstairs.

"Andie," I said, returning to the phone. "Okay, now I can talk. Where were we? Oh yes . . . about packing and stuff."

"Why not?" she insisted. "Remember, Sean's expecting to see you."

She didn't have to remind me. "Which brings me to something," I added. "I want you to give him a message for me—you know, explain why I couldn't come."

"So . . . you're giving up. Well, I'm not interested in passing along secondhand information," she said. "You're going to the choir competitions, and that's final!"

"Please, Andie, you're blowing this out of proportion," I said.

"It's not that I don't want to go; I do. But what would you do if you were me?"

"It wouldn't be easy, that's for sure. But like I said at school, now that your mom's had her baby, why can't your stepdad help out?"

I shrugged. Did I dare ask him?

"Please just think about it?" she pleaded.

"Well, if he doesn't come home too tired, maybe I will."

"Too tired?" Andie was beside herself. "You can't just let this go. Maybe I should come over there."

"Not a good idea."

So, once again, I thought things were settled. At least about what step I should take next, which was pretty much zilch.

♥ ♥ ♥

I never even heard Uncle Jack come home.

By the time I fussed and fought with Carrie, and later with Stan, who couldn't spare some time to take us to the hospital to see the baby, I was exhausted. And feeling blue.

I had a very suspicious feeling that Stan was actually putting off seeing our new sister. For some strange—probably macho—reason.

Mark and Phil were much easier to handle than the girls, and when I told them to clean up their rooms after supper and do their homework, they did it. I was shocked.

Fortunately, I had less homework than usual. I headed for my room and started working, only to find that I kept falling asleep at my desk.

When I looked at the clock, it was midnight.

Oh no, I thought. *I've completely lost my chance!*

And sure enough, when I tiptoed down the hall to see if Uncle Jack was home, I spotted his bathrobe lying at the foot of the bed. And, listening for a moment, I heard snoring.

Uncle Jack was home . . . and I'd totally missed him!

Sad and desperate, I headed downstairs for some milk and cookies. The burden of responsibility had already begun to lessen somewhat, just having an adult back in the house, especially at night. But knowing what I was about to miss made me angry.

There was plenty of milk in the fridge—a whole gallon. I reached for it, thankful for a man like Uncle Jack in our lives. Even without a grocery list, he'd taken it upon himself to remember a few of the basic food groups consumed in this household.

Slowly, I poured a glass of milk.

Glancing down, I noticed Goofey. "Did you come to keep a lonely girl company?" I picked him up.

He purred, eyeing my glass. "All right," I said, putting him down and getting his bowl. "If I'm up, you have to be up, too . . . is that it?"

Goofey meowed.

Then I heard a sound in the dining room and turned to see Uncle Jack coming toward the kitchen. "What's this? A midnight snack?" He grinned. "Mind if I join you?"

"Okay."

He sat on a barstool and leaned forward on his elbows. "Guess I should've wakened you earlier."

"That's fine," I said, glad to have this opportunity, at least. "I think I was probably wiped out."

"It certainly looked that way to me. And I must say, not a very good way for a young lady to start out on an important trip."

I turned away from the cookie jar and stared at him. I'd scarcely been listening at this point, thinking he was just coming downstairs to chitchat or have a snack. But this—what had he just said?

"I'm sorry, could you repeat that?" I held my breath.

"I've got you covered, Holly-Heart," he said with a broad grin. "You're going to Washington, D.C."

I ran to him, and stifling a shriek of joy, I hugged the daylights out of him.

"Now, then, do you need some help getting ready?" he asked.

"I'll just do a quick load of laundry, if that's all right." I was fully awake, adrenaline rushing through my veins!

He nodded his approval.

"Oh, thank you, Uncle Jack," I said again. "I hope this isn't going to be a hardship on you. Or Mom."

"Not at all. And Stan's going to have a golden opportunity to learn firsthand what family life's all about."

"Stan?" I gulped. "He's going to be in charge?"

"Not totally. But he'll be in training of sorts, that's for certain."

"In training?"

"Yes, Mrs. Hibbard has agreed to oversee things before and after school till I can get home from work."

I laughed out loud. "Our next-door neighbor? You're kidding! Does Stan know about this?"

"He knows, and he'll have to live with it."

I chuckled, heading upstairs to think through the items of clothing and things I needed for my trip. Mrs. Hibbard, the pickiest little old lady in Dressel Hills, was going to whip Stan Patterson into shape!

Was this poetic justice or what?

Chapter 12

I had only one regret about leaving my family behind: not getting to lay eyes on my baby sister before I left.

Mrs. Duncan was overjoyed about my coming. So was Andie. And if I'm not too presumptuous to say so, I think Jared looked very pleased, too.

I, however, could hardly contain myself as we filed into the coach section of the airplane. "You'll never believe what I was doing at one o'clock this morning," I said, settling into the aisle seat next to Andie.

"Dirty laundry?" She laughed. "I told you, and you didn't listen!"

"Well, for once, you were right." I stuffed my carry-on bag beneath the seat directly in front of me, still wiggling with excitement, not to mention the effects of several glasses of soda.

Uncle Jack would surely have freaked if he'd known what I'd had to drink for breakfast. But adrenaline doesn't last forever, and when you've had only a few hours' sleep, well . . .

The shuttle flight to Denver lasted about forty minutes, and then all of us experienced the fun of finding our way—while trying to stay together—through the maze of security checks, concourses, and underground shuttles at Denver International Airport.

But soon we were seated in the waiting area, ready for the Boeing 737 to fly us to Chicago. There, we'd be changing planes again.

"What will you do when you see Sean?" asked Andie right out of the blue.

"Run up to him, throw my arms around him, and give him a big pucker." I chuckled sarcastically. "What do you think I'll do, silly?"

"Hey, I'm serious."

"So am I." We giggled about it, and when we'd calmed down a bit, I told her that I was actually feeling awkward about meeting Sean again, especially with the whole choir hanging around.

"Aw, it's nothing, right? You're just friends."

I shook my head at her. She had me good.

"So . . . I'm right, there is more to the Sean Hamilton-Holly Meredith story."

"Not really."

"Uh-huh." And she rolled her eyes at me.

♥ ♥ ♥

Chicago's O'Hare International Airport was bustling with people coming and going, and although we didn't have to rush off to catch our connecting flight, I could see that it was difficult for Mrs. Duncan and the three adult sponsors to keep track of us. We were like sheep being herded—all twenty-five of us.

But even as we waited to go down the escalator, I couldn't help thinking about my new sister back home.

Shoot, I hadn't even had a chance to say "thanks" to Mom before I left. And I was pretty sure she had been responsible for my getting to go at the last minute. I decided to call her once we were settled in the hotel.

One by one we stepped onto the moving walkway in the

underground level of the connection terminal, surrounded by some very cool neon and strobe lights.

"What do you think, Holly?" Jared called back to me. "Check out what you would've missed."

"It's fabulous," I replied, watching a chartreuse-orange design blink off the wall.

"Sure is!" Andie poked my back.

Paula crowded in from behind. "Who does your baby sister look like?"

"Uncle Jack says she's a charmer, but since I haven't seen her yet, I really don't know."

"You haven't seen her?" Kayla said, all aghast. "Why not?"

"It's a long story," I explained, "beginning with *S* and ending with *N*."

That's all that needed to be said. She figured it out, especially with Andie's help—who turned around, mouthing nasties about Stan.

"Well, I guess you *are* lucky to be here," Paula said.

"Considering everything, yeah," I replied.

♥ ♥ ♥

That night I wrote in my journal.

Friday, April 19: I can't believe it! Several times during the flight I pinched myself to make sure it wasn't just a glorious dream.

We're staying in this magnificent, old, historic hotel. (We're getting a special rate because there are so many of us.) From the penthouse, Andie, Paula, Kayla, and I checked out the Mall in the distance—what a view! It's not a shopping mall, though. It's a park—a wide, grassy carpet two miles long, running between the Washington Monument and Capitol Hill.

This evening, after we checked into the hotel, we went to the John F. Kennedy Center for the Performing Arts

*building—it's huge, made of marble, and surrounded by
pillars. It also overlooks the Potomac River. That's where our
competition is tomorrow.*

*I'm so excited . . . nervous, too. So is everyone else. Mrs.
Duncan has been great about soothing our fears, encouraging us with her "we can do it" comments. Still, it's fraz-
zling. I mean, here we are. We made districts, state, and
regionals. And the best of the best are competing along with
us.*

Do we have what it takes to win?

I packed my journal-notebook back into the bottom of my
suitcase. Of course, I knew I could trust my girl friends. It wasn't
like being back home with two little snoopers scoping out every
tidbit of my life.

When the Miller twins finished talking to their parents, I used
my cell phone and called the Dressel Hills General Hospital. Two
thousand miles away!

"Mom, hi . . . it's me, Holly."

"Oh, honey, you're there already." She sounded a little
drugged up.

"It's two hours later here."

"That's right." She yawned. "I hope you and your friends are
having a good time."

"Yes, but how are you?"

"Still a bit groggy."

"How's the baby?" I asked.

"Aw, April's so sweet and pretty. She's ready to go home,
but we're stuck here another couple of days."

"That's probably good, Mom. Take your time getting your
strength back, okay?" I didn't want to tell her that she should
stay in the hospital as long as possible. What awaited her at 207
Downhill Court would discourage any surgery patient!

I kept talking. "I didn't get a chance to thank you for talking Uncle Jack into letting me come."

"Oh, I didn't talk him into it. Your brother talked *me* into it."

"What?"

"Stan called last night, sometime after supper, I think. He said you were dying to go with the choir."

"He said that?"

"He certainly did, and when Jack and I talked it over, we decided to ask Mrs. Hibbard to supervise."

"Wow, I had no idea Stan—"

"Yes, you have your stepbrother to thank for this," she said again, beginning to sound a bit droopy. I had a feeling she was going to fall asleep on me.

"Well, I hope you're feeling better real soon, Mom. I love you."

"Love you, too."

"Good-bye. And give April a kiss for me."

"I will."

When I hung up, I told Andie and the twins what Mom had said about Stan. "Can you figure this?"

"Maybe Stan isn't as horrid as you think," Kayla spoke up. But, of course, she didn't really count; she'd been sweet on him since day one.

"He's horrid, all right," I stated. "It's just that he got tired of hearing me hound him about shirking his duty. That's got to be the only reason."

"Well . . . maybe." Andie wore a sly smile.

"Hey, wait a minute." I grabbed a pillow and flung it at her. "Did you have something to do with this?"

"Me? I promised . . . remember?" But her eyes told another story.

"Andie, how can I ever trust you again?" I said, laughing.

"I got you here—didn't I?"

The answer to that was a perfectly fabulous pillow fight—minus a zillion feathers. Nope. These state-of-the-art hotel pillows were the absolute best around.

Hopefully, so was the Dressel Hills Show Choir.

Chapter 13

I don't remember encountering air as thick with anticipation as it was the next afternoon. Right after lunch, no less. Everyone in the choir felt it, too. I could see it on their faces—the brightness, the urgency. The desire to sing to our utmost ability.

We used our allotted time to vocalize, but as warmed up and mellow as we sounded, there were still a few bugs to work out. Things like confidence and poise—all-important elements. Things that, if missing, were sure to stand out.

Since we didn't want to look like hicks from the sticks—not here, surrounded by all the grandeur of the nation's capital—we listened carefully as Mrs. Duncan gave us our final "polishing."

"She's fine-tuning us again," Andie said softly.

I grinned back at my friend. "Yep, Mrs. Duncan is the best."

All lined up and waiting in the wings, we agonized through the melodious sounds of two other choirs ahead of us. One group hailed from West Virginia, not far from here. The other choir was an all-black, all-girl choir from New York City. After hearing their performance, I was worried. These babes were out-of-this-world good, and there was no getting around it—we were up against style and charisma—a total class act.

I caught Mrs. Duncan's eye and shrugged during the audience applause. Promptly, she poked up her thumb and flashed a plucky grin. She believed in us.

And . . . we were next.

The emcee was introducing us as we crept over the silent, velvety floor behind the main curtains. "And now, from colorful Colorado, I give you the Dressel Hills High School Show Choir!"

Of course the audience was jazzed—the last group had wound them up. Anyway, we were greeted with a thunderous welcome. And when the side curtains parted automatically, we walked onto the stage, single file, finding our way to our appointed spots on the risers.

There was no seeing the audience, because the spotlights on us were so hot and bright. Somewhere, out in the sea of blackness, the Miller twins' relatives were watching . . . along with the vice-president of the United States!

I don't know why, but once we stood there, I realized how very high these risers were compared to the ones back home. For a split second, I thought I might become dizzy and, heaven forbid, pass out in front of half the population of . . .

This was déjà vu—recalling a scene from another time and another place—our seventh-grade musical, more than two years back. I could even hear a familiar voice saying, *"Holly Meredith, you're turning green!"* But I shoved that ridiculous thought out of my mind.

Mrs. Duncan gave a cue for Andie to play the four-note chord that started us off on our a cappella madrigals. Thank goodness, the illusion disappeared, and I focused hard on remembering my part—as did each of my choir-member friends.

We sang from our hearts. No question.

Mrs. Duncan's face reflected our enthusiasm. And the coolest thing—we sounded great!

After our performance, we left the stage via another magical portal, unseen by the audience. This was the stuff of fairy tales, and once all of us were in the same place again, we were given a tour of the building. We saw six beautiful theatres housed inside the center. My favorites were the Eisenhower Theatre, mainly for plays, and the Terrace Theatre, where people from all over the world come to experience poetry readings, modern dance, and drama.

I couldn't help wondering what it would be like to play Maria von Trapp—female lead in *The Sound of Music*—on one of those incredible stages.

Next, we took the Metro, an underground subway system with the coolest curved and indented walls and roof—reminding me of Mom's Saturday-morning waffles. Only these were warped!

Lincoln Memorial, next stop. Everyone, it seemed, had to have individual pictures taken in front of Lincoln's huge statue—nineteen feet high. Tears sprang to my eyes as I read the opening lines of the Gettysburg Address, etched in marble. *Four score and seven years ago . . .*

What a place!

Mrs. Duncan gathered all of us for a group shot. Before we disbanded, she asked, "How many want to see Ford's Theatre? We still have time."

Unanimous.

"Anyone tired?" she asked.

No one would admit it. We were in fabulous Washington, D.C., for pete's sake!

Andie, Paula, and I stuck together. Kayla and Amy-Liz were close behind us when we caught the Metro again. Soon we were being whisked downtown . . . and back in time.

The old theater on Tenth Street had been restored to its appearance on that fateful night in 1864, when Abraham Lincoln had been fatally shot. During the story of the assassination—dramatically told by the guide—Andie literally jumped at the shot of the blank gun.

Exhausted but delighted with the events of the day, we headed to the nearest pizza place for supper.

♥ ♥ ♥

"How did your performance go?" Uncle Jack asked later that evening when I called the hospital again.

"Mrs. Duncan says we were great."

"How did you like the Kennedy Center?" he asked.

"Perfect. I think it must be acoustically flawless. I mean, not only could we hear our voices coming through the giant stage speakers, we actually got the feel of the auditorium, even though it was so huge. It's an incredible place." I sighed. "I don't know, I guess it's hard to put into words."

He chuckled a bit. "I guess that's how you might describe the little dumplin' I have here in my arms. You couldn't begin to describe *her* with words."

"Oh . . . you must be holding April," I cooed.

"Just a minute, the whole family's here for a visit." He gave the phone to Mom.

"Hi, Holly-Heart. Did the competition go well?" She sounded pretty much herself again.

"I wish you could've heard us sing."

"Oh, I'm so happy for you, honey."

There was mumbling going on in the background—someone was telling Stan to sit down with the baby.

I almost cracked up. "What's Stan doing?"

"Oh, he asked to hold his baby sister," Mom explained. "And I don't think he quite remembers how. It's been a long time since Stephie was this tiny."

"For sure," I muttered, but I was confused. I really couldn't picture it. Stan—holding a two-day-old infant?

Carrie got on the line next. "Hey, Holly, I think something came in the mail for you, from that publisher person. You know, the one in Chicago?"

"Really? What's the writing look like?"

"Huh?"

"The address on the envelope—whose writing is it?" I knew if it were mine—the self-addressed, stamped envelope—it was a definite rejection.

"I think it was typewritten," she replied.

"Large or small envelope?"

"Small."

"Yes!" This was so fabulous. I couldn't wait to tell Jared.

Briefly, I talked to Mom again, then said good-bye. But even as I hung up the phone, I could not imagine Stan holding baby April.

When I told my roommates about it, they hooted with laughter. None of them could believe it—especially not Andie. Kayla, yeah, because, like I said, she had this major thing for my brousin.

Andie had ordered room service, of all things. "It's part of the deal, right?" she said, laughing it off.

"It's not like we have carte blanche," I reprimanded her. "This stuff is expensive, and the taxpayers of Dressel Hills aren't picking up the tab. We're on our own."

Paula nodded. "Which reminds me, Mrs. Duncan said to go easy on expenditures."

"No kidding." I stared at Andie.

She whipped out a handful of twenties and waved them around. "Maybe, but my dad said we could live it up . . . just a little."

It turned out she'd ordered root beer floats for all of us. When? Who knows. But I have a sneaking suspicion it was while Paula, Kayla, and I went exploring the pool room and spa right after we got back from our tour around the city.

Anyway, we slurped them up, found an old black-and-white

movie on cable TV, and snuggled down for a night of girl talk and giggling.

♥ ♥ ♥

Two hours later, Andie gasped, clutching her throat. Honestly, I thought she was choking. "You haven't called Sean yet, have you?"

I grinned. "Wouldn't you like to know?"

"Holly! C'mon—don't forget who's responsible for getting you here."

"Uh-huh." I grinned back at her.

She leaped onto my bed, followed by Kayla and Paula. "So tell us, is the love of your life coming with us Monday?"

There was no keeping it quiet any longer. "My *friend* is joining us for the FBI tour, and it looks like he'll be able to hang out with us most of the day."

"With us." Andie teased. "C'mon, Holly, we all know it's *you* he wants to see."

I shrugged, thinking they were probably right. Only thing was, how would Sean fit into the group dynamics here? After having established a comfortable long-distance friendship, well, I just didn't know how things would work out in person. I guess I'd find out.

Sooner or later.

Chapter 14

Sunday morning our choir performed a couple of sacred numbers at two different churches in the downtown area. Most of the regional finalists had been scheduled to do the same around town.

One of the locations turned out to be where the president and first lady attended church. Man, did we go through major security rigamarole before entering! But it was definitely worth it to look out into the crowd and see their familiar faces.

Later, after lunch, we sat in on several more performances at the Kennedy Center. Relaxing there beneath one of the dazzling chandeliers, I honestly wondered how the judges could ever begin to choose a winner. Every group sounded fantastic.

Andie, however, was partial to the ensembles with piano accompaniment. Personally, I liked a cappella better. Maybe because there was something almost ethereal about the sound of pure, unaccompanied voices. Anyway, sitting out in the spectacular auditorium sent shivers up my spine. And it whet my appetite for tonight's dinner-theater entertainment to come.

♥ ♥ ♥

Somehow, Jared landed a seat next to me at the table that evening. I was glad, though. This was the perfect opportunity to discuss the status of my manuscript. "I think there might be something waiting for me at home—a response about the story I sent to your uncle."

"Your novella?"

I nodded. "If Carrie's right, I might have an acceptance letter."

He grinned. "I'm not surprised."

"You know about this?" I stared at him incredulously.

He filled me in on the details, and as it turned out, his short story had also been chosen for publication.

"Once again, we'll be published together," I said, remembering the story he'd written under a female pen name—for a girl's magazine, no less!

"Yeah." He gave my arm a teeny squeeze, and even though a bunch of kids from choir witnessed the gesture, I didn't mind. Jared was actually super cool.

♥ ♥ ♥

The next morning, at eight o'clock, Sean met up with us as we waited on E Street for a tour of the J. Edgar Hoover Federal Bureau of Investigation Building. I spotted his short blond hair, and after being nudged nearly out of line by giggly Andie, I called to him.

Sean hurried over, almost sprinting. I was surprised to see how much taller he was—and really tan. "Hey, Holly. It's good to see you again." His smile was warm and endearing.

"Same here," I said, trying to tune out the running dialogue between Andie and the twins behind me. "I'd like you to meet some of my friends."

I spotted Mrs. Duncan ahead of us and led Sean over to meet our choir director and the adult sponsors. I could tell Andie was having a fit by the way she glared at me as we got back in line a few minutes later.

To appease her, I reintroduced Sean to her. "I'm sure you remember Andie Martinez."

He extended his hand like a true gentleman. "Hey, Andie. How's it going?"

While I was introducing Paula and Kayla, Jared happened to come over. "This is Jared Wilkins," I told Sean. Then turning to Jared, I said, "I'd like you to meet my California friend, Sean Hamilton."

The two of them shook hands, too, Jared taking the initiative and striking up a conversation with Sean. I was terribly impressed with Jared's maturity as I observed them together. He'd come a long way since his "jealousy days"!

Soon the long line of eager tourists began to move. Mrs. Duncan had informed us that this was the week for the White House spring garden tour. "That's why America's hometown is overcrowded with sightseers," she explained.

Personally, I was glad the competition had been held this month. I couldn't begin to imagine how crowded Washington, D.C., would be in the summer with school out.

Sean fell into step with me. We talked about his cross-continental flight and where the Dressel Hills choir stood with the competition so far. "A decision will be made by tonight," I told him. "The first-place choir gets to sing at the Capitol, in the rotunda, tomorrow at noon."

"Cool." He grinned. "In front of lots of congressmen?"

"And women."

He laughed. "Of course."

Soon we were led through the entrance to the block-long building—the John Dillinger "death mask" and the Ten Most Wanted list exhibits greeted us. A gripping crime show!

Danny Myers and some of the other guys asked questions, but the guide wasn't stumped by any of them. In fact, he seemed to have an answer for everything, along with additional stories—complete with blood-curdling details.

Because Sean was pursuing a career in medicine, he was most interested in the crime labs, where technicians did all sorts of scrutinizing work. Things like analyzing handwriting and fibers and determining blood types.

Next, we were taken to a room filled with over four thousand guns and twelve thousand different kinds of ammunition. Some of the guys in the group got overtly macho suddenly but not Sean. He listened and observed, like the young gentleman he was.

Last but not least, we witnessed the FBI's very own indoor firing range—noisy and action-packed. We viewed it from behind a glass wall, of course. Personally, I was glad to get out of there!

After the FBI tour we caught the Metrorail, which sped us away to the National Air and Space Museum. Mrs. Duncan told us, before we ever stepped inside, that this was the most-visited museum in the world. More than nine million people visited each year.

When our group was divided in half by our adult sponsors, Andie sulked about it—which meant she wasn't thrilled about her and the Miller twins being separated from Sean and me. I figured she'd get over it. Besides, it was a much better arrangement . . . at least for my guy friend and me.

The place was literally soaring with airplanes, rockets, and missiles—from the Wright brothers' 1903 Flyer to the Viking Lander from Mars. I had a hard time keeping up with our small group, though, because I really wanted to just stand and gawk at each exhibit. And the space probes and satellites floating overhead.

"C'mon, Holly," Sean called to me once. "I'd hate to see you 'space out' in here."

I laughed. "You're pun-ny," I said about his play on words. And he was. A real wit and a half!

About an hour later, while we were exploring the huge

Skylab space station, suddenly our group vanished. It seemed so weird, especially because just seconds before, we'd all been together—right here in this huge, silver, barrel-shaped orbital workshop.

"If we hurry, maybe we can track 'em down," Sean suggested.

So we rushed through the long middle hall, trying to spot anyone familiar. We even backtracked through each of the two-story hallways, searching everywhere.

After checking the Albert Einstein Planetarium section, we decided it was futile; besides, we didn't want to waste valuable sightseeing time. We would go it alone. And secretly, I was thrilled.

"I hope Mrs. Duncan and the others won't worry," I said as we made our way outside into the warm, bright sunshine.

"Oh, there's a good chance we'll run into them," Sean assured me. "Any idea where they'd be headed next?"

"Probably somewhere for lunch, but beats me where."

My cell phone battery was dead, so I really wasn't sure about the best approach to take for locating our group. Neither was Sean, but he had a great idea. "Let's grab a snack. I don't know about you, but I'm starved."

We walked to a hot dog stand one block away. While we waited in line, Sean and I talked—mostly about the monuments and the attractions. But I really wanted to know his impressions of George Washington University and the college days activities over the past weekend. I decided not to be nosy, though—I'd wait till he brought it up.

With the sun shining down on us through the newly formed leaves, Sean asked, "What's your favorite attraction so far?"

"That's hard to say," I replied, telling him about the splendor of the Lincoln Memorial and the drama of Ford's Theatre. "We saw those Saturday." I paused for a moment. "What I think I really liked best was the space museum—touching the moon rock was so cool. What about you?"

"Has to be the FBI building."

I wasn't surprised. The place was perfect for a guy interested in blood and other medical stuff.

We were finally close enough to the food stand to read the prices—three times higher than in Dressel Hills—probably than any other place in the world, too.

"How hungry are you?" he asked with a grin.

"A little." But I certainly didn't want him to think he had to pay for me. Quickly, I pulled out my wallet. The face of George Washington on my one-dollar bills gave me an idea. "Hey, want to visit the Bureau of Engraving and Printing this afternoon? My stepdad highly recommended it."

Sean promptly found his tourist guide and map. "Sounds like fun. I hear they print more than thirty-five million bills every day."

I was surprised at how agreeable he was. Andie would say he was only trying to impress me. But I had a different take on the way Sean handled himself around me. And it had nothing to do with trying to sway or influence me. Nope. Sean was a well-bred, very nice Christian guy.

Secretly, I hoped our friendship might continue for a long time. At least, until he and I came to know God's plans for our lives. Of course, no way would I discuss the book I'd read recently. Not with Sean. I wouldn't want him to think I was bold or, as my mother called it, forward. According to her, no one ever attracted a nice boy by chasing him.

Surprisingly enough, I'd found this to be true in the past. The best way to attract friendships with boys was to allow them to do the pursuing.

And over hot dogs, fries smothered in ketchup, and plenty of soda, I let Sean do just that.

Chapter 15

Sean did end up paying for my lunch, even though I told him I was quite capable of handling my own financial affairs.

He wouldn't hear of it. So I guess I could actually say this had just been my very first real date—even though I'd tried to convince myself that I wasn't interested in the formal dating thing much anymore.

Mom had made a rule years ago that I had to be fifteen to go out on an actual date with a guy. Oh sure, I'd spent lots of time in groups with boys from our church, but for some reason, I'd built up this whole date thing in my mind. Longing, waiting for the second I turned fifteen.

Funny thing, though. My thinking had begun to change, partly because of that cool book, and for another reason, too. Sean was my good friend. The way I saw it, our relationship was fabulous—and absolutely appropriate for our age—just the way things were. To think of him in a romantic, gushy sense would surely spoil things. I couldn't risk anything happening to the beautiful rapport we shared.

So I was determined to shove out the first-date notion and focus on simply sharing with and listening to my friend.

After lunch we walked nearly three blocks on the Mall, toward the Bureau of Engraving and Printing. Ordinary sights and sounds captured our attention along the way—little kids from a day care having a picnic, and a group of older folk on bicycles.

We soaked up the gentle, warm breezes of a romantic April afternoon . . . er, I mean a pleasant one.

Finally I couldn't wait any longer. I simply had to ask the question burning inside me. "What do you think of the university here?" I blurted.

Sean smiled as we walked, glancing at me as if he might be ready to discuss it. "I want to check out two others before I make my final decision. You know, take my time about it."

"So you're not really wild about George Washington University?"

"It's great—but too far away from California."

"Where are the other schools?" I asked, genuinely interested.

"One's KU—Kansas University." He paused for a moment, a wide grin spreading across his face. "And the other is UCCS—the University of Colorado at Colorado Springs."

"You're kidding! You might go to school in *my* state?"

He stopped walking and turned to me. "Wouldn't it be cool, Holly? And so handy for me to see you more often."

"That'd be fun," I admitted as a curious feeling caught me by surprise.

I was glad it was his turn to ask questions. "Any idea where you might go to school?"

We resumed our walk, the smell of daffodils in the air. Letting my hair blow freely, I told him some of my future aspirations. "Well, I'm really interested in becoming a published book author . . . someday. It's hard to say what school I should attend for that sort of thing. I know I want to study plenty of English and American literature before I attempt a novel or anything serious. Besides, Mrs. Ross, my English teacher, says a writer needs to live and experience life for a long while before attempting a book."

Sean listened with rapt attention. In fact, both of us were so caught up in conversation, we almost missed turning south at Fourteenth Street.

"What are the chances of your show choir taking first place?" Sean asked later as we waited for the next available tour in front of the gray building—where America's paper money was printed.

"Well, if you could've heard the other groups sing, you might think we had zero chance."

"Really? Which ones were best?"

I told him my three top picks—one of them included the all-girls group from New York. "I guess when it comes right down to it, we'll have to trust the judges' vote." I shook my head. "Man, I'd hate to be the one picking."

He stepped back a bit, studying me. "What if—just what if—your choir is chosen? When would you be going to Austria for the international competition?"

"Why do you want to know?" I wondered what he was really asking.

"This summer?" he persisted.

"Sometime in mid-June, I think."

By the way he nearly chuckled, I had a funny feeling he was fishing for something.

"C'mon," I pleaded. "What's up?"

"Let's just see if your choir wins or not." That's all he would say.

I was beginning to feel comfortable with him. Really comfortable. That's when I decided to bring up the subject of the book I'd read. And I was careful not to be too forward about it, either. "It's really incredible—the concepts in the book, I mean."

"Who's the author?" he asked. "It sounds familiar."

I began to tell him more. Afterward I hoped I'd done the right thing. "So, what do you think?" I asked, noting a sign warning tourists about taking photographs. "Is it a radical idea?"

"There'd sure be a lot fewer broken hearts in the world."

I agreed. And I didn't tell him, but I knew that the minute I let a boy hold my hand, the relationship had already begun to change. I didn't want physical attraction to become more important than friendship.

We talked more about it, and soon he was pulling out his wallet and asking me for the name of the author. I waited while he jotted it down, inching along with the crowd.

At last we were inside and listening to an informative but brief spiel on the production of currency. How it was designed, engraved, and printed. Progressing along, we watched as thousands of dollars zipped through the printing presses. There were forklifts hauling crisp, green dollar bills, and other interesting things to see, like tons of postage stamps and passports.

Seeing the passports made me think of Sean's secretive comment. Why did he want to know about Austria? Was he going there this summer?

Partway into the tour, Sean leaned over, and before I could stop him, he aimed his camera and it flashed.

"Halt right there, young man!" a deep voice bellowed into the crowd. The burly guard whipped out his two-way radio and began reporting the infraction as he headed straight for us.

Tugging on Sean's shirtsleeve, I said, "Didn't you see the sign back there?" I was sure he hadn't. But that didn't seem to hinder the guard.

"Hand over that camera!" the stern command was given.

I cringed. Was my friend going to jail?

"It's against the law to take pictures in a federal building." The guard was obviously wired up.

"I'm very sorry, sir," Sean spoke up. "I didn't see any sign, otherwise I would've kept my camera in its case."

I worried that Sean's expensive camera might be confiscated—his precious pictures erased.

"How could you miss seeing the signs?" the guard demanded, now out of breath and surveying Sean's camera. "They're posted everywhere."

Sean glanced at me and said tenderly, "I was lost in conversation with my girlfriend."

That helped. The guard hesitantly returned the camera—backing off. But my heart sure didn't. It was going berserk. And after all our logical, serious talk about the fabulous book.

After all that . . .

Girlfriend!

Shoot, I was so bewildered by the unexpected comment, that at the end of the tour in the visitor's center, I purchased a bag of shredded money as a souvenir!

What *was* I thinking?

Chapter 16

"Do you think we'll ever catch up with Mrs. Duncan and the choir?" I asked, still rather dazed, yet reluctant to end our private talk.

A boyish grin spread across Sean's handsome face. "Let's see the Washington Monument next." He studied his map and discovered it was only a few blocks north of us. "It's not far—look for the park and fifty American flags."

I checked my watch. Two o'clock—still plenty of time.

"Is it true the monument stays open till midnight?" I asked. "A friend of mine once told me he climbed all 898 steps and rode the elevator down at midnight." I didn't tell him the friend was Jared Wilkins, who had visited it while on summer vacation with his family.

Sean held my hand briefly as we crossed the street, but I knew it was only out of concern for my safety. Besides, I wasn't complaining. After all, my own father, now a Christian, had approved of Sean Hamilton right from the start—another one of the important principles taught in the book I'd read.

♥ ♥ ♥

As it turned out, none of the Dressel Hills choir members was anywhere near the tall marble monument or its reflecting pool to the west. But Sean and I had fun riding the elevator to the top. The view was great, too. Exceptionally clear. We could see for a zillion miles in all four directions.

"Just think," I joked, "if we had binoculars, we might be able to find Mrs. Duncan and the choir from up here."

Sean laughed, but I sensed he wasn't terribly worried about catching up to the others. Not yet. The day was young. And since we were in the vicinity, we paid a solemn visit to the Vietnam Veterans' Memorial. Sean found his uncle's name on the black granite wall and asked one of the park employees to make a rubbing of the name.

Baskets of flowers and personal letters, along with many other gifts, had been left behind at the wall. People in uniform, and others not, stood and cried openly. After a few moments of observing this perpetual silent yet emotional drama, I began to have a modest understanding of the pain and loss that comes with war.

Slowly and thoughtfully, Sean and I walked back to the reflecting pool. There, we sat on the grass and watched the ducks, talking softly about the effects of human cruelty.

After we'd rested our feet, we caught the Tourmobile to the Tomb of the Unknown Soldier and the Eternal Flame at John Kennedy's gravesite in Arlington National Cemetery. Sean went camera-crazy, insisting on taking shots of me at each of the famous landmarks—even at some general's gravestone I'd never heard of. Actually, it got to be comical, but I knew it would be a long time before we might see each other again, so I cooperated and put on my best smile for him.

♥ ♥ ♥

Back at the hotel, I waited—actually sacked out on the bed

for an hour—before Andie and the twins ever returned. And what a joyful reunion it was!

"We thought you'd eloped or something," Andie joked.

I sat up and blinked my sleepy eyes. "Was Mrs. Duncan worried?"

"Not really," Paula chimed in. "Anyone can take one look at Sean and see he's a responsible guy."

Kayla was nodding her approval. "It was nice, probably, that it worked out this way . . . right?"

"If you're asking if I planned it, well, I didn't."

"But if you could do it over, would you get lost again? That's the real question." Andie was being silly. But she was right, and I knew it.

Somehow or other, it had seemed almost providential that Sean and I spent the afternoon together.

"Is he coming to the Kennedy Center tonight?" Paula asked as she plopped onto the bed with an exhausted grunt.

"I hope so." I got up and started brushing my hair. "So . . . what do you think of him?" I asked rather sheepishly.

Andie jumped right on it. "Aha! She's a goner—I knew it. We should've brought that no-dating, just-waiting book along with us on this trip."

I studied my friends carefully. "It's okay, I can take a joke." But I wasn't going to share the intimate thoughts going through my mind. Not now. I had some tall praying to do before I told anyone what I was thinking about Sean Hamilton.

♥ ♥ ♥

After supper at a Chinese restaurant, we took the Metrorail once again—for the last time this trip—to the Kennedy Center.

Sean showed up in time to sit with us. All of us wore our patriotic competition outfits—navy blue pants or skirts with white Oxford shirts, and the guys wore red dress ties—in case we were winners.

"You look great," he whispered.

"Thanks, so do you." And I meant it. Sean was a fabulous dresser, wearing khaki-colored trousers and a light blue shirt. I was proud to be seen with him. And Mrs. Duncan obviously approved, too, because when I caught her eye, she winked at us.

The announcer started the evening by thanking the many choral groups from around the country. I glanced at Andie and saw that she had her fingers crossed. I hoped she wouldn't be too disappointed if we didn't make it. Andie would be talking of nothing else back home, probably for the rest of the school year. On the other hand, if we did win, she'd be packing and planning for all of us between now and June something.

The man in the black tuxedo stood before the microphone, waiting for the echo from the trumpet fanfare to fade completely. "I would like to begin by announcing the second runners-up."

In other words, third place, I thought.

Ceremoniously, he pulled an envelope out of his coat. We waited as he glanced at the card inside. "Second runners-up, all the way from Oregon—the Portland High School Choral-aires!"

Everyone applauded, and I felt myself getting tense. Did we have a chance?

The group from Oregon headed for the stage. They were happy, from the smiles on their faces. They'd get to go to Austria this summer only if the first-place winners and the first runners-up couldn't make it. Phooey. I wouldn't have been smiling!

The emcee continued with his dramatic charade. I'd turned to look at Andie and the Miller twins, and the guy started saying something about the choir from Colorado. I'd almost missed it because of my daydreaming!

I was paying attention now. All ears.

"From the majestic Colorado Rockies—the Dressel Hills Show Choir—our first runners-up!"

Mrs. Duncan motioned for us to stand. Sean was beaming, and I heard him say, "Cool!"

I followed the rest of my friends as we headed down the long, carpeted aisle to stand onstage.

Hard as I tried, it was impossible to see Sean's smiling face in the audience as I stood there on the wide, expansive stage. The spotlights were so powerful and the place so charged with excitement, I started to hold my breath again.

"Breathe," Andie said to me over the applause.

And I did. Still, I could hardly believe we were up here. I mean, this was really big-time stuff!

None of us were too surprised when the all-girl choir from New York City took first place. They deserved the highest honors.

♥ ♥ ♥

Later, at a glitzy ice-cream parlor, Mrs. Duncan congratulated us. "Most likely we won't be going to Vienna in two months, but we've certainly accomplished a worthy goal. I know—and I speak for the principal and all the teachers at Dressel Hills High—you students are absolutely tops. And I'm so very honored to be your director."

Now it was our turn to cheer her. And we did, complete with whistles from some of the guys.

Sean grinned, apparently thrilled to be in the middle of this celebratory commotion. Later, when things died down a bit and we could actually hear each other without shouting, he told me why he'd asked about Austria earlier. "Your father has some business there this summer," he explained. "He wants me to go along."

"Daddy's going to Europe?" This was the first I'd heard of it.

"I'm going to assist him, I guess you'd say." He smiled. "More as a traveling companion, though."

"So my stepmom doesn't want to leave Tyler?" He was her young son. "Is that why?"

Sean nodded. "Saundra thinks someone should be with your dad because of his heart problems."

I sighed. "Well, lucky you."

He held the door for me as we left the ice-cream place. "Who knows, maybe you'll get there yet."

"That would be nothing shy of a miracle—I mean, those New York singers aren't going to miss out on the international competition. No way!"

"Miracles happen," he replied. That would have been the last exchange of words between us if it hadn't been for Mrs. Duncan—fabulous teacher that she was.

Discreetly, she came over and said the rest of the group would head on to the Metro station if Sean didn't mind escorting me back to the hotel.

"Sure, I'll be happy to," he said gallantly.

The choir and sponsors strolled down the street, and when they were out of sight, Sean and I began walking slowly back to my hotel.

"Thanks for sharing the evening with me," I began. "It was really special." I almost said, "because of you," but didn't. I had a feeling he already knew.

"I wouldn't have missed this for anything, Holly." We looked out over the beautiful Potomac River in the distance. The sky still had a touch of color and light in it. "I wouldn't have missed you."

His words touched my heart. They were trustworthy and good. Just the way he was.

I was almost afraid to look up at him, worried that he might see in my eyes the things I felt.

"Do you mind if I call you occasionally?" he asked. "Is it okay with your family?"

I nodded. "It's fine. I'd like that."

"And we'll keep writing, both regular letters and email."

"Yes," I whispered, scarcely finding my voice.

We were silent for a moment, listening to the sounds of dusk. Then he said, "Your director is really terrific, you know. Please tell her thanks for me."

I glanced up at him, grinning.

He added, "Some teachers might've had a problem with our getting lost today."

"I know what you mean. But Mrs. Duncan's the best."

He reached for my hand unexpectedly. "She's actually quite terrific, but she's not the best."

I was looking into his face now, no longer bashful. But I was determined not to get emotional. Shoot, I wanted to be able to see this wonderful friend of mine clearly. Besides, tears on a night like this were way overrated.

"Well, I guess this is good-bye," I offered. "Have a good flight home."

"Thanks." He turned to face the river then, our shoulders touching as we looked out toward the sunset. "More sightseeing tomorrow?"

"We're scheduled to see the White House and the Capitol with our state senator."

He teased, "Watch your camera!"

"Don't worry." We walked on slowly now. "I honestly thought you were going to be hauled off to jail today," I said.

He chuckled. "We made some interesting memories together, didn't we?"

"No kidding."

"And," he said softly, "hopefully they won't be the last."

I should've been prepared for what came next. He looked at

me and said, "You'll be in my prayers, Holly-Heart. I want God's will for both of us, individually and otherwise."

It was sweet. A direct result of the conversation we'd had earlier.

"I'll be praying for you, too." It was a promise I would keep.

IT'S A GIRL THING

Chapter 17

We, the fabulous first runners-up from Colorado, toured the Red, Blue, and Green rooms of the White House the next morning. Then came the East Room, where the president held press conferences, followed by the State Dining Room. We received special treatment from our state senator because of our newly acquired status. Hotshot show choir members we were!

Somehow, he arranged for us to meet the Secretary of State, and later we "accidentally" ran into the First Dog, who seemed rather pleased about being made over by so many doting teenagers. I almost took a picture of the perfectly groomed pet to show to my ordinary fluff-ball kitty back home, but I remembered Sean's advice about flash photography and refrained.

Overhead were enormous, crystal-laden chandeliers—one of the things that really grabbed me about this place. And the wide, wood molding around the fireplaces, doors, and windows. Maybe I was beginning to change my taste—old, historic things really were cool.

The Oval Office—the president's workplace in the west wing—was off limits to the tour, of course, as were the First Family's private quarters upstairs. I was curious what those rooms looked like, but having seen as much as I had here on the tour, my imagination took over. I decided the very next time anyone ran a special on the White House, I would tune in.

Overall, my assessment of the magnificent mansion was that it was old. Very old. Two hundred years old, to be exact.

"So, what did you think?" I asked Andie as we made our way outside afterward.

"Too stuffy. A house ought to be a place to relax."

I smiled at her reaction. "Where you can put your feet up and not worry about it, right?" I thought of my dad's elegant beach house in Southern California. Now, there was a study in serious interior design. But that was Daddy's—and Saundra's—style.

"Do you miss Sean?" she asked later, as we headed for Capitol Hill.

"He just left, for pete's sake." I purposely evaded the question.

"Well, I have a feeling you'll be seeing him again." She tilted her curly head.

"He's really very special."

"I can see that," Paula piped up.

"Hey, whoa—don't forget about that dating book," Kayla urged.

I grinned. "Get this. Sean's planning to read it."

Andie clutched her throat. "Oh no, it *is* serious."

We joked about it, but underlying all of our talk was a sense of doing what was right. We were growing up, trying on new ideas—eager to follow what the Bible said. Yep, we were nearing the end of our freshman year, all right, more mature than ever. But we were far from the end of our coming-of-age.

Next year, and the next, we would attempt to keep our eyes on Jesus, the ultimate grown-up and best example. And, in years to come, we might tell our own children about how we'd tripped and fallen but gotten back up and plugged ahead.

Late Wednesday afternoon we arrived in Dressel Hills, tired but perfectly elated about the outcome of our trip. Mrs. Duncan couldn't stop talking about how wonderful we were—musically and otherwise.

"I think she's secretly hoping for a chance at Vienna," Andie said as we waited in the baggage claim area.

Jared had overheard. "How could that ever happen?"

"Let her dream," I answered. "She deserves it."

"Yeah. Some people deserve it more than others." And he was off to grab his bags, leaving us girls to wonder what he meant.

"That Jared," Andie said as we pulled each other's luggage off the conveyor, "does he ever say what he means?"

"He used to," I chimed in. "Personally, I'm glad those days are over!"

Andie caught my eye. "You and me both."

♥ ♥ ♥

It wasn't long before Uncle Jack, Carrie, and Stephie showed up. The girls squeezed in hard against me as my stepdad gave me a hug.

"We missed you, Holly," Carrie said.

"We sure did!" Stephie remarked. "Mrs. Hibbard was—"

She stopped when her dad shook his head. "Our neighbor did her best" was all he said.

Carrie scrunched up her nose, and I figured there'd been some conflicts. Maybe with Stan. But I was smart enough not to go there.

We headed for the automatic doors and to the parking lot.

"Someone's at home, waiting to see you," Uncle Jack said as he loaded my suitcases into the back of the van.

"I can't wait."

Stephie grabbed my hand. "Oh, Holly, our baby's so-o pretty!"

"Does she look like you?" I asked.

"Almost exactly," Carrie said. "And Stephie doesn't mind not being the baby of the family anymore."

"I never said that," wailed Stephie.

I winked at her, letting her push in beside me on the van's second seat. "These things take time," I whispered in her ear, and she leaned her head against my arm.

Carrie crawled up front, riding shotgun with Uncle Jack. "You just wait till you hold April," she said, smiling back at me.

"She's all cuddly and sweet," my stepdad said. "But then, so were all of you at that age."

"And we're not *now*?" Carrie demanded.

He reached over and swished her long ponytail. "Now you're cuddly and . . . and . . . sometimes a little bit sour." It was just a joke, and Carrie loved it. We all did. Uncle Jack was so cool.

♥ ♥ ♥

The biggest surprise came when I walked into the house. There, in the Boston rocker, sat Stan—holding April.

I couldn't help it. I stared. Probably longer than I should've. "Wow, this is going to take some getting used to."

"So get over it," he muttered back at me.

"Hey, I think I must've missed something." I knelt down beside Stan and touched the tiny hand sticking out of the blanketed bundle.

"You missed everything," Stan said quietly. "But it made all the difference."

The guys in my life—when would they ever start saying what they meant?

"Are you telling me you're glad I went to Washington? That you wouldn't have fallen in love with your baby sister if I hadn't?"

He tried to conceal the smile. "Don't be smug," he said. "Wanna hold her?"

"What do *you* think?"

He stood up and let me sit in Mom's rocker, then placed

my sister gently in my arms. "Oh, April," I cooed down into the precious, tiny face. "I'm so glad to meet you."

"We changed her name," Stan said flatly.

"How come?" I asked, shocked.

"She didn't exactly look like an April," he said.

I couldn't tell if he was serious or not. "Well, she does to me," I replied.

Carrie was giggling now. "Our baby has a nickname," she chanted. "Can you believe it?"

That figured. Uncle Jack was the master giver of weird and wacky names.

"I almost hate to ask," I said.

Mom came slowly downstairs just then, looking tired but radiant in her prettiest bathrobe. "Welcome home, honey."

"Did you honestly change April's name?" I asked as she kissed the top of my head.

She headed for the couch and Uncle Jack. "Modified it, I guess you'd say."

"To what?"

"April-Love," Stan said at last. "Because she reminds Mom of you."

"Oh, really?" I studied the rosebud face. "Maybe it's the shape of her chin."

"I thought you said she looked like *me*!" Stephie insisted.

Uncle Jack put his arm around Mom and they snuggled, admiring their first child together—now asleep in my arms. "April is a combination of all of us." And my stepdad went right down the line. "She has her mother's eyes . . . and my good nature."

We laughed, then settled down for the rest of his comments.

"She has Stan's determination, Phil's smarts, and Mark's appetite."

"Poor kid," whispered Carrie.

"Now, hold on a minute," Uncle Jack said. He looked at

Mom and gave her a peck on the end of her nose. "The baby has Stephie's dimples, Carrie's little nose, and Holly's . . ." He stopped, adding to the suspense. "She has Holly's good heart—and that's all there is to it."

I made the chair rock gently and felt the first, sweet stirrings of tiny April. Here we all were together. The people who mattered most in my life . . . and this new little one.

"By the way, Stan," I said, looking up, "thanks for what you did . . . helping me be able to go to Washington."

"It was nothing" came the reply.

"Well, thanks anyway," I repeated.

"Hey . . . whatever." Stan was much too cool to show his true feelings, this brousin of mine. But maybe, just maybe, April-Love would help him with that macho stuff. From what I'd seen, she was already beginning to soften him up.

"Congratulations," Mom said about show choir. "Wish we could've heard you sing."

"Oh, you will," I told her. "Mrs. Duncan has some big plans for us . . . media coverage, the works. Dressel Hills hasn't heard the end of us yet."

We sat there, taking turns talking. Later, Uncle Jack decided to have a short devotional. While he read from the Bible, I watched April's wee face, noting the family marks. The set and color of Mom's eyes, Carrie's nose, and Stephie's demure dimples . . . but most of all, the blessing of God.

Someday, I decided, if it was God's will, I would have a husband and a family. Maybe it was a girl thing to be thinking like this. Or simply a direct result of having had a fabulous weekend with Sean. Whatever, it was a good thing. And so very right.

♥ ♥ ♥

That night a big, white moon shone brightly through my window as I looked out over the mountains of the continental divide. I remembered watching for Santa's elves to tiptoe over those mountains when I was a little girl. Of course, I was way beyond that now—too grown-up to believe in such childish things. I had better things to believe in. *Someone* to believe in. A Savior and friend—Jesus Christ.

When I slept in my own soft, four-poster bed, I dreamed I could hear the angels whispering "Holly-Heart" to me outside my window. And in their heavenly voices I heard the excitement of tomorrow—my future. The future that my all-wise heavenly Father lovingly held in His hands.

And in my sleep, I felt a flurry of joy.

Acknowledgments

Thanks to all who have helped to make the HOLLY'S HEART series a successful reality. I'm forever grateful to Charette Barta and Sharon Madison, who believed in Holly-Heart from her earliest beginnings, as well as to my superb editor, Rochelle Glöege, whose suggestions and encouragement are so valuable to me.

Big hugs to my terrific teen consultants—Shanna, Larissa, Mindie, Amy, Brandy, Cindy, Kelly, Jonathan, Janie, and Julie. With their fantastic ideas and input, they made the HOLLY'S HEART series even more fun to create!

Hurrah for my SCBWI critique group, as well as reviewer Barbara Birch, my witty sis, who dreamed up the idea of Holly and friends being snowbound at school.

Three cheers for my husband, Dave, whose thoughtful comments, loving support, and super sandwiches made this series possible.

And finally, my deep appreciation to my many fans who think Holly really *does* live somewhere in Colorado. Your many cards, letters, and email messages have brought joy and encouragement to this writer's heart. I've enjoyed every minute spent writing HOLLY'S HEART just for you!

From Bev . . . to You

I'm thrilled that you've chosen to read HOLLY'S HEART. As my first young-adult protagonist, Holly Meredith remains dear to my heart, and I laughed and cried with her as I wrote every one of these books.

Holly-Heart and I have quite a lot in common. While growing up in Lancaster County, Pennsylvania, I wrote zillions of secret lists and journal entries (and still do!). I also enjoy my many e-pals, and sending snail mail letters and notes to encourage family and friends has always been one of my favorite things to do. And I know all about the importance of having a true-blue best friend. Mine was Sandi Kline, and while we didn't have Loyalty Papers, we did write secret-coded messages to each other. Once, we even hid a few under the carpet of the seventh step leading to the sanctuary of my dad's church!

Thanks to my books, I've had the opportunity to develop friendships with people of all ages, from the grade-schoolers who love my picture books to the teens and senior adults who enjoy my novels. Through the years, some of you have even written to confide in me or share some of the difficulties you've faced. Growing up can definitely be tough sometimes. I've always found hope in the words of Psalm 139, which describes the amazing love of our Creator-God. It's comforting to know that the same God who formed us in our mother's womb, who knows the number of individual hairs we're washing and blow-drying each day, also sees the fears and concerns of our lives. Our heavenly Father sees and understands. What an enormous blessing that is!

To learn more about my writing, sign up for my e-newsletter, or contact me, visit my Web site, *www.beverlylewis.com.*

Only Girls Allowed: More Fun Reads From Beverly Lewis

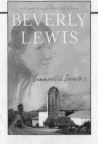

Meet Merry Hanson, a fifteen-year-old girl who happens to live in Amish country—only she isn't Amish. When strange things seem to be happening there, it's up to Merry to get to the bottom of it. Like when her friend's mom mysteriously disappears.

Whether she's solving mysteries, learning the ways of the Amish, helping friends, or just trying to stay out of trouble, you won't want to miss a single adventure with Merry.

SUMMERHILL SECRETS: Volume 1
Whispers Down the Lane, Secret in the Willows, Catch a Falling Star, Night of the Fireflies, A Cry in the Dark

SUMMERHILL SECRETS: Volume 2
House of Secrets, Echoes in the Wind, Hide Behind the Moon, Windows on the Hill, Shadows Beyond the Gate

Join Olivia Hudson, Jenna Song, Heather Bock, and Miranda Garcia as they follow their dreams of competing in the Olympics. From figure skating to gymnastics to skiing, cheer on your new friends as they go through life's challenges and triumphs.

GIRLS ONLY
Dreams on Ice, Only the Best, A Perfect Match, Reach for the Stars, Follow the Dream, Better Than Best, Star Status